THE LIAR'S KEY

THE LIAR'S KEY

THE RED QUEEN'S WAR
◆ BOOK TWO ◆

MARK LAWRENCE

ACE BOOKS, NEW YORK

An imprint of Penguin Random House LLC
375 Hudson Street, New York, New York 10014

This book is an original publication of Penguin Random House LLC.

Library of Congress Cataloging-in-Publication Data

Lawrence, Mark, 1966– author.
The liar's key / Mark Lawrence. — First edition.
pages ; cm. — (The Red Queen's War ; Book two)
ISBN 978-0-425-26880-3 (hardcover)
I. Title.
PS3612.A9484L53 2015
813'.6—dc23
2015002214

FIRST EDITION: June 2015

PRINTED IN THE UNITED STATES OF AMERICA

10 9 8 7 6 5 4 3 2 1

Cover illustration by Jason Chan.
Interior text design by Laura K. Corless.
Map reprinted by permission of HarperCollins Publishers Ltd © 2014 Andrew Ashton.

Penguin
Random
House

Dedicated to my mother, Hazel

ACKNOWLEDGMENTS

Many thanks to the good folk at Ace Books who have made this all happen and put the book in your hands. Special thanks to Diana Gill for taking the helm, and to the art department for working with Jason Chan to produce another splendid cover. A bucket of gratitude for Sarah Chorn too, who read an early version of the book and provided valuable feedback.

Finally another round of applause for my agent, Ian Drury, and the team at Sheil Land for all their sterling work.

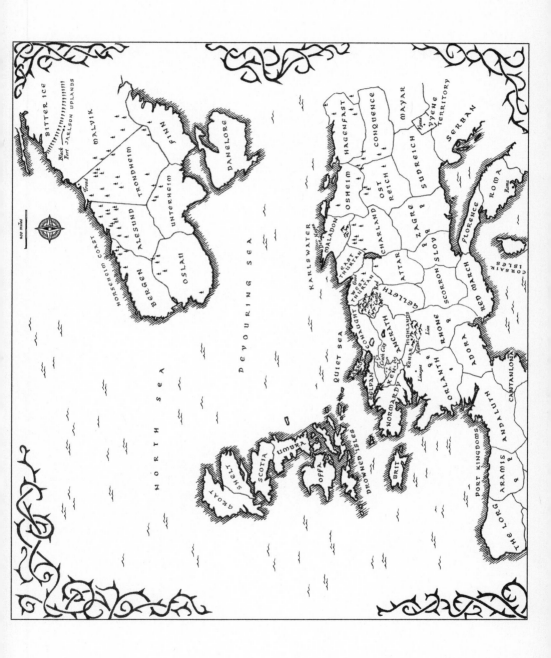

AUTHOR'S NOTE

For those of you who have had to wait a year for this book I provide a brief note to Book 1, *Prince of Fools*, so that your memories may be refreshed and I can avoid the exquisite pain of having to have characters tell each other things they already know for your benefit.

Here I carry forward only what is of importance to the tale that follows.

1. Jalan Kendeth (grandson of the Red Queen) and Snorri ver Snagason (a very large Viking) set off from Red March (northern Italy) for the Bitter Ice (northern Norway), bound together by a spell that cursed one of them to be light-sworn and the other dark-sworn.

2. Jalan is now dark-sworn and visited each sunset by a female spirit called Aslaug.

3. Snorri is light-sworn and visited each sunrise by a male spirit called Baraqel.

4. They travelled to the Black Fort to rescue Snorri's wife and surviving child from Sven Broke-Oar and agents of the Dead King, including necromancers, unborn, and Edris Dean. This rescue failed. Snorri's family did not survive.

5. Jalan, Snorri, and Tuttugu, a fat and slightly timid Viking, are the three survivors of the quest to the Black Fort. They have returned to the port town of Trond and spent the winter there.

6. Snorri has Loki's key, a magical key that will open any lock. The Dead King wants this key very much.

7. Of their enemy at the Black Fort it is possible that Edris Dean and a number of the Hardassa (Red Vikings) survived, along with a handful of necromancers from the Drowned Isles.

8. Jalan's grandmother, the Red Queen, remains in Red March with her elder sister, known as the Silent Sister, and her misshapen elder brother, Garyus. It was the Silent Sister's spell that bound Snorri and Jalan together.

9. A number of powerful individuals use magic to manipulate events in the Broken Empire, often standing as the controlling interests behind many of the hundred thrones. The Dead King, the Lady Blue, the ice witch Skilfar, and the dream-mage Sageous are four such individuals. Jalan met Skilfar and Sageous on the way to the Black Fort. The Dead King has attempted to kill Jalan and Snorri several times. The Lady Blue is engaged in some long and secret war against the Red Queen and appears to be guiding the Dead King's hand, though perhaps he doesn't know it.

PROLOGUE

Two men in a room of many doors. One tall in his robes, stern, marked with cruelty and intelligence, the other shorter, very lean, his hair a shock of surprise, his garb a changing motley confusing the eye.

The short man laughs, a many-angled sound as likely to kill birds in flight as to bring blossom to the bough.

"I have summoned you!" The tall man, teeth gritted as if still straining to hold the other in place, though his hands are at his side.

"A fine trick, Kelem."

"You know me?"

"I know everyone." A sharp grin. "You're the door-mage."

"And you are?"

"Ikol." His clothes change, tattered yellow checks on blue where before it was scarlet fleur de lis on grey. "Olik." He smiles a smile that dazzles and cuts. "Loki, if you likey."

"Are you a god, Loki?" No humour in Kelem, only command. Command and a great and terrible concentration in stone-grey eyes.

"No." Loki spins, regarding the doors. "But I've been known to lie."

"I called on the most powerful—"

"You don't always get what you want." Almost sing-song. "But sometimes you get what you need. You got me."

"You are a god?"

"Gods are dull. I've stood before the throne. Wodin sits there, old one-eye, with his ravens whispering into each ear." Loki smiles. "Always the ravens. Funny how that goes."

"I need—"

"Men don't know what they need. They barely know what they want. Wodin, father of storms, god of gods, stern and wise. But mostly stern. You'd like him. And watching—always watching—oh the things that he has seen!" Loki spins to take in the room. "Me, I'm just a jester in the hall where the world was made. I caper, I joke, I cut a jig. I'm of little importance. Imagine though . . . if it were *I* that pulled the strings and made the gods dance. What if at the core, if you dug deep enough, uncovered every truth . . . what if at the heart of it all . . . there was a lie, like a worm at the centre of the apple, coiled like Oroborus, just as the secret of men hides coiled at the centre of each piece of you, no matter how fine you slice? Wouldn't that be a fine joke now?"

Kelem frowns at this nonsense, then with a quick shake of his head returns to his purpose. "I made this place. From my failures." He gestures at the doors. Thirteen, lined side by side on each wall of an otherwise bare room. "These are doors I can't open. You can leave here, but no door will open until every door is unlocked. I made it so." A single candle lights the chamber, dancing as the occupants move, their shadows leaping to its tune.

"Why would I want to leave?" A goblet appears in Loki's hand, silver and overflowing with wine as dark and red as blood. He takes a sip.

"I command you by the twelve arch-angels of—"

"Yes, yes." Loki waves away the conjuring. The wine darkens until it's a black that draws the eye and blinds it. So black that the silver tarnishes and corrupts. So black it is nothing but the absence of light. And suddenly it's a key. A black glass key.

"Is that . . . ?" There's a hunger in the door-mage's voice. "Will it open them?"

"I should hope so." Loki spins the key around his fingers.

"What key is that? Not Acheron's? Taken from heaven when—"

"It's mine. I made it. Just now."

"How do you know it will open them?" Kelem's gaze sweeps the room.

"It's a good key." Loki meets the mage's eyes. "It's every key. Every key that was and is, every key that will be, every key that could be."

"Give it to—"

"Where's the fun in that?" Loki walks to the nearest door and sets his fingers to it. "This one." Each door is plain and wooden but when he touches it this door becomes a sheet of black glass, unblemished and gleaming. "This is the tricky one." Loki sets his palm to the door and a wheel appears. An eight-spoked wheel of the same black glass, standing proud of the surface, as if by turning it one might unlock and open the door. Loki doesn't touch it. Instead he taps his key to the wall beside it and the whole room changes. Now it is a high vault, clean lines, walls of poured stone, a huge and circular silver-steel door in the ceiling. The light comes from panels set into the walls. A corridor leads off, stretching further than the eye can see. Thirteen silver-steel arches stand around the margins of the vault, each a foot from the wall, each filled with a shimmering light, as if moonbeams dance across water. Save for the one before Loki, which is black, a crystal surface fracturing the light then swallowing it. "Open this door and the world ends."

Loki moves on, touching each door in turn. "Your death lies behind one of these other doors, Kelem."

The mage stiffens then sneers. "God of tricks they—"

"Don't worry." Loki grins. "You'll never manage to open that one."

"Give me the key." Kelem extends his hand but makes no move toward his guest.

"What about that door?" Loki looks up at the circle of silver-steel. "You tried to hide that one from me."

Kelem says nothing.

"How many generations have your people lived down here in these caves, hiding from the world?"

"These are not caves!" Kelem bridles. He pulls back his hand. "The world is poisoned. The Day of a Thousand Suns—"

"—was two hundred years ago." Loki waves his key carelessly at the ceiling. The vast door groans, then swings in on its hinges, showering earth and dust upon them. It is as thick as a man is tall.

"No!" Kelem falls to his knees, arms above his head. The dust settles on him, making an old man of him. The floor is covered with soil, with green things growing, worms crawl, bugs scurry, and high above them, through a long vertical shaft, a circle of blue sky burns.

"There, I've opened the most important door for you. Go out, claim what you can before it all goes. There are others repopulating from the east." Loki looks around as if seeking an exit of his own. "No need to thank me."

Kelem lifts his head, rubbing the dirt from his eyes, leaving them red and watering. "Give me the key." His voice a croak.

"You'll have to look for it."

"I command you to . . ." But the key is gone, Loki is gone. Only Kelem remains. Kelem and his failures.

ONE

Petals rained down amid cheers of adoration. Astride my glorious charger at the head of Red March's finest cavalry unit, I led the way along the Street of Victory toward the Red Queen's palace. Beautiful women strained to escape the crowd and throw themselves at me. Men roared their approval. I waved—

Bang. Bang. Bang.

My dream tried to shape the hammering into something that would fit the story it was telling. I've a good imagination and for a moment everything held together. I waved to the highborn ladies adorning each balcony. A manly smirk for my sour-faced brothers sulking at the back of—

Bang! Bang! Bang!

The tall houses of Vermillion began to crumble, the crowd started to thin, faces blurred.

BANG! BANG! BANG!

"Ah hell." I opened my eyes and rolled from the furs' warmth into the freezing gloom. "Spring they call this!" I struggled shivering into a pair of trews and hurried down the stairs.

The tavern room lay strewn with empty tankards, full drunks, toppled benches, and upended tables. A typical morning at the Three Axes. Maeres sniffed around a scatter of bones by the hearth, wagging his tail as I staggered in.

BANG! BANG—

"All right! All right! I'm coming." Someone had split my skull open with a rock during the night. Either that or I had a hell of a hangover. Damned if I knew why a prince of Red March had to answer his own front door, but I'd do anything to stop that pounding tearing through my poor head.

I picked a path through the detritus, stepping over Erik Three-Teeth's ale-filled belly to reach the door just as it reverberated from yet another blow.

"God damn it! I'm here!" I shouted as quietly as I could, teeth gritted against the pain behind my eyes. Fingers fumbled with the lock bar and I pulled it free. "What?" And I hauled the door back. "What?"

I suppose with a more sober and less sleep-addled mind I might have judged it better to stay in bed. Certainly that thought occurred to me as the fist caught me square in the face. I stumbled back, bleating, tripped over Erik, and found myself on my arse staring up at Astrid, framed in the doorway by a morning considerably brighter than anything I wanted to look at.

"You bastard!" She stood hands on hips now. The brittle light fractured around her, sending splinters into my eyes but making a wonder of her golden hair and declaring in no uncertain terms the hour-glass figure that had set me leering at her on my first day in Trond.

"W-what?" I shifted my legs off Erik's bulging stomach, and shuffled backward on my behind. My hand came away bloody from my nose. "Angel, sweetheart—"

"You bastard!" She stepped after me, hugging herself now, the cold following her in.

"Well—" I couldn't argue against "bastard," except technically. I put my hand in a puddle of something decidedly unpleasant and got up quickly, wiping my palm on Maeres, who'd come over to investigate, tail still wagging despite the violence offered to his master.

"Hedwig ver Sorren?" Astrid had murder in her eyes.

I kept backing away. I might have half a foot over her in height but she was still a tall woman with a powerful right arm. "Oh, you don't want to believe street talk, my sweets." I swung a stool between us. "It's only natural that Jarl Sorren would invite a prince of Red March to his halls once he knew I was in town. Hedwig and I—"

"Hedwig and you what?" She took hold of the stool as well.

"Uh, we— Nothing really." I tightened my grip on the stool legs. If I let go I'd be handing her a weapon. Even in my jeopardy visions of Hedwig invaded my mind, brunette, very pretty, wicked eyes, and all a man could want packed onto a short but inviting body. "We were barely introduced."

"It must have been a pretty *bare* introduction if it has Jarl Sorren calling out his housecarls to bring you in for justice!"

"Oh shit." I let go of the stool. Justice in the north tends to mean having your ribs broken out of your chest.

"What's all the noise?" A sleepy voice from behind me.

I turned to see Edda, barefoot on the stairs, our bed furs wrapped around her middle, slim legs beneath, and milk pale shoulders above, her white-blond hair flowing across them.

Turning away was my mistake. Never take your eye off a potential foe. Especially after handing them a weapon.

"Easy!" A hand on my chest pushed me back down onto a floor that felt thick with grime.

"What the—" I opened my eyes to find a "someone" looming over me, a big someone. "Ouch!" A big someone poking clumsy fingers at a very painful spot over my cheekbone.

"Just removing the splinters." A big fat someone.

"Get off me, Tuttugu!" I struggled to get up again, managing to sit this time. "What happened?"

"You got hit with a stool."

I groaned a bit. "I don't remember a stool, I— OUCH! What the hell?" Tuttugu seemed set on pinching and jabbing at the sorest part of my face.

"You might not remember the stool but I'm pulling pieces of it out of your cheek—so keep still. We don't want to spoil those good looks, now do we?"

I did my best to hold still at that. It was true, good looks and a title were most of what I had going for me and I wasn't keen to lose either. To take my mind off the pain I tried to remember how I had managed to get beaten with my own furniture. I drew a blank. Some vague recollection of high-pitched screaming and shouting . . . a memory of being kicked whilst on the floor . . . a glimpse through slitted eyes of two women leaving arm in arm, one petite, pale, young, the other tall, golden, maybe thirty. Neither looked back.

"Right! Up you get. That's the best I can do for now." Tuttugu hauled on my arm to get me on my feet.

I stood swaying, nauseous, hung over, perhaps still a little drunk, and—though I found it hard to credit—slightly horny.

"Come on. We have to go." Tuttugu started to drag me toward the brightness of the doorway. I tried digging in my heels but to no avail.

"Where?" Springtime in Trond had turned out to be more bitter than a Red March midwinter and I'd no interest in exposing myself to it.

"The docks!" Tuttugu seemed worried. "We might just make it!"

"Why? Make what?" I didn't remember much of the morning but I hadn't forgotten that "worried" was Tuttugu's natural state. I shook him off. "Bed. That's where I'm going."

"Well if that's where you want Jarl Sorren's men to find you . . ."

"Why should I give a fig for Jarl Sorr—oh." I remembered Hedwig. I remembered her on the furs in the jarlshouse when everyone else was still at her sister's wedding feast. I remembered her on my cloak during an ill-advised outdoors tryst. She kept my front warm but damn my arse froze. I remembered her upstairs at the tavern that one time she slipped her minders . . . I was surprised we didn't shake all three axes down from above the entrance that afternoon. "Give me a moment . . . two moments!" I held up a hand to stay Tuttugu and charged upstairs.

Once back in my chamber a single moment proved ample. I stamped on the loose floorboard, scooped up my valuables, snatched an armful of clothing, and was heading back down the stairs before Tuttugu had the time to scratch his chins.

"Why the docks?" I panted. The hills would be a quicker escape—and then a boat from Hjorl on Aöefl's Fjord just up the coast. "The docks are the first place they'll look after here!" I'd be stood there still trying to negotiate a passage to Maladon or the Thurtans when the jarl's men found me.

Tuttugu stepped around Floki Wronghelm, sprawled and snoring beside the bar. "Snorri's down there, preparing to sail." He bent down behind the bar, grunting.

"Snorri? Sailing?" It seemed that the stool had dislodged more than the morning's memories. "Why? Where's he going?"

Tuttugu straightened up holding my sword, dusty and neglected from its time hidden on the bar shelf. I didn't reach for it. I'm fine with wearing a sword in places where nobody is going to see it as an invitation—Trond was never such a place.

"Take it!" Tuttugu angled the hilt toward me.

I ignored it, wrestling myself into my clothes, the coarse weave of the north, itchy but warm. "Since when did Snorri have a boat?" He'd sold the *Ikea* to finance the expedition to the Black Fort—that much I did remember.

"I should get Astrid back here to see if another beating with a stool might knock some sense into you!" Tuttugu tossed the sword down beside me as I sat to haul my boots on.

"*Astrid?* . . . Astrid!" A moment returned to me with crystal clarity—Edda coming down the stairs half-naked, Astrid watching. It had been a while since a morning went so spectacularly wrong for me. I'd never intended the two of them to collide in such circumstances but Astrid hadn't struck me as the jealous sort. In fact I hadn't been entirely sure I was the only younger man keeping her bed warm whilst her husband roamed the seas a-trading. We mostly met at her place up on the Arlls Slope, so stealth with Edda hadn't been a priority. "How did Astrid even know about Hedwig?" More importantly, how did she reach me before Jarl Sorren's housecarls, and how much time did I have?

Tuttugu ran a hand down his face, red and sweating despite the spring chill. "Hedwig managed to send a messenger while her father was still raging and gathering his men. The boy galloped from Sorrenfast and started asking where to find the foreign prince. People directed him to Astrid's house. I got all this from Olaaf Fish-hand after I saw Astrid storming down the Carls Way. So . . ." He drew a deep breath. "Can we go now, because—"

But I was up and past him, out into the unwholesome freshness of the day, splattering through half-frozen mud, aimed down the street for the docks, the mast tops just visible above the houses. Gulls circled on high, watching my progress with mocking cries.

TWO

If there's one thing I like less than boats it's being brutally murdered by an outraged father. I reached the docks painfully aware that I'd put my boots on the wrong feet and slung my sword too low so it tried to trip me at each stride. The usual scene greeted me, a waterfront crowded with activity despite the fishermen having put to sea hours earlier. The fact that the harbour lay ice-locked for the winter months seemed to set the Norsemen into a frenzy come spring—a season characterized by being slightly above the freezing point of brine rather than by the unfurling of flowers and the arrival of bees as in more civilized climes. A forest of masts painted stark lines against the bright horizon, longboats and Viking trade ships nestled alongside triple-masted merchantmen from a dozen nations to the south. Men bustled on every side, loading, unloading, doing complicated things with ropes, fishwives further back working on the nets or applying wickedly sharp knives to glimmering mounds of last night's catch.

"I don't see him." Snorri was normally easy to spot in a crowd—you just looked up.

"There!" Tuttugu tugged my arm and pointed to what must be the smallest boat at the quays, occupied by the largest man.

"That thing? It's not even big enough for Snorri!" I hastened after Tuttugu anyway. There seemed to be some sort of disturbance up by the harbour master's station and I could swear someone shouted "Kendeth!"

I overtook Tuttugu and clattered out along the quay to arrive well ahead of him above Snorri's little boat. Snorri looked up at me through the black and windswept tangle of his mane. I took a step back at the undisguised mistrust in his stare.

"What?" I held out my hands. Any hostility from a man who swings an axe like Snorri does has to be taken seriously. "What did I do?" I did recall some kind of altercation—though it seemed unlikely that I'd have the balls to disagree with six and a half foot of over-muscled madman.

Snorri shook his head and turned away to continue securing his provisions. The boat seemed full of them. And him.

"No really! I got hit in the head. What *did* I do?"

Tuttugu came puffing up behind me, seeming to want to say something, but too winded to speak.

Snorri let out a snort. "I'm going, Jal. You can't talk me out of it. We'll just have to see who cracks first."

Tuttugu set a hand to my shoulder and bent as close to double as his belly would allow. "Jal—" Whatever he'd intended to say past that trailed off into a wheeze and a gasp.

"Which of us cracks first?" It started to come back to me. Snorri's crazy plan. His determination to head south with Loki's key . . . and me equally resolved to stay cosy in the Three Axes enjoying the company until either my money ran out or the weather improved enough to promise a calm crossing to the continent. Aslaug agreed with me. Every sunset she would rise from the darkest reaches of my mind and tell me how unreasonable the Norseman was. She'd even convinced me that separating from Snorri would be for the best, releasing her and the light-sworn spirit Baraqel to return to their own domains, carrying the last traces of the Silent Sister's magic with them.

"Jarl Sorren . . ." Tuttugu heaved in a lungful of air. "Jarl Sorren's men!" He jabbed a finger back up the quay. "Go! Quick!"

Snorri straightened up with a wince, and frowned back at the dock wall where chain-armoured housecarls were pushing a path through the crowd. "I've no bad blood with Jarl Sorren . . ."

"Jal does!" Tuttugu gave me a hefty shove between the shoulder blades. I balanced for a moment, arms pinwheeling, took a half step forward, tripped over that damn sword, and dived into the boat. Bouncing off Snorri proved marginally less painful than meeting the hull face first, and he caught hold of enough of me to make sure I ended in the bilge water rather than the seawater slightly to the left.

"What the hell?" Snorri remained standing a moment longer as Tuttugu started to struggle down into the boat.

"I'm coming too," Tuttugu said.

I lay on my side in the freezing dirty water at the bottom of Snorri's freezing dirty boat. Not the best time for reflection but I did pause to wonder quite how I'd gone so quickly from being pleasantly entangled in the warmth of Edda's slim legs to being unpleasantly entangled in a cold mess of wet rope and bilge water. Grabbing hold of the small mast, I sat up, cursing my luck. When I paused to draw breath it also occurred to me to wonder why Tuttugu was descending toward us.

"Get back out!" It seemed the same thought had struck Snorri. "You've made a life here, Tutt."

"*And* you'll sink the damn boat!" Since no one seemed inclined to do anything about escaping I started to fit the oars myself. It was true though— there was nothing for Tuttugu down south and he did seem to have taken to life in Trond far more successfully than to his previous life as a Viking raider.

Tuttugu stepped backward into the boat, almost falling as he turned.

"What are you doing here, Tutt?" Snorri reached out to steady him whilst I grabbed the sides. "Stay. Let that woman of yours look after you. You won't like it where I'm bound."

Tuttugu looked up at Snorri, the two of them uncomfortably close. "Undoreth, we." That's all he said, but it seemed to be enough for Snorri. They were after all most likely the last two of their people. All that remained of the Uuliskind. Snorri slumped as if in defeat then moved back, taking the oars and shoving me into the prow.

"Stop!" Cries from the quay, above the clatter of feet. "Stop that boat!"

Tuttugu untied the rope and Snorri drew on the oars, moving us smoothly away. The first of Jarl Sorren's housecarls arrived red-faced above the spot where we'd been moored, roaring for our return.

"Row faster!" I had a panic on me, terrified they might jump in after us. The sight of angry men carrying sharp iron has that effect on me.

Snorri laughed. "They're not armoured for swimming." He looked back at them, raising his voice to a boom that drowned out their protests, "And if that man actually throws the axe he's raising I really will come back to return it to him in person."

The man kept hold of his axe.

"And good riddance to you!" I shouted, but not so loud the men on the quay would hear me. "A pox on Norsheim and all its women!" I tried to stand and wave my fist at them, but thought better of it after nearly pitching over the side. I sat down heavily, clutching my sore nose. At least I was heading south at last, and that thought suddenly put me in remarkably good spirits. I'd sail home to a hero's welcome and marry Lisa DeVeer. Thoughts of her had kept me going on the Bitter Ice, and now with Trond retreating into the distance she filled my imagination once again.

It seemed that all those months of occasionally wandering down to the docks and scowling at the boats had made a better sailor of me. I didn't throw up until we were so far from port that I could barely make out the expressions on the housecarls' faces.

"Best not to do that into the wind," Snorri said, not breaking the rhythm of his rowing.

I finished groaning before replying, "I know that, *now*." I wiped the worst of it from my face. Having had nothing but a punch on the nose for breakfast helped to keep the volume down.

"Will they give chase?" Tuttugu asked.

That sense of elation at having escaped a gruesome death shrivelled up as rapidly as it had blossomed and my balls attempted a retreat back into my body. "They won't . . . will they?" I wondered just how fast Snorri could row. Certainly under sail our small boat wouldn't outpace one of Jarl Sorren's longships.

Snorri managed a shrug. "What did you do?"

"His daughter."

"Hedwig?" A shake of the head and laugh broke from him. "Erik Sorren's chased more than a few men over that one. But mostly just long enough to make sure they keep running. A prince of Red March though . . . might go the extra mile for a prince, then drag you back and see you handfasted before the Odin stone."

"Oh God!" Some other awful pagan torture I'd not heard about. "I barely touched her. I swear it." Panic starting to rise, along with the next lot of vomit.

"It means 'married,'" said Snorri. "Handfasted. And from what I heard you barely touched her repeatedly and in her own father's mead-hall to boot."

I said something full of vowels over the side before recovering myself to ask, "So, where's our boat?"

Snorri looked confused. "You're in it."

"I mean the proper-sized one that's taking us south." Scanning the waves I could see no sign of the larger vessel I presumed we must be aiming to rendezvous with.

Snorri's mouth took on a stiff-jawed look as if I'd insulted his mother. "You're in it."

"Oh come on . . ." I faltered beneath the weight of his stare. "We're not seriously crossing the sea to Maladon in this rowboat are we?"

By way of answer Snorri shipped the oars and started to prepare the sail.

"Dear God . . ." I sat, wedged in the prow, my neck already wet with spray, and looked out over the slate-grey sea, flecked with white where the wind tore the tops off the waves. I'd spent most of the voyage north unconscious and it had been a blessing. The return would have to be endured without the bliss of oblivion.

"Snorri plans to put in at ports along the coast, Jal," Tuttugu called from his huddle in the stern. "We'll sail from Kristian to cross the Karls-water. That's the only time we'll lose sight of land."

"A great comfort, Tuttugu. I always like to do my drowning within sight of land."

Hours passed and the Norsemen actually seemed to be enjoying them-selves. For my part I stayed wrapped around the misery of a hangover, leavened with a stiff dose of stool-to-head. Occasionally I'd touch my nose to make sure Astrid's punch hadn't broken it. I'd liked Astrid and it sorrowed me to think we wouldn't snuggle up in her husband's bed again. I guessed she'd been content to ignore my wanderings as long as she could see herself as the centre and apex of my attentions. To dally with a jarl's daughter, someone so highborn, and for it to be so public, must have been more than her pride would stand for. I rubbed my jaw, wincing. Damn, I'd miss her.

"Here." Snorri thrust a battered pewter mug toward me.

"Rum?" I lifted my head to squint at it. I'm a great believer in hair of the dog, and nautical adventures always call for a measure of rum in my largely fictional experience.

"Water."

I uncurled with a sigh. The sun had climbed as high as it was going to get, a pale ball straining through the white haze above. "Looks like you made a good call. Albeit by mistake. If you hadn't been ready to sail I might be handfasted by now. Or worse."

"Serendipity."

"Seren-what-ity?" I sipped the water. Foul stuff. Like water generally is.

"A fortunate accident," Snorri said.

"Uh." Barbarians should know their place, and using long words isn't it. "Even so it was madness to set off so early in the year. Look! There's still ice floating out there!" I pointed to a large plate of the stuff, big enough to hold a small house. "Won't be much left of this boat if we hit any." I crawled back to join him at the mast.

"Best not distract me from steering then." And just to prove a point he slung us to the left, some lethal piece of woodwork swinging scant inches above my head as the sail crossed over.

"Why the hurry?" Now that the lure of three delicious women who had fallen for my ample charms had been removed I was more prepared to listen to Snorri's reasons for leaving so precipitously. I made a vengeful note to use "precipitously" in conversation. "Why so precipitous?"

"We went through this, Jal. To the death!" Snorri's jaw tightened, muscles bunching.

"Tell me once more. Such matters are clearer at sea." By which I meant I didn't listen the first time because it just seemed like ten different reasons to pry me from the warmth of my tavern and from Edda's arms. I would miss Edda, she really was a sweet girl. Also a demon in the furs. In fact I sometimes got the feeling that I was her foreign fling rather than the other way around. Never any talk of inviting me to meet her parents. Never a whisper about marriage to her prince . . . A man enjoying himself any less than I was might have had his pride hurt a touch by that. Northern ways are very strange. I'm not complaining . . . but they're strange. Between the three of them I'd spent the winter in a constant state of exhaustion. Without the threat of impending death I might never have mustered the energy to leave. I might have lived out my days as a tired but happy tavernkeeper in Trond. "Tell me once more and we'll never speak of it again!"

"I told you a hundr—"

I made to vomit, leaning forward.

"All right!" Snorri raised a hand to forestall me. "If it will stop you puking all over my boat . . ." He leaned out over the side for a moment, steering the craft with his weight, then sat back. "Tuttugu!" Two fingers toward his eyes, telling him to keep watch for ice. "This key." Snorri patted the front of his fleece jacket, above his heart. "We didn't come by it easy." Tuttugu snorted at that. I suppressed a shudder. I'd done a good job of forgetting everything between leaving Trond on the day we first set off for the Black Fort and our arrival back. Unfortunately it only took a hint or two for memories to start leaking through my barriers. In particular the screech of iron hinges would return to haunt me as door after door surrendered to the unborn captain and that damn key.

Snorri fixed me with that stare of his, the honest and determined one that makes you feel like joining him in whatever mad scheme he's espousing—just for a moment, mind, until common sense kicks back in. "The Dead King will be wanting this key back. Others will want it too. The ice kept us safe, the winter, the snows . . . once the harbour cleared the key had to be moved. Trond would not have kept him out."

I shook my head. "Safe's the last thing on your mind! Aslaug told me what you really plan to do with Loki's key. All that talk of taking it back to my grandmother was nonsense." Snorri narrowed his eyes at that. For once the look didn't make me falter—soured by the worst of days and made bold by the misery of the voyage I blustered on regardless. "Well! Wasn't it nonsense?"

"The Red Queen would destroy the key," Snorri said.

"Good!" Almost a shout. "That's exactly what she *should* do!"

Snorri looked down at his hands, upturned on his lap, big, scarred, thick with callus. The wind whipped his hair about, hiding his face. "I will find this door."

"Christ! That's the last place that key should be taken!" If there really was a door into death no sane person would want to stand before it. "If this morning has taught me anything it's to be very careful which doors you open and when."

Snorri made no reply. He kept silent. Still. Nothing for long moments but the flap of sail, the slop of wave against hull. I knew what thoughts ran through his head. I couldn't speak them, my mouth would go too dry. I couldn't deny them, though to do so would cause me only an echo of the hurt such a denial would do him.

"I will get them back." His eyes held mine and for a heartbeat made me believe he might. His voice, his whole body shook with emotion, though in what part sorrow and what part rage I couldn't say.

"I will find this door. I will unlock it. And I will bring back my wife, my children, my unborn son."

THREE

"Jal?" Someone shaking my shoulder. I reached to draw Edda in closer and found my fingers tangled in the unwholesome ginger thicket of Tuttugu's beard, heavy with grease and salt. The whole sorry story crashed in on me and I let out a groan, deepened by the returning awareness of the swell, lifting and dropping our little boat.

"What?" I hadn't been having a good dream, but it was better than this.

Tuttugu thrust a half-brick of dark Viking bread at me, as if eating on a boat were really an option. I waved it away. If Norse women were a high point of the far north then their cuisine counted as one of the lowest. With fish they were generally on a good footing, simple, plain fare, though you had to be careful or they'd start trying to feed it to you raw, or half-rotted and stinking worse than corpse flesh. "Delicacies" they'd call it . . . The time to eat something is the stage between raw and rotting. It's not the alchemy of rockets! With meat—what meat there was to be found clinging to the near vertical surfaces of the north—you could trust them to roast it over an open fire. Anything else always proved a disaster. And with any other kind of eatable the Norsemen were likely to render it as close to inedible as makes no difference using a combination of salt, pickle, and desiccated nastiness. Whale meat they preserved by pissing on it! My theory was that a long history of raiding each other had driven them to make their foodstuffs so foul that no one in their right mind would want to steal it. Thereby ensuring that, whatever else the enemy might carry off, women, children, goats, and gold, at least they'd leave lunch behind.

"We're coming in to Olaafheim," Tuttugu said, pulling me out of my doze again.

"Whu?" I levered myself up to look over the prow. The seemingly endless uninviting coastline of wet black cliffs protected by wet black rocks had been replaced with a river mouth. The mountains leapt up swiftly to either side, but here the river had cut a valley whose sides might be grazed, and left a truncated floodplain where a small port nestled against the rising backdrop.

"Best not to spend the night at sea." Tuttugu paused to gnaw at the bread in his hand. "Not when we're so close to land." He glanced out west to where the sun plotted its descent toward the horizon. The quick look he shot me before settling back to eat told me clear enough that he'd rather not be sharing the boat with me when Aslaug came to visit at sunset.

Snorri tacked across the mouth of the river, the Hœnir he called it, angling across the diluted current toward the Olaafheim harbour. "These are fisher folk and raiders, Jal. Clan Olaaf, led by jarls Harl and Knütson, twin sons of Knüt Ice-Reaver. This isn't Trond. The people are less . . . cosmopolitan. More—"

"More likely to split my skull if I look at them wrong," I interrupted him. "I get the picture." I held a hand up. "I promise not to bed any jarl's daughters." I even meant it. Now we were actually on the move I had begun to get excited about the prospect of a return to Red March, to being a prince again, returning to my old diversions, running with my old crowd, and putting all this unpleasantness behind me. And if Snorri's plans led him along a different path then we'd just have to see what happened. We'd have to see, as he put it earlier, who cracked first. The bonds that bound us seemed to have weakened since the event at the Black Fort. We could separate five miles and more before any discomfort set in. And as we'd already seen, if the Silent Sister's magic did fracture its way out of us the effect wasn't fatal . . . except for other people. If push came to shove Aslaug's advice seemed sound. Let the magic go, let her and Baraqel be released to return to their domains. It would be far from pleasant if last time was anything to go by, but like pulling a tooth it would be much better afterward. Obviously though, I'd do everything I could to avoid pulling that particular tooth—unless it meant traipsing into mortal danger on Snorri's quest. My own plan involved getting him to Vermillion and having Grandmother order her sister to effect a more gentle release of our fetters.

We pulled into the harbour at Olaafheim with the shadows of boats at anchor reaching out toward us across the water. Snorri furled the sail, and Tuttugu rowed toward a berth. Fishermen paused from their labours, setting down their baskets of hake and cod to watch us. Fishwives laid down half-stowed nets and crowded in behind their men to see the new arrivals. Norsemen busy with some or other maintenance on the nearest of four longboats leaned out over the sides to call out in the old tongue. Threats or welcome I couldn't tell, for a Viking can growl out the warmest greeting in a tone that suggests he's promising to cut your mother's throat.

As we coasted the last yard Snorri vaulted up onto the harbour wall from the side of the boat. Locals crowded him immediately, a sea of them surging around the rock. From the amount of shoulder-slapping and the tone of the growling I guessed we weren't in trouble. The occasional chuckle even escaped from several of the beards on show, which took some doing as the clan Olaaf grew the most impressive facial hair I'd yet seen. Many favoured the bushy explosions that look like regular beards subjected to sudden and very shocking news. Others had them plaited and hanging in two, three, sometimes five iron-capped braids reaching down to their belts.

"Snorri." A newcomer, well over six foot and at least that wide, fat with it, arms like slabs of meat. At first I thought he was wearing spring furs, or some kind of woollen overshirt, but as he closed on Snorri it became apparent that his chest hair just hadn't known when to stop.

"Borris!" Snorri surged through the others to clasp arms with the man, the two of them wrestling briefly, neither giving ground.

Tuttugu finished tying up and with a pair of men on each arm the locals hauled him onto the dock. I clambered quickly up behind him, not wishing to be manhandled.

"Tuttugu!" Snorri pointed him out for Borris. "Undoreth. We might be the last of our clan, him and I . . ." He trailed off, inviting any present to make a liar of him, but none volunteered any sighting of other survivors.

"A pox on the Hardassa." Borris spat on the ground. "We kill them where we find them. And any others who make cause with the Drowned Isles." Mutters and shouts went up at that. More men spitting when they spoke the word "necromancer."

"A pox on the Hardassa!" Snorri shouted. "That's something to drink to!"

With a general cheering and stamping of feet the whole crowd started to move toward the huts and halls behind the various fisheries and boat sheds of the harbour. Snorri and Borris led the way, arms over each other's shoulders, laughing at some joke, and I, the only prince present, trailed along unintroduced at the rear with the fishermen, their hands still scaly from the catch.

I guess Trond must have had its own stink, all towns do, but you don't notice it after a while. A day at sea breathing air off the Atlantis Ocean tainted with nothing but a touch of salt proved sufficient to enable my nostrils to be offended by my fellow men once more. Olaafheim stank of fresh fish, sweat, stale fish, sewers, rotting fish, and uncured hides. It only got worse as we trudged up through a random maze of split-log huts, turf roofed and close to the ground, each with nets at the front and fuel stacked to the sheltered landward side.

Olaafheim's great hall stood smaller than the foyer of my grandmother's palace, a half-timbered structure, mud daubed into any nook or cranny where the wind might slide its fingers, wooden shingles on the roof, patchy after the winter storms.

I let the Norsemen crowd in ahead of me and turned back to face the sea. In the west clear skies showed a crimson sun descending. Winter in Trond had been a long cold thing. I may have spent more time than was reasonable in the furs but in truth most of the north does the same. The night can last twenty hours and even when the day finally breaks it never gets above a level of cold I call "fuck that"—as in you open the door, your face freezes instantly to the point where it hurts to speak, but manfully you manage to say "fuck that," before turning round, and going back to bed. There's little to do in a northern winter but to endure it. In the very depths of the season sunrise and sunset get so close together that if Snorri and I were to be in the same room Aslaug and Baraqel might even get to meet. A little further north and they surely would, for there the days dwindle into nothing and become a single night that lasts for weeks. Not that Aslaug and Baraqel meeting would be a good idea.

Already I could feel Aslaug scratching at the back of my mind. The sun hadn't yet touched the water but the sea burned bloody with it and I could hear her footsteps. I recalled how Snorri's eyes would darken when she used to visit him. Even the whites would fill with shadow, and become for a minute or two so wholly black that you might imagine them holes into some endless night, from which horrors might pour if he but looked your way. I held that to be a clash of temperaments though. If anything my vision always seemed clearer when she came. I made sure to be alone each sunset so we could have our moment. Snorri described her as a creature of lies, a seducer whose words could turn something awful into an idea that any reasonable man would consider. For my part I found her very agreeable, though perhaps a little excessive, and definitely less concerned about my safety than I am.

The first time Aslaug came to me I had been surprised to find her so close to the image Snorri's tales had painted in my mind. I told her so and she laughed at me. She said men had always seen what they expected to see but that a deeper truth ran beneath that fact. "The world is shaped by mankind's desires and fears. A war of hope against dread, waged upon a substrate that man himself made malleable though he has long forgotten how. All men and all men's works stand on feet of clay, waiting to be formed and reformed, forged by fear into monsters from the dark core of each soul, waiting to rend the world asunder." That's how she introduced herself to me.

"Prince Jalan." Aslaug stepped from the shadows of the hall. They clung to her, dark webs, not wanting to release their hold. She pulled clear as the sun kissed the horizon. No one would mistake her for human but she wore a woman's form and wore it well, her flesh like bone, but dipped in ink so it soaked into every pore, revealing the grain, gathering black in any hollow. She fixed me with eyes that held no colour, only passions, set in a narrow and exquisite face. Oil-dark hair framed her, falling in unnatural coils and curls. Her beauty owed something to the praying mantis, something to the inhumanity of Greek sculpture. Mask or not though, it worked on me. I'm easily led in matters of the flesh. "Jalan," she said again, stepping around me. She wore tatters of darkness as a gown.

I didn't answer, or turn to follow her. Villagers were still arriving, and the cheers and laughter from inside the hall were drawing more by the minute. None of them would see Aslaug but if they saw me spinning around and talking to the empty air it wouldn't look good. Northmen are a superstitious lot, and frankly with what I'd seen over the last few months they were right to be so. Superstition though does tend to have a sharp end, and I didn't want to find myself impaled on it.

"Why are you out here in the wilds with all these ill-smelling peasants?" Aslaug reappeared at my left shoulder, her mouth close to my ear. "And why"—a harder edge to her tone, eyes narrowing—"is that light-sworn here? I can smell him. He was going away . . ." A tilt of her head. "Jalan? Have you followed him? Tagged along like a dog at heel? We've talked about this, Jalan. You're a prince, a man of royal blood, in line for the throne of Red March!"

"I'm going home." I whispered it, hardly a twitch in my lips.

"Leaving your beauties behind?" She always held a note of disapproval when it came to my womanizing. Obviously the jealous type.

"I thought it time. They were getting clingy." I rubbed the side of my head, not convinced that Tuttugu had gotten all the splinters out.

"For the better. In Red March we can begin to clear your path to succession." A smile lit her face, the sky crimson behind her with the sun's death throes.

"Well . . ." My own lips curled with an echo of her expression. "I'm not one for murder. But if a whole bunch of my cousins fell off a cliff I wouldn't lose any sleep over it." I'd found it paid to play along with her. Whilst I'd rejoice in any misfortune that fate might drop upon my cousins, three or four of them in particular, I've never had an appetite for the more lethal games played at some courts with knife and poison. My own vision for my glorious path to the throne involved toadying and favourit-ism, lubricated with tales of heroism and reports of genius. Once selected as Grandmother's favourite and promoted unfairly into the position of heir it would just be a case of the old woman having a timely heart attack and my reign of pleasure would begin!

"You know that Snorri will be plotting your destruction, Jalan?" She reached an arm around me, the touch cold but somehow thrilling too, filled with all the delicious possibilities that the night hides. "You know what Baraqel will be instructing. He told you the same when Snorri kept me within him."

"I trust Snorri." If he had wanted me dead he could have done it many times over.

"For how long, Prince Jalan? For how long will you trust him?" Her lips close to mine now, head haloed with the last rays of the sunset. "Don't trust the light, Prince Jalan. The stars are pretty but the space between them is infinite and black with promise." Behind me I could almost hear her shadow mix with mine, its dry spider-legs rustling one against the next. "Returning with your body and the right story to Vermillion would earn Snorri gratitude in many circles for many reasons . . ."

"Good night, Aslaug." I clenched what could be clenched and kept from shuddering. In the last moments before the dark took her she was always at her least human, as if her presence outlasted her disguise for just a heartbeat.

"Watch him!" And the shadows pulled her down as they merged into the singular gloom that would deepen into night.

I turned and followed the locals into their "great" hall. My moments with Aslaug always left me a touch less tolerant of sweaty peasants and their crude little lives. And perhaps Snorri did bear watching. He had after all been on the point of abandoning me when I most needed help. A day later and I could have been subjected to all the horrors of hand-fasting, or some even crueller form of Viking justice.

FOUR

Three long tables divided the mead-hall, now lined by men and women raising foaming horn and dripping tankard. Children, some no more than eight or nine, ran back and forth with pitchers from four great barrels to keep any receptacle from running dry. A great fire roared in the hearth, fish roasting on spits set before it. Hounds bickered around the margins of the room, daring a kicking to run beneath the tables should anything fall. The heat and roar and stink of the place took a moment's getting used to after plunging in from the frigid spring evening. I plotted a course toward the rear of the hall, giving the dogs a wide berth. Animals are generally good judges of character—they don't like me—except for horses which, for reasons I've never understood, give me their all. Perhaps it's our shared interest in running away that forms the bond.

Snorri and Borris sat close to the fire, flanked by Olaafheim's warriors. Most of the company appeared to have brought their axes out for the evening's drinking, setting them across the tabletop in such a crowd that putting down a drink became a tricky task. Snorri turned as I approached, and boomed out for a space to be made. A couple of grumbles went up at that, soon silenced with mutters of "berserker." I squeezed down onto a narrow span of arse-polished bench, trying not to show my displeasure at being wedged in so tightly among hairy brigands. My tolerance for such familiarities had increased during my time at the Three Axes as owner and operator . . . well, in truth I paid for Eyolf to keep bar and Helga and Gudrun to serve tables . . . but still, I was there in spirit. In any event, although my tolerance had increased it still wasn't high and at least in Trond you got a better quality of bearded, axe-wielding barbarian. Faced with the present situation though, not to mention a table full of axes, I did what any man keen on leaving with the same number of limbs that he entered with would do. I grinned like an idiot and bore it.

I reached for the brimming flagon brought to me by a blond and barefoot child and decided to get drunk. It would probably keep me out of trouble, and the possibility that I might pass the whole trip to the continent in a state of inebriation did seem inviting. One worry stayed my hand however. Though it pained me to admit it, my grandmother's blood did seem to have shown in me. Snorri or Tuttugu had already mentioned my . . . disability to our hosts. In the troll-wrestling heart of the north being a berserker seemed to carry a good deal of cachet, but any right-thinking man would tell you what a terrible encumbrance it is. I've always been sensibly terrified of battle. The discovery that if I get pushed too far I turn into a raging maniac who throws himself headlong into the thickest of the fighting was hardly comforting. A wise man's biggest advantage is in knowing the ideal time to run away. That sort of survival strategy is somewhat impaired by a tendency to start frothing at the mouth and casting aside all fear. Fear is a valuable commodity, it's common sense compressed into its purest form. A lack of it is not a good thing. Fortunately it took quite a lot of pushing to get my hidden berserker out into the open and to my knowledge it had only ever happened twice. Once at the Aral Pass and once in the Black Fort. If it never happened again that would be fine with me.

". . . Skilfar . . ." A one-eyed man opposite Snorri, speaking into his ale horn. I picked out the one word, and that was plenty.

"What?" I knocked back the rest of my own ale, wiping the suds from my whiskers, a fine blond set I'd cultivated to suit the climate. "I'm not going back there, Snorri, no way." I remembered the witch in her cavern, her plasteek legion all around. She'd scared the hell out of me. I still had nightmares . . .

"Relax." Snorri gave me that winning smile of his. "We don't have to."

I did relax, slumping forward as I let go of a tension I hadn't known was there. "Thank God."

"She's still in her winter seat. Beerentoppen. It's a mountain of ice and fire, not too far inland, it'll be our last stop before we leave the north just a few days down the coast and strike out for Maladon across open sea."

"Hell no!" It had been the woman that scared me, not the tunnels and statues—well, they had too, but the point was that I wasn't going. "We'll head south. The Red Queen will have any answers we need."

Snorri shook his head. "I have questions that won't wait, Jal. Questions that need a little northern light shed on them."

I knew what he wanted to talk about—that damned door. If he took the key to Skilfar, though, she'd probably take it off him. I didn't doubt for a moment that she could. Still, it would be no skin off my nose if she stole it. A thing that powerful would be safer in the old witch's keeping anyhow. Far from where I intended to be and out of the Dead King's reach.

"All right." I cut across the one-eyed warrior again. "You can go. But I'm staying in the boat!"

The fellow across from Snorri turned a cold blue eye my way, the other socket empty, the firelight catching the twitch of ugly little muscles in the shadowed hollow. "This fit-firar speaks for you now, Snorri?"

I knew the insult to be a grim one. The Vikings can think of nothing worse to call you than "land man," one who doesn't know the sea. That's the trouble with these backwater villages—everyone's tetchy. They're all ready to jump up at a moment's notice and spill your guts. It's over-compensation of course, for living in freezing huts on an inhospitable beach. At home I'd damn the fellow's eyes . . . well eye at least . . . and let one half of the palace guard hold me back while the other half beat him out of town. The trouble with a friend like Snorri is that he's the sort to take things at face value and think I really did want to defend my own honour. Knowing Snorri he'd stand by clapping while the savage carved me up.

The man, Gauti I think Snorri had called him, had one hand on the axe before him, casual enough, fingers spread, but he kept that cold eye on me and there was little to read in it that wasn't murder. This could go very wrong, very quickly. The sudden urge to piss nearly overtook me. I smiled the bold Jalan smile, ignoring the sick feeling in my stomach, and drew my dagger, a wicked piece of black iron. That got some attention, though less than in any place I'd ever seen an edge drawn before. I did at least get the satisfaction of seeing Gauti flinch, his fingers half closing about his axe hilt. To my credit, I do *look* like the kind of hero who would demand satisfaction and have the skill to take it.

"Jal . . ." Snorri with a half frown, gesturing with his eyes at the eight inches of knife in my hand.

I pushed aside some axe hafts and in a sudden move inverted my blade so the point hovered a quarter inch above the table. Again Gauti's eye twitched. I saw Snorri quietly lay his hand on the man's axe head. Several warriors half rose then settled back in their places.

One great asset in my career as secret coward has been a natural ability to lie fluently in body language. Half of it is . . . what did Snorri call it? Serendipity. Pure lucky accident. When scared I flush scarlet, but in a fit young man overtopping six foot by a good two inches it usually comes across as outrage. My hands also rarely betray me. I may be quivering with fright inside but they hold steady. Even when the terror is so much that they do finally shake it's often as not mistaken as rage. Now though, as I set knifepoint to wood, my hands kept firm and sure. In a few strokes I sketched out an irregular blob with a horn at the top and lobe at the bottom.

"What is it?" The man across from me.

"A cow?" A woman of middle years, very drunk, leaning over Snorri's shoulder.

"That, men of the clan Olaaf, is Scorron, the land of my enemies. These are the borders. This . . ." I scored a short line across the bottom of the lobe. "This is the Aral Pass where I taught the Scorron army to call me 'devil.'" I looked up to meet Gauti's singular glare. "And you will note that not one of these borders is a coastline. So if I were a man of the sea it would mean, in my country, that I could never close with my enemy. In fact every time I set sail I would be running away from them." I stuck the knife firmly in the centre of Scorron. "Where I come from 'land men' are the only men who can go to war." I let a boy refill my tankard. "And so we learn that insults are like daggers—it matters which way you point them, and where you stand." And I threw my head back to drain my cup.

Snorri pounded the table, the axes danced, and the laughter came. Gauti leaned back, sour but his ill-temper having lost its edge. The ale flowed. Codfish were brought to table along with some kind of salty grain-mash and dreadful little sea-weed cakes burned nearly black. We ate. More ale flowed. I found myself talking drunkenly to a greybeard with more scar than face about the merits of different kinds of longboat— a subject I acquired my "expertise" on in many separate pieces during innumerable similar drunken conversations with regulars back at the Three Axes. More ale, spilled, splashed, gulped. I think we'd got onto knots by the time I slipped gracefully off the bench and decided to stay where I was.

"Hedwig," I grumbled, still half-asleep. "Get off me, woman."

The licking paused, then started up again. I wondered vaguely where I was, and when Hedwig's tongue had got quite so long. And sloppy. And stinky.

"Get off!" I swiped at the dog. "Bloody mutt." I raised myself on one elbow, still at least half-drunk. The hearth's glowing embers painted the hall in edge and shadow. Hounds slunk beneath the tables, searching for scraps. I could make out half a dozen drunks snoring on the floor, lying where they fell, and Snorri, stretched out along the central table, head on his pack, deep in his slumbers.

I got up, unsteady, stomach lurching. Although the hall smelled as if pissing in it might improve matters, I wove a path toward the main doors. In the gloom I might hit a sleeping Viking and it would prove hard to talk my way out of that one.

I reached the double doors and heaved open the one on the left, the hinges squealing loud enough to wake the dead—but apparently nobody else—and stepped out. My breath plumed before me and the moonlit square lay glittering with frost. Another fine spring night in the north. I took a pace to the left and started to answer nature's call.

Beneath the splash of borrowed ale lay the slap of waves against the harbour wall, beneath that the murmur of surf slopping half-heartedly up the distant beach that slanted down to the river, and beneath that . . . a quiet that prickled the hairs at the back of my neck. I strained my ears, finding nothing to warrant my unease, but even in my cups I have a sense for trouble. Since Aslaug's arrival the night seemed to whisper to me. Tonight it held its tongue.

I turned, still fumbling to lace my fly, and found instead that I needed to go again, right away. Standing no more than ten yards from me was the biggest wolf ever. I'd heard tall stories aplenty in the Three Axes and I'd been prepared to believe the north bred bigger wolves than might be found down south. I'd even seen a direwolf with my own eyes, albeit stuffed and mounted in the entrance hall to Madam Serene's Pleasure Palace down on Magister Street, Vermillion. The thing before me had to be one of the Fenris breed they spoke about in Trond. It stood as tall as a horse, wider in its shaggy coat, its mouth full of sharp ivory gleaming in the moonlight.

I stood there, stock still, still draining onto the ground between my feet. The beast moved forward, no snarl, no prowling, just a quick but slightly ungainly advance. It didn't occur to me to reach for my sword. The wolf looked as though it might simply bite the sharp end off in any case. Instead I just stood there, making a puddle. I normally pride myself on being the type of coward who acts in the moment, running away when it counts rather than being rooted to the spot. This time however the weight of terror proved too great to run with.

Not until the huge beast charged past me, crashing open the double doors and rushing on into the great hall did I find the presence of mind to start my escape. I ran, holding my breath against the carrion reek of the thing. I got as far as the edge of the square, driven by the awful screams and howls behind me, before my brain dropped anchor. Dogs from the hall ran yelping past me. I came up short, panting—mostly in fear since I hadn't run very far—and drew my sword. Ahead of me in the blind night could be any number of similar monsters. Wolves hunt in packs after all. Did I want to be alone in the dark with the beast's friends, or would the safest place be with Snorri and a dozen other Vikings facing the one I'd seen?

All across Olaafheim doors were being kicked open, flames kindled. Hounds that had been taken unawares now gave voice, and cries of "To arms!" started to ring out. Gritting my teeth, I turned back, making no effort to hurry. It sounded like hell in there: men's screams and oaths, crashing and splintering, but strangely not a single snarl or wolf-howl. I'd seen dog fights before and they're loud affairs. Wolves, it seemed, were given to biting their tongues—yours too, no doubt, if they got a chance!

As I drew closer to the hall the cacophony from within grew less loud, just groans, grunts, the scrape of claw on stone. My pace slowed to a crawl. Only the sounds of activity at my back kept me moving at all. I couldn't be seen to be just standing there while men died only yards away. Heart racing, feet anything but, I made it to the doorway and eased my head around so one eye could see within.

Tables lay upended, their legs a short and drunken forest shifting in the fire glow. Men, or rather pieces of men, scattered the floor amid dark lakes and darker smears. At first I couldn't see the Fenris wolf. A grunt of effort drew my eyes to the deepest shadow at the side of the hall. The beast stood hunched over, worrying at something on the ground. Two axes jutted from its side, one stood bedded in its back. I could see its great jaws wide about something, and a man's legs straining beneath its snout, covered in a black slime of blood and slobber. Somehow I knew who it was, trapped in that maw.

"Snorri!" The shout burst from me without permission. I clapped a hand to my mouth in case any more foolishness might emerge. The last thing I wanted was for that awful head to turn my way. To my horror I found that I'd stepped into the doorway—the absolute worst place to be, silhouetted by moonlight, blocking the exit.

"To arms!"

"To the hall!" Cries from all directions now.

Behind me I could hear the pounding of many feet. No retreat that way. The Norse will string a coward up by his thumbs and cut off bits he needs. I stepped in quickly to make myself a less obvious target, and edged along the inner wall, trying not to breathe. Vikings started to arrive at the doorway behind me, crowding to get through.

As I watched the wolf, a hand, looking child-size against the scale of the creature, slid up from the far side of its head and clamped between its eyes. A glowing hand. A hand becoming so brilliant that the whole room lit almost bright as day. Exposed by the light, I did what any cockroach does when someone unhoods a lantern in the kitchens. I raced for cover, leaping toward the shelter of a section of table fallen on its side partway between us.

The light grew still more dazzling, and half-blinded I staggered across a torso, fell over the table, and sprawled forward with several lunging steps, desperate to remain on my feet. My outstretched sword sunk into something soft, grating across bone, and a moment later an immense weight fell across me, taking away all illumination. And all the other stuff too.

FIVE

". . . underneath! It's taken six men to get him out." A woman's voice, tinged with wonder.

I felt as if I were lifted up. Carried away.

"Steady!"

"Easy . . ."

A warm wet cloth passed across my forehead. I snuggled into the softness cradling me. The world lay a pleasant distance away, only snatches of conversation reaching me as I dozed.

In my dream I wandered the empty palace of Vermillion on a fine summer's day, the light streaming in through tall windows overlooking the city's basking sprawl.

". . . hilt deep! Must have reached the heart . . ." A man's voice.

I was moving. Borne along. The motion halfway between the familiar jolt of a horse and the despised rise and fall of the ocean.

". . . saw his friend . . ."

"Heard him shout in the doorway. 'Snorri!' He roared it like a Viking . . ."

The world grew closer. I didn't want it to. I was home. Where it was warm. And safe. Well, safer. All the north had to offer was a soft landing. The woman holding me had a chest as mountainous as the local terrain.

". . . charged straight at it . . ."

". . . dived at it!"

The creak of a door. The raking of coals.

". . . berserker . . ."

I turned from the sun-drenched cityscape back into the empty palace gallery, momentarily blind.

". . . Fenris . . ."

The sunspots cleared from my eyes, the reds and greens fading. And I saw the wolf, there in the palace hall, jaws gaping, ivory fangs, scarlet tongue, ropes of saliva, hot breath . . .

"Arrrg!" I jerked upright, my head coming clear of Borris's hairy man-breasts. Did the man never wear a shirt?

"Steady there!" Thick arms set me down as easily as a child onto a fur-laden cot. A smoky hut rose about us, larger than most, people crowded round on all sides.

"What?" I always ask that—though on reflection I seldom want to know.

"Easy! It's dead." Borris straightened up. Warriors of the clan Olaaf filled the roundhouse, also a matronly woman with thick blond plaits and several buxom younger women—presumably the wife and daughters.

"Snorri—" I started before noticing him lying beside me, unconscious, pale—even for a northman—and sporting several nasty gashes, one of them an older wound sliced down across his ribs, angry and white-crusted. Even so he looked in far better shape than a man should after being gnawed on by a Fenris wolf. The markings about his upper arms stood out in sharp contrast against marble flesh, the hammer and the axe in blue, runes in black, trapping my attention for a moment. "How?" I didn't feel up to sentences containing more than one word.

"Had a shield jammed in the beast's mouth. Wedged open!" Borris said.

"Then you killed it!" One of his daughters, her chest almost as developed as his.

"We got your sword out." A warrior from the crowd, offering me my blade, hilt first, almost reverential. "Took some doing!"

The creature's weight had driven the blade home as it fell.

I recalled how wide the wolf's mouth had been around Snorri, and the lack of chewing going on. Closing my eyes I saw that brilliant hand pressed between the wolf's eyes.

"I want to see the creature." I didn't, but I needed to. Besides, it wasn't often I got to play the hero and it probably wouldn't last long past Snorri regaining his senses. With some effort I managed to stand. Drawing breath proved the hardest part. The wolf had left me with bruised ribs on both sides. I was lucky it hadn't crushed them all. "Hell! Where's Tuttugu?"

"I'm here!" The voice came from behind several broad backs. Men pulled aside to reveal the other half of the Undoreth, grinning, one eye closing as it swelled. "Got knocked into a wall."

"You're making a habit of that." It surprised me how pleased I was to see him in one piece. "Let's go!"

Borris led the way, and flanked by men bearing reed torches I hobbled after, clutching my ribs and cursing. A pyramidal fire of seasoned logs now lit the square and a number of injured men were laid out on pallets around it, being treated by an ancient couple, both shrouded in straggles of long white hair. I hadn't thought from my brief time in the hall that anyone had survived, but a wounded man has an instinct for rolling into any cranny or hidey hole that will take him. In the Aral Pass we'd pulled dead men from crevices and fox dens, some with just their boots showing.

Borris took us past the casualties and up to the doors of the great hall. A small man with a big warty blemish on his cheek waited guard, clutching his spear and eyeing the night.

"It's dead!" The first thing he said to us. He seemed distracted, scratching at his overlarge iron helm as if that might satisfy whatever itched him.

"Well of course it's dead!" Borris said, pushing past. "The berserker prince killed it!"

"Of course it's dead," I echoed as I passed the little fellow, allowing myself a touch of scorn. I couldn't say why the thing had chosen that moment to fall on me, but its weight had driven my sword hilt-deep, and even a wolf as big as a horse isn't going to get up again after an accident like that. Even so, I felt troubled. Something about Snorri's hands glowing like that . . .

"Odin's balls! It stinks!" Borris, just ahead of me.

I drew breath to point out that of course it did. The hall had stunk to heaven but to be fair it had been only marginally worse than the aroma of Borris's roundhouse, or in fact Olaafheim in general. My observations were lost in a fit of choking though as the foulness invaded my lungs.

Choking with badly bruised ribs is a painful affair and takes your mind off things, like standing up. Fortunately Tuttugu caught hold of me.

We advanced, breathing in shallow gasps. Lanterns had been lit and placed on the central table, now set back on its feet. Some kind of incense burned in pots, cutting through the reek with a sharp lavender scent.

The dead men had been laid out before the hearth, parts associated. I saw Gauti among them, bitten clean in half, his eye screwed shut in the agony of the moment, the empty socket staring at the roof beams. The wolf lay where it had fallen whilst savaging Snorri. It sprawled on its side, feet pointing at the wall. The terror that had infected me when I first saw it now returned in force. Even dead it presented a fearsome sight.

The stench thickened as we approached.

"It's dead," Borris said, walking toward the dangerous end.

"Well of course—" I broke off. The thing reeked of carrion. Its fur had fallen out in patches, the flesh beneath grey. In places where it had split worms writhed. It wasn't just dead—it had been dead for a while.

"Odin . . ." Borris breathed the word through the hand over his face, finding no parts of the divine anatomy to attach to the oath this time. I joined him and stared down at the wolf's head. Blackened skull would be a more accurate description. The fur had gone, the skin wrinkled back as if before a flame, and on the bone, between eye sockets from which ichor oozed, a handprint had been seared.

"The Dead King!" I swivelled for the door, sword in fist.

"What?" Borris didn't move, still staring at the wolf's head.

I paused and pointed toward the corpses. As I did so Gauti's good eye snapped open. If his stare had been cold in life now all the winters of the Bitter Ice blew there. His hands clawed at the ground, and where his torso ended, in the red ruin hanging below his ribcage, pieces began to twitch.

"Burn the dead! Dismember them!" And I started to run, clutching my sides with one arm, each breath sharp-edged.

"Jal, where—" Tuttugu tried to catch hold of me as I passed him.

"Snorri! The Dead King sent the wolf for Snorri!" I barged past wart-face on the door and out into the night.

What with my ribs and Tuttugu's bulk neither of us was the first to get back to Borris's house. Swifter men had alerted the wife and daughters. Locals were already arriving to guard the place as we ducked in through the main entrance. Snorri had got himself into a sitting position, showing off the over-muscled topology of his bare chest and stomach. He had the daughters fussing around him, one stitching a tear on his side while another cleaned a wound just below his collarbone. I remembered when I had been light-sworn, carrying Baraqel within me, just how much it took out of me to incapacitate a single corpse man. Back on the mountainside just past Chamy-Nix, when Edris's men had caught us, I'd burned through the forearms of the corpse that had been trying to strangle me. The effort had left me helpless. The fact that Snorri could even sit after incinerating the entire head of a giant dead-wolf spoke as loudly about his inner strength as all that muscle did about his outer strength.

Snorri looked up and gave me a weary grin. Having been at different times both light-sworn and now dark-sworn I have to say the dark side has it easier. The power Snorri and I had used on the undead was the same healing that we had both used to repair wounds on others. It drew on the same source of energy, but healing undead flesh just burns the evil out of it.

"It came for the key," I said.

"Probably died on the ice and was released by the thaw." Snorri winced as the kneeling daughter set another stitch. "The real question is how did it know where to find us?"

It was a good question. The idea that any dead thing to hand might be turned against us at any point on our journey was not one that sat well with me. A good question and not one I had an answer for. I looked at Tuttugu as if he might have one.

"Uh." Tuttugu scratched his chins. "Well it's not exactly a secret that Snorri left Trond sailing south. Half the town watched." Tuttugu didn't add "thanks to you" but then again he didn't need to. "And Olaafheim would be the first sensible place for three men in a small boat to put in. Easily reachable in a day's sailing with fair winds. If he had an agent in town with some arcane means of communication . . . or maybe necromancers camped nearby. We don't know how many escaped the Black Fort."

"Well that makes sense." It was a lot better than thinking the Dead King just knew where to find us any time he wanted. "We should, uh, probably leave now."

"Now?" Snorri frowned. "We can't sail in the middle of the night."

I stepped in close, aware of the two daughters' keen interest. "I know you're well liked here, Snorri. But there's a pile of dead bodies in the great hall, and when Borris and his friends have finished dismembering and burning their friends and family they might think to ask why this evil has been visited upon their little town. Just how good a friend is he? And if they start asking questions and want to take us upriver to meet these two jarls of theirs . . . well, do you have friends in high places too?"

Snorri stood, towering above the girls, and me, pulling on his jerkin. "Better go." He picked up his axe and started for the door.

Nobody moved to stop us, though there were plenty of questions.

"Need to get something from the boat." I said that a lot on the way down to the harbour. It was almost true.

By the time we reached the seafront we had quite a crowd with us, their questions merging into one seamless babble of discontent. Tuttugu kept a reed-torch from Borris's roundhouse, lighting the way around piled nets and discarded crates. The locals, lost in the surrounding shadows, watched on in untold numbers. A man grabbed at my arm, saying something about waiting for Borris. I shook him off.

"I'll check in the prow!" It took me a while to master the nautical terminology but ever since learning prow from stern I took all opportunities to demonstrate my credentials. I clambered down, gasping at the pain that reaching overhead caused. I could hear mutters above, people encouraging each other to stop us leaving.

"It might be in the stern . . . that . . . thing we need." Tuttugu could take acting lessons from a troll-stone. He dropped into the other end of the boat, causing a noticeable tilt.

"I'll row us away," Snorri said, descending in two steps. He really hadn't got the hang of deception yet, which after nearly six months in my company had to say something bad about my teaching skills.

To distract the men at the harbour wall from the fact we were smoothly pulling away into the night I raised a hand and bid them a royal farewell. "Good-bye, citizens of Olaafheim. I'll always remember your town as . . . as . . . somewhere I've been."

And that was that. Snorri kept rowing and I slumped back down into the semi-drunken stupor I'd been enjoying before all the night's unpleasantness started. Another town full of Norsemen left behind me. Soon I'd be lazing in the southern sun. I'd almost certainly marry Lisa and be spending her father's money before the summer was out.

Three hours later dawn found us out in the wide grey wilderness of the sea, Norseheim a black line to the east, promising nothing good.

"Well," I said. "At least the Dead King can't get at us out here."

Tuttugu leaned out to look at the wine-dark waves. "Can dead whales swim?" he asked.

SIX

Our hasty departure from Olaafheim saw us putting in two days later at the port of Haargfjord. Food supplies had grown low and although Snorri wanted to avoid any of the larger towns, Haargfjord seemed to be our only choice.

I patted our bag of provisions. "Seems early to restock," I said, finding it more empty than full. "Let's get some decent vittles this time. Proper bread. Cheese. Some honey maybe . . ."

Snorri shook his head. "It would have lasted me to Maladon. I wasn't planning on feeding Tuttugu, or having you borrow rations then spit them out into the sea."

We tied up in the harbour and Snorri set me at a table in a dockside tavern so basic that it lacked even a name. The locals called it the dockside tavern and from the taste of the beer they watered it with what they scooped from the holds of ships at the quays. Even so, I'm not one to complain and the chance to sit somewhere warm that didn't rise and fall with the swell was one I wasn't about to turn down.

I sat there all day, truth be told, swigging the foul beer, charming the pair of plump blond serving girls, and devouring most of a roast pig. I hadn't expected to be left so long but before I knew it I had reached that number of ales where you blink and the sun has leapt a quarter of its path between horizons.

Tuttugu joined me late in the afternoon looking worried. "Snorri's vanished."

"A clever trick! He should teach me that one."

"No, I'm serious. I can't find him anywhere, and it's not that big a town."

I made show of peering under the table, finding nothing but grime-encrusted floorboards and a collection of rat-gnawed rib bones. "He's a big fellow. I've not known a man better at looking after himself."

"He's on a quest to open death's door!" Tuttugu said, waving his hands to demonstrate how that was the opposite of looking after oneself.

"True." I handed Tuttugu a leg bone thick with roast pork. "Look at it this way. If he *has* come to grief he's saved you a journey of months . . . You can go home to Trond and I'll wait here for a decent-sized ship to take me to the continent."

"If you're not worried about Snorri you might at least be worried about the key." Tuttugu scowled and took a huge bite from the pig leg.

I raised a brow at that but Tuttugu's mouth was full and I was too drunk to hold on to any questions I might have.

"Why are you even doing this, Tuttugu?" I ran ale over my loose tongue. "Hunting a door to Hell? Are you planning to follow him in if he finds it?"

Tuttugu swallowed. "I don't know. If I'm brave enough I will."

"Why? Because you're from the same clan? You lived on the slopes of the same fjord? What on earth would possess you to—"

"I knew his wife. I knew his children, Jal. I bounced them on my knee. They called me 'uncle.' If a man can let go of that he can let go of anything . . . and then what point is there to his life, what meaning?"

I opened my mouth, but even drunk I hadn't answers to that. So I lifted my tankard and said nothing.

Tuttugu stayed long enough to finish my meal and drink my ale, then left to continue his search. One of the beer-girls, Hegga or possibly Hadda, brought another pitcher and the next thing I knew night had settled around me and the landlord had started making loud comments about people getting back to their own homes, or at least paying over the coin for space on his fine boards.

I heaved myself up from the table and staggered off to the latrine. Snorri was sitting in my place when I came back, his brow furrowed, an angry set to his jaw.

"Snolli!" I considered asking where he'd been but realized that if I was too drunk to say his name I'd best just sit down. I sat down.

Tuttugu came through the street doors moments later and spotted us with relief.

"Where have you been?" Like a mother scolding.

"Right here! Oh—" I swivelled around with exaggerated care to look at Snorri.

"Seeking wisdom," he said, turning to narrow blue eyes in my direction, a dangerous look that managed to sober me up a little. "Finding my enemy."

"Well that's never been a problem," I said. "Wait a while and they'll come to you."

"Wisdom?" Tuttugu pulled up a stool. "You've been to a völva? Which one? I thought we were headed for Skilfar at Beerentoppen?"

"Ekatri." Snorri poured himself some of my ale. Tuttugu and I said nothing, only watched him. "She was closer." And into our silence Snorri dropped his tale, and afloat on a sea of cheap beer I saw the story unfold before me as he spoke.

After leaving me in the dockside tavern Snorri had gone over the supply list with Tuttugu. "You got this, Tutt? I need to go up and see Old Hrothson."

"Who?" Tuttugu looked up from the slate where Snorri had scratched the runes for salt, dried beef, and the other supplies, together with tally marks to count the quantities.

"Old Hrothson, the chief!"

"Oh." Tuttugu shrugged. "My first time in Haargfjord. Go, I can haggle with the best of them."

Snorri slapped Tuttugu's arm and turned to go.

"Of course even the best haggler needs *something* to pay with . . ." Tuttugu added.

Snorri fished in the pocket of his winter coat and pulled out a heavy coin, flipping it to Tuttugu.

"Never seen a gold piece that big before." Tuttugu held it up to his face, so close his nose almost bumped it, the other hand buried in his ginger beard. "What's that on it? A bell?"

"The great bell of Venice. They say beside the Bay of Sighs you can hear it ring on a stormy night, though it lies fifty fathoms drowned." Snorri felt in his pocket for another of the coins. "It's a florin."

"Great bell of where?" Tuttugu turned the florin over in his hand, entranced by the gleam.

"Venice. Drowned like Atlantis and all the cities beneath the Quiet Sea. It was part of Florence. That's where they mint these."

Tuttugu pursed his lips. "I'll find Jal when I'm done. That's if I can carry all the change I get after spending this beauty. I'll meet you there."

Snorri nodded and set off, taking a steep street that led away from the docks to the long halls on the ridge above the main town.

In his years of warring and raiding Snorri had learned the value of information over opinion, learned that the stories people tell are one thing but if you mean to risk the lives of your men it's better to have tales backed up by the evidence of your eyes—or those of a scout. Better still several scouts, for if you show a thing to three men you'll hear three different accounts, and if you're lucky the truth will lie somewhere between them. He would go to Skilfar and seek out the ice witch in her mountain of fire, but better to go armed with advice from other sources, rather than as an empty vessel waiting to be filled with only her opinion.

Old Hrothson had received Snorri in the porch of his long hall, where he sat in a high-backed chair of black oak, carved all over with Asgardian sigils. On the pillars rising above him the gods stood, grim and watchful. Odin looked out over the ancient's bowed head, Freja beside him, flanked by Thor, Loki, Aegir. Others, carved lower down, stood so smoothed by years of touching that they might be any god you cared to name. The old man sat bowed under his mantle of office, all bones and sunken flesh, thin white hair crowning a liver-spotted pate, and a sharp odour of sickness about him. His eyes, though, remained bright.

"Snorri Snagason. I'd heard the Hardassa put an end to the Undoreth. A knife in the back on a dark night?" Old Hrothson measured out his words, age creaking in each syllable. The younger Hrothson sat beside him in a lesser chair, a silver-haired man of sixty winters. Honour guards clad in chain mail and furs flanked them, long axes resting against their shoulders. The two Hrothsons had sat here when Snorri last saw them, maybe five years earlier, gazing down across their town and out to the grey sea.

"Two only survived," Snorri said. "Myself and Olaf Arnsson, known as Tuttugu."

The older Hrothson leaned forward and hawked up a mess of dark phlegm, spitting it to the boards. "That for the Hardassa. Odin grant you vengeance and Thor the strength to take it."

Snorri clapped his fist to his chest though the words gave him no comfort. Thor might be god of strength and war, Odin of wisdom, but he sometimes wondered if it wasn't Loki, the trickster god, who stood behind what unfolded. A lie can run deeper than strength or wisdom. And hadn't the world proved to be a bitter joke? Perhaps even the gods themselves lay snared in Loki's greatest trick and Ragnarok would hear the punch line spoken. "I seek wisdom," he said.

"Well," said Old Hrothson. "There's always the priests."

All of them laughed, even the honour guards.

"No really," the younger Hrothson spoke for the first time. "My father can advise you about war, crops, trade, and fishing. Do you speak of the wisdom of this world or the other?"

"A little of both," Snorri admitted.

"Ekatri." Old Hrothson nodded. "She has returned. You'll find her winter hut by the falls on the south side, three miles up the fjord. There's more in her runes than in the smokes and iron bells of the priests with their endless tales of Asgard."

The son nodded, and Snorri took his leave. When he glanced back both men were as they had been when he left them five years before, gazing out to sea.

◆ ◆ ◆

An hour later Snorri approached the witch's hut, a small roundhouse, log-built, the roof of heather and hide, a thin trail of smoke rising from the centre. Ice still fringed the falls, crashing down behind the hut in a thin and endless cascade, pulses of white driving down through the mist above the plunge pool.

A shiver ran through Snorri as he followed the rocky path to Ekatri's door. The air tasted of old magic, neither good nor ill, but of the land, having no love for man. He paused to read the runes on the door. Magic and Woman. Völva it meant. He knocked and, hearing nothing, pushed through.

Ekatri sat on spread hides, almost lost beneath a heap of patched blankets. She watched him with one dark eye and a weeping socket. "Come in then. Clearly you're not taking no answer for an answer."

Snorri ducked low to avoid the door lintel and then to clear the herbs hanging from the roof stays in dry bunches. The small fire between them coiled its smoke up into the funnel of the roof, filling the single room with a perfume of lavender and pine that almost obscured the undercurrent of rot.

"Sit, child."

Snorri sat, taking no offence. Ekatri looked to be a hundred, as wizened and twisted as a clifftop tree.

"Well? Do you expect me to guess?" Ekatri dipped her clawed hand into one of the bowls set before her and tossed a pinch of the powder into the embers before her, putting a darker curl into the rising smoke.

"In the winter assassins came to Trond. They came for me. I want to know who sent them."

"You didn't ask them?"

"Two I had to kill. The last I disabled, but I couldn't make him speak."

"You've no stomach for torture, Undoreth?"

"He had no mouth."

"A strange creature indeed." Ekatri drew out a glass jar from her blanket, not a thing northmen could make. A thing of the Builders, and

in the greenish liquid within, a single eyeball, turning on the slow current.
The witch's own perhaps.

"They had olive skin, were human in all respects save for the lack of
a mouth, that and the ungodly quickness of them." Snorri drew out a gold
coin from his pocket. "Might be from Florence. They had the blood price
on them, in florins."

"That doesn't make them Florentines. Half the jarls in Norseheim
have a handful of florins in their warchests. In the southern states the
nobles spend florins in their gambling halls as often as their own currency." Snorri passed the coin over into Ekatri's outstretched claw. "A
double florin. Now they are more rare."

Ekatri set the coin upon the lid of the jar where her lost eye floated.
She drew a leather bag from her blankets and shook it so the contents
clacked against each other. "Put your hand in, mix them about, tip them
out . . . here." She cleared a space and marked the centre.

Snorri did as he was bidden. He'd had the runes read for him before.
This message would be a darker one, he fancied. He closed his hand
around the tablets, finding them colder and heavier than he had expected,
then drew his fist out, opened it palm up and let the rune stones slip
from his hand onto the hides below. It seemed as though each fell through
water, its path too slow, twisting more than it should. When they landed
a silence ran through the hut, underwriting the finality of the pronounce-
ment writ in stone between the witch and himself.

Ekatri studied the tablets, her face avid, as if hungry for something she
might read among them. A very pink tongue emerged to wet ancient lips.

"Wunjo, face down, beneath Gebo. A woman has buried your joy, a
woman may release it." She touched another two face up. "Salt and Iron.
Your path, your destination, your challenge, and your answer." A gnarled
finger flipped over the final runestone. "The Door. Closed."

"What does all that mean?" Snorri frowned.

"What do you think it means?" Ekatri watched him with wry
amusement.

"Am I supposed to be the völva for you?" Snorri rumbled, feeling
mocked. "Where's the magic if *I* tell you the answer?"

"I let you tell me your future and you ask where the magic lies?" Ekatri reached out and swirled the jar beside her so the pickled eyeball within spun with the current. "The magic might be in getting into that thick warrior skull of yours the fact that your future stands on your choices and only you can make them. The magic lies in knowing that you seek both a door and the happiness you think lies behind it."

"There's more," Snorri said.

"There is always more."

Snorri drew up his jerkin. The scrapes and tears the Fenris wolf had given him were scabbed and healing, bruises livid across his chest and side, but across his ribs a long single slice lay glistening, the flesh about it an angry red, and along the wound's length a white encrustation of salt. "My gift from the assassins."

"An interesting injury." Ekatri reached forward with withered fingers. Snorri flinched but kept his place as she set her hand across the slit. "Does it hurt, Snorri ver Snagason?"

"It hurts." Through gritted teeth. "It only gives me peace when we sail. The longer I stay put the worse it gets. I feel a . . . tug."

"It pulls you south." Ekatri removed her hand, wiping it on her furs. "You've felt this kind of call before."

Snorri nodded. The bond with Jal exerted a similar draw. He felt it even now, slight, but there, wanting to pull him back to the tavern he'd left the southerner in.

"Who has done this?" He met the völva's one-eyed gaze.

"Why is a better question."

Snorri picked up the stone Ekatri had named the Door. It no longer felt unduly cold or heavy, just a piece of slate, graven with a single rune. "Because of the door. And because I seek it," he said.

Ekatri held her hand out for the Door and Snorri passed the stone to her, feeling a twinge of reluctance at releasing it.

"Someone in the south wants what you carry, and they want you to bring it to them." Ekatri licked her lips, again—the quickness of her tongue disturbing. "See how one simple cut draws all the runes together?"

"The Dead King did this? He sent these assassins?" Snorri asked.

Ekatri shook her head. "The Dead King is not so subtle. He is a raw and elemental force. This has an older hand behind it. You have something everyone wants." Ekatri touched the claw of her hand to her withered chest, the motion just glimpsed beneath the blankets. She touched on herself the same spot where Loki's key lay against Snorri's flesh.

"Why just the three? Sent in the midst of winter. Why not more, now that travelling is easy?"

"Perhaps he was testing something? Does it seem reasonable that three such assassins should fail against one man? Perhaps the wound was all they were intended to give you. An invitation . . . of a kind. If it wasn't for the light within you battling the poison on that blade you would belong to the wound already, busy rushing south. There would be no question of any delay or diversion to speak to old women in their huts." She closed her eye and seemed to study Snorri with her empty socket a while. "They do say Loki's key doesn't like to be taken. Given, surely, but taken? Stolen, of a certainty. But taken by force? Some speak of a curse on those who own it through strength. And it doesn't do to anger gods, now does it?"

"I mentioned no key." Snorri fought to keep his hands from twitching toward it, burning cold against his chest.

"Ravens fly even in winter, Snagason." Ekatri's eye hardened. "Do you think if some southern mage knew of your exploits weeks ago, old Ekatri would not know of it by now in her hut just down the coast? You came seeking wisdom: don't take me for a fool."

"So I must go south and hope?"

"There is no 'must' about it. Surrender the key and the wound will heal. Perhaps even the wounds you can't see. Stay here. Make a new life." She patted the hides beside her. "I could always use a new man. They never seem to last."

Snorri made to stand. "Keep the gold, völva."

"Well, it seems my wisdom is valued today. Now that you've paid for it so handsomely perhaps you might heed it, child." She made the coin vanish and sighed. "I'm old, my bones are dry, the world has lost its savour, Snorri. Go, die, spend yourself in the deadlands . . . it matters little to me, my words are a pretty noise for you, your mind is set. The waste sorrows me, young and full of juice you are, but in the end, in the end we're all wasted by the years. Think on it, though. Did those who stand in your path just start to covet Loki's key this winter?"

"I—" Snorri knew a moment of shame. His thoughts had been so narrowed on the choice he'd made that the rest of the world had escaped him.

"As your tragedies draw you south . . . wonder how those tragedies came to be and whose hand truly lay behind them."

"I've been a fool." Snorri found his feet.

"And you'll keep being one. Words can't turn you from this course. Maybe nothing can. Friendship, love, trust, childish notions that have left this old woman . . . but, whatever the runes have to say, these are what rule you, Snorri ver Snagason, friendship, love, trust. They'll drag you into the underworld, or save you from it. One or the other." She hung her head, stared into the fire.

"And this door I seek? Where can I find it?"

Ekatri's wrinkle of a mouth puckered into consideration. "I don't know."

Snorri felt himself deflate. For a moment he had thought she might tell him, but it would have to be Skilfar. He started to turn.

"Wait." The völva raised a hand. "I don't know. But I can guess where it might lie. Three places." She returned her hand to her lap. "In Yttrmir the world slopes into Hel, so they say. In the badlands that stretch to the Yöttenfall the skies grow dim and the people strange. Go far enough and you'll find villages where no one ages, none are born, each day follows the next without change. Further still and the people neither eat nor drink nor sleep but sit at their windows and stare. I've not heard that there is a door—but if you wish to go to Hel, that is a path. That is the first. The second is Eridruin's Cave on the shore of Harrowfjord. Monsters dwell there. The hero Snorri Hengest fought them, and in his saga it speaks of a door that stands in the deepest part of those caverns, a black door. The third is less sure, told by a raven, a child of Crakk, white-feathered in his dotage. Even so. There is a lake in Scorron, the Venomere, dark as ink, where no fish swim. In its depths they say there is a door. In older days the men of Scorron threw witches into those waters, and none ever floated to the surface as corpses are wont to do."

"My thanks, völva." He hesitated. "Why did you tell me? If my plan is such madness?"

"You asked. The runes put the door in your path. You're a man. Like most men you need to face your quarry before you can truly decide. You won't let go of this until you find it. Maybe not even then." Ekatri looked down and said no more. Snorri waited a moment longer, then turned and left, watched by a single eye floating in its jar.

"Assassins?" I lifted my head, the room continuing to move after I stopped. "Nonsense. You never mentioned any attack."

Snorri lifted his jerkin. A single ugly wound ran down his side, far back, just past the ribs, salt crusted as he'd described. I may have seen it when Borris's daughters were washing him back in Olaafheim after the Fenris wolf got hold of him, or perhaps he had been turned the wrong way . . . in any event I didn't recall it in my inebriation.

"So how much does it cost to hire assassins then?" I asked. "Just for future reference. And . . . where's the money? You should be rich!"

"I gave most of it to the sea, so that Aegir would grant us safe passage," said Snorri.

"Well that didn't bloody work!" I banged the table, perhaps a little harder than I meant to. I can be an excitable drunk.

"Most of it?" Tuttugu asked.

"I paid a völva in Trond to treat the wound."

"Did a piss-poor job from what I could see," I interjected, holding on to the table to keep from sliding past it.

"It was beyond her skill, and while we stay here it only grows worse. Come, we'll sail at dawn."

Snorri stood and I guess we followed, though I've no memory of it.

SEVEN

I woke the next morning under sail and with a head sore enough to keep me curled in the prow groaning for the mercy of death until well past noon. The previous evening returned to me in fragments over the course of the next few days but it took an age to assemble the pieces into anything that made sense. And even then it didn't make much sense. I consoled myself with our steady progress toward home and the civilized comforts thereof. As my head eased I planned out who I would see first and where I'd spend my first night. I would probably ask for Lisa DeVeer's hand, assuming she hadn't been dragged to the opera that night and burned with the rest. She was the finest of the old man's daughters and I'd grown very fond of her. Especially in her absence. Thoughts of home kept me warm, and I huddled in the prow, waiting to get there.

The sea is always changing—but mostly for the worse. A cold and relent-less rain arrived with the next morning and plagued us all day, driven by winds that pushed the ocean up before them into rolling hills of brine. Snorri's dreadful little boat wallowed around like a pig trying to drown, and by the time evening threatened even the Norsemen had had enough.

"We'll put in at Harrowheim," Snorri told us, wiping the rain from his beard. "It's a little place I know." Something about the name gave me a bad feeling but I was too eager to be on solid ground to object, and I guessed that even driven as he was the Norseman would rather spend the night ashore.

So, with the sun setting behind us we turned for the dark coastline, letting the wind hurl us toward the rocks until at the last the mouth of a fjord revealed itself and we sailed on in. The fjord proved itself a narrow one, little more than two hundred yards wide, its shores rising steeper than a flight of stairs, reaching for the serrated ridges of sullen rock that cradled the waters.

Aslaug spoke to me while the two Norsemen busied themselves with rope and sail. She sat beside me in the stern, clad in shadow and suggestion, impervious to the rain and the tug of the wind.

"How they torment you with this boat, Prince Jalan." She laid a hand on my knee, ebony fingers staining the cloth, a delicious feeling soaking into me. "Baraqel guides Snorri now. The Norseman doesn't have your strength of will. Where you were able to withstand the demon's preaching Snorri is swayed. His instincts have always been—"

"Demon?" I muttered. "Baraqel's an angel."

"You think so?" She purred it close by my ear and suddenly I didn't know what I thought, or care overmuch that I didn't. "The creatures of the light wear whatever shapes you let them steal from legend. Beneath it all they are singular in will and no more your friend or guardians than the fire."

I shivered in my cloak wishing I had a good blaze to warm myself by right now. "But fire is—"

"Fire is your enemy, Prince Jalan. Enslave it and it will serve, but give it an inch, give it any opportunity, and you'll be lucky to escape the burning wreckage of your home. You keep the fire at arm's length. You don't take a hot coal to your breast. No more should you embrace Baraqel or his kind. Snorri has done so and it has left his will in ashes—a puppet for the light to work its own purposes through. See how he looks at you. How he watches you. It's only a matter of time before he acts openly against you. Mark these words, my prince. Mark—"

The sun sank and Aslaug fell into a darkness that leaked away through the hull.

We drew up at the quays of Harrowheim in the gathering gloom, guided in by the lights of houses clustered on the steepness of the slope. To the west some sort of cove or landslip offered a broad flattish area where crops might be grown in the shelter of the fjord.

An ancient with a lantern waved us alongside his own boat where he'd been sat picking the last fish from his nets.

"You'll be wannin' me ta walk you up," he said, all gums and wisps of beard.

"Don't trouble yourself, Father." Tuttugu getting onto the quay with far more grace than he showed on land. He stooped low over the man's boat. "Herring, eh? White-Gill. Nice catch. We don't see them for another few weeks up in Trond."

"Ayuh." The old man held one up, still flipping half-heartedly in his fingers. "Good 'uns." He put it down as Snorri clambered out, leaving me to stagger uncertainly across the rolling boat toward the step. "Still. Better go with you. The lads are twitchy tonight. Raiders about—it's the season for 'em. Might fill you full of spear before you know it."

My boot, wet with bilge water, slipped out from under me at "raiders" and I nearly vanished into the strip of dark water between quay and boat. I caught myself painfully on the planks, biting my tongue as I clutched the support. "Raiders?" I tasted blood and hoped it wasn't a premonition.

Snorri shook his head. "Not serious stuff. The clans raid for wives come spring. Here it'll be Guntish men."

"Ayuh. And Westerfolk off Crow Island." The old man set down his nets and came to join us, making an easier job of it than I had.

"Lead on." I waved him forward, happy to trail behind if it meant him getting speared rather than me.

Now that Snorri had mentioned it I did recall talk of the practice back at the Three Axes. The business of raiding for girls of marriageable age seemed something that the people of Trond felt beneath them, but they loved to tell tales about their country bumpkin cousins doing it. Mostly it seemed to be an almost good-natured thing with a tacit approval from both sides—but of course if the raider proved sufficiently unskilled to get caught then he'd earn himself a good beating . . . and sometimes a bad one. And if he picked a girl that didn't want to get caught she might give him worse than that.

Men emerged from the shadows as we walked up between the huts. Our new friend, Old Engli, put them quickly at their ease and the mood lightened. Some few recognized Snorri and many more recognized his name, leading us on amid a growing crowd. Lanterns and torches lit around us, children ran into the muddy streets, mothers and daughters eyed us from glowing doorways, the occasional girl, bolder than the rest, hanging from a window recently unboarded in the wake of winter's retreat. One or two such caught my eye, the last of them a generously proportioned young woman with corn-coloured hair descending in thick waves and hung with small copper bells.

"Prince Jalan—" I managed half a bow and half an introduction before Snorri's big fist knotted in my cloak and hauled me onward.

"Best behaviour, Jal," he hissed between his teeth while offering a wide smile left and right. "I know these people. Let's try not to have to leave in a hurry this time."

"Yes, of course!" I shook myself free. Or he let me go. "Do you think I'm some sort of wild beast? I'm always on my best behaviour!" I stomped on behind him, straightening my collar. Damn barbarian thinking he could teach a prince of Red March manners . . . she did have a very pretty face though . . . and squeezable—

"Jal!"

I found myself marching past the entrance into which everyone else had turned. A quick reversal and I was through the mead-hall's doorway into the smoke and noise. Mead-hut I'd call it—it made Olaafheim's hall look big. More men streamed in behind me while others found their seats around the long benches. It seemed our arrival had occasioned a general call to broach casks and fill drinking horns. We'd started the party rather than crashed in on it. And that gives you a pretty good picture of Harrowheim. A place so desolate and starved of interest that the arrival of three men in a boat is cause for celebration.

"Jal!" Snorri slapped the tabletop to indicate a space between him and Tuttugu. It seemed well meaning enough but something in me bridled at the gesture, ordering me to my place, somewhere he could keep an eye on me. As if he didn't trust me. Me! A prince of Red March. Heir to the throne. Being watched over by a hauldr and a fisherman as if I might disgrace myself in a den of savages. Me, being watched over by Baraqel even though I no longer had to suffer him in my head. I sat down still smiling, but feeling brittle. I snatched up the drinking horn before me and took a deep swig. The dark and sour ale within did little to improve my mood.

As the general cacophony of disputes over seating and cries for ale settled into more distinct conversations, I began to realize that everyone around me was speaking Norse. Snorri gabbled away with a lean old stick of a man, spitting out words that would break a decent person's jaw. On my other side Tuttugu had found a kindred spirit, another ginger Norseman whose red beard spilled down over a stomach so expansive it forced him to sit far enough back from the table that reaching his ale became a problem. They too were deep in conversation in old Norse. It was starting to seem that the very first person we met was the only one among them who could speak like a man of Empire.

Back in Trond most of the northmen knew the old tongue but every one of them spoke the language of Empire and would use it over beers, at work, and in the street. Generally the city folk avoided the old tongue and its complications of dialect and regional variation, sticking instead to the language of merchants and kings. In fact the only time the good folk of Trond tended to slip into Norse was when seeking the most appropriate swear word for the situation. Insulting each other is a national sport in Norseheim and for the very best results competitors like to call on the old curses of the north, preferably raiding the stock of cruel-things-to-say-about-someone's-mother that is to be found in the great sagas.

Out in the sticks however it proved to be a very different story—a story told exclusively in a language that seemed to require you swallow a live frog to pronounce some words and gargle half a pint of phlegm for the rest. Since my grip on Norse was limited to calling someone a shithead or telling them they had very pert breasts I scowled at the company and opted to keep my mouth shut unless of course I was pouring ale into it.

The night rolled on and whilst I was deeply glad to be out of that boat, out of the wind, and to have a floor beneath me that had the decency to stay where it had been put, I couldn't really enjoy being crammed among two score ill-smelling Harrowheimers. I had to wonder at Engli's tale of raiding since the whole male population seemed to have jammed themselves into the mead-hall at the first excuse.

"—Hardassa!" Snorri's fist punctuated the word against the table and I became aware that most of the locals were listening to him now. From the hush I guessed he must be telling the tale of our trip to the Black Fort. Hopefully he wouldn't be mentioning Loki's key.

To my mind the Norse vilification of Loki seemed an odd thing. Of all their heathen gods Loki was clearly the most intelligent, capable of plans and tactics that could help Asgard in its wars against the giants. And yet they spurned him. The answer of course was all around me in Harrowheim. Their daughters weren't being wooed, or seduced, they were being taken by raiders. In the ancient tales, to which each Viking aspired, strength was the only virtue, iron the only currency that mattered. Loki with his cunning, whereby a weaker man might outdo a stronger one, was an anathema to these folk. Little wonder then if his key carried a curse for any that sought to take it by main strength.

Had Olaaf Rikeson taken it by force and drawn down Loki's curse, only to have his vast army freeze on the Bitter Ice? Whoever had given Snorri that wound had more sense than the Dead King. Using half a ton of Fenris wolf to claim the key might seem a more certain course but such methods might also be a good way to find yourself on the wrong end of a god's wrath.

"Ale?" Tuttugu started filling my drinking horn without waiting on my answer.

I pursed my lips as another thought struck me—why the hell did they call them mead-halls? I'd emptied several gallons from various drinking horns, flagons, tankards . . . even a bucket one time . . . in half a dozen mead-halls since coming north and never once been offered mead. The closest the Norse came to sweet was leaving the salt out of their ale. While pondering this important question I decided it time to go empty my used beer into the latrine and stood with just the hint of a stagger.

"Still getting my land legs." I set a hand to Tuttugu's shoulder for support and, once steady, set off for the door.

My lack of the local lingo didn't prove an impediment in the hunt for the latrine—I let my nose lead me. On my return to the hall the faintest jingle of bells caught my attention. Just a brief high tinkle. The sound seemed to have come from an alley between two nearby buildings, large, log-built structures, one sporting elaborate gables . . . possibly a temple. With a squint I could make out a cloaked figure in the gloom. I stood, blinking, hoping to God that this wasn't some horny but myopic clansman who was going to attempt to carry me off to a distant village even more depressing than Harrowheim.

The figure held its ground, sheltered in the narrow passage. Two slim hands emerged from dark sleeves and pushed back the hood. Bells tinkled again, and the girl from the window revealed herself, a saucy quirk to her smile that required no translation.

I cast a quick glance at the glowing rectangle of the mead-hall door-way, another toward the latrines, and seeing nobody looking in my direc-tion, I hastened across the way to join my new friend in the alley.

"Well, hello." I gave her my best smile. "I'm Prince Jalan Kendeth of Red March, the Red Queen's heir. But you can call me Prince Jal."

She reached out to lay a finger across my lips before whispering something that sounded as delicious as it was incomprehensible.

"How can I say no?" I whispered back, setting a hand to her hip and wondering for a moment what the Norse for "no" actually was.

She wriggled out from beneath my palm, bells tinkling, setting her fingers between her collarbones. "Yngvildr."

"Lovely." My hands pursued her while my tongue considered wrestling with her name and decided not to.

Yngvildr skipped away laughing and pointed back between the build-ings, more sweet gibberish spilling from her mouth. Seeing my blank look she paused and repeated herself slowly and clearly. The trouble is of course that it doesn't matter how slowly and how clearly you repeat gib-berish. It's possible the word "pert" was in there somewhere.

High above us the moon showed its face and what light it sent down into our narrow alley caught the girl's lines, illuminating the curve of her cheek, her brow, leaving her eyes in darkness, gleaming on her bell-strewn hair, silver across the swell of her breasts, shadows descending toward a slender waist. Suddenly it didn't really matter what she was saying.

"Yes," I said, and she led the way.

We passed between the temple and its neighbour, between huts, edged around pigsties where the hogs snored restless in their hay, and out past log stacks and empty pens to where the slope mellowed toward Harrowheim's patch of farmland. I snatched a candle-lantern hanging outside one of the last huts. She hissed and tutted, half-smiling, half-disapproving, gesturing for me to put it back, but I declined. A tallow stub in a poorly blown glass cowl was hardly grand theft and damned if I were ending the night with a broken leg or knee-deep in a slurry pit. Wherever Yngvildr planned to get her first taste of Red March I intended to get there fit enough to give good account of myself.

So we stumbled on in our small circle of light, out across a gentle slope, the earth rutted by agriculture, holding hands now, her occasionally saying something which sounded seductive but might well have been an observation on the weather. A little more than a hundred yards out from the last of the huts a tall barn loomed up at us out of the night. I stood back and watched as Yngvildr lifted the locking bar and drew back one of the plank-built double doors set into the front of the crude log structure. She looked back over her shoulder, smiling, and walked on in, swallowed by the darkness. I considered the wisdom of the liaison for about two seconds and followed her.

The lamp's light couldn't reach the roof or the walls but I could see enough to know the place held hay bales and farm implements. Not many of either, but plenty to trip over. Yngvildr tried once more to make me abandon the lamp, pointing to the doorway, but I smiled and pulled her close, kissing the arguments off her lips. In the end she rolled her eyes and broke free to close the door once more.

Taking my hand Yngvildr led the way deeper into the barn to a point where a ladder led up to a split-level above the main hay store. I followed her up, taking time to admire the grubby but well-formed legs disappearing into the shadows of her skirts. At the top a large pile of loose hay had been formed into something vaguely nest-shaped.

Now a hay barn in Red March in the spring or fall can be a half-decent place to tumble the odd peasant girl or friendly farm lass, though they never tell you quite how itchy straw is in those bawdy tales, or how sharp, or how it gets into all manner of places where neither partner in the enterprise really ever wants to get anything sharp or itchy. A hay barn in Norseheim in the spring however is akin to an icehouse. A place where no sane man, however keen he might be for a spot of slap and tickle, would part with any layers, and where anything that pokes its head into the frigid air is apt to shrivel and die. I set the lamp down beside us, and with my breath pluming before me, wondered if there were any way I could slip back to the mead-hall right now while retaining some shred of pride. Yngvildr on the other hand seemed keen to proceed as planned and with smiles, gestures, and presently with impatient jerks of the head as she went to all fours, indicated that I should hurry up with my end of the bargain.

"Just give me a minute, Y—Yng—. . . dear lady." I held my hands out over the lamp to warm them. "Cold air is never flattering to a man . . ."

Norse women can be quite proactive and Yngvildr proved no exception, backing me to the wall and rucking up a considerable number of coarse skirts to initiate proceedings. A bit of numb-fingered fumbling and with the bare minimum of undressing Yngvildr and I were locked together in a style not uncommon in farmyards, with me providing the somewhat abused filling in a sandwich between the barn wall and my latest "conquest."

Despite the biting cold, the itchy straw, and the hard planks I did eventually start to enjoy myself. Yngvildr was after all attractive, enthusiastic and energetic. I even began to warm up a bit and start ringing her bells. Reaching forward I took hold of her shoulders and put some effort into seeing what kind of notes I could get out of her. The ringing became louder as our excitement mounted . . . and more deep throated . . .

"That's it! Louder! I'll bet no Norseman has rung your—"

The realization that even the best lover in the world wouldn't be able to coax so deep or multitudinous a clanging from Yngvildr's tiny copper bells caught me in mid boast. I opened my eyes and, still being rhythmically pounded back against the wall, peered over the edge of the upper floor to see that the lower barn was full of cattle, with more of the beasts coming in through the door, each with a large cow-bell around its neck.

"You—offff! You didn't—offff! Close the door properly!"

Yngvildr appeared too occupied to care or notice and seemed to think my commentary was me urging her to greater efforts. For a few moments more I knelt there, trying not to let my head bang the timbers.

"Yes . . . perhaps we could quiet things down . . ." Her enthusiasm appeared to be attracting more cattle by the second. "Sssh!" It made no impression on her. I stared, somewhat helpless, down at the bovine sea below and those that weren't busy helping themselves to the hay, or just crapping on the floor, stared back up at me. It wasn't until I heard over the noise of Yngvildr's bells, her panting, and the clanging of cow-bells, the sound of men approaching that I started to panic.

"Dear lady, if you could just—offff!" I banged my head quite hard that time, adding anger into the mix of rising panic and involuntary lust. "Shut up!"

It sounded as if there were quite a few Harrowheimers approaching, their voices more curious than alarmed. Presumably when they saw that the cows had entered the barn it would inject a little more urgency into the situation. Lord knew what they'd do if they caught the foreigner in the act of despoiling their maiden!

"Time to stop, Y—" I banged my head again while struggling for her name. "Stop! They're coming!"

Unfortunately Yngvildr seemed to take my urgency as further encouragement and proved wholly disinclined to stop. I could just make out the glow of a lantern off in the field through a small window above the doors.

"Get! Off!" And with considerable effort I managed to shove Yngvildr far enough to disengage and free myself from the wall. As she fell forward, onto her face unfortunately, her shoulder caught the lamp and sent it tumbling.

"Oh shit!" It's remarkable how quickly fire takes hold of straw. I backed away on my arse, kicking out at the burning clumps nearest to me. They promptly dropped over the edge into the main barn. Seconds later a great mooing went up from below us, rising rapidly into notes of animal panic. Yngvildr rolled over, hay stuck to her mouth, and looked about in bewilderment—an expression that moved quickly through fury to terror.

"No! No, no, no, no, no!" I tried beating at the burning hay but just helped the fire to spread. Meanwhile down below the cattle had gone into full stampede, ripping off the barn doors in their eagerness to be outside. By the high-pitched yells just audible over the general din of the herd it seemed as though the locals drawn by the cows' unusual behaviour were having their curiosity rewarded with a good trampling.

"Come on!" Always the gentleman I led the way to ensure it was safe, sliding down the ladder at reckless speed without a care for splinters. Already the air hung thick with smoke, hot as sin. Choking and wheezing I made for the back of the barn, reasoning there must be a door there and that would be closer. Also, although the fire headed my list of priorities in a big way, I didn't want to jump from it directly into the frying pan. Slipping out the back might allow me to escape unobserved and weasel out of the whole thing.

"Shit!" I stopped in my tracks, confronted by a small door blocked by several bales of hay, all already smouldering. Yngvildr staggered into my back, sending me stumbling forward toward the nearest bale, across which flames flickered into being as though angered by my approach. The smoke blinded me, filling my eyes with tears and swirling around so thickly that only flames showed through. Yngvildr thrust something into my hand, choking out words rendered no less comprehensible by her lack of breath. It appeared to be some kind of farm implement, two sharp iron spikes on the end of a wooden haft. Somewhere at the back of my mind the word "pitchfork" bubbled up, though I probably would have applied the same label to any number of peasant tools. More gibberish as Yngvildr shook my arm and pushed me forward. The girl had clearly gone mad with fear but keeping a cool head and showing the innovative thinking we Kendeths are famed for I set to hefting the burning hay aside with the device. The severity of the situation must have coaxed new strength from my muscles as I managed to toss the bales left and right despite my lack of breath and each of them outweighing me. With the last of my energy and with the fire roaring at my back I kicked the door open and the both of us burst out together.

The light of the blaze through the doorway cast a sudden cone of illumination into the darkness, catching five or six grey-clad men hurrying away across the field. I didn't care what they were up to but in the heat of the moment, and discovering with a yell that the pitchfork I held clutched before me was on fire, I threw the thing at them. My interest in the implement ended the second it left my scorched hands as I realized that my cloak was also ablaze.

Yngvildr and I hobbled back across the field, accompanied by the agitated lowing of the herd and lit from behind by the spiralling inferno that had consumed the barn within moments of us escaping it. As we reached the margins of the village we found our path blocked by dozens of Harrowheimers, all standing around their huts and hovels, open mouthed, their faces glowing with the reflection of the fire at our backs. Snorri loomed large among them.

"Tell me you didn't . . ." The look he shot my way made me fairly sure that bits of my cloak were still smoking.

"I—" I didn't get a chance to start lying before Yngvildr wriggled out from beneath my arm where I'd been using her for support and began talking at a startling rate and volume. I stood, somewhat bewildered, as the wench gestured her way through some great pantomime of what I presumed must be recent events. Part of me expected her to drop to all fours for a full display of just how the southern monster had despoiled the flower of Harrowheim.

Yngvildr paused to snatch a breath and Tuttugu called to me, "Which way did they go?"

"Um—" Fortunately Yngvildr saved me from having to invent an answer while guessing what she'd said. With her lungs refilled she launched into the next stage of her tale.

"A pitchfork?" Snorri asked, glancing from Yngvildr to me, an eyebrow raised.

"Well, one improvises." I shrugged. "We princes can turn most objects into a weapon in a pinch."

Yngvildr still had plenty of go in her and continued to spill her story with the same volume but the crowd's attention wandered from her, drawn into the shadows where three warriors were emerging from the field, one brandishing what looked to be the pitchfork in question and barking out something that sounded uncomfortably like an accusation. I took Yngvildr protectively by the shoulders to use as a shield.

"Now see here! I—" My bluster ran out temporarily while I tried to think what defence I might offer that wouldn't get me used as a target for axe-throwing practice.

"He says, when they caught up with the raiders they were pulling this out of their friend's backside," Snorri said, a grin cracking within the close-cropped darkness of his beard. "So, you rescued Yngvildr and chased off, what? Six of them? With a pitchfork? Splendid." He laughed and slapped Tuttugu across the shoulders. "But why would they fire the barn? That's the bit I don't understand. There'll be hell to pay over it come the clan-meet!"

"Ah," I said, trying to give myself pause for all the lies to sink in. Yngvildr appeared to be a highly creative girl under pressure. "I think maybe that was an accident? One of the idiots must have taken a lamp into the barn—probably they were planning to collect a few girls there before setting off for home. Must've got knocked over in the excitement . . ."

Snorri repeated what I'd said in Norse for the gathered crowd. A silence trailed his last word and two score and more of Harrowheim's eyes stared hard at me through the flame-lit gloom. I figured if I shoved Yngvildr at the feet of the nearest ones and ran for it I might lose them in the night. I'd tensed for the shove when without warning a cheer went up, beards split into broad smiles full of bad teeth, and before I knew what was happening we'd been swept along the muddy streets and back into the mead-hall. This time they managed to squeeze twice as many bodies into the place, half of them female. As the ale started to flow once more and I found myself squashed between Yngvildr and an older but no less comely woman that Snorri assured me was her sister rather than her mother, I started to think a night in Harrowheim might have its charms after all.

* * *

We left on the morning tide with sore heads and foggy recollections of the night's events. The rain had let up, the relentless wind had relented, and the true story of how their largest barn got burned flat had yet to emerge. It seemed the best time to depart. Even so I would have dallied a day or three, but Snorri had an urgency about him, his humour gone. When he thought no one watching I saw him hold his side above the poisoned wound and I knew then that he felt that pull, drawing him south.

Sad to say neither Yngvildr nor her still less pronounceable sister came to see me off at the quay, but they had both managed a smile when Snorri hauled me from the furs that morning and I let that warm me against the cold wind as we set sail.

As the distance took Harrowheim I didn't feel quite so well rid of this Norse town as I had of Trond, Olaafheim, and Haargfjord. Even so, the glories of Vermillion beckoned. Wine, women, song . . . preferably not opera . . . and I'd certainly search out Lisa DeVeer, perhaps even marry her one day.

"We're going the wrong way!" It had taken me the best part of half an hour to realize it. The fjord had narrowed a touch and there was no sign of the sea.

"We're sailing up the Harrowfjord." Snorri at the tiller.

"Up?" I looked for the sun. It was true. "Why? And where do I know that name from?"

"I told it to you four nights ago. Ekatri told me—"

"Eridruin's Cave. Monsters!" It all came back to me, rather like unexpectedly vomiting into your mouth. The völva's mad tale about a door in a cave.

"It was meant to be. Fated. My namesake sailed here three centuries ago."

"Snorri Hengest died here." Tuttugu from the prow. "We should see

Skilfar. She'll know of a better way. Nobody comes here, Snorri. It's a bad place."

"We're looking for a bad thing."

And that was that. We kept going.

"So, who was Eridruin?" Sailing on a fjord is infinitely preferable to sailing on the sea. The water stays where it's put and the shore is so close that even I might make it there if it came to swimming. This said, I would rather be sailing over rough seas away from any place famed for monsters than sailing toward it on the flattest of millponds. "I said, who was—"

"I don't know. Tuttugu?" Snorri kept his eyes on the left shore.

Tuttugu shrugged. "It must ache Eridruin's spirit to be famed enough for his name to survive but not quite enough for anyone to remember why they remember it."

A stiff breeze had carried us inland. The day kept grey, the sun showing only brief and weak. By late afternoon we'd covered perhaps thirty miles and seen no sign of habitation. I had thought Harrowheim's raiders came from further up the fjord, but nobody lived here. Tuttugu had the right of it. A bad place. Somehow you could tell. It wasn't anything as simple as dead and crooked trees, or rocks with sinister shapes . . . it was a feeling, a wrongness, the certain knowledge that the world grew thin here, and what waited beneath the surface loved us not. I watched the sun sinking toward the high ridges and listened. The Harrowfjord wasn't silent or lifeless, the water lapped our hull, the sails flapped, birds sang . . . but each sound held a discordant tone, as if the skylarks were just a note away from screaming. You could almost catch it . . . some dreadful melody played out just beneath hearing.

"There." Snorri pointed to a place high upon the stepped shore to our left. Like a dark eye amid the stony slopes, Eridruin's Cave watched us. It couldn't be any other.

The Norsemen lowered the sails and brought us into the shallows. Fjords have deep shallows, diving down as steeply as the valleys that contain them. I jumped out a yard from the shore and managed to wet myself to the hips.

"You're just going up there . . . right now?" I looked about for the promised monsters. "Shouldn't we wait and . . . plan?"

Snorri shouldered his axe. "You want to wait until it gets dark, Jal?"

He had a point. "I'll guard the boat."

Snorri wound the boat's line around a boulder that emerged from the water. "Come on."

The Norsemen set off, Tuttugu at least looking as though he would rather not and casting glances left and right. He carried a rope coiled many times about him, and two lanterns bounced on his hips.

I hurried after them. Somehow I could think of no horror worse than being alone in that place, sitting by the still water as the night poured down the slopes.

"Where are the monsters?" It wasn't that I wanted to see any . . . but if they were here I'd rather know where.

Snorri paused and looked about. I immediately sat down to catch my breath. He shrugged. "I can't see any. But then how many places live up to their reputation? I've been to plenty of Giant's This and Troll's That, without a sniff of either. I climbed the Odin's Horn and didn't meet him."

"And the Fair Maidens are a great disappointment." Tuttugu nodded. "Who thought to set that name on three rocky isles crammed with ugly hairy men and their ugly hairy wives?"

Snorri nodded up the slope again and set off. In places it was steeper than stairs and I reached out ahead of me, clambering up.

I climbed, expecting attack at any moment, expecting to see bones among the rocks, drifts of them, tooth-marked, some grey with age, some fresh and wet. Instead I discovered just more rocks and that the growing sense of wrongness now whispered around me, audible but too faint to break apart into words.

Within minutes we stood at the cave mouth, a rocky gullet, fringed with lichen above and stained with black slime where the water oozed. Twenty men could march in abreast, and be swallowed.

"Do you hear it?" Tuttugu, more pale than he had ever looked.

We heard it, though perhaps the cave spoke different words to each of us. I heard a woman whispering to her baby, soft at first, promising love . . . then sharper, more strained, promising protection . . . then terrified, hoarse with agony promising— I spoke aloud to overwrite the whispers. "We need to leave. This place will drive us mad." Already I found myself wondering, if I threw myself down the slope would the voice stop?

"I don't hear anything." Snorri walked in. Perhaps his own demons spoke louder than the cave.

I took a step after him, out of habit, then caught myself. Fingers in my ears did nothing to block out the woman's voice. Worse, I realized there was something familiar about it.

Snorri's progress slowed as the cave floor sloped away, as steep as the valley behind us, but slick with slime and lacking handholds. The gradient steepened further, the cave narrowing to a black and hungry throat.

"Do not."

A tall man stood between Snorri and me, in the shadow of the cave, in the space through which Snorri had just walked. A young man, clad in a strange white robe, sleeved and open at the front. He watched us through stony grey eyes, unsmiling. All the other voices retreated when the man spoke—my woman with her dead child, and the others behind her, not gone but reduced to the pulsing hiss you can hear in a seashell.

Snorri turned, taking the axe from his back. "I need to find a door into Hel."

"Such doors are closed to men." The man smiled then—no kindness in it. "Take a knife to your veins and you will find yourself there soon enough."

"I have a key," Snorri said, and made to resume his descent.

"I said, do not." The man raised his hand and we heard the bones of earth groan. Plates of stone shattered away from the cavern roof, dust drifting in their wake.

"Who are you?" Snorri faced him again.

"I came through the door."

"You're dead?" Snorri took a step toward the man, fascinated now. "And you came back?"

"This part of me is dead, certainly. You don't live as long as I have without dying a little. I have echoes of me in Hel." The man tilted his head, as if puzzled, as if considering himself. "Show me your key."

"Who are you?" Snorri repeated his first question.

Across from me Tuttugu stopped pressing the heels of his hands to his ears. His eyes widened from the slits they had been. He grabbed up his axe from the rocks and crawled to my side.

"Who? Who was I? That man is dead, an older one wears his skin. I'm just an echo—like the others echoing here, though my voice is the strongest. I am not me. Just a fragment, unsure of my purpose . . ."

"Who—"

"I won't bandy my name before a light-sworn warrior." The dead man seemed to gather himself. "Show me your key. It must be the reason I am here."

Snorri pursed his lips then released one hand from the axe to draw Loki's key from beneath his jerkin. "There. Now, if you won't help me, shade, begone."

"Ah. This is good. This is a good key. Give it to me." A hunger in him now.

"No. Show me the door, ghost."

"Give me the key and I'll allow you to continue along your path."

"I need the key to open the door."

"I thought that once. I had many failures. I called myself door-mage but so many doors resisted me. The key you hold was stolen from me, long ago. Death was the first door I opened without it. Some doors just require a push. For others a latch must be lifted, some are locked, but a sharp mind can pick most locks. Only three still resist me. Darkness, Light, and the Wheel. And when you give me the key I will own those too."

Snorri looked my way and beckoned me. "Jal, I need you to lock the door after me. Take the key and give it to Skilfar. She will know how to destroy it."

"I have something you want, barbarian."

The door-mage had a child at his side, gripping her neck from behind. A small girl in a ragged woollen smock, bare legs, dirty feet, her blond hair thrown across her face as the man forced her head down.

"Einmyria?" Snorri breathed the name.

In one hand the child held a peg doll.

"Emy?" A shout. He sounded terrified.

"The key, or I'll break her neck."

Snorri reached into his jerkin and tore the key from its thong. "Take it." He strode forward pressing it carelessly into the mage's hand, eyes on his daughter, bending toward her. "Emy? Sweet-girl?"

Two things happened together. Somehow the mage dropped Loki's key, and in reaching to catch it as it fell he let go of the child's neck. She looked up, hair falling to the sides. Her face was a wound, the dark red muscle of her cheeks showed through, stripped of skin and fat. She opened her mouth and vomited out flies, thousands of them, a buzzing scream. Snorri fell back and she leapt on him, black talons erupting from the flesh of her hands.

I glimpsed Snorri amid the dark cloud, on his back, struggling to keep the child-thing from ripping out his eyes. Tuttugu lumbered forward, shielding his face, swinging his axe in an under-arm looping blow. Somehow he missed Snorri but caught the demon, the force of the impact knocking her clear. For a second she scrabbled at the muddy slope, shrieking at an inhuman pitch, then fell away, wailing, into the consuming blackness. The flies followed her, like smoke inhaled by an open mouth.

With that deafening buzz receding I noticed the laughter for the first time. Looking away from the cave's throat I saw that the mage remained crouched on the ground, the key still before him on the rock. He wasn't looking at Snorri, just the key. He tried again to pick it up but somehow his fingers passed through it. Another awful, bitter laughter broke from him, a noise that ran through my teeth and made them feel brittle.

"I can't touch it. I can't even touch it."

Snorri scrambled to his feet and rushed the man, throwing him back with a roar. The mage went tumbling, fetching up hard against a rock. Snorri scooped up the key and rubbed his shoulder where he'd barged his foe aside, an expression of disgust on his face, as if the contact sickened him.

"What have you done with my daughter?" Snorri advanced on the mage, axe raised.

The man didn't seem to hear. He stood, staring at his hands. "All these years and I couldn't pick it up . . . Loki must have his little jokes. You'll bring it to me though. You'll bring me that key."

"What have you done with her?" Snorri, as murderous as I'd ever heard him.

"You can't threaten me. I'm dead. I'm—"

Snorri's axe took the man's head. It hit the ground, bounced once and rolled away. The body remained standing for long enough to ensure it would feature in my nightmares, then toppled, the neck stump bloodless and pale.

"Come on." Snorri started to climb down the cave's black gullet, backing into it on all fours, feet first, questing for edges to hold his weight. "Leave him!"

I turned away from the remains of the man, the ghost, the echo, whatever it was.

The whispers rose again. I could hear the woman crying, the sound rasping on my sanity.

"Jal!" Snorri calling me.

"I said, *do not!*"

I turned, looking for the voice. My eyes settled on the severed head. The thing was staring at me.

I struggled to speak, but a voice deeper than my own answered instead. Somewhere deep below us the earth rumbled, the sound of stones that had held their peace ten thousand years and more now speaking all at once, and not in a whisper but a distant roar.

"What?" I looked to where Snorri hung, confusion on his face.

"Better run." The head spoke from the floor, lips writhing as the words sounded inside my skull.

The roar and rumble of falling rock rushed toward us, rising from deep below, a terrible gnashing, as if the intervening space were being devoured by stone teeth.

"Run!" I shouted, and took my own advice. My last glimpse of the cave showed me Tuttugu running my way and Snorri behind him, still trying to haul himself clear of the drop-off.

I sprinted out beneath the hanging lichen and recoiled off Tuttugu as our paths crossed. The impact sent me sprawling and probably saved my life as my terror would have seen me racing out onto a killingly steep descent toward the fjord.

"Quick!" I wheezed the word while trying to haul air back into my recently emptied lungs.

Tuttugu and I staggered out onto the slope, clinging to each other, a rolling cloud of pulverized stone billowing behind us. We fell to the ground and looked back as the cave exhaled dust, like smoke whooshing from the mouth of some vast dragon. Buried thunder vibrated through us, resonating in my chest.

"Snorri?" Tuttugu asked, staring at the cave mouth without hope.

I made to shake my head, but there, emerging from the cloud, grey from foot to head, came Snorri, spitting and coughing.

He collapsed beside us, and for the longest time none of us spoke.

Finally, with the last traces of dust drifting out across the water far below, I stated the obvious. "No key in the world is going to open that for you."

EIGHT

We returned to coast-hopping, the Norseheim shore leading us south. Given that Snorri's options appeared to have reduced to the wastes of Yttrmir in the distant and unwelcoming kingdom of Finn, or a poisoned lake in still more distant Scorron, he settled for seeking out Skilfar as originally planned, his quest so far having added only questions rather than answers.

Aslaug came to me that first night, just as on the previous one on the fjord while we sailed away from the collapse of Eridruin's Cave, and warned me against the Norseman's plans.

"Snorri is led by that key and it will be his ruin, just as it will ruin any who keep his company."

"They say it's Loki's key," I told her. "You don't trust your own father?"

"Ha!"

"Can't the daughter of lies see through her father's tricks?"

"I lie." She smiled that smile which makes a man smile back. "But my lies are gentle things compared to those my father sews. He can poison a whole people with four words." She framed my face with her hands, her touch dry and cool. "The key is locking you in to your fate even as it opens every door. The best liars always tell the truth—they just choose which parts. I might truthfully tell you that if you fight a battle at the equinox your army will be victorious—perhaps though, your army would have won on every day that month, but only on the equinox would *you* not survive the battle to see the enemy routed."

"Well, believe *me* when I say I'm stopping in Vermillion. Horses, wild or otherwise, couldn't drag me to Kelem's doorstep."

"Good." Again the smile. "Kelem seeks to own night's door. It would be better it were never opened than that old mage gain control over it. Get the key for yourself though, Prince Jalan, and you and I might open that particular door together. I would make you King of Shadows and be your queen . . ."

She broke apart in the gloom as the sun set, her smile last to depart.

We restocked on staples and water at isolated communities, and passed the larger ports by. Seven days' sailing from Harrowheim's quays brought us to within sight of Beerentoppen, our last landfall in the lands of Norseheim. Seven days best forgotten. I thought I'd seen the worst of travel by sea when the *Ikea* brought us north. Before I passed out I'd seen waves big as a man slamming into the longboat, the whole vessel rolling about and seemingly out of control. Between Harrowheim and Beerentoppen however a storm overtook us that even Snorri acknowledged as "a bit windy." The gale rolled up waves that would overtop houses, setting the whole ocean in a constant heaving swell. One moment our tiny boat sat deep in a watery valley, surrounded by vast dark mountains of brine, the next second would see us hoisted skyward, lifted to the very crest of a foam-skinned hill. It seemed certain the whole craft would be flipped into the air by one wave only to come crashing down into the arms of the next for a final embrace. Somewhere in that long wet nightmare Snorri decided our boat was called the *Sea-Troll*.

The only good reason to let dawn find you awake is that the previous night's wine has not yet run out, or that a demanding young woman is keeping you up. Or both. Being cold and wet and seasick was not a good reason, but it was mine.

The predawn glow revealed Beerentoppen hunched amid the marches of its smaller kin who crowded the coast. The faintest wisp of smoke marked it out, rising from a blunt peak. The range lay on the westmost tip of the jarldom of Bergen and from these shores we would head out into open seas for the final crossing to the continent.

I watched the mountains with deep mistrust while Tuttugu angled us toward the distant shore. Snorri slept as if the ocean swell were a cradle, looking so comfortable it made me want to kick him.

Snorri had told me that any child of the north knew Skilfar could be found at Beerentoppen. *Come the freezing of the sea, 'til the spring thaw, Skilfar bides in Beeren's Hall.* Few though, even of the elders, snaggle-toothed and grey, perched upon their bench in the jarl's hall, could tell you *where* upon the fire-mountain she might bide. Certainly Snorri appeared to have no idea. I glanced across at the big and shadowed lump of him and was considering where best to kick him when he looked up, saving me the effort.

As the sun rose across the southern shoulder of the distant volcano Baraqel walked along its rays. He strode over the sea, advancing when each wave caught the day's sparkle. His great wings captured the light and seemed to ignite, the fire reflecting in each bronze scale of the armour that encompassed him. I tried to sink out of sight in the boat's prow. I hadn't thought I would still be able to see the angel, and not being in the habit of greeting the dawn with Snorri, I hadn't put the assumption to the test.

"Snorri!" The valkyrie stood before us, feet upon the waves, looking down from a height little shorter than the *Sea-Troll*'s mast. I registered his voice with mild horror. Had Snorri been able to see Aslaug and hear everything I said to her? That would be awkward, and the bastard had never said a word about it . . .

"I need to find Skilfar." Snorri sat up, holding the boat's side. He hadn't much time, Baraqel would be gone when the sun cleared the mountain. "Where is her cave?"

"The mountain is a place of both darkness and light." Baraqel pointed back toward the Beerentoppen with his sword, the sunlight burning on bright steel. "It is fitting that you and . . ." Baraqel peered toward me and I lowered my head out of sight. ". . . he . . . are bound there together. Do not trust him though, this copper prince. The dark whore has his ear now and whispers poison. He will try to take the key from you before long. It must be destroyed, and quickly. Do not give him time or opportunity to work her will. Skilfar can do—"

"The key is mine and I will use it."

"It will be stolen from you, Snorri, and by the worst of hands. You serve only the Dead King's cause in this madness. Even if you evade his minions and find the door . . . nothing good can come through it. The Dead King—the very one who has worked these wrongs upon you—wants death's door opened. His desire that it be opened is the sole reason your people, your wife, your children died. And now you seek to do that work for him. Who knows how many unborn are gathered on the far side waiting to come through in the moment that key turns in the lock?"

Snorri shook his head. "I will bring them back. Your repetition will not change this, Baraqel."

"The breaking of day changes all things, Snorri. Nothing endures beyond the count of the sun. Pile a sufficient weight of mornings upon a thing and it *will* change. Even the rocks themselves will not outlast the morning."

The sun now stood upon the Beerentoppen's shoulder. In moments it would be clear.

"Where will I find Skilfar?"

"Her cave looks to the north, from the mountain's waist." And Baraqel fell into golden pieces, sparkling and dying on the waves, until in the end they were no more than the dancing of the morning's light amid the waters.

I lifted my head to check the angel had really gone.

"He's right about the key," I said.

Tuttugu shot me a puzzled look.

Snorri snorted, shook his head, and set to trimming the sail. He took the tiller from Tuttugu and angled the *Sea-Troll* toward the base of the mountain. Before long gulls spotted the craft, circling about it on high, their cries added to the wind's keening and the slap of waves. Snorri drew the deepest breath and smiled. Beneath a mackerel sky with the morning bright around him it seemed that even the most sorrow-laden man could know a moment's peace.

When we made shore later in the day Snorri and Tuttugu had to drag me out of the boat like a sack of provisions. Days of puking had left me dehydrated and weak as a newborn. I curled up on my cloak a few yards above the high tide line, determined never to move again. Black sand, streaked with unhealthy yellows, stretched down to the breakers. I poked half-heartedly at the stuff, coarse and intermixed with pieces of black rock made brittle by innumerable bubbles held within the stone.

"Volcanic." Snorri set down the sack he'd carried from the boat and took a handful of the beach, working it through his fingers.

"I'll guard the beach." I patted the sand.

"Up you get, the walk will do you good." Snorri reached for me.

I fell back with a wordless bleat of complaint, resting my head against the sand. I wanted to be back in Vermillion, far from the sea and somewhere a sight warmer than the godforsaken beach Snorri had chosen.

"Should we hide the boat?" Tuttugu looked up from securing the last strap of his pack.

"Where?" I flopped my head to the side, staring across the smooth black sands to the tumble of rocks that ended the cove.

"Well—" Tuttugu puffed out his cheeks as he was wont to do when puzzling.

"Don't worry, I'll keep an eye on it for you." I reached out and slapped his shin. "You say hello to Skilfar for me. You'll like her. Lovely woman."

"You're coming with us." Snorri looming over me, blocking out the pale morning sun.

"No, really. You go traipsing up your mountain of ice and fire after your witch. I'll have a little rest. You can tell me what she said when you get back."

In silhouette Snorri was too dark for me to see his face but I could sense his frown. He hesitated, shrugged, and moved away. "All right. I can't see any barns for you to burn or women for you to chase. Should be safe enough. Watch out for any wolves. Especially dead ones."

"The Dead King wants you, not me." I heaved onto my side to watch them start up the slope toward the rocky hinterland. The land stepped rapidly up toward the Beerentoppen foothills. "He wants what you're carrying. You should have dropped it in the ocean. I'll be safe enough." Neither of them turned or even paused. "I'll be safe enough!" I shouted at their backs. "Safer than you two, anyhow," I muttered to the *Sea-Troll*.

To a city man like me there's something deeply unsettling about being in the middle of nowhere. Excepting Skilfar, I doubted another soul lived within fifty miles of my lonely little cove. No roads, no tracks, no hint of man's work. Not even scars left by the Builders back in the misty long-ago. On one side the bulk and heave of mountains, impassable to all but the most determined and well-equipped traveller, and on the other side the wide ocean stretching to unimaginable distances and depths. The Vikings had it that the sea held its own god, Aegir, and he had no use for men, taking their ventures upon its surface as impertinence. Looking out across to the bleak horizon I could well believe it.

A light rain began to fall, driven across the sands at a shallow angle by the wind off the sea.

"Bugger." I took shelter behind the boat.

I sat with my back to the hull, the damp sand under my arse, legs out before me, boot heels pushing little trenches into the stuff. I could have got in and wedged myself back into the prow but I'd had enough of boats to last a lifetime.

I retreated again into my dream of Vermillion, eyes fixed on the black sand but seeing the sun-baked terracotta roofs of the west town, threaded by narrow alleys and divided by broad avenues. I could smell the spice and smoke, see the pretty girls and highborn ladies walking where merchants sold their wares on carpet and stall. Troubadours filled the evening with serenades and the old songs that everyone knows. I missed the crowds, relaxed and happy, and the warmth. I would have paid a gold crown for just an hour of a summer day in Red March. The food too. I just wanted to eat something that hadn't been pickled or salted or blackened on an open fire. Along the Strada Honorous or in Adam's Plaza the hawkers roamed with trays of sweetmeats or pastry trees laden with dangling delicacies . . . my stomach rumbled loud enough to break the spell.

Gull cries rang out, mournful across the desolation of that shore. Shivering, I huddled deeper into my cloak. Snorri and Tuttugu had long since vanished over the first ridge. I wondered if Tuttugu was wishing he'd stayed behind yet. In Vermillion I would have a day of hawking with Barras Jon, or be out at the horse track with the Greyjar brothers. Evening would see us all gathered at the Royal Jug, or down by the river in the Ale Gardens, preparing for a night of wenching, or should Omar join us, dice and cards at the Lucky Sevens. God, I missed those days . . . Mind, if I turned up at the Lucky Sevens now how long would it be before Maeres Allus heard I was under one of his roofs and invited me to have a private word? A smile twisted my lips as I remembered Snorri hacking the arm from Cutter John, Maeres's torturer. Even so, Vermillion would not be a healthy place for me until that bit of unpleasantness was sorted out.

The cries of the gulls, earlier so poignant against the bleakness of the landscape, had grown raucous and swollen to cacophony.

"Bloody birds." I looked for a stone but none lay to hand.

Throwing the first stone . . . a simple pleasure. Once my life had been one simple pleasure after the next. I wondered what Barras and the boys would make of me, returning in my heathen rags, leaner, my sword notched, scars to show. Less than a year would have passed but would things still be the same? Could they? Would those old pastimes still satisfy? When I finally rode through the Red Gates would I really be back . . . or had the moment somehow passed, never to be recaptured? I'd seen too much on my journey. Learned too much. I wanted my ignorance back. And my bliss.

Something splatted on my forehead. I reached to wipe the dribbles from my cheek, fingers coming away gooey with white muck.

"Fucking bloody . . ." Weakness forgotten, I lurched to my feet, fist raised in impotent rage at the gulls circling overhead. "Bastards!" I wheeled seaward, intent on finding a stone lower down the beach.

Not until I'd found my stone—a nice flatish piece of black-grey slate, smoothed by the waves and with that perfect round-in-the hand feel—and started to straighten up for my reckoning with the gulls did I notice the longboat. Still a ways out among the very first breakers, sail furled, forty oars splashing rhythmically as they drove it forward. I stood, jaw hanging, shocked into stillness. To either side of the prow a red eye had been painted, staring forward, heavy with threat.

"Shit." I dropped my stone. I'd seen this before. A memory from our trek north. Looking down upon the Uulisk Fjord. A longboat made tiny with the distance. A red dot at its prow. These were Hardanger men. Red Vikings. They might even have Edris Dean with them if the bastard had escaped the Black Fort. Two Vikings stood in the prow, round rune-marked shields, wolf-skin cloaks, red hair streaming around their shoulders, axes ready, close enough to see the iron eye rings and nose guards on their helms. "Shit." I scrambled back, grabbed my sword, snatched up the smallest of three bags of provisions, started running.

A winter of over-eating and over-boozing had done little for my fitness, the only exercise I got happening under the furs. The breath came ragged from my lungs before I even reached the first ridge. What had been a dull ache of ribs crushed beneath the weight of the Fenris wolf rapidly flared into the pain of dagger-driven-into-lung with each gasp of air. On reaching the higher ground I risked pausing to turn around. The Hardanger men had their longboat beached with a dozen of them busy around it. At least twice that number had already started up the slope on my trail, scrambling over the rocks as if catching a southerner would make their day. And yes, in the midst of them, bareheaded, a solid fellow in a studded leather jerkin, sword hilt jutting over his shoulder, iron-grey hair with that blue-black streak and bound at the back into a tight queue. "Edris fucking Dean." I seemed to be making a habit of being chased up mountains by the man.

The land rose toward Beerentoppen as if it were in a dreadful hurry. I panted my way through dense clumps of gorse and heather, struggled through stands of pine and winter-ash, and scrabbled over the patches of bedrock that lay exposed where the wind wouldn't allow the meagre soil to gather. A little higher and the trees gave up trying, and before long my path angled across bare rock unbroken by any splash of green. I kept on, cursing Snorri for leaving me, cursing Edris for giving chase. No doubts now remained about who had been keeping watch on us in Trond. And if Edris was here and dead things were hunting us too it seemed certain that at least one necromancer escaped the Black Fort with him. Quite possibly the scary bitch from Chamy-Nix who'd stood the mercenaries Snorri killed back up again.

Snorri and Tuttugu had left no trail so Beerentoppen's broken peak was all I had to guide me. Baraqel had told them where Skilfar was but damned if I could remember what he'd said. I stumbled gasping and spluttering around the vast boulders that decorated any even vaguely flat surface, and skittered a dangerous path across slopes littered with brittle stones that may have been spat from the volcano . . . or dropped by pixies for all I knew.

One skitter took me a little too far. I hit a rock, tripped, and sprawled, coming to a halt not more than a foot from a drop big enough to be the killing kind. "Shit." The closest of my pursuers were three hundred yards off and moving fast. I got to my feet, hands bloody.

I'm very good at running away. For best results put me in a city. Among streets and houses I do well. In such surroundings a good sprint, tight cornering, and an open mind when it comes to hiding places will see a man clear under most circumstances. The countryside is worse— more things to trip you up, and the best hiding spots are often taken. On a bleak mountainside it comes down to endurance, and when a fellow has been wrung out by sea sickness, not to mention rolled on by the kind of wolf that would only need two friends to bring down a mammoth . . . well, it's not going to end well.

Fear is a great motivator. It returned me to my feet and set me jogging on. I didn't dare look back for fear of missing my footing again. I clutched my side, rasped in one breath after the next, and tried to keep from weaving across the slope. Hope is almost as bad as fear for goading a man past the point at which he should give up. Hope persuaded me I was opening a lead. Hope convinced me the next rise would reveal Snorri and Tuttugu just ahead. When, in a sudden pounding of footsteps, the Hardassa man caught up with me and brought me down, I fell with a wheeze of surprise, despite it having been inevitable from the moment I spotted their longboat closing on the beach.

The Viking crashed down on top of me, pressing my face to the rock. I lay panting while the rest of the pursuit gathered round. My view offered only their boots but I didn't need to see any more than that to know they would be a fearsome bunch.

"Prince Jalan Kendeth. Good to meet you again." A southern accent, a touch winded.

The weight lifted from me as my captor rolled clear. I took my time getting into a sitting position. Looking up, I found Edris Dean staring down at me, feet braced against the slope, hand on hip. He seemed pleased. The dozen Red Vikings arrayed around him looked less pleased. More of them stretched out back down the slope, toiling upward.

"Don't kill me!" It seemed like a good place to start.

"Give me the key and I'll let you go," Edris said, still with the smile.

The thing about staying alive is staying useful. As a prince I'm always useful . . . as an heir and a figurehead. As a debtor I was useful as long as Maeres believed I might be able to pay him back. As Edris's captive, too far from home to be a good prospect for ransom, my only real use lay in being a link to Loki's key. "I can take you to it." It might only mean a few more hours of life but I'd sell my own grandmother for that. And her palace.

Edris waved a couple of the Hardassa men forward. One took the rations sack I'd been too preoccupied to ditch, the other started to go through my clothes, and not gently. "My friends here tell me there's only one reason to put in at this shore." He pointed up at Beerentoppen. "I don't need you to find the witch."

"Ah!" The Viking was being particularly thorough and his hands were freezing. "Uh. But. You need me to . . ." I hunted for a reason. "Skilfar! Snorri's got the key and he's going to give it to Skilfar. You've got to catch him before he gets to her."

"I don't need you for that either." Edris took the dagger from his belt. A plain iron pig-sticker.

"But . . ." I eyed the blade. He had a good point. "He'll trade the key for me. You don't want to fight him—didn't go so well last time. And . . . and . . . he might throw the key away. If he threw it as you charged him you could spend a week hunting these slopes and still not find it."

"Why would he trade Loki's key against your life?" Edris sounded doubtful.

"Blood debt!" It came to me in a flash. "He owes me his life. You don't know Snorri ver Snagason. Honour's all he has left. He'll pay his debt."

Edris twitched his mouth in a sneer, quickly gone. "Alrik, Knui, he's your responsibility. Take his weapons."

The pair searching me and my belongings took away my sword and knife. Edris strode past, setting a good pace, the others following in his wake. "You keep up now, my prince, or we'll have to cut you loose and take our chances."

Alrik, a dark-bearded thug, started me off with a shove between the shoulders. "Quick." The Red Vikings spoke the old tongue among themselves and some had a few words of Empire. Knui followed on. I had no illusions concerning what was meant by "cutting me loose."

Hurrying after Edris, I kept a good eye on the ground ahead, knowing a twisted ankle would see me gutted and left to die. Now and then I stole a glance at the mountain slopes to either side. Somewhere out there the necromancer might be watching, and even in these direst of straits I had time to be scared of her.

Climbing to the Beerentoppen crater with Edris in the lead proved every bit as horrific as running before him. Staggering up ever-steeper rockfaces, hands and knees raw, feet blistered and bruised, panting hard enough to vomit a lung, I actually wished I could be back in the *Sea-Troll* bobbing about on the ocean.

Hours passed. Noon passed. We got high enough to see across the snow-laden peaks north and south, the going becoming even more vertical and more treacherous, and still no Snorri. It astonished me that without knowing he was pursued Snorri had kept ahead of us. Especially with Tuttugu. The man was not made for climbing mountains. Rolling down them he'd be good at.

Afternoon crawled into evening and I crawled after Edris, driven on by the threat of Alrik's hatchet and by well-placed kicks from Knui. The peak of the mountain looked to be broken off, ending in a serrated rim. The slopes took on a peculiar folded character, as if the rock had congealed like molten fat running from a roasting pig. We got to within a few hundred yards of the top when Edris's scouts returned to report. They yabbered in the old tongue while I lay sprawled, willing some hints of life back into limp legs.

"No sign of Snorri." Edris loomed over me. "Not out here, not in the crater."

"He must be somewhere." I half wondered if Snorri had lied, if he'd gone off on some different quest. Maybe the next cove held a fishing town, a tavern, warm beds . . .

"He's found the witch's cave, and that's bad news for all of us. Especially you."

I sat up at that. Fear of imminent death always helps a man find new reserves of energy. "No! Look—" I forced my voice to come out less shrill and panicky. Weakness invites trouble. "No. *I* wanted Snorri to give Skilfar the key—but he didn't agree. Chances are he'll still have it when he comes out. He's a hard man to argue with. And then you can trade."

"When a man starts changing his story it's difficult to give credence to anything he says." Edris eyed me speculatively, a look that had probably been the last thing half a dozen men ever saw. Even so, the blind terror that had held me since sighting their longboat had started to ebb. There's an odd thing about being among men who are casually considering your murder. On my ventures with Snorri I'd been plunged into one horror after another, and run screaming from as many of them as I could. The terror that a dead man inspires, trailing his guts as he lurches after you, or that cold chill the hot breath of a forest fire can bring, these are reactions to wholly alien situations—the stuff of nightmare. With men though, the regular everyday sort, it's different. And after a winter in the Three Axes I'd come to see even the most hirsute axe-clutching reavers as fairly common fellows with the same aches, pains, gripes and ambitions as every other man, albeit in the context of summers spent raiding enemy shores. With men who bear you no particular ill will and for whom your murder will be more of a chore than anything else, entailing both the effort of the act and of the subsequent cleaning of a weapon, the business of dying starts to seem a bit everyday too. You almost get swept up in the madness of the thing. Especially if you're so exhausted that death seems like a good excuse for a rest. I returned his stare and said no more.

"All right." Edris ended the long period of decision and turned away. "We'll wait."

The Red Vikings distributed themselves across the slopes to seek the entrance to Skilfar's lair. Edris, Alrik, and Knui stayed with me.

"Tie his hands." Edris settled down against a rock. He drew his sword from its scabbard and took a whetstone to its edge.

Alrik bound my hands behind me with a strip of hide. None of them had brought packs, they'd just given chase. They had no food other than what they'd stolen from me, and no shelter. From our elevation we could see along the mountainous coast for several miles in each direction, and out across the sea. The beach and their longboat lay hidden by the volcano's shoulder.

"Is *she* here?" The necromancer plagued my thoughts, images of dead men rising kept returning to me, unbidden.

Edris let a long moment pass before a slow turn of the head brought his gaze my way. He gave me an uneasy smile. "She's out there." A wave of his hand. "Let's hope she stays there." He held his sword toward me. "She gave me this." The thing put an ache in my chest and made me shiver, as if I remembered it from some dark dream. Script ran along its length, not the Norse runes but a more flowing hand reminiscent of the markings the Silent Sister used to destroy her enemies. "Kill a babe in the womb with this piece of steel and the poor wee thing is given to Hell. Just waits there for its chance to return unborn. The mother's death, the death of any close relative, opens a hole into the drylands, just for that lost child, and if you're quick, if you're powerful, all that potential can be born into the world of men in a new and terrible form." He spoke in a conversational tone, his measure of regret sounding genuine enough—but at the same time a cold certainty wrapped me. This was the blade that had slain Snorri's son in his wife's belly, Edris the man who started the foul work that the necromancers continued and that ended with Snorri facing his unborn child in the vault at the Black Fort's heart. "You watch the slopes, young prince. The necromancer's out there, and that one you really don't want to meet."

Alrik and Knui exchanged glances but said nothing. Knui took off his helm, setting it on his knees, and rubbed his bald scalp, scraping his nails through sweat-soaked straggles of red-blond hair to either side. In places the helm had left him raw, bouncing back and forth on the long climb. The day had taken its toll on all of us and despite the awfulness of my predicament my head started to nod. With the horror of Edris's words rattling about in my brain I knew I wouldn't ever sleep again, but I lay back to rest my body. I closed my eyes, sealing away the bleakness of the sky. A moment later oblivion took me.

"Jalan." A dark and seductive voice. "Jalan Kendeth." Aslaug insinuated herself into my dream, which up until that point had been a dull repetition of the day, climbing the Beerentoppen all over again, endless images of rocks and grit passing under foot, hands reaching for holds, boots scrabbling. I stopped dead on the dream-slopes and straightened to find her standing in my path, draped in shadow, bloody with the dying sun. "What a drab place." She looked about herself, tongue wetting her upper lip as she considered our surroundings. "It can't really be this bad? Why don't you wake up so I can see for real."

I opened a bleary eye and found myself staring out at the setting sun, the sky aflame beneath louring clouds. Alrik sat close by sharpening his hatchet with a whetstone. Knui stood a little way off where the slope dropped away, watching the sun go down, or pissing, or both. Edris seemed to have disappeared, probably to check on his men.

Aslaug stood behind Alrik, looking down on the dark mass of his hair and broad shoulders as he tended his weapon. "Well this won't do at all, Jalan." She leaned to peer behind me at my hands, wedged between my back and the rock. "Tied up! And you, a prince!"

I couldn't very well answer her without drawing unwanted attention, but I watched, filled with the dark excitement her visits always provoked. It wasn't that she made me brave exactly, but seeing the world when she stood in it just took the edge off everything and made life seem simpler. I tested the bonds on my wrists. Still strong. She made life simple . . . but not *that* simple.

Aslaug set one bare foot on the helmet Alrik had set beside him, and laid her finger against the side of his head. "If you launched yourself at him and struck the top of your forehead against this spot . . . he would not get up again."

I gestured with my eyes toward Knui, just ten yards down the slope.

"That one," she said. "Is standing next to a fifteen foot drop . . . How quickly do you think you could reach him?"

Under normal circumstances I'd still be arguing about the head butt. I would have guessed as zero the likelihood that I could pick myself up, cover the distance to Knui without falling on my face. To then knock Knui off the cliff while not following him over was surely impossible. I also wouldn't have the nerve to try it, not even to save my life. But with Aslaug looking on, an ivory goddess smoking with dark desire, a faint mocking smile on perfect lips, the odds didn't seem to matter any more. I knew then how Snorri must have felt when he battled with her beside him. I knew an echo of the reckless spirit that had filled him when the night trailed black from the blade of his axe.

Still I hesitated, looking up at Aslaug, slim, taut, wreathed in shadows that moved against the wind.

"Live before you die, Jalan." And those eyes, whose colour I could never name, filled me with unholy joy.

I tilted away from the boulder that supported me, rocked onto my toes, and started to fall forward before straightening my legs with a sudden thrust. Suppressing the urge to roar I threw myself like a spear, forehead aimed for the spot on Alrik's temple where Aslaug had laid her finger.

The impact ran through me, filling my vision with blinding pain. It hurt more than I had thought it would—a lot more. For a heartbeat or two the world went away. I recovered to find myself lying across Alrik's unresisting form, head on his chest. I rolled clear, trying to see out of eyes screwed tight against the pain. Down the slope Knui had turned from the cliff edge and his contemplation of the sea.

Getting on your feet on a steep incline with your hands bound behind you is not easy. In fact I didn't quite manage it. I lurched, half-stood, unbalanced, and set off down the mountainside flat out, desperately trying to get each foot in front of me in time to keep from diving face first into the rock.

Knui moved quickly. I aimed at him as the only chance for stopping my headlong dash. He'd already advanced a couple of yards and was unslinging his axe when, totally out of control, I cannoned into him. Even braced against the impact, Knui had no chance. Wiry and tougher than leather he might be, but I was the bigger man and carrying more momentum than anyone on a mountainside would ever want. Bones crunched, I carried him backward, we held for a broken second teetering on the cliff edge, and with a single cry we both went over.

Hitting Alrik had been harder and more painful than I wanted or expected. Hitting Knui proved much worse. Both were gentle taps compared to hitting the ground. For the second time in under a minute I passed out.

I came to lying face down on something soft. And damp. And . . . smelly. I couldn't see much or move my arms.

"Get up, Jalan." For a moment I couldn't understand who was speaking. "Up!"

Aslaug! I couldn't get up—so I rolled. The softness proved to be Knui. Also the dampness and the smell. His face registered surprise, the expression frozen in. The back of his head had . . . spread, the rocks crimson with it. I struggled to my knees, hurting myself on the stones. Aslaug stood beside me, against the cliff, her head and shoulders rising above the edge where Knui had stood. Shadow coiled up about her, vine-like, her features darkening.

"Y—You said the drop was fifteen foot!" I spat blood.

"I was next to you, Jalan. How could I see?" An infuriating smile on her lips. "It got you moving though. And any fall on a mountain can kill a man, with a little luck."

"You! Well . . . I." I couldn't find the right words, the fear had started to catch up with me.

"Better get your hands free . . ." She pressed back against the stone, crouching now, indistinct as the horizon ate the sun and gloom swelled from every hollow.

"I . . ." But Aslaug had gone and I was speaking to the rocks.

Knui's axe lay a little further down the slope. I shuffled toward it and with considerable difficulty positioned myself so I could start to saw at the hide strip around my wrists, watching all the while for other Hardassa men or Edris himself to come running into view.

Even a sharp axe takes a god-awful long time to cut through tough hide. Sitting there by Knui's corpse it felt like forever. Every few seconds I let my gaze slip from lookout duty to check he hadn't moved. I had a poor record with killing men on mountainsides. They tended to get up again and prove more trouble dead than alive.

At last the hide parted and I rubbed my wrists. Looking up, Aslaug's second lie became apparent. She had said if I head butted Alrik where she pointed that he wouldn't be getting up again. Yet there he was, standing at the top of the four-foot "cliff" that Knui and I sat at the bottom of. He didn't seem pleased. More importantly, he had his hatchet in one hand and a wide-bladed knife with a serrated back in the other.

"Edris will want me alive!" I considered running but didn't want to bet against how well Alrik could throw that hatchet. Also he could probably catch me. I thought about the axe lying on the rocks behind me. But I'd never swung one. Not even for splitting logs.

The Viking's glance flitted to Knui, lying there with the rocks painted a dark scarlet all around him. "Fuck Edris."

Two words told me all I needed to know. Alrik was going to murder me. He tensed, readying himself to jump down. And an axe hit him in the side of his head. The blade sheared through his left eye, across the bridge of his nose, and stopped midway along the eyebrow on the other side. Alrik fell to the ground and Snorri stepped into view. He put one large foot on the side of Alrik's face and levered his axe free with an awful cracking sound that made me retch.

"How's the *Sea-Troll*?" Snorri asked.

"*I'm* fine! Thank you very much." I remained seated and patted myself down. "No, not fine. Bruised and damn near murdered!" Seeing Snorri suddenly made it all seem much more real and the horror of it all settled on me. "Edris Dean was going to gut me with a knife and—"

"Edris?" Snorri interrupted. "So he's behind this?" He rolled Alrik's corpse off the drop with his foot.

Tuttugu came into view, glancing nervously over his shoulder. "The southerner? I thought it might just be the Hardassa . . ." He caught sight of me. "Jal! How's the boat?"

"What is it with northmen and their damn boats? A prince of Red March nearly died on this—"

"Can you carry us away from the Red Vikings?" Snorri asked.

"Well no, but—"

"How's the damn boat then?"

I took the point. "It's fine . . . but it's about a spear's length from the longboat that these two came in." I nodded to the corpses at my outstretched feet. "And there are over a dozen more with it, and two dozen on the mountain."

"Good that Snorri found you then!" Tuttugu rubbed his sides like he always did when upset. "We were hoping they'd come ashore somewhere else . . ."

"How—" I stood up, thinking to ask how it was that Snorri *did* find me. Then I saw her. A little further back from the edge from where Snorri and Tuttugu looked down on me. A Norse woman, fair hair divided into a score of tight braids, each set with an iron rune tablet, a style I'd seen among older women in Trond, though none ever sported more than a handful of such runes.

Snorri saw my surprise and gestured at the woman. "Kara ver Huran, Jal." And at me. "Jal, Kara." She spared me a brief nod. I guessed her to be about halfway between me and Snorri in age, tall, her figure hidden beneath a long black cape of tooled leather. I wouldn't call her pretty . . . too weak a word. Striking. Bold-featured.

I bowed as she drew closer. "Prince Jalan Kendeth of Red March at your ser—"

"My boat is in the next cove. Come, I'll lead you there." She pinned me with remarkably blue eyes as if taking an uncomfortably accurate measure of me, then turned to go. Snorri and Tuttugu made to follow.

"Wait!" I stumbled about, trying to gather my wits. "Snorri!"

"What?" Glancing back over his shoulder.

"The necromancer. She's here too!"

Snorri turned back after Kara, shaking his head. "Better hurry then!"

I set both hands to the top of the "cliff" and prepared to heft myself up onto the slope above when I saw my sword hilt jutting over Alrik's shoulder. He lay on his side, not far from Knui. Above the nose his head was little more than skull fragments, hair and brain. I hesitated. I'd killed my first man with that sword, albeit mostly by accident—at least he was the first one I remembered. I'd notched that sword battling against the odds in the Black Fort, wedged it hilt-deep in a Fenris wolf. If I'd ever done anything that might truly count as manly, honourable, or brave it was done holding that blade.

I took a step toward Alrik. Another. The fingers of his right hand twitched. And I ran like hell.

NINE

Deep gullies, rain-carved through ancient lava flows, brought us down to the cove where Kara's boat lay at anchor.

"It's a long way out," I said, peering through the gloom. The footing in the gullies would have been dangerous in full day. Coming down in deep shadow had been practically begging for a broken ankle. And now with the night thick about us Kara expected me to swim toward a distant and slightly darker clot of sea that was allegedly a boat. I could see the gentle phosphorescence of the waves as the foam surged over the jagged rocks where the beach should be, and beyond them . . . nothing else. "A very long way out!"

Snorri laughed as if I'd made a joke and started to strap his weapons onto the little raft Kara had towed ashore when she arrived. I hugged myself, shivering. The rain had returned. I had expected snow—the night felt cold enough for it. And somewhere out there the necromancer hunted us . . . or had already found us and now watched from the rocks. Out there, Knui and Alrik would be stumbling along our trail, oozing, broken, filled with that dreadful hunger that invades men when they return from death.

While the others prepared themselves I watched the sea with my usual silent loathing. The moon broke from behind a cloudbank, lighting the ocean swell with glimmers and making white bands of the breaking waves.

Tuttugu appeared to share some of my reservations but at least like a walrus he had his bulk to keep him warm and to add buoyancy. My swimming might accurately be described as drowning sideways.

"I'm not good in the water."

"You're not good on land," Snorri retorted.

"We'll come in closer." Kara glanced my way. "I can bring her closer now the tide's in."

So one by one, with their bulkier clothing on the raft in tight-folded bundles, the three of them waded into the surf and struck out for the boat. Tuttugu went last and at least acknowledged how icy the sea was with some most un-Viking-like squeals and gasps.

I stood on the beach alone with the sound of the waves, the wind, and the rain. Freezing water trickled down my neck, my hair hung in my eyes, and the bits of me that weren't numb with cold variously hurt, ached, throbbed, and stung. Moonlight painted the rocky slopes behind the shingle in black and silver, rendering a confused mosaic into which my fears could construct the slow advance of undead horrors. Perhaps the necromancer watched from those dark hollows even now, or Edris urged the Hardassa toward me with silent gestures . . . Clouds swallowed the moon, leaving me blind.

Eventually, after far longer than I felt it reasonable for them to take, I heard Snorri calling. The moonlight returned, reaching through a wind-torn hole in the clouds, and the boat resolved from the darkness, picked out in silver. Kara's looked to be a more seaworthy craft than Snorri's rowing boat, longer, with more elegant lines and a deeper hull. Snorri ceased his labour at the oars still fifty yards clear of the shore and the hidden rocks further in. The tall mast and furled sails wagged to and fro as waves rolled beneath, gathering themselves to break upon the beach.

"Jal! Get out here!" Snorri's boom across the water.

I stood, unwilling, watching the breakers smash, collapse into foam, and retreat, clawing at the shingle. Further out the sea's surface danced with rain.

"Jal!"

In the end one fear pushed out another. I found myself more afraid of what might be descending from the mountain beneath the cover of darkness than of what might lurk beneath the waves. I threw myself into the surf, shouting oaths at the shocking coldness of it, and tried to drown in the direction of the boat.

My swim consisted of a long and horrific repetition. First of being plunged beneath icy water, then thrashing to the surface, gasping a blind breath and finally a few seconds of beating at the brine before the next wave swamped me. It ended abruptly when a hooked pole snagged my cloak and Snorri hauled me into the boat like a piece of lost cargo.

For the next several hours I lay sodden and almost too exhausted to complain. I thought the cold would be the death of me, but hadn't any solution to the problem or the energy to act on it if an idea had occurred. The others tried to wrap me in some stinking furs the woman had stashed away onboard but I cursed them and wouldn't cooperate.

Dawn found us adrift beneath clear skies a mile or two off the coast. Kara unfurled the sail and set a course south.

"Hang your clothes on the line, Jal, and get under these." Snorri thrust the furs at me again. Bearskins by the look of them. He pointed to his own rags flapping on one of the ropes that secured the sail. A woollen robe I'd not seen before strained to cover his chest.

"I'm fine." But my voice emerged as a croak and the cold wouldn't leave me despite the sunshine. A few minutes later I snatched up the furs with poor grace and stripped, shivering violently. I struggled to keep from toppling arse up between the benches, face in the bilge water, and I kept my back to Kara since a man is never flattered by a cold wind—not that she seemed interested in any case.

Wrapped in something that used to wrap a bear, I huddled down out of the wind close to Snorri and tried not to let my teeth chatter. Most parts of me ached and the bits that didn't ache were really painful. "So what happened?" I needed something to take my mind off my fever. "And who is Kara?" Did he still have that damn key was what I really wanted to know.

Snorri looked out over the sea, the wind whipping a black mane behind him. I supposed he looked well enough in that rough-hewn bar-barian sort of way but it always astonished me that a woman would look twice at him when young Prince Jal was on offer.

"I think I'm hallucinating," I said, somewhat more loudly. "I'm sure I asked a question."

Snorri half-startled and shook his head. "Sorry, Jal. Just thinking." He slid down closer to me, sheltering. "I'll tell you the story."

Tuttugu came forward to listen, as if he hadn't seen the tale unfold before him the previous day. He sat tented in sailcloth while his clothes flapped on the mast. Only Kara stayed back, hand on the tiller, gaze to the fore, occasionally glancing up at the stained expanse of the sail, pregnant with the wind.

"So," began Snorri, and just as so often before on our travels he wrapped that voice around us and drew us into his memories.

Snorri had stood in the prow, watching the coast draw near.

"We'll beach her? Yes?" Tuttugu paused by the anchor, a crude iron hook.

Snorri nodded. "See if you can wake Jal." Snorri mimed a slap. He knew Tuttugu would be more gentle. The fat man's presence cheered him in ways he couldn't explain. With Tuttugu around Snorri could almost imagine these were the old days again, back when life had been more simple. Better. In truth when the pair of them, Jalan and Tuttugu, had turned up on the quay in Trond Snorri's heart had risen. For all his resolve he had no love of being alone. He knew Jal had been pushed into the boat by circumstance rather than jumping of his own accord, but Tuttugu had no reason to be there other than loyalty. Of the three of them only Tuttugu had started to make a life in Trond, finding work, new friends, a woman to share his days. And yet he'd given that up in a moment because an old friend needed him.

An hour later and the beach lay far behind them. Snorri had climbed high enough to break clear of the pines, thick about Beerentoppen's flanks. Tuttugu came puffing from the tree-line a minute later. They turned north and wound around the mountain on a slow and rising spiral. Snorri aimed to bring them to the north face where they could ascend directly, searching for the cave. They saw few signs of life, once an eagle, wings spread wide to embrace a high wind, once a mountain goat, racing away across broken slopes that looked all but impassable.

Within two hours they had the north to their backs and were ready to climb in earnest.

"Troll country, I'd say." Tuttugu took a suspicious sniff, nose to the wind.

Snorri snorted and put his water flask to his lips. Tuttugu had never so much as smelled a troll, let alone seen one. Still he had a point: the creatures did seem to like volcanoes. Wiping his mouth Snorri started up the slope.

"There!" After another hour's clambering Tuttugu proved to have the sharper eyes, jabbing a finger toward an overhang several hundred yards to their left.

Snorri squinted. "Could be." And led off, placing each foot on the treacherous surface with caution. Between their path and the cave lay a dark scree slope where any slip would likely see them sliding halfway back down in an ever-growing avalanche of loose, frost-shattered stone. Twice Tuttugu went down sharply on his backside with a despairing wail. Their luck held though and they made it to the firmer footing at the base of the cliffs into which the cave was set.

Snorri led again, Tuttugu in his wake sniffing. "I can smell something. It's trolls. I knew it." He fumbled for his axe. "Bloody trolls! I should have stayed with Jal—"

"It's not trolls." Snorri could smell it too. Something powerful, animal, the kind of rankness that only a predator can afford. He shrugged the axe from across his shoulders, and took it in two hands, his father's axe, recovered from the *Broke-Oar* on the Bitter Ice. Slow steps took him closer to the cave mouth, the dark interior yielding secrets as it grew to encompass his vision.

"Hel's teats!" Snorri breathed the oath out before closing his jaw, which had fallen open. In the shadows a monster slumbered. A hound that might stand taller than a shire horse, and wide as the elephant in Taproot's circus. It had that blunt yet wrinkled face of dogs bred for fighting rather than the hunt. One canine, of similar size to Snorri's fingers and thumb all funnelled up together, protruded from the lower jaw, escaping slobbery jowls to point toward a wet nose.

"It's asleep." A hoarse whisper at his shoulder. "If we're very quiet we can get away."

"This is her cave, Tutt. There aren't going to be two. And this must be her guardian. It's not here by chance."

"We could . . ." Tuttugu rubbed furiously at his beard as if hoping to dislodge an answer. "You could lure it out and I could drop a rock on it from up there!" He pointed to the cliff top.

"I think that might . . . irritate her. I've met this woman, Tutt. She's not someone you want to irritate."

"What then? We can't very well walk up and pat the puppy."

Snorri took a hand from his axe and dug beneath his furs to touch Loki's key. Immediately he felt them, Emy, Egil, Karl, Freja, as if it were their skin beneath his fingers, not the slickness of obsidian. "That's exactly what we'll do."

With the need to run trembling in every limb, Snorri advanced into the cave, axe lowered, quiet but not creeping. A few yards in and he sensed he was alone. Turning, he beckoned Tuttugu. The other half of the Undoreth stood no further forward than when they last spoke, huddled in his leathers and quilted jacket, arms so tight about himself he almost squeezed his bulk thin. Snorri beckoned again, with more urgency. Tuttugu offered a despairing look at the heavens and hurried into the cave.

In close file the pair of them trod a silent path toward a tunnel leading from the back of the cave, some yards past the vastness of the dog. The size of the beast overwhelmed Snorri's senses, the powerful dog-stink, the warmth of its breath as he passed within feet of that great muzzle. His back scraped the cave wall with each step. And at the closest point one huge eye rolled open amid the folded topology of the dog's face, regarding Snorri with an unreadable look. For a moment he froze, hand tight on his axe, raising the weapon an inch or two before remembering how poorly it would serve him. With his gaze fixed on the tunnel mouth Snorri moved on, Tuttugu wheezing behind him as if terror had taken hold of his throat.

Twenty paces later they stood out of the hound's sight in a tunnel too small for any pursuit. Snorri felt his body unclench. When the Fenris wolf came for him he had been able to attack, channelling his energy into the battle. Holding back all those instincts had wound every fibre of him to within a hair of snapping.

"Come." He nodded ahead to the glow reflecting on the tunnel walls.

Another convolution of the passage brought them to a cavern, lit from above by fissures running through the thickness of the mountainside to a distant sky. A small pool lay beneath these vents, glowing with the light. The chamber, large as any jarl's hall, lay strewn with the business of living. A pallet heaped with bed furs, a blackened hearth by some natural chimney in the rock, a cauldron before it, other pots stacked to one side, here and there sea-chests, some closed, others open to display clothes, or sacks of stores. Two women sat close together in oak chairs carved in the Thurtan style. Between them they held a scroll, the younger woman tracing a finger along some line of it while the elder watched and nodded.

"Come in if you must." Skilfar raised an arm. Her flesh lay as white as it had when she held audience amid the conjunction of Builders' tracks, guarded by Hemrod's plasteek army, but it no longer smoked with coldness. Her eyes held that same wintry blue but they were the eyes of an old woman now, not some frost-sworn demon.

Snorri took a few paces into the chamber.

"Ah, the warrior. But no prince this time? Not unless he filled out . . . a little." Skilfar cocked her head, looking past Snorri to Tuttugu, trying unsuccessfully to hide in his shadow. The younger woman with the braided hair put down her scroll, unsmiling.

Snorri took another step then realized he still had his axe in hand.

"Sorry." He secured it across his back. "That beast of yours scared the hell out of me! Not that an axe would have helped much."

A thin smile. "So you braved my little Bobo did you?" Her glance flitted to the entrance behind him. Snorri turned. A small dog, stubby-legged, wrinkle-faced, and broad-chested had followed Tuttugu. It sat now, looking up at the fat man with sad eyes, one tooth protruding from its lower jaw above the folds of its muzzle.

"How—"

"Everything in this world depends upon how you look at it, warrior. Everything is a matter of perspective—a matter of where you stand."

"And where do I stand, völva?" Snorri kept his voice respectful, and in truth he had always respected the wisdom of the völvas, the rune-sisters as some called them. Witches of the north as Jal had it. Though they stood at odds with the priests of Odin and of Thor the rune-sisters always gave advice that seemed at its core more honest, darker, filled with doubt in place of hubris. Of course the völvas Snorri had dealt with in the past were neither so famed nor so unsettling as Skilfar. Some said she was mother to them all.

Skilfar looked to the woman beside her, "Kara?"

The woman, a northerner with maybe thirty summers on her, frowned. She fixed Snorri with a disconcerting stare and ran the iron runes at the ends of her braids through her fingers. They marked her as wise beyond her years.

"He stands in shadow," she said. "And in light." Her frown deepened. "Past death and loss. He sees the world . . . through a keyhole?" She shook her head, runes clattering.

Skilfar pursed her lips. "He's a difficult one, I grant you." She took another scroll from the pile beside her, tight-wrapped and ending in caps of carved whale tooth. "First dark-sworn and clinging to a lost hope. Now light-sworn and holding to a worse one. And carrying something." She set a bony hand to her narrow and withered chest. "An omen. A legend. Something made of belief."

"I'm looking for the door, völva." Snorri found his own hand at his chest, resting above the key. "But I don't know where it lies."

"Show me what you have, warrior." Skilfar tapped her breastbone.

Snorri watched her a moment. Hardly a kindly grandmother, but far more human than the creature he and Jal had found amid her army of plasteek warriors the previous year. Which was her true face? he wondered. Maybe neither of them. Maybe her dog was neither the monster he'd first seen nor the toy that seemed to sit now by the tunnel mouth. When a man can't trust his eyes what does he fall back on . . . and what does the choice he makes reveal about him? Lacking answers, Snorri drew forth the key on the thong that hung about his neck. It made slow rotations in the space before his eyes, from some angles reflecting the world, from others dark and consuming. Did Loki really fashion this? Had the hands of a god touched what he had touched? And if so, what lies had the trickster left there, and what truths?

Three slow claps, sounding to the tempo of the key's revolutions. "Extraordinary." Skilfar shook her head. "I underestimated our Silent Sister. You actually did it. And tweaked the nose of this upstart 'king of the dead.'"

"Do you know where the door is?" Snorri almost saw their faces in the flashes between reflection and absorption, Emy's eye glimpsed in the moment, as if through a closing crack. The fire of Freja's hair. "I need to know." He could taste the wrongness. He knew the trap, and that he reached to close it around himself. But he saw them, felt them . . . his children. No man could step away. "I need to know." His voice rough with the need.

"That is a door that should not be opened." Skilfar watched him, neither kind nor cruel. "Nothing good will come of it."

"It's my choice," he said, not sure if it was or not.

"The Silent Sister cracked the world to fill you and that foolish prince with magic. Magic enough to thwart even the unborn. Time was when you put a crack in the world it would heal quickly, like a scratch on skin. Now such wounds fester. Any crack is apt to grow. To spread. The world has become thin. Pressed on too many sides. The wise can feel it. The wise fear it.

"Given time enough, and peace, the wound you bear will heal. Time still heals all wounds, for now. And the scars left behind are our legacy of remembrance. But pick at it and it will fester and consume you. This is true both of the crack the Sister ran through your marrow, and of the hurt the Dead King gave."

Snorri noted she didn't speak of the assassin's cut. He didn't trust her enough to volunteer the information, and instead set his teeth against the growing ache of it and the southward tug that seemed to pull on him by each rib.

"Give me the key and I will set it beyond men. The spirits you have borne, both the dark and the light, are of a piece. Like fire and ice they are no friends of our kind. They exist at the extremes, where madness dwells. Man treads the centre line and when he wanders from it, he falls. You carry an avatar of light now but he lies as sweetly as the darkness."

"Baraqel told me to destroy the key. To give it to you. To do anything but use it." Snorri had endured the same speech dawn after dawn.

"The dark then, whatever face it took to persuade you, you must not believe it."

"Aslaug cautioned me against the key. She said Loki bled lies, breathed them, and his tricks would lay creation in ruins given but an inch. Her father would feed all darkness to the wyrm just as soon as break the light. Anything to upset the balance and drown the world in chaos."

"This is truly your will, warrior? Yours alone?" Skilfar leaned forward in her chair now, her gaze a shiver that travelled the length of him. "Tell me—I will know the truth of it." The age of her wavered in her voice, a frightening weight of years that sounded little different from pain. "Tell me."

Snorri set the key back against his chest. "I am Snorri ver Snagason, warrior of the Undoreth. I have lived a Viking's life, raw and simple, on the shore of the Uulisk. Battle and clan. Farm and family. I was as brave as it was in me to be. As good as I knew. I have been a pawn to powers greater than myself, launched as a weapon, manipulated, lied to. I cannot say that no hand rests on my shoulder even now—but on the sea, in the wild of the evening storm and the calm of morning, I have looked inside, and if this is not true then I know no true thing. I will take this key that

I won through battle and blood and loss. I will open death's door and I will save my children. And if the Dead King or his minions come against me I will sow their ruin with the axe of my fathers."

Tuttugu came to stand at Snorri's shoulder, saying nothing, his message clear.

"You have a friend here, Snorri of the Undoreth." Skilfar appraised Tuttugu, her fingers moving as if playing a thread through her hands. "Such things are rare. The world is sweetness and pain—the north knows this. And we die knowing there is a final battle to come, greater than any before. Leave your dead to lie, Snorri. Sail for new horizons. Set the key aside. The Dead King is beyond you. Any of the hidden hands could take this thing from you. I could freeze the marrow in your bones and take it here and now."

"And yet you won't." Snorri didn't know if Skilfar's magics could overwhelm him, but he knew that having sought his motivations and intent with such dedication the völva would not simply take the key.

"No." She released a sigh, the coldness of it pluming in the air. "The world is better shaped by freedom. Even if it means giving foolish men their head. At the heart of all things, nestled among Yggdrasil's roots, is the trick of creation that puts to shame all of Loki's deceptions. What saves us all are the deeds of fools as often as the acts of the wise.

"Go if you must. I tell you plain, though—whatever you find, it will not be what you sought."

"And the door?" Snorri spoke the words low, his resolve never weaker.

"Kara." Skilfar turned to her companion. "The man seeks death's door. Where will he find it?"

Kara looked up from the study of her fingers, frowning in surprise. "I don't know, Mother. Such truths are beyond me."

"Nonsense." Skilfar clicked her fingers. "Answer the man."

The frown deepened, hands rose, fingers knotted among the rune-hung braids, an unconscious gesture. "The door to death . . . I . . ."

"Where *should* it be?" Skilfar demanded.

"Well . . ." Kara tossed her head. "Why should it be anywhere? Why should death's door be any place? If it were in Trond how would that be right? What of the desert men in Hamada? Should they be so far from—"

"And the world is fair?" Skilfar asked, a smile twitching on thin lips.

"It—No. But it has a beauty and a balance to it. A rightness."

"So if there is a door but it isn't anywhere—what then?" A pale finger spinning to hurry the young woman along.

"It must be everywhere."

"Yes." Skilfar turned her winter-blue eyes upon Snorri once more. "The door is everywhere. You just have to know how to see it."

"And how do I see it?" Snorri looked about the cavern as if he might find the door had been standing in some shadowed nook all this time.

"I don't know." Skilfar raised a hand to stop his protest. "Must I know everything?" She sniffed the air, peering curiously at Snorri. "You're wounded. Show me."

Without complaint Snorri opened his jacket and drew up his shirt to show the red and encrusted line of the assassin's knife. The two völvas rose from their seats for a closer inspection.

"Old Gróa in Trond said the venom on the blade was beyond her art." Snorri winced as Skilfar jabbed a cold finger at his ribs.

"Warts are beyond Gróa's art." Skilfar snorted. "Useless girl. I could teach her nothing." She pinched the wound and Snorri gasped at the salt sting of it. "This is rock-sworn work. A summons. Kelem is calling you."

"Kelem?"

"Kelem the Tinker. Kelem, master of the emperor's coin. Kelem the Gate-keeper. *Kelem!* You've heard of him!" An irritable snap.

"I have now." Snorri shrugged. The name did ring a bell. Stories told to children around the fire in the long winter nights. Snorri thought of the assassins' Florentine gold, remembering for a moment the fearsome swiftness of the men. Each coin stamped with the drowned bell of Venice. The ache of his wound built, along with his anger. "Tell me more about him . . . please." A growl.

"Old Kelem stays salted in his mine, hiding from the southern sun. He's buried deep but little escapes him. He knows ancient secrets. Some call him the last Mechanist, a child of the Builders. So old he makes me look young."

"Where—"

"Florence. The banking clans are his patrons. Or he is theirs. That relationship is harder to unravel than any knot Gordion ever tied. Perhaps the clans sprang from his loins back along the centuries when he quickened. Like many children though they are eager to inherit—of late the banks of Florence have been flexing their muscles, testing the old man's strength . . . and his patience." Skilfar's gaze flitted to Kara, then back to Snorri. "Kelem knows every coin in this Broken Empire of ours and holds the beating heart of its commerce in his claw. A different type of power to imperial might or the Hundred's thrones, but power none the less." In her palm lay a golden coin, a double florin, minted by the southern banks. "A different power but in its way more mighty than armies, more insidious than dancing in the dreams of crowned heads. A double-edged sword perhaps, but Kelem has lived for centuries and has yet to cut himself."

"I thought him a story. A children's tale."

"They call him the Gate-keeper too. He finds and opens doors. It's clear enough why he's called you to him. Clear enough why you need to be rid of this key and soon."

"Gate-keeper?" Snorri said. "Do they call him a door-mage as well?" He felt his hands tighten into fists and saw for a moment a demon wearing Einmyria's form, leaping at him, released by the mage in Eridruin's Cave.

"Once upon a time he called himself that, back in the long ago."

"And he is rock-sworn, you say?"

Skilfar tilted her head to study Snorri from a new angle. "To live so long a man must swear to many masters, but gold is of the earth and it was always his first love."

"I've met him . . . or a shadow of him. He barred the way to Hel against me, said I would bring the key to him." Snorri paused, remembering the demon and how his heart had leapt when he thought it his little girl. He forced his hands to unclench. "And I will."

"That's madness. After the Dead King there is no one worse to give the key to."

"He knows where death's door is though. Can you show it to me? Is there another choice? A better choice? One Kelem cannot deny me?" Snorri tucked the key away and closed his jacket. "Get a codfish on the line and you have dinner. Get a whale on the line and you might *be* the dinner." He set a hand against the blade of his axe. "Let him reel me in, and we shall see."

"At least it saves me trying to ease his hook out of you without killing you," Skilfar said, her lips pursed. "Kara will go with you."

"What?" Kara looked up at that, head turning sharp enough to fan out her hair.

"No. I—" Snorri couldn't think of an objection other than it felt wrong. The sharp challenge in the woman's regard had sparked an instant attraction in him. She reminded him of Freja. And that felt like betrayal. A foolish notion but an honest one, deep as bones.

"But—" Kara shook her head. "A warrior? What's to be learned watching him swing his axe?"

"You'll go with him, Kara." Skilfar became stern. "A warrior? Today he is a warrior. Tomorrow, who knows? A man casts a million shadows, and yet you trap him within such a singular opinion. You travelled here seeking wisdom, girl, but all that I have here on these scrolls is information. The wise come into their majority out in the world, amid the muck and pain of living. It's not all the dropping of runes and the wrapping of old platitudes in gravitas. Get out there. Go south. Burn in the sun. Sweat. Bleed. Learn. Come to me older, tempered, hardened." She tapped a finger to the scroll case on her lap. "These words have waited here an age already—they will wait on you a little longer. Read them with eyes that have seen the wideness of the world and they will mean more to you. There is a singular benefit in Snorri's choosing of Kelem to show him the door. A thousand-mile benefit. On such a journey a man might grow, and change, and find himself a new opinion. Perhaps you can help him."

Snorri stretched beside me. "And that was that." He stood, the boat shifting beneath his weight, and glanced at Kara. "Skilfar shooed us out and her little dog followed to see that we left. Kara followed on minutes later. She said there were men hunting us on the mountain and that we'd find you near the crater on the west face."

I looked between them, Snorri, Tuttugu, Kara—the madman, the faithful hound, the baby witch. Three of them against the Dead King, and if he didn't take them then Kelem waited at the end of their journey. And the prize if they won was to open death's door and let hell out . . .

"Florence, eh? The best path to Florence leads through Red March. You can drop me off there."

TEN

Perhaps Kara had a magic about her that permeated her boat, or maybe I had found my sea legs at long last—either way, the voyage south from the Beerentoppen proved less horrendous than the many days with Snorri in the *Sea-Troll*. Kara had named her boat *Errensa*, after the valkyrie that swim beneath the waves to gather the war dead for Ragnarok. She knew the winds and kept her sails full, driving us south faster than a man can run.

"She's a fine-looking woman," I told Snorri when he came to join me, huddled in the prow. The boat wasn't large but the wind gave us privacy, overwriting our conversation and snatching the words away.

"That she is. She's got a strength about her. Didn't think she'd be your type, Jal. And haven't you been mooning over this Lisa of yours ever since we left Trond?"

"Well, yes, I mean Lisa's a lovely girl . . . I'm sure I'll climb her balcony once or twice when I get back but . . ." But a man has to think about the here and now, and right there and right then, Kara had all my attention.

Life aboard a small sailboat is not to be recommended, however attractive the company, and even when you don't have to spend most of each day emptying yourself over the side. The food proved cold, monotonous, and in short supply. The nights continued to try to reinstate winter. My fever continued to keep me weak and shivering. And any hopes I had of exercising my charms on Kara died early on. For one thing it's hard to play the enigmatic prince of romance when the object of your affections gets to watch you shit into the sea twice a day. For another, the very first time my hand wandered her way Kara took a long knife from out beneath the many pleats of her skirt and explained with unnecessary volume how she would use it to pin that hand to my groin should it wander again. Snorri and Tuttugu just watched me and rolled their eyes as if it were my fault! I cursed the lot of them for miserable peasants and retreated to nibble on our diminishing store of dry oatcakes—revolting things.

At sunset Aslaug came, rising through the boards of the hull as if the inky depths had kept her safe while day scoured the world. Tuttugu glanced my way, shuddered and busied himself with a net that needed repairs. Snorri stared hard at the spot from which Aslaug rose, his gaze unreadable. Did he miss her company? He hadn't the look of a man who saw her clearly though, his eyes sliding past her as she moved toward me. I hope her words slid past his ears just as well.

"Jalan Kendeth. Still huddled among northmen? Yours is the palace of Red March, not some creaking tub."

"You have a faster means of getting there?" I asked, my mood still soured.

Aslaug made no reply but turned slowly as if hunting a scent, until she faced the stern where Kara stood beside the tiller. The völva saw Aslaug in the moment the avatar's gaze fell upon her. I could tell it in an instant. Kara made no attempt to conceal that recognition, or her anger. Without taking her gaze from the spirit she tied off the tiller and stepped forward. She compensated for the swell, advancing as if the boat were set in rock.

"Out!" Loud enough to startle Snorri and Tuttugu, and to have me jump half out of my seat. "Out, night-spawn. Out, lie-born. Out, daughter of Loki! Out, child of Arrakni!" Kara's eyes blazed with the sunset. She advanced, one hand held before her, clutching something that looked rather like a human bone.

"Well she's a pretty thing!" Aslaug said. "Snorri will take her from you. You know that don't you, Jalan?"

"Out!" Kara roared. "This boat is mine!" She struck the bone to the mast and all about the hull runes lit, burning with a wintery light. In that instant Aslaug seemed to collapse, flowing into some smaller shape, the size of a large dog, so wreathed in darkness it was hard to see any detail . . . other than it had too many legs. In a quick thrashing of long dry limbs Aslaug scurried over the side and was gone without a splash. I shuddered and looked up at Kara who returned my gaze, her lips set in a thin line. I opted to say nothing. The völva held like that, still with the bone to the mast, for another minute, then another, and then, with the sun gone behind the world, she relaxed.

"She is not welcome here," Kara said, and returned to steering the boat.

"She and Baraqel are all Snorri and I have in our corner. They're ancient spirits, angel and . . . well . . . There are people after us, *things*, after us that work magic as easily as breathing. We need them. The Red Queen's sister gave us—"

"The Red Queen moves you on her board like all her other pawns. What she gives you is as much a collar as a weapon." Kara took up the tiller again. Adjusted course. "Don't be fooled about these creatures' nature. Baraqel is no more a valkyrie or angel than you or me. He and Aslaug were human once. Some among the Builders copied themselves into their machines—others, when the Wheel first turned, escaped their flesh into new forms."

"Aslaug never told me—"

"She's the daughter of lies, Jalan!" Kara shrugged. "Besides, she probably doesn't remember. Their spirits have been shaped by expectation for so long. When the Day of a Thousand Suns came their will released them and they were free. Gods in an empty world . . . then we came back. New men, roaming the earth as the poisons faded. New will. And slowly, without us knowing it, or them, our stories bound about the spirits and *our* will made them into something suited to our expectations."

"Uh." I leaned back, trying to make sense of the völva's words. After a while my head started to hurt. So I stopped, and watched the waves instead.

We sailed on. Snorri and Kara seemed to find excitement in each newly revealed stretch of dreary Norse coastline. Even the sea itself could fascinate them. The swell is doing that, the wind is turning, the rocks are this, the current is westerly. Pah. I'd heard more interesting discussions between herdmen cataloguing the ailments of sheep. Or I probably would have if I'd listened.

A consequence of boredom is that a man is forced to look either to the future or the past, or sideways into his imagination. I tend to find my imagination too worrisome to contemplate, and I had already exhausted the possible scenarios for my homecoming. So, sulking in the *Errensa's* prow I spent long hours considering the circumstances of my abduction from Red March and forced march across half of Empire to the Black Fort. Time and again my thoughts returned to great uncle Garyus and his silent sister—born a conjoined monstrosity, the rightful king and queen of Red March. Their father, Gholloth, had set the chirurgeons to splitting them, but neither could ever be set upon the throne when age claimed him. He passed them over for Alica, the younger sister. My grandmother. A less obvious monster. But which of them ruled? Which of them had truly set Snorri and myself upon our path north? Which of them had gambled my life and soul against the Dead King? The blood-men with their sharp knives and blunt opinions had cut Garyus from his sister, but the twins had not split even. Garyus a broken teller of stories, his nameless sister a silent voyeur of years yet to come. And Grandmother, the Red Queen, the beating heart of the Marches for a generation, the iron queen with no give in her, her armies feared across the south, her name reviled.

In the empty hours memories plagued me as they are wont to do with nothing to drown out their whispering. Garyus had given me Mother's locket, and over years I'd so wrapped it in lies that I couldn't see its value when sat in my palm. Perhaps I'd been equally blind to its purpose. Dr. Taproot, the man who had known obscure facts about the Scraa slopes and Nfflr ridges of the Uuliskind, had told me a thing about my mother and I had laughed at his mistake. Had I wrapped her life in as many lies as her locket? Did I look at her death with the same blindness that had hidden the locket's nature from me?

It's not like me to brood on the past. I'm not comfortable with uncomfortable truths. I prefer to round off the edges and corners until I have something worth keeping. But a boat and the wide sea give a man little else to do.

"Show me the key," I said.

Snorri sat beside me trailing a line and hook into the sea. He'd caught nothing in all the hours he'd been at it.

"It's safe." He placed a hand on his chest.

"I don't think that thing can be described as safe." I sat up to face him. "Show it to me."

With reluctance Snorri tied his line to the oarlock and drew the key from his shirt. It didn't look like part of the world. It looked as if it had no place there in the daylight. As the key turned on its thong it seemed to change, flickering from one possibility to the next. I supposed a key that could open any lock had to entertain many shapes. I reached for it, but Snorri pushed my hand aside.

"Best not."

"You're worried I'll drop it in the sea?" I asked.

"You might."

"I won't." Hand held out.

Snorri raised a brow. A simple but eloquent expression. I had been known to lie before.

"We came as close to dying for this thing as men can come, Snorri. Both of us. I have a right."

"It wasn't for the key." Voice low, eyes seeing past me now. "We didn't go for the key."

"But it's all we got," I said, angry that he should deny me.

"It's not a thing you want to touch, Jal. There's no joy in it. As a friend I say don't do this."

"As a prince of Red March I say give me the fucking key."

Snorri lifted the thong from about his neck and with a sigh dangled the key into my palm, still retaining the tie.

I closed my hand about it. For the briefest moment I considered ripping it free and arcing it out across the water. In the end I lacked either the courage or the cruelty to do it. I'm not sure which.

"Thank you." The thing seemed to shift in my grasp and I squeezed it to force one form upon it.

There isn't much I remember about my mother. Her hair—long, dark, smelling of softness. I recall how safe her arms felt. I remember the comfort in her praise, though I could summon none of the words to mind. The sickness that took her I recollected as the story I told about it when people asked. A story without drama or tragedy, just the everyday futility of existence. A beautiful princess laid low by common disease, wasted away without romance by a flux. Isolated by her contagion—her last words spoken to me through a screen. The betrayal a child feels when a parent abandons them returned to me now—still sharp.

"Oh." And without transition the key was no longer a key. I held my mother's hand, or she held mine, a seven-year-old boy's hand encompassed in hers. I caught her scent, something fragrant as honeysuckle.

Snorri nodded, his eyes sympathetic. "Oh."

Without warning the boat, the sea, Snorri, all of it vanished, just for the beat of a heart. A blinding light took its place, dazzling, dying away as I blinked to reveal a familiar chamber with star-shaped roundels studding the ceiling. A drawing room in the Roma Hall where my brothers and I would play on winter nights. Mother stood there, half bent toward me, a smile on her face—the face in my locket, but smiling, eyes bright. All replaced a moment later with the boat, the sky, the waves. "What?" I dropped the key as though it had bitten me. It swung from Snorri's hand on the thong. "What!"

"I'm sorry." Snorri tucked the key away. "I warned you."

"No." I shook my head. *Too young she was for the assassin's blade.* Taproot's words, as if he spoke them in my ear. "No." I stood up, staggered by the swell. I closed my eyes and saw it again. Mother bending toward me, smiling. The man's face looming over her shoulder. No smile there. Half-familiar but not a friend. Features shadowed, offered only in rumour, hair so black as to be almost the blue beneath a magpie's wing, with grey spreading up from the temples.

The world returned. Two steps brought me to the mast and I clung for support, the sail flapping inches from my nose.

"Jal!" Snorri called, motioning for me to come back and sit before the sweep of the boom took me into the water.

"There *was* a blade, Snorri." Each blink revealed it, light splintering from the edge of a sword held low and casual, the fist at his side clenched about its hilt. "He had a sword!" I saw it again, some secret hidden in the dazzle of its steel, putting an ache in my chest and a pain behind my eyes.

"I want the truth." I stared at Kara. Aslaug hadn't arrived with the setting sun. To me, that was proof enough of the völva's power. "You can help me," I told her.

Kara sighed and bound the tiller. The wind had fallen to a breeze. The sails would soon be furled. She sat beside me on the bench and looked up to study my face. "Truth is rarely what people want, Prince Jalan."

"I need to know."

"Knowledge and truth are different things," Kara said. She brushed stray hair from her mouth. "I want to know, myself. I want to know many things. I braved the voyage to Beerentoppen, sought out Skilfar, all in search of knowing. But knowledge is a dangerous thing. You touched the key—against Snorri's strongest advice—and it brought you no peace. Now I advise you to wait. We're aimed at your homeland. Ask your questions there, the traditional way. The answers are likely not secrets, just facts you've avoided or misplaced whilst growing up."

"I can't wait." The boat had become a prison, the sea an endless wall. I sat trapped there, with neither space nor answers. *Too young she was for the assassin's blade.* I remembered, on the journey north, wiping the soup from my locket and at Snorri's insistence really seeing it for the first time in years. The scales had fallen from my eyes and I had discovered a treasure. Now I feared what I might see if I looked again at my past— but not looking had ceased to be an option. The key had unlocked the door to memories long buried. Now I had to throw that door wide. "Help me to remember."

"I have little skill, Prince Jalan." Kara looked down at her hands, folded in her lap, nails bitten short, fingers callused by ropework. "Find another way . . . Perhaps the key—"

"It's Loki's key," I snapped, filling the words with more harshness than intended. "It's black with lies. I need to know if what I saw, what I remember, are true memories, or the trickery of some pagan spirit."

Evening thickened, spreading across the face of the sea, the glow of the swallowed sun faded among the clouded western skies. A fat raindrop struck my hand, another grazed my cheek. Snorri watched us from the prow, huddled in his cloak. Tuttugu sat closer, whittling some piece of driftwood he'd snagged from the water.

"All I know of memory is in the blood," Kara said. "A man's blood can tell the secrets of his line. The story of his life lies there, the story of his father too, and his father's father. But—"

"Let's do that then. I like a good story, and if it's about me—all the better!"

"But," she kept to her thread with the tone that always means the speaker is heading toward "no." "I am a novice. It takes a lifetime to learn the blood-tongue. Skilfar might show you a day of your choosing, or hunt out some secret held too deep for speaking. My art is less . . . precise."

"Try?" I used that vulnerable look that makes women melt.

Kara pressed her lips together in a thin line and studied my face. Her eyes, very blue, moved as if I were a book she could read. I saw her pupils dilate. Somehow she was falling for my puppy dog routine. I felt slightly disappointed. I had wanted her to be more . . . magic. Stronger. I've found over the years that women want to save me. No matter how bad I am. No matter how bad they *see* me being—perhaps I've cast aside their friends when I've had my fun, or cheated with a handful of court wives, a new one each day—if I but show them some small hope that I might be redeemed, many, even some of the cleverest of them, the most moral, the most wise, step into my trap. It seems that the prospect of taming a dangerous reprobate who is unlikely to truly care for them is sweeter honey to some than, say, a strong and moral man like Snorri. Don't ask me why. It makes no sense to me—I just thank God for making the world this way.

There in the boat though, wanting the truth, wanting for perhaps the first time in my life to know myself, I would rather have been sat beside a woman who could see right through me.

"Please," I said, widening my eyes. "I know this will help me to be a better man."

And like that she fell for it. "If you're sure, Jalan." She started to rummage in the covered space beneath the bench.

"I am." I wasn't sure of much except that the experience was damned unlikely to make me a better man. I was sure though that it was what I wanted, and getting what I want has always been my main priority. Aslaug says it shows strength of character. I forget what Baraqel called it.

"Here!" She pulled out a long case of polished bone from the locker and sat up. A single rune had been burned into the front of the box. It looked familiar.

"Thorns." Kara set a finger to the rune in answer to the query in my raised eyebrow. "The first thing we'll be needing is some blood. And for that—a thorn." She clicked the case open to reveal the longest needle I'd ever seen.

"Ah," I said, making to get up. "Perhaps we could do this later." But Snorri and Tuttugu had crowded around now, both snorting as though I were play-acting for their amusement.

The weight of their expectation pressed me back into my seat. "Ha. As if I were scared of a little needle." I managed a dry laugh. "Have at me, madam witch."

"I have to say the incantations first." She offered a small smile and all of a sudden despite the foot-long needle that sat between us, and the fact she'd promised to meet my next advance with a knife to the balls, I found myself wanting her. She hadn't Astrid's voluptuousness or Edda's slender form, or the prettiness of either . . . maybe it was just being forbidden that sparked my lust, but more than that it was the strength in her. Old witches aside, like Skilfar and my grandmother, I'd never met a woman more capable. Like Snorri she had something about her that made it impossible to believe she would ever let you down, ever be afraid, ever run.

Kara lit a lantern. Speaking in the old tongue of the north, she dipped the needle into the sea, then ran it through the flame. She spoke my name in the mix. More than once. It sounded well upon her lips.

"When the needle is blooded you must taste it. Then whatever is to be revealed will come."

"I've tasted my blood before. It didn't tell me much." I must have swallowed a gallon of the stuff when Astrid punched me. Once my nose starts bleeding it never wants to stop.

"This will be different." Again that smile. "Hold out your hand."

So I did. I wasn't sure how deep the needle would prick but I steeled myself. Squealing like a little girl probably wouldn't help me in my new quest to bed her.

Kara took my hand, fingers probing, as if to find the ideal spot. I sat still, content to have her hold my hand, feeling a heat build between us.

"Now . . ." She circled the needle over my palm as if searching.

"Ow! Dear God! Sweet Jesu! The bitch stabbed me!" I yanked my hand away, transfixed by the needle that Kara had driven entirely through it in one smooth motion. "Jesu!" Six inches of crimson-beaded steel protruded from the back of my hand.

"Quick! Taste it. The longer you delay the further back the memories!" Kara grabbed my wrist and tried to steer the hand toward my mouth.

"You fucking stabbed me!" I couldn't quite believe it. Blackness crowded my vision and I felt faint with shock. Curiously there wasn't much pain.

"Help me with him." Kara glanced at Snorri and used both hands on my wrist. The bloody needle lurched toward my face. Damned if I was letting her do it though. She'd stab the thing through my mouth given half a chance! I pushed back. "Stop fighting me, Jalan. There's not much time."

Snorri lent his strength to the task and a moment later the needle wiped the complaint off my tongue. Kara pulled the steel free then. That's when it started to hurt—as the needle grated across the small bones in my palm.

"Concentrate now, Jalan! This bit is important." She clamped my face between her treacherous stabby hands. She probably said some other stuff after that, but by then I'd fainted clean away.

◆　◆　◆

I'm flying. Or I'm the sky. These things are equal. The day is ending and far below me the land folds, falls, and rises. The mountains still catch the sun, forests sweep out in shadow, rivers run, or dawdle, each according to their nature, but all bound for the sea. The ocean lies distant, crinkled with the dying light.

Lower.

The country below runs from plains, green with growing, toward arid hills, stone crested. Trails of smoke lace the air like threads, twisted by the wind. Fields lie blackened where the fire has consumed them. A wood, acres wide, stands ablaze.

Lower.

A castle sprawls across a high ridge, commanding views into two valleys that run toward the garden lands. A huge castle, its outer wall thick as a house, taller than trees, punctuated by seven round towers. Enclosed within this perimeter, a small town in stone and Builder-brick, then a second wall, yards thick and higher than the first, and within that, barracks, armouries, a well-house, and a keep tower. The keep I recognize—or think I do. It reminds me of the Ameroth Tower that stands on the edge of the Scorpions, a range of hills straddling the region where Red March, Slov, and Florence meet. I visited the tower once. I must have been ten. Father had sent Martus to be squired to Lord Marsden who keeps his household there. Darin and I tagged along as part of our education. The tower had been the tallest building I'd ever seen. It still is. A work of the Builders. An ugly rectangular structure, fashioned from poured stone, without windows or ornament. I recall that it had been surrounded by rubble and the village lay a mile off, the locals too fearful of ghosts to dwell any closer. Darin and I had ridden the surrounding hills, being still young enough to explore and play. I remember that the rocks thereabouts sported peculiar scorch marks. Geometric patterns fractured into them in ways I couldn't explain.

Lower.

An army stands camped about the castle, arrayed for siege. An army so numerous that the tents of the different units colour the ground like crops in great fields. The horses for their cavalry are corralled in herds thousands strong. Forests have been felled to build the machinery that waits at the foremost edge of the host. Rocks are piled beside each in pyramids ten, twenty, thirty feet high. The throwing arms of trebuchet, catapults and mangols are drawn back, loaded, ready to unleash.

Lower.

The stink and the cacophony of the horde are intolerable. Such a press of humanity and animals in such close confines. On the higher ground pavilions stand, decked with crests of arms. The great houses of Slov are there. The high and the mighty have come with their knights and levies. Among the forests of standards are the arms of nobles from Zagre, Sudriech, even Mayar. There cannot be less than thirty thousand men here. Perhaps fifty thousand.

I'm falling. Falling. Toward the outer wall. Unseen I descend among the troops that crowd the top of the east-most wall tower. There are a hundred archers here, smooth iron skullcaps fluted across the neck, chain-mail coifs, leather jerkins set with iron plates, skirts of overlapping leather strips, iron-studded. I have seen such armour on stands along the long gallery of Roma Hall. As a child I used to hide behind one suit in particular, by the west stair, and leap out to shock the maids.

A scorpion bolt-lobber stands at the front of the tower, aimed out between the crenulations at the distant foe. The operating crew are holding back a respectful distance whilst gathered immediately behind the engine a small group of nobility debate some issue.

In a moment I stand amongst them. Next to me is a huge warrior in battered platemail, heavy-duty stuff fashioned in the old style from black iron. He glances my way but he sees through me.

"We can hold for relief. If it takes two months we can hold," he says, eyes fierce and dark, set in a brutal face, a black beard bristling over his lantern jaw, threaded by a pale scar.

"Damn that!" The speaker whirls from her contemplation of the enemy. She stands four fingers over six foot, her build athletic, strong, young with it . . . maybe eighteen. Her armour is gilded, and worked in enamels across it are the burning spears of the Red March. No vanity this though, the steel is full gauge and without ornament. A soldier's armour. "If we let them bide here the Czar's path west lies open. The Steppes will be at Vermillion's gates before the harvest."

I watch her face, broad and angular, pale for a woman of the March— beneath a shock of dark red hair, angry hazel eyes, full lips. I know this face.

"Contaph." She advances on the knight beside me. Even a woman of her stature has to look up at the man. "Can we attack? Sally forth? They won't be expecting an attack."

An intake of breath at this from the men around her, knight captains and lords by their armour. I can understand this. There are not enough troops within the castle to challenge the host outside. I know this without looking. The castle could not hold so many.

"They won't be expecting an attack, princess," says Contaph. "But they are ready for one, even so. Kerwcjz is no fool."

"A deputation!" This from a man at the wall, with a spyglass to his eye.

The princess leads the nobles to the battlements, archers parting to make space. "Tell me," she says.

"Ten riders under a white flag. An emissary. And a prisoner. A woman. A girl—"

The princess snatches the spyglass and sets it to her own eye. "Gwen!"

"Kerwcjz has your sister?" Contaph's fist tightens on the pommel of his sword, the iron plates of his gauntlet grating one against the next. "This means Omera has fallen."

"Give me your bow," the princess demands of the nearest archer.

"Alica!" A strained whisper from the man beside her, smaller but similar in his colouring.

"Princess," she says. The bow is in her hands, her eyes on his— dangerous. "Call me by my name again, cousin, and I will drop you from this wall."

She pulls an arrow from the archer's quiver. "It's a good bow?"

"Y-yes . . . princess." The archer stutters it out. "Pulls a hair to the left if you over-draw. But that's not a worry—it's too much bow for a wo—"

Princess Alica strings the arrow and draws it to her ear, pointing up at the great keep tower back beyond the second wall. "Yes?"

"A hair to the left, your majesty." The man backs away. "Two fingers on a fifty-yard target."

"They've drawn up." The cousin at the wall.

The princess lets the bow relax and comes to watch. Nine of the men have spread into a line on their horses. The emissary and the captive ride forward five more yards. The girl is in silks, side-saddle, she looks no more than thirteen, maybe fourteen. The man is fat, his armour adjusted for it, his neck thick and reddened by the Red March sun. He wears a blue plumed helm and a long turquoise cloak.

"Hail, the castle!" His voice reaches them, thinned by the distance.

Princess Alica's face is stone. She strings the arrow to her bow once more and draws it.

"The flag . . ." Contaph stares at her, a frown throwing his brow into deep furrows. Out among the enemy contingent the white flag flutters.

She looks once, out across the wall. "A mistake," she says. "It helps me adjust for the wind." She arches her spine, drawing the bowstring back further across her breastplate . . . and the arrow is gone, just the hiss of it left behind amid our silence.

The princess drops the bow and steps away from the wall. Behind her a high-pitched cry rings out. A pause. The sound of galloping.

"Princess Gwen—" The cousin runs out of words.

"Shot her sister . . ." The whisper ripples along the wall.

Alica whirls back around to face them all. "No negotiation. No surrender. No terms."

Another sharp turn and she's striding toward the stairs at the tower's centre. Contaph jogs, clanking to catch her, the others strung out behind. I'm at her shoulder. So close I can hear the tightness of her breath.

She doesn't turn her head as Contaph draws level at the head of the stair. "Kerwcjz would have had her staked over a fire for us all to watch by morning. He'd have set her singing my troops a song of pain and kept her at it as long as his torturers' skills allowed." The cousin and three others arrive behind us. Alica keeps her shoulders to them. Back at the wall the first rock explodes against the battlements. All along the enemy line engines of war release their pent up forces with throaty twangs.

"We win this, or we die. There is no third way."

And in that moment I knew my grandmother.

And rock rained down upon us.

ELEVEN

"I'm *so* hungry."

"Finally he wakes!" Snorri's voice close by.

I opened my eyes. "I've gone blind!" Panic seized me and I struggled up, banging my head on something hard.

"Relax!" He sounded amused. A big hand pushed me down. The old magic sizzled unpleasantly at the contact points.

"My eyes! My fuc—"

"It's night time."

"Where are the damn stars then?" I touched my forehead where I'd bashed it. My fingers came away sticky.

"It's cloudy."

"Where's the lantern?" I had him this time. We always kept the lantern burning on dark nights, wick trimmed low. Better to waste a little oil than trip overboard in the dark when nature called.

"You broke it when you fell over."

I remembered it all. *That woman! My hand!*

"My hand!" I shouted, stupidly grabbing the place she stabbed me and yelping in pain.

Tuttugu uttered a sleepy complaint and stopped snoring. These days I only really noticed his snoring when he stopped.

"Why am I so hungry?"

"You're a pig." I heard Snorri turn over and gather his covers.

"You've been asleep the best part of two nights and a day." Kara's voice from the other end of the boat.

"Well . . ." I paused to consider that. "Well, it didn't work. You mutilated me for nothing."

"You saw nothing?" She sounded unconvinced.

"I saw my grandmother. When she was younger than I am now. She was a scary bitch back then too! Worse, if anything."

"You delayed too long before tasting the blood," Kara said.

"Well excuse me for being busy staring at the six inches of steel sticking out of the back of my hand!" I still couldn't believe she didn't warn me.

"You may see more when you next dream. Perhaps what you seek." She didn't sound bothered—sleepy more than anything.

I glowered at her in the darkness, but judging by the soft sounds all around me the three of them had already fallen back into their slumbers. I couldn't follow them. I'd slept enough. Instead I sat staring into the darkness, rocked by the waves, until the skies shaded into pale to herald the dawn.

I spent those cold dark hours staring at memories of memories. At my grandmother a lifetime ago, at the sacrifices she made to deny her enemy, at the fire in her that drove her to attack long after hope had fled the battlefield. Like Snorri. Or rather, like Snorri had been.

In the grey predawn I watched the northman slumped across the tiller, the slits of his eyes dark as he watched me back. Baraqel would talk to him soon. The angel would walk across the waves and speak of light and purpose, and still Snorri would steer this boat south, aimed toward death.

"You're a coward, Snorri ver Snagason." Perhaps it was the lack of sleep, or the Red Queen's blood still running hot in my veins, or even an honest desire to help the man, but something set the words spilling from my mouth, my normal desire to avoid any chance of being hit overridden for the moment.

"How so?" He didn't move or raise his voice. In truth I'd never seen the violence he displayed in battle spill over into conversation—even those that ran against him. Perhaps I just judged him by what I'd do if I were a big scary Viking.

"This key. It's built of lies, you know that. Taking it to death's door—" I waved an arm in the air. "It's just looking for a way out, an escape. You may as well have cut a hole in the sea ice back in Trond harbour and jumped through. Same result, less effort, and fewer people inconvenienced." I would have told him he wasn't going to get his wife back, or his children, or the unborn baby. I would have told him it was all nonsense and that the world doesn't work that way. I would have said that but perhaps I'm not that cruel, or perhaps I didn't trust his temper that far . . . but most likely it didn't need to be said. He knew it already.

Snorri didn't speak. Nothing but the moan of the wind and the slap of waves against the hull. Then, "Yes. I am a coward, Jal."

"So, throw the key over the side and come with me to Vermillion."

"The door is my quest now." Snorri sat up. "The door. The key. It's all I have." He touched the place where the key hung beneath his jerkin. "And what is the key if not a chance to face the gods and to demand an explanation for the world . . . for your life?"

I knew this wasn't about gods. Whatever he said. His family drew him on. Freja, Emy, Egil, Karl. I still kept their names and the stories he'd told about them, and they weren't even mine. It's not in me to care about such things, but even so, I saw that little girl, her peg doll, Snorri running to save her. I'd expected him to speak of them again over the long winter. Expected it and dreaded it. Known that one night, deep in his cups, he must break and drunkenly he would rage against the loss. But he never did. No matter how dark the night nor how long, or how much of my ale he consumed, Snorri ver Snagason made no complaint, spoke no word of his loss. I hadn't expected to speak of it at last in a small boat, bound on every side by cold miles of restless sea.

"That's not—"

"Sixty beats of a heart would be enough. If I could hold them. Let them know I came for them no matter what stood in my way. It would be enough. Sixty beats of a heart past that door would outweigh sixty years in this world without them. You've not loved, Jal, not held your child, newborn and bloody, soft against a hard world, and promised that child you'd keep it safe. And Freja. I don't have the words for it. She woke me. I'd spent my time in red dreaming, biting at any hand that tried to feed me. She woke me—I saw her—and she was all I wanted to see—all I could see."

Kara and Tuttugu hadn't moved from their benches but I saw in the stillness of them that both lay awake, listening.

"There's no place in this world for me any more, except as a weapon, except as the anger behind a sharp edge, bringing sorrow. I'm done, Jal. Broken. Past my time."

I hadn't anything to say to that, so I said nothing, and let the sea speak. In time the sun found us, and Baraqel must have flowed into the northman's mind, though whether he had any words to offer up after Snorri's own I couldn't say.

TWELVE

That first day after I woke from the blood dream I spent cradling my hand in my lap and glowering at Kara. She kept her peace though. At least until I started fumbling at the laces of my trews to answer nature's call. It's a difficult business at the best of times, standing up in a small boat to relieve oneself over the side. Trying to stand in choppy seas whilst unlacing with an injured hand is doubly difficult.

"This would be a hell of a lot easier if some lunatic hadn't stabbed me!" The laces confounded my awkward fingers yet again. "Christ's whore!" I may have uttered a few more oaths, and called a certain völva's good name into disrepute . . .

"In the north we call that a little prick," Kara replied, not looking over from her place at the tiller.

I'm sure she meant the injury, but Tuttugu and Snorri, being ignorant barbarians, laughed themselves hoarse at my expense, and thereafter I manfully ignored my wound, having found the edge of Kara's tongue to be sharper than her needle.

Tuttugu and I kept our eyes north as often as not, watching for the sails of a longship. Any flash of white had us wondering if a pair of red eyes waited beneath, and behind that a deckful of the Hardassa. Thankfully we saw no sign of them. Perhaps after the events at the Black Fort the Dead King no longer held sufficient sway over the Red Vikings to have them dog our trail all the way to the continent. Or maybe we had simply outrun them.

◆ ◆ ◆

In three days' sail from Beerentoppen the *Errensa* had borne us so far south that the Norseheim coast now curved away from us, heading east. The Devouring Sea lay ahead, the last barrier to the continent, spreading out toward the shores of Maladon. Kara said her prayers, the Undoreth called on Odin and Aegir, I made one-sided bargains with the Almighty, and we parted company from the north for good or ill.

The Devouring Sea, or the Karlswater as those on its southern shores name it, has a poor reputation with sailors. Storms from the great ocean are often funnelled down into the Karlswater by the Norseheim highlands. Such storms are perilous enough out in the deeps, but in the shallow waters where we now sailed they would on occasion whip up rogue waves so huge that no ship could survive them. Such waves were rare but they could sweep the Karlswater clear. Aegir's Broom the Vikings called them. The sea-god cleaning house.

I hung at the *Errensa*'s stern, watching Norseheim diminish behind us, compressed between sea and sky into a dark and serrated line. Then just a line. Then imagination. And finally memory.

"When I get to Maladon I'm paying a barber to shave this beard." I ran my fingers up into the curls, bleached white-blond by the newly arrived sun, thick with salt and grease. My old crowd wouldn't even recognize me, all scars, lean muscle, and wild hair. Still, nothing that a tailor, a man with a razor, and a month of comfortable living couldn't set right.

"It suits you." Kara looked up at me under her brows, blue eyes unreadable. She sat repairing a cover for one of the storage units. She'd warmed to me a little over the course of the journey, checking on my hand wound without apology but with a gentle touch. Twice a day she rubbed a sweet-smelling unguent at the entry and exit holes. I enjoyed the attention so much I somehow forgot to mention it had stopped hurting.

In exchange for Kara's medical care I entertained her with tales of the Red March court. It never hurts to mention you're a prince—a lot.

Especially if you are one. She seemed to find my stories amusing, though I wasn't sure she was always laughing at the parts I thought were funny . . .

"A fish!" Snorri leapt up, rocking the boat. "Thor's teeth! I caught one!"

He had too, a foot and a half of black slimy fish jerking back and forth in his hands, the line still trailing from its mouth.

"Only took you twelve days at sea!" I'd told him to give it up an age ago.

"I got one!" Snorri's triumph couldn't be dented by my jibes.

Tuttugu came over to slap him on the back. "Well done! We'll make a fisherman of you yet."

Of course Tuttugu had only to drop a hook over the side and it seemed the fish fought each other for the privilege of swallowing it. He must have hauled a score of them from the waves since we set sail. He'd taken to coaching Snorri and confided to me that the warrior had been a poor farmer too. Tuttugu worried that Snorri had nothing to fall back on—he had a talent for war but in the peace he might find life challenging.

"A fine one." Kara joined them, standing close beside Snorri. "A black-cod should always be boiled and eaten with winter greens." The two of them seemed at ease in each other's company. I watched them with a strange mixture of jealousy and satisfaction. Part of me half wanted Snorri and the völva to find the furs together. A good woman was the only hope for him. He needed something other than his grief.

I found it rather worrying that I might be considering sacrificing the pleasure I hoped to take in Kara. That didn't sound like me at all. Especially after all the hours I'd spent imagining the ways I'd set her rune-charms clicking one against the other . . . still . . . if Snorri found himself a woman he might be able to let go of the madness that possessed him to seek a door into death and recover his lost family. And, whatever my plans, there was always a chance I would get dragged into the insanity. So after all I was giving up Kara in my own interest. I relaxed. That sounded more like me.

In the midst of the Devouring Sea, as far from land as I had ever been, I sat amid the heave and the swell on Kara's small wooden boat and, with little to fix my mind upon, focused on Snorri instead. I watched him, leaning into the prow now, the wind streaming dark hair behind him, eyes on the southern horizon. As fierce a warrior as I'd ever known, with no give in him, no fear in the face of sword or axe. I knew why I was bound south—to claim the comforts and privilege of my birthright and live to a disgraceful old age. I knew what drew Snorri and, despite what he'd said days before, I couldn't marry his words to any kind of sense. I'd seen plenty of what came back from the deadlands and none of it had been pretty.

I'd also noticed that since my long sleep he wore the key on a piece of rusting chain—as if he'd read my mind when I considered tearing it free and tossing it overboard. I felt a little hurt by his mistrust, however justified. I considered broaching the subject but watching him there, hunched around the pain of his poisoned wound and the older pain of his loss . . . I let it lie. Instead I followed his gaze to the dark stain on the horizon that held his attention.

"That looks bad." It looked worse than bad.

"Yes." A nod. "Could get rough."

The storm caught us half a day from the shores of Maladon. A cataclysmic war of the elements that even the Vikings called a storm. It made everything that I'd suffered on the sea before seem like mild discomfort. The wind became a fist, the rain its spears, gripped tight and driven into flesh. And the waves . . . those waves will haunt my dreams until the day something worse comes along. The sea changed scale around us. A man out on the ocean always feels small, but amid waves that could overtop and sweep away castles, you understand what it is to be a beetle among stampeding elephants.

The wind drove us, without sails, skidding across foam-skinned behemoths. Turn to face it and the rain made you blind, the wind filling you as you tried to scream. Turn away and it became a fight to snatch a breath, so unwilling was the air to pause long enough to be captured.

I guess Snorri and the others were busy. They certainly seemed to do a lot of shouting and throwing themselves about. What they were busy with though I couldn't tell you. Nothing they did could make any difference in the face of that assault. For my part I clung to the mast with both arms, and at times both legs. No lovers' clinch was ever as tight as the embrace in which I held that wooden pole, and despite waves that washed across me until my lungs hammered for a chance to breathe, I kept my grip.

Small boats are, it turns out, highly resilient to being sunk. They bob up again and again in defiance of reason and expectation. My eldest brother, Martus, when ten or eleven, used to go to Morano Bridge with his friends, and sometimes Darin and I would sneak along to watch. The older boys would swim in the shallows, or go onto the bridge and drop their lines in the Seleen. When they got bored with not catching any fish they'd start looking for mischief. Martus would lead them along the many-pillared bridge wall, and piss on passing boats, or taunt local boys, safe in the knowledge that Father's guards would protect him. Father always sent four guards with Martus, him being the heir.

One fine spring morning at the Morano Bridge Martus decided on a naval warfare simulation. In practice this meant having his friends haul large stones from the riverbank up onto the bridge and then him dropping them on passing mother ducks and the long trains of ducklings following in their wake. The thing is that it's quite hard to sink a duckling with a rock. Especially when they're coming out from under the bridge. The delay between the spotters on the upstream side and the emergence of the targets has to be judged, along with the exit point and the drop time. So for the best part of two hours Darin and I watched from the riverbank as Martus dropped a hundredweight of stones, some larger than his head, on a stream of fluffy ducklings led under the bridge by ill-advised mother ducks. And despite enormous splashes on all sides, the sucking drag of drowning stones, and a tumult of sizeable waves, those fluffy little bas-tards sailed on indefatigably, unsinkable yellow balls of downy defiance that drove Martus into ever greater rage. He didn't get a single one, and when he raced down to tackle the last of them mano-a-duckling in the shallows, an angry swan burst from the reeds, evaded all four guards, and broke his wrist for him with a savage peck. Best day ever!

Anyway, Kara's boat was rather like those ducklings. It had to be a kind of magic, but whatever the storm threw at us, it kept on floating.

The storm didn't end, just weakened by degrees, each time resurging as my hopes grew, until by dawn it was merely torrential rain driven by a gale. I fell asleep still hugging the mast, soaked and frozen, knowing the sun had begun its climb into the sky but unable to see it behind the storm wrack.

I woke, shivering, and feverish once more, to the sound of gulls and the distant crash of breakers.

"Tie the jib off!" Kara's voice.

"Turn her! Turn her!" Snorri, tight with anxiety.

"Big one coming!" Tuttugu, sounding as weary as I felt.

I lifted my head, unhooked a sore arm from the mast, and rubbed the salt crusts from my eyes. The sky lay a pale blue, ribboned with the remnants of rainclouds. The sun stood overhead, bright but without much warmth. I inched myself round to face the way the *Errensa* was pointing, unwilling to completely relinquish my grip on the mast. The wave before us ran on ahead, revealing a dark coastline of cliffs and coves, the high ground topped with grass and bushes. And beyond the headlands . . . nothing . . . no surly Norse mountains reaching for the sky and telling you to sod off. At last we'd reached Maladon. A rough enough dukedom to be sure, but with the decency to do whatever had to be done on the level rather than perched on the side of a ridiculously steep slope or huddled in the narrow margin between snowy uplands and icy sea. A weight lifted off my heart.

A delicious few seconds of hope, and then I noticed how the only sail we had was a scrap of tattered cloth strung between the bow and the mast, and just how big those breakers were, and how white they foamed before drawing back to reveal the black teeth of the rocks. The next second I noticed how upside-down we were and how cold the water rushing into my mouth was. For several minutes after that I spent most of my time thrashing wildly and gasping for air in between the breaking crests of waves that plunged me under then rolled me over and over before releasing their grip just in time for the next one.

I don't recall finally crawling ashore, just the sand-level view of Snorri walking along the beach to find me. Somehow he'd kept his axe.

"Maladon," I said, grabbing a handful of it as he hauled me to my feet. "I could almost kiss you."

"Osheim," Snorri said.

"What?" I spat out grit and tried to frame a better question. "What?" I asked again. *Nobody goes to Osheim.* And there's a bloody good reason for it.

"The storm blew us east. We're fifty miles past Maladon." Snorri puffed his cheeks out and looked across the sea. "You all right?"

I patted myself down. No major injuries. "No," I said.

"You're fine." Snorri let go of me and I managed not to fall. "Kara's down the beach with Tutt. He cut his leg on the rocks. Lucky it's not broken."

"Seriously, *Osheim*?"

Snorri nodded and set off back, walking where the waves swept the sand, each of his footprints erased before he'd taken another ten steps. I spat some more grit and a decent-sized pebble from my mouth and followed with a sigh.

The Builders left us quite a few reminders of their era. Reminders that even someone like me, whose primary use for history books was for beating smaller princelings around the head with, could hardly ignore. A man who ignored the borders of Promised Land would find his skin falling off while twisted monsters ate his face. The Engine of Wrong in Atta, the bridges and towers still left scattered across the continent, the Vault of Voices in Orlanth, the time bubbles on the Bremmer Slopes, or the Last Warrior—trapped on Brit . . . all these were well known, but none sent the same shiver up my spine as the Wheel of Osheim. It seemed that almost every fairy tale our nurses had spun to entertain my brothers and me when we were small had happened in Osheim. The worst of them happened closest to the Wheel. The tales Martus demanded, the most bloody and most twisted, all started, "Once upon a time, not far from the Wheel of Osheim," and from there on it was time to hide behind your hands or cover your ears. Come to think of it, the women who looked after us when we were little were an evil bunch of old witches. They should have been hanged, the lot of them, not set to watch over the sons of a cardinal.

We sheltered in a dell behind the headlands, Snorri and me, while Kara poked around on the nearby heath and Tuttugu returned to the beach to see what might be salvaged from the wreck or lying washed up on the sands. Tuttugu's leg still bore an angry red scar, but Snorri's healing touch had rendered it serviceable, closing an ugly wound that had turned my stomach to look at. The effort had left Snorri flat on his back but far less incapacitated than on other occasions and before long he was sitting up to fiddle with his axe. Steel and saltwater are a poor mix and no warrior will leave his blade wet. I watched him work, pursing my lips. His swift recovery struck me as odd since the Silent Sister's spell was supposed to have faded over the winter according to Skilfar, and such things should be harder, not more easy.

"Eggs." Kara came back from rummaging across the heather-covered slope behind us. In her cupped hands half a dozen blue gulls' eggs. You could probably tip the contents of all of them into a decent-sized chicken's egg and not fill it. She sat down on grass between Snorri and me, crossing her long legs, bare and scratched and grimy and delicious. "How long do you think it will take to get to Red March?" Looking at me as if I would know.

I spread my hands. "With my luck, a year."

"We'll need horses," Snorri said.

"You hate horses, and they hate you." It was true though, we did need some. "Can Kara even ride? Can Tuttugu? Is Kara actually coming with us?" It seemed a hell of a journey to make on the whim of an old witch in a cave.

"If I still had the *Errensa* under me it would be a difficult decision," Kara admitted. "But perhaps the storm was trying to tell us something. No going back until we're done."

Snorri raised a brow at that but said nothing.

"No going anywhere for me. Ever. I'm not leaving Red March again. Not if I live to be a hundred. Hell, I doubt I'll set foot outside the walls of Vermillion again once I'm through the gates." Righteous indignation swelled, driven past the bounds of my usual stoic good humour. I blame my fever and the fact of being sat in a grassy hollow, soaked, cold, exhausted, days from the nearest warm bed, flagon of ale, or hot meal. I kicked at the sod. "Fucking Empire. Fucking oceans. Who needs any of it? And now we're in fucking Osheim. That's just great. Fuck dark-sworn or light-sworn. I want some future-sworn. Could have seen that storm coming and got out of the way."

"The Builders watched the weather from above." Kara tilted a finger toward the heavens. "They could tell what storms would come but they still couldn't stop the storm that was big enough to sweep them all away."

"Every fortune-teller I ever met was a faker. First thing you should do to a soothsayer is poke them in the eye and say, 'Didn't see that coming, did you?'" My mood still ran sour. I couldn't believe we'd been delivered up on the shores of a place where all my childhood nightmares ran riot.

"What will happen when I let go?" Kara held out one of her tiny eggs between thumb and forefinger, positioning her hand above a stone breaking through the sod between us.

"You'll mess up this fine stone," I said.

"Now you're seeing the future." A grin. She looked younger when she smiled. "And if you lunged forward and tried to stop me?"

My lips echoed her smile. I quite liked that idea. "I don't know. Should we try?"

"And that's the curse of the future-sworn. None of us can see past our own actions—not us, not the future-sworn, not the Silent Sister, not Luntar, not the Watcher of Parn, none of them." Kara offered me the egg.

"Raw?" The sun had broken through and I was starting to feel human enough to eat. I couldn't remember when I'd last had a good meal. Even so, my appetite hadn't returned to the degree where raw gull's egg looked like something I wanted oozing over my tongue. "No?" Kara shrugged, and putting her head back she broke the egg into her mouth.

Watching her it was hard to imagine that Skilfar or the Silent Sister might have been like this once—young women overburdened with cleverness and ambition, setting foot on the path to power.

"I wonder what it is that the Silent Sister sees with that blind eye of hers. Things she can't even speak of."

Kara wiped her mouth with the back of her hand. "And if she moves to change them . . . she can no longer see how they will end. So how terrible does the future have to look before you reach in to that clear pool to change it and have the silt rise up all around your hand so you're as blind as everyone else—knowing it won't settle again until the day, the hour, the moment of the thing you most fear?"

"I'd change everything bad that ever looked like happening to me." I could think of a long list of things I would have avoided, with "leaving Red March" right at the top of it. Or maybe getting into debt with Mae-res Allus should be at the top, because leaving Red March did actually save me from a horrific death at his torturer's hands. But then getting into debt had been such fun . . . hard to imagine all those years living as a pauper . . . I suppose I could have pawned Mother's locket . . . My head started to spin. "Well . . . I suppose . . . It's a complicated business."

"And if you changed those bad things how would you know that the change wouldn't lead to worse things that would now wait for you unseen in the years to come?" Kara ate another of the eggs and handed the rest to Snorri. They looked lost in the wideness of his palm.

"Hmmm. Perhaps the evil old witch got what she deserved after all." It sounded as though looking into the future might be as much of a pain as looking into the past. The *moment* was clearly the place to be. Except this moment which was wet and cold.

An hour later Tuttugu returned carrying a makeshift sailcloth sack into which he'd loaded his salvage. There wasn't much of it, and nothing to eat save a tub of butter that had already been rancid when purchased in Haargfjord more than a week back.

"We should go!" Snorri slapped his thighs and stood.

"Better than starving here, I suppose." I set off, unburdened with sword, pack, rations, or any other defence against danger and privation other than the knife at my hip. A fine knife it must be said, also purchased in Haargfjord, a brutal bit of sharp iron, intended for intimidation, and not yet used in any more deadly endeavour than peeling fruit.

Snorri and Tuttugu followed in my wake.

"Where are you going?" Kara remained where we'd left her.

"Um." I squinted at the sun. "South . . . east-ish?"

"Why?"

"I . . ." It had seemed *right*. It occurred to me as I considered the question that something good waited for us in the direction I'd led off in. Something very good. We should probably hurry.

"It's the draw of the Wheel," she said.

Snorri frowned. Tuttugu ferreted about in his beard, hunting inspiration.

"Crap." Nanna Willow had told us this one a dozen times. Nanna Willow had come to us from my grandmother's personal staff, a stick of a woman, dry as bones, and not given to taking any shit from unruly princes. When the mood took her she'd tell us fairy tales—some so dark they'd even have Martus wanting a nightlight and a kiss to ward off the spirits. And practically every victim in the abattoir of Nanna Willow's bedtime tales was led into Osheim by the draw of the Wheel.

"This is the right way." Tuttugu nodded as if to convince himself and pointed ahead.

For my part I turned on a heel and hurried back to Kara's side. "Crap," I repeated myself. Part of me still wanted to follow the line Tuttugu indicated. "It's all true, isn't it? Tell me there aren't boggen and flesh-mauls too . . ."

"The path to the Wheel grows strange." Kara spoke the words as if quoting them. "And then more strange. If a man ever reached the Wheel he would find all things are possible. The Wheel gives anything a man could want."

"Well . . . that doesn't sound too bad." And so help me my feet started taking me south again. South and a little east. Tuttugu set off again too, just ahead of me.

"It's the monsters that stop them reaching the Wheel." Kara's voice, an unwelcome nagging behind me. Even so, the word "monsters" was enough to stop both me and Tuttugu. We'd both seen more monsters than we ever wanted to.

"What monsters? You said anything a man could want!" I turned back, unwilling.

"Monsters from the id."

"From the what?"

"The dark places in your mind where you make war on yourself." Kara shrugged. "That's how the sagas have it. You think you know what you want, but the Wheel reaches past what you think you know into the deep places where nightmares are born. The Wheel grows stronger as you get closer. At first it answers your will. As you get closer it answers your desire. And closer still it dances to your imagination. All your dreams, each shadowed corner of your mind, each possibility you've considered . . . it feeds them, makes them flesh, sends them to you."

Tuttugu joined us. I caught a whiff of him as he drew close. Old cheese and wet hound. It was only when we had a moment apart that you noticed it. We probably all reeked after too long in that little boat and it would take more than a quick sinking to wash it off. "You lead us, völva," he said.

Only Snorri remained where he was, out on the moor with long grass dancing to the beat of the wind all about him. He stood without motion, still staring south where the sky held a purplish taint, like a fading bruise. At first I'd thought it was clouds. Now I wasn't sure.

"After you." I gestured for Kara to lead us. My imagination proved torment enough to me from one day to the next. Absolutely no way was I heading somewhere that could put flesh on any bone I dreamed up. Men are dragged down by their fears all the time, but in Osheim apparently that had to be taken far more literally.

Snorri remained where he'd first stopped, close enough to hear our conversation but making no move to return or go on. I knew what he would be thinking. That the great Wheel of the Builders might turn for him and bring his children back. They wouldn't be real though, just images born of his imagination. Even so—to Snorri the exquisite pain of such torture might be something he couldn't step away from. I opened my mouth to make some remonstration . . . but found I had no words for it. What did I know of the bonds that bind father to son or husband to wife?

Raised in a culture of war and death I would have pegged a Viking warrior to be the most able of any man to put such tragedy behind him and walk on. But Snorri had never been the man I'd thought would lie behind the beard and the axe. Somehow he was both less than the fantasy and more at the same time.

I turned and walked back toward him. Anything I had to say seemed shallow beside the depth of his grief. Words are awkward tools at best, too blunt for delicate tasks.

I almost set a hand to his shoulder, then let it fall. In the end I settled for, "Come on then."

Snorri turned, looked at me—as if from a thousand miles away—then twitched his lips, hinting at a smile. He nodded and we both went back together.

"Sail!" Tuttugu had returned to the ridge above the dell whilst I went to retrieve Snorri. Now he pointed out toward the ocean as we returned.

"Maybe we won't have to walk after all," I said as we reached Kara.

She shook her head at my ignorance. "You can't just wave down a ship."

"Why's he jumping up and down then?"

"I don't know." Snorri said the words in a voice that suggested a slow-dawning suspicion. He left us and jogged up the slope toward the ridge. Kara followed on at a more relaxed pace and I dogged her heels.

Both men were crouched by the time we reached them and Snorri waved us down too. "Edris," he hissed.

I edged alongside Tuttugu on my elbows, adding more mud to my costume.

"Shit." I squinted at the flash of sail miles and more off the coast. "How the hell can you tell?"

I felt Tuttugu shrug beside me. "I just know. It's the cut of the sails . . . just the way of it . . . Hardassa for sure."

"How is it even possible?" I asked, becoming aware of Kara moving up beside me, her braid runes tapping as the wind played them out.

"The unborn knew where to dig for Loki's key," she said.

"It was under the Bitter Ice! Anyone who listened to the stories knew—oh." The Bitter Ice stretched for scores of miles of ice cliffs and then reached back an unknown distance into the white hell of the north. How *did* they know where to dig?

"Something draws them to it," she said.

"There's unborn on that ship?" Suddenly I wanted to be home very badly.

Kara shrugged. "Maybe. Or some other servant of the Dead King who can sense the key."

I shuffled back from the ridge. "We'd better move fast then." At least running away was something I understood.

THIRTEEN

"We've got to move fast, but in which direction?" Snorri asked.

"We need to be away from the coast." Tuttugu hugged his belly with nervous arms, perhaps imagining a Hardassa driving his spear into it. "Take away their advantage. Otherwise they'll pace us at sea and come in for us by night. And if they're forced to beach they'll have to leave men to guard the longboat."

"We'll aim south-west." Kara pointed to a low hill on the horizon. "We should reach the Maladon border in three or four days. If we're lucky we'll be close to Copen."

"Copen?" Tuttugu asked. I offered him silent thanks for not making me be the one to display my ignorance yet again.

"A small city on the Elsa River. The duke winters there. A good place to rest and gather our resources," Kara said. By which she no doubt meant "for Jalan to buy us food and horses." At this rate I'd arrive at Vermillion as poor as I thought I was when I left it.

We set off at a good pace, knowing the Hardassa men would be better provisioned, better equipped . . . probably just plain better in all regards given that our second best warrior was likely a woman with a knife.

The sun came out to mock us, and Kara led the way, winding a path across slopes thick with heather and dense clumps of viciously spiked gorse.

"We're getting closer to the Wheel aren't we?" I asked an hour later, footsore already.

"Yes, we'll just cut through the outer edge of its . . . domain."

"You can feel it too?" Snorri fell back to walk beside me, his stride free as if his wound no longer pained him.

I nodded. Even with four hours until sunset I could sense Aslaug prowling, impatient. Each patch of shadow seethed with possibilities despite the brightness all about. Her voice lay beneath all other sounds, urgent but indistinct, rising with the wind, scratching behind Snorri's question. "It's like the world is . . . thinner here." Even with an arm's length between Snorri and me that old energy crackled across the shoulder facing him, buzzing in my teeth, a brittle sensation, as if I might shatter if I fell. With the old feeling came new suspicions, all of Aslaug's warnings creeping into my mind. Baraqel's hold on the northman would be strengthening with each yard closer to the Wheel. How long could I trust Snorri for? How long before he became the avenger Baraqel intended him to be, smiting down anyone tainted with the dark . . .

"You look . . . better," I told Snorri.

"I feel better." He patted his side.

"All magic is stronger here," Kara called back without turning. "Quicker to answer the will. Snorri is more able to resist Kelem's call, the light in him is battling the poison." She picked up the pace, and glanced my way. "It's a bad place to use enchantment, though. Like lighting a fire in a hay barn." I wondered if Snorri had mentioned Harrowheim to her.

"What is this 'wheel' anyway? Some sort of engine?" I imagined a huge wheel turning, toothed like the gears in a watermill.

"No one alive has seen it, not even the wrong-mages who live as close in as they can stand. The sagas say it's the corpse of a god, Haphestur, not of Asgard but a stranger from without, a wanderer. A smith who forged weapons for Thor and Odin. They say he lies there rotting and the magic of making leaks from him as his flesh corrupts." Kara glanced up at me, as if to gauge my reaction.

I kept my face stiff. I've found heathens to be a touchy lot if you laugh at their stories. "That's what the priests say. What do the völvas believe?"

"In King Hagar's library on Icefjar there are remnants of books copied directly from the works of the Builders themselves. I understood them to say that the Wheel is a complex of buildings laid above a vast underground ring, a stone tunnel, many miles long and going nowhere. A place where the Builders saw new truths."

I mulled on this one, walking another hour in silence. I pictured the Builders' ring of secrets, seeing it all aglow in my mind's eye while I tried to ignore each new blister. Less painful than the blisters, but somehow more distressing, was the sensation that each step took us closer to the Wheel, the world becoming fragile, a skin stretched too tight across bone, ready to give suddenly and without warning, and leave us falling into something new and much, much worse.

"Look!" Tuttugu, behind us but pointing ahead.

I squinted at the dark spot down in the shallow valley before us. "I didn't think anyone lived in Osheim."

"Lots of people live in Osheim, idiot." Snorri made to deliver one of those playful punches to the shoulder that leave my arm dead for the next six hours. He paused though, feeling the old crackle of magic, as fierce across his knuckles as it was across my side. "Most of them live far south, around Os City, but there are farmers everywhere."

I glanced around. "Farming what exactly? Rocks? Grass?"

"Goats." Kara pointed to some brown dots closer at hand. "Goats and sheep."

We hastened across the valley toward the lone hut. Somewhere in the back of my mind Aslaug whispered that Snorri had raised his hand against me, yet again, insulted me to my face. A low-born barbarian insulting a prince of the March . . .

Coming closer we saw that the dwelling was a stone-built round-house, the roof thatched with dried heather and river-reeds. Apart from a shed a single winter from no longer being a shed, and a drystone wall for stock to shelter behind come the snows, there were no outbuildings, and no other dwellings lay in sight.

A handful of mangy goats bleated at our arrival, one from the roof. An axe stood bedded in a log before the doorless opening. The place seemed deserted.

"See if they left any furs." I nodded at the door as Tuttugu drew up alongside us. "I'm freezing." My clothes still felt damp and were doing a poor job of keeping out the wind.

Tuttugu looked up at Snorri who shrugged and walked on over to the doorway.

"Halloo, the house?" Snorri paused as though he heard something, though I couldn't make out anything but the goat on the roof, bleating as if it were wondering how to get down again.

Snorri stepped up to the entrance. And then stepped back again. The long and gleaming prongs of some kind of farm implement following him out. "I'm alone here and have nothing you might want." A voice gone rusty with the years. "Also no intention of letting you take it." By inches a yard of wooden haft emerged, and finally on the other end an old man, tall but stooped, his hair, eyebrows, and short beard all white like snow, but thick, as if a thaw might give us back the younger man.

"More of you, eh?" He narrowed rheumy eyes at Kara. "Völva?" He lowered his pitchfork.

Kara inclined her head and spoke a few words in the old tongue. It sounded like a threat but the ancient took it well and gestured to his hut. "Come in. I'm Arran Vale, born of Hodd, my grandfather—" He glanced back at us. "But perhaps you've travelled too far to have heard of Lotar Vale?"

"You need to leave here, Arran." Snorri stepped in closer, making his words clear. "Gather only what you need. Hardassa are coming."

"Hardassa?" Arran repeated as if uncertain of the word, or of his hearing. He tilted his head, peering up at the Norseman.

"Red Vikings," Snorri said. Old Arran knew those! He turned quickly, vanishing into his home.

"It's us they're after! We should take what we need and go!" I glanced back at the distant lip of the valley, half expecting to see Edris's friends pouring down the slopes.

"That's exactly what *they* will do when they spot this place," Tuttugu said. "Take what they want. Re-provision. Their longship can hold a lot of goats." Something in his eyes told me his own thoughts were circling the idea of goat stew even now.

"Hurry!" Snorri slapped a hand to the lintel-stone, leaning in.

I looked back again and a lone figure stood on the ridge, little more than a mile away. "Shit." I'd been expecting it all this time, but that didn't stop the truth of it from being a cold shock.

Arran re-emerged carrying nothing but his pitchfork and in the other hand a butcher's knife. Across his back he'd secured a bow that looked as old as him and as likely to snap if bent.

"I'll stay." The old man looked to the horizon. "This is my place."

"What part of Viking horde did you not understand?" I took a pace forward. Bravery of any kind generally makes me uncomfortable. Bravery this stupid just made me angry.

Arran didn't look my way. "I'd be obliged if you'd take the boy though. He's young enough to leave."

"Boy?" Snorri rumbled. "You said you were alone."

"I misled you." The faintest smile on the bitter line of the old man's lips. "My grandson is with the goats in the south vale. The völva will know what's best for him—but don't bring him back here . . . not after."

"You're not even going to slow them down with that . . . fork."

"Come with us," Tuttugu said, his face clouded. "Look after your grandson." He said it like he meant it, even though it was clear the man had no intention of leaving. And if he did it would just slow us down.

"You can't win." Snorri, frowning, his voice very deep.

The old man gave a slow nod and a double tap on Snorri's shoulder with the fist that held the knife. A gesture that reminded me he had not always been old, nor was age what defined him.

"It doesn't matter if you win—it only matters that you make a stand," he said. "I am Arran, son of Hodd, son of Lotar Vale, and this is my land."

"Right . . . You do know that if you just ran away they'd probably ignore you?" I said. Somewhere just behind the conversation Aslaug's screams scratched to get through. *Run!* The message bled out into each pause. I didn't need instruction—running filled my mind, top to bottom. "Well . . ." I glanced once more at the doorway to the roundhouse, imagining it thick with fur cloaks inside. "We should . . . go." A look at the ridge revealed half a dozen figures now, close enough that I could make out their round shields. I started walking to galvanize the others into action.

"May the gods watch you, Arran Vale." Kara bowed her head. "I will do my best for your grandson." She spoke the words as if she were playing a role but in the unguarded moment as she turned away I saw her doubts—her runes and wisdom perhaps as much a facade as my title and reputation. She started to follow me. Dig deep enough into anyone and you'll find a scared little boy or scared little girl trying to get out. It's just a question of how deep you have to scratch to find them—that and the question of what it really is that scares the child.

"Shit." I saw the boy, running toward us down the long and gentle slope of the valley's southern edge, a ragged child, red hair streaming behind. Snorri followed my gaze. I picked up my pace, angling to intercept the boy's path, though several hundred yards still separated us. Kara veered left to cover that approach should he try to evade me.

Only the Undoreth stayed where they were. "Snorri!" I called back.

"Get him to safety, Jal." A raw tone that stopped me in my tracks.

"Come on!" I turned back, beckoning them on. Tuttugu stood beside Snorri, axe in hands.

"It matters that we make a stand." Snorri's words reached me though he didn't raise his voice.

"Christ." They'd bought into the old man's nonsense. I could understand it from Arran, addled by age and a step from the grave in any case . . . but Snorri? Had Baraqel stolen his mind? And what the hell was Tuttugu staying for?

"Kara!" I shouted. "They won't come!"

A score and more of the Hardassa advanced down the northern slope now in a rough skirmish line, their cloaks of tartan, of wolfskin, and of bear blowing about their shoulders, shields low, axes held above the heather, their iron helms robbing any expression.

"Take the boy!" She started back toward Snorri.

"Wait! What?" Her face didn't look like someone preparing to argue Snorri out of it. "Hell." With Aslaug screaming at me to run, my own instincts screaming louder still, and Kara telling me to do it . . . I ran.

The little bastard dodged round me but I managed to overhaul him in a dozen paces and catch his hair. We both went down amongst the tussock grass. The kid couldn't have been more than ten, skinny with it, but he had a desperate strength, and sharp teeth.

"Ow!" I snatched my hand back, putting knuckle to mouth. "You little fucker!" He scrambled away, earth showering me where his toes gouged at the ground. I lunged after him, getting my feet under me and charging half a dozen steps—well aware I was heading in the opposite direction to the one I wanted to go in. A tussock caught my foot and I went down, diving, arms stretched. My fingers closed on the kid's ankle as my face hit the grass.

The air exploded from my lungs and refused to return. I lay, gripping the boy tight enough to break bones and desperately willing myself to draw breath. Lifting my head, I could see, past the black spots swimming in my vision, to the line of Hardassa, closing around the three men before the hut. Kara stood halfway between me and the fight.

This was it. We were all going to die.

With a shout the Hardassa advanced, spears and axes raised, shields on high.

Snorri's battle-cry rose with those of the Red Vikings, that old note of violent joy ringing out. He didn't wait for them to close but launched himself toward the biggest of the enemy. The attack took the Hardassa by surprise, so confident were they in their numbers. Snorri leapt, setting a foot to the boss of his foe's raised shield and climbing above him as the man braced himself, then collapsed beneath the weight. Snorri rode the shield down, swinging his axe in an arc that smashed it through one helm, another, and sent the third spinning away.

Tuttugu and the old man followed, roaring out their challenge. It occurred to me, as the air started to leak back into my chest, that Tuttugu would be killed within the next ten seconds, and that I'd miss him despite his being a fat, ill-smelling, and low-born heathen.

I saw Arran shove his fork at a red-bearded Viking. Part of me, the part raised on story-book knights and legends of past heroes, had been expect-ing some display of martial excellence from the man, something to match the gravitas of his words. At the end of it though, for all his bravery, Arran Vale proved to be only what he was, a farmer, and an old one at that. His fork turned on a shield, scoring two grooves through the paintwork, whilst the Viking's axe bit into his neck, lost in a crimson deluge.

The Hardassa closed around Snorri and Tuttugu. Hopelessly outnumbered and having no defence other than the axes in their hands, the last of the Undoreth stood no chance. The leg I had hold of stopped tugging as the boy also started to accept the reality of the situation.

I could still see Snorri, or at least his head, above the melee, roaring, seemingly illuminated by his own light like the actors on a Vermillion stage followed by the candle-mirror. Of Tuttugu there was no sign.

Kara stood maybe ten yards from the backs of the closest Vikings, no weapon in her hand. I didn't know how they might treat her after the killing was done. Did völvas enjoy the same protected status that priests did in Christendom . . . and were those traditions of sanctuary trampled over as often up north as down south?

Snorri's axe rose above the crowd, trailing gore, a scarlet spray flicking off the blade as it reversed and hammered down. The arm that held it glowed so bright it made shadows of the blood smeared along its length. So bright it hurt to look at it. And then, with a sound that I felt in my chest rather than heard, a brilliance lit within the Viking throng, making a black forest of limbs and torsos. For a moment I could see nothing but the after-images seared into the back of my eyes, the silhouette of axe and shield, the tangle of arms. Blinking them clear I made out a figure surging through the melee, barging men aside, dragging something. A bright figure.

"Snorri!" I rose to my knees, releasing the boy and pressing the heels of my palms to both eyes to rid them of the last traces of blindness.

Snorri came on, hauling Tuttugu by the foot. He paused by Kara, twisted round, and ripped out the spear that transfixed Tuttugu's stomach. He tossed the bloody shaft aside, the light dying from him with each moment, and strode on, pulling his friend along with a grunt of effort. Behind him the Vikings cursed and clawed at their eyes. At least one felled a comrade, swinging his axe in a wild arc when barged by a blind man seeking escape.

Kara made no move to follow. She stood, still facing the enemy, raising her hands to her head. With a sudden motion she ripped free two handfuls of the runes from her hair, and scattered them across the ground before her like a farmer sowing grain.

Snorri reached me and the boy and collapsed to his knees. He had a gash on his upper arm, another on his hip. Ugly wounds, but by rights he should have been little more than bloody chunks. Behind him Kara strode back and forth where her runes fell, chanting something.

"Why in hell?" I had too many questions and my mounting outrage wouldn't let me frame them.

"Couldn't let him stand alone, Jal. Not after we'd led them to his home."

"But . . ." I waved an arm at everything in general. "Now we're running away? With Tuttugu dead?"

"The old man died." Snorri glanced at the boy. "Sorry, son." He shrugged. "It's not my land. Nothing to stay for after Arran fell."

"I'm not dead." A weak voice behind him. Then, less certain, "Am I?"

"No." Kara hurried past us. "Let's go." She called the last part over her shoulder. A few runes still bounced across her back but most of her braids had lost theirs.

Tuttugu sat up, patting himself, a bewildered look on his face. He poked at the blood-soaked hole where his jerkin strained across his stomach. I understood then why Snorri was on his knees, head down.

"You healed him! And the light . . ." I trailed off, looking past the Undoreth to where the Red Vikings stood, rubbing their eyes, some rising from where they'd fallen, looking around as they regained their sight. In between us, where Kara sowed her runes the ground seemed to heave in one place, sink in another. One of the Hardassa ceased blinking away his blindness and spotted us. He gave chase, axe high for the strike.

"Hell." I glanced about. Snorri and Tuttugu looked in no state for battle. Kara, if she drew it, would have a thin knife to face down the axeman. That left me, my dagger, and a weaponless boy. I wasn't sure of his age—ten? Eleven? Twelve? What did I know about children. I considered shoving the boy forward first.

The Red Viking ran a dozen more paces. To his left the ground rippled, the sod tore, and a vast snake arced from beneath the earth. It took him in its mouth, dived back, and in two heartbeats was swallowed by the soil as if it were a sea serpent on the ocean.

"What—?" I managed, an expression of my disbelief rather than a question. More snakes broke the surface, smaller ones no thicker than a man, seen only for scattered moments and gone. And the colour of them, drawn from no pallet I had ever seen, a pattern of crystalline brown and umber, confusing the eye, as if they were a thing apart from the world.

"Children of the Midgard Serpent—the great wyrm that wraps the world." Kara sounded as amazed as I was.

"How long will they stay?" The snakes kept to where Kara had cast her runes, forming a barrier to protect us. Now that the other Hardassa were regaining their sight they backed away, shields raised, as if a shield could stop such serpents any more than could a castle wall.

"I don't know." Like me, Kara couldn't look away. "This has never happened before. The casting can make a person imagine snakes, make them believe that the grass writhes before them and fear to tread there . . . this is beyond . . ."

"It's the Wheel." Tuttugu, still examining his torn and bloody jerkin where the spear impaled him.

"Let's go." Snorri stood with an effort. "It won't take long for them to think to just go round."

We opened a good lead while the Hardassa paused to take stock, tend their wounds, and consider their snake problem. In the hills and ridges beyond the valley we even lost sight of them, though it couldn't be long before they overhauled us again.

"We're heading closer to the Wheel?" It took an hour for me to notice: the business of putting one foot before the next had been consuming all my energy.

"Our only chance lies in magic—we can't outrun them or outfight them." Kara glanced back at the pursuit. "In this direction we grow stronger."

Kara might be growing stronger but I felt weaker by the yard. Of all of us only the boy, Hennan, had any go left in him. The distant strain of a horn reached us and I found I could walk a little faster after all.

"Seems to me." I took a few more steps before finding the effort required to finish the sentence. "That the Wheel has drawn you in too. Just took a bit longer."

That was how Nanna Willow had it. The Wheel would pull you in. Quick or slow, but in the end you'd come, thinking it was your idea, full of good reasons for it. I wondered how Hennan and his grandfather had lived here so long without succumbing. Perhaps such resistance lay in their blood, passed one generation to the next.

The stain in the sky had grown darker and the oddly shaped rocks that broke the sod cast long shadows. Somehow my dread at meeting Aslaug in this place felt only a little less intense than my healthy fear of the sharp edges the Red Vikings were carrying after me.

We struggled on through an increasingly twisted land, across a wild heath where the occasional tree clawed slantwise toward the sky, angled by the north wind. Stones broke the sod with increasing regularity. Dark pieces of basalt that looked as if they had erupted from the bedrock but which must have been set standing by men. In places fields of such stones stood in rows, marching into the distance, aiming in toward the Wheel. I had no strength left to marvel at them. Later we passed black shards of volcanic glass, some pieces taller than a man, sharp as the blades the ancients made from the stuff. I saw my face reflected in gleaming obsidian surfaces, warped as if drowning in horror within the stone—and looked no more. Further still and the obsidian grew up in twisted and razor-edged trees.

Closer to the Wheel the rocks took on disturbingly human shapes, on a scale ranging from the size of a man's head to larger than my father's halls. I tried not to see the faces or what they were doing to each other.

I cast the occasional glance at Snorri as we went—trying to judge what kind of hold Baraqel might be gaining on him as we came nearer to the Wheel. Several times I caught him sneaking furtive glances my way, only confirming my doubts about him.

In one place we came across a ring of obsidian pieces, knife-sharp, each taller than Snorri, and aimed skyward though splayed as if some great force at the centre of the circle had pushed them outward. For fifty yards on every side the heath lay blasted, blackened earth with only the occasional twist of heather stem now turned to charcoal. Something silvery gleamed at the centre. Despite our need for haste, Kara angled us toward the ring.

"What is it?" Snorri posed the question to Kara's back as she approached the standing stones. It looked as if softly glowing pearls laced the black earth within the ring, forming a rough outline of some explosion within. Kara passed between two of the shards and entered the circle. She went to one knee and scraped at the burnt soil with her blade. It seemed as though the glow intensified around her. A moment later she stood, something shining in her hands, making dark sticks of her fingers.

When she reached us I saw that what she held was neither silver nor a pearl. "Orichalcum." She withdrew one hand. A bead of metal the size of a fist rested upon the palm of the other, its surface gleaming, lit with its own silvery light, but broken with sheens of colour like oil on water, moving one into the other, a slow dance, mingling and separating as I watched.

"Will it help us fight the Hardassa?" Snorri asked.

"No." Kara led the way on. "Take it, Tuttugu."

Tuttugu accepted the over-sized bead. Immediately the light in it died and it became merely shiny metal, like a solid drop of quicksilver.

"A magic was worked in that circle long ago." Kara took the bead back and the glow returned. "Orichalcum leaks into the world at such sites, though I've never heard of it being found in such quantity. Skilfar has a piece." She held her thumb and finger out to show how small, pea-sized. "One use for it is to assess a would-be völva's potential. It has nothing to say of wisdom, but of affinity for enchantment it speaks volumes. This glow is my potential. Training and wisdom will help me put it to good use, as a warrior hones their strengths into skills."

"And when Skilfar held it out for you to take?" Snorri asked.

Kara shook her head. "She bid me take it from a bowl upon a shelf in her cave. Though weeks later I saw her pass beneath that shelf and the glow from within the bowl was brighter than when I hold it now in my hand." She held it out to Snorri. "Try it."

Snorri reached for it, without slowing his pace, and she dropped the orichalcum into his palm. Immediately it lit from within, so bright it made me glance away. "Warm!" He passed it back quickly.

"Interesting." Kara didn't seem disappointed at being outshone. "I can see why the Silent Sister chose you. Jal, you try." She held the bead for me to take.

"I've had enough of heathen spell-mongering." I kept my distance and hid my hands beneath my armpits. "Last time we did something like this I ended up being stabbed." In truth I didn't want to be shown as dull before her. Tuttugu might seem pleased at sparking nothing from the metal—but a prince should never be seen to fail. Especially by a woman he's hoping to impress. And was that a grin I saw on Snorri's face as he outshone me, yet again? Aslaug had said the northman sought to usurp me, and now the whispers rose at the back of my mind to confirm it. For a moment I imagined that the Red Vikings *had* killed him. Would that have been so bad?

"Frightened?" Kara still held the orichalcum toward me.

To change the subject I asked, "Chose him? Nobody chose him—or me. It was accident that wrapped us in the Sister's curse. A chance escape, a meeting against the odds." I'd been expendable, a minor prince-ling left to die in her fire, an acceptable price to pay for ending an unborn. And my "meeting" with Snorri had hardly been planned. I'd run straight into him in a blind terror whilst trying to escape the crack spreading from my great aunt's broken spell.

"I don't think so." Kara said no more as we struggled up a rise. At the top she continued. "The Silent Sister's spell wouldn't fit into just any man. It's too powerful. I've never heard of its like. Even Skilfar was amazed— she never said it in so many words, but I could tell. A spell like the Sister's needed two people to carry it, and to grow its strength from the first seed. Two people—opposites—one for the dark part, one for the light. It wouldn't be left to chance. No, this must have been planned an age in advance . . . to bring two such rare individuals together."

I'd heard enough. Opposite to Snorri. Coward to his hero, thief to his honesty. Lech to his fidelity. Magic as mud to his shining potential.

All I had to console myself with was prince to his pauper . . . I was glad at least to find myself as suited to sorcery as a paving slab. Magic always struck me as hard and dangerous work . . . not that there are any words you can put before "work" that makes it sound attractive. Certainly not "dangerous" or "hard."

Our marching order changed as the miles passed. The boy grew weary and fell back with Tuttugu whose burst of energy from being healed now seemed spent. Snorri, Kara, and I, however, shed our tiredness. I found a dark excitement building in me. Each time I trod through the shadows cast by standing stones I heard Aslaug, her message now a simple promise—"I come." And, although I feared her arrival, the threat of it bubbled through me like black joy, twisting my lips into a smile that might scare me if I had a mirror to see it in.

Cresting a ridge somewhat higher than the rest we paused, and turning back saw the enemy for the first time since the hut. We waited for Tuttugu and Hennan to struggle up to our position.

"I count twenty of them," Snorri said.

"There were that many at Arran's roundhouse before they attacked," said Tuttugu, panting. "Close on a score."

"Didn't you manage to kill *any* of them?" I didn't try to keep the complaint from my voice.

"Six, I think," Snorri grunted. "They're following us with the others."

"Ah." I turned to Kara. "Did you remember the necromancer when you said magic was our only hope? Because it looks like she's following us in."

Five or six hundred yards across a broad vale our enemy came on in a tight knot, their pace unhurried but relentless. I took a few steps to put more distance between Snorri and me. The skin along the side facing him burned and I swear for a moment I saw cracks reach out toward him from my arm, like black lightning forking into the air.

We pressed on, hurrying down the far side of the ridge, the heather catching at our ankles. At the bottom we waited for Tuttugu to draw level with us again.

"The sun will set soon. We'll make our stand then." Snorri cast a sideways glance my way. "Baraqel will lend me strength then too. He comes closest at dawn, but the dying of the light is another time when he can draw near—especially here."

I nodded, suddenly not trusting the Norseman an inch. Every word he uttered sounded like a lie and when I blinked I could almost see Baraqel's wings spreading from Snorri's shoulders. Even so, ahead of us lay the Wheel and every nightmare ever whispered of in fireside tales. I wouldn't run into it to avoid an axe. Besides, once Aslaug showed up I had the feeling that she wouldn't be letting me run anywhere other than straight at the foe, whoever they might be.

The wind still blew, fitful now, edged with memories of winter. The land lay strangely silent, the lone cry of a curlew seeming an impertinence. I could smell rain approaching.

"Not much go left in them," I told Kara as Tuttugu drew near. Hennan looked half-dead on his feet, though I'd heard no word of complaint from him. The boy wiped at his nose as he came closer, dry mud still in his hair from where I had brought him down when he raced to stand with his grandfather.

Tuttugu drew level and lifted his axe in greeting, the blade dark with dried blood, exhaustion written in the gesture.

Snorri grabbed the back of Hennan's jerkin as he passed and hoisted him off the ground and onto his shoulders with one arm. "You can ride," he said. "No charge."

Tuttugu looked my way. "And Jal carries me?"

I laughed despite myself and slapped a hand to his shoulder. "You should come to Vermillion, Tutt. Fish off the bridge for your living and come out with me of an evening to scandalize the highborn. You'd love it. If the heat doesn't melt Vikings."

Tuttugu grinned. "The war chief of the Undoreth endured it."

"Ah, but even Snorri went crispy at the edges, and he did spend most of his time in nice dark prison cells . . ."

"Wh—" Tuttugu bit his reply off and stopped to stare.

As we crested another fold in the terrain an archway stood revealed in our path. Weathered stone, tall as a tree, narrow, and set with deep graven runes. Kara hurried ahead to examine the carvings.

"Well, that's nice." I walked through it, ignoring Kara's hiss of warning. A considerable part of me had hoped, albeit without conviction, that I'd find myself somewhere new on emerging from the other side of the arch. Somewhere safe. Sadly, I just arrived on the grass opposite and looked back at the Norse, their hair wild across their faces in a sudden gust.

"What is it?" I asked.

"Something to set our backs against," said Snorri.

"A work of the wrong-mages." Kara craned her neck to stare at the runes above her. "A doorway to other places. But opening it is beyond any skill of mine. And like as not those places are worse than this one."

"Sounds like any one of these wrong-mages could take the Empire throne and bend the Hundred to his will if their magic is so strong." I followed her gaze up the stonework. Runes had been worked on my side too. Some of them reminded me of those the Silent Sister set climbing across the walls of the opera house and suddenly I felt those awful violet flames again, my ears filled with the screams of those I left to burn.

"Hel, they could take the whole world with magics like that." Tuttugu set his back to the stone and slid down to sit against the base. Snorri shrugged Hennan from his back and lifted his axe to inspect the blade.

"The wrong-mages are bound to the Wheel," Kara said. "And in time it breaks each of them. Their power diminishes swiftly as they move further from the centre. Not that many of them have the willpower to leave in any case. Kelem was the only wrong-mage to truly escape this place." Her fingers moved among her braids, freeing most of the runes still hanging there, preparing for the fight.

"You said opening the doorway was beyond you . . ." I frowned at the völva, her face resigned yet still fierce. "But before today the spell you summoned serpents with had only ever rippled the grass . . ."

She looked up at Snorri, standing beside her. "Give me the key—there's not much to lose at this point . . . I'll try to open the way."

"What?" He eyed the open space between us. "It's an arch. There's no lock."

Kara touched her rune-filled left fist to a symbol on the left support, eyes narrowed in concentration, the echo of some internal litany twitching on her lips. She crossed to the opposite side and struck a second carving with her right fist. "Give me the key. I can work this."

Snorri looked suspicious. I felt a little glow to know it wasn't just me he didn't trust with Loki's gift. "Direct me," he said.

The völva shot him a narrow look. "We don't have time to argue, just—"

"Show me how and I'll do it." I could hear the growl in his voice. This wasn't up for debate.

Kara glanced toward the closest ridge where the Hardassa would soon appear. "From the runes it seems this arch was an attempt to open the doors to many places where men were not meant to go. Here," she pointed to the first character she had touched, "darkness, and there, light. To step across miles in this world you have to take shortcuts through such places."

"Open the door to light," Snorri said.

"Damn that!" I saw his plan now, to unleash Baraqel and his kind on the Broken Empire. "Take the dark path—Aslaug can guide us."

"No!" It was perhaps the first time since he faced Sven Broke-Oar that I'd heard true rage in his voice. A nimbus of light lit around him, tinged with the red of the western sky. "We'll not take that road."

A fury of my own rose at the snarl on the northman's treacherous face. A black anger running through my veins, dark and thrilling. The idea that I had ever feared Snorri seemed as ridiculous as the idea I had ever trusted him. Right now I knew the strength of mere muscle would count for nothing when I reached out to crush him. I held his gaze. The bastard wanted Baraqel out in the world. Everything Aslaug had said was true. Snorri was the light's servant now. "Kara, open the night-door."

"No." Snorri stepped forward and I matched him, until we stood face to face beneath the empty arch. Darkness smoked off my skin and I could feel Aslaug's hands upon my shoulders, cool and steadying. The light that burned around Snorri bled from his eyes now. There's light that is the warmth and comfort of the first days of summer, then there's the glare of a desert sun where that light moves from comfort to cruelty—the light

Baraqel sent through Snorri went beyond that into something not meant for men, so harsh that it held no place for any living thing.

"Kara!" I barked at her. "Open it."

Snorri raised his fist, perhaps unconscious of the axe clutched in it. "I won't have that night-whore—"

I hit him. Without thought. And the impact of it near deafened me. A burst of dark-light threw both of us yards back, but we found our feet in moments, throwing ourselves at each other, howling.

Only Tuttugu stepping into the archway and interposing himself prevented a second, more violent clash. Snorri found himself holding his father's axe above the head of the only other living Undoreth. I found myself, hands outstretched into claws, reaching for Tuttugu's face.

Snorri withdrew his hand and let the axe drop. "What . . . what are we doing?" The moment of madness passed.

I'd been going to leap on an axe-wielding Snorri, barehanded. "Christ—it's this place!" Neither of us owned our actions any more. A little longer and we'd both be puppets for the avatar we carried inside us. "We need to get out of here before it kills us."

"The Red Vikings will probably beat Osheim to it." Kara insinuated herself past Tuttugu to stand between us. She pushed both of us back. "I'll try to open the door that I think I have most chance of success with." She looked up at Snorri. "And if you won't let go of your precious key then, yes, I will direct you." She wiped the frustration from her face and pushed Snorri back another couple of feet before turning to face the archway, eyes doing that defocused "witchy" thing of hers. "There!" She moved beside him, pointing to an arbitrary point in the air, her head cocked to one side, staring past her finger into some infinity.

With a frown, Snorri fished out the key on its chain and, stepping closer, raised it to the point indicated. The blackness of the thing looked wrong against the thickening gloom. It had nothing of darkness about it, that black, but was something else again, perhaps the colour of lies, or sin.

"Nothing." Snorri put the key away. "All that fuss and . . . nothing." He bent to pick up his axe. "I'm sorry, Jal. I'm a poor friend."

I held up a hand to forgive him, ignoring the fact I'd hit him first.

Snorri stepped away from us swinging his axe. The enemy would be upon us soon enough. He needed to make ready. The axe cut glimmering arcs as he wove a figure of eight, then turning with the swing, reversed into an upward slice. Snorri made it seem almost an art, even with so crude a weapon. To my left Tuttugu readied himself, tightening his belt and wiping clean his blade with his sailcloth sack. Courage didn't come naturally to him, at least not the kind that warriors laud, but he'd taken his death blow once already this day and now prepared to die again.

"We could just give them the key." I felt someone should state the obvious. "Leave it here and head west for Maladon."

They all ignored me. Even the boy—and he hadn't a clue what I was talking about, so that seemed harsh. Ten or eleven years were surely too few to see past Prince Jalan's glossy exterior?

I would have set off by myself but the Silent Sister's trap had grown stronger with each stride we took toward the Wheel. I doubted I could get a hundred yards before the crack tore wide and Baraqel ripped from Snorri while Aslaug poured out of me.

"The sun's coming down," Kara said unnecessarily.

"I know." The arch's shadow stretched toward the Wheel, dark with possibility. I felt Aslaug's breath on the back of my neck again—heard the dry scratching at the door that held her back.

The Red Vikings came on over the ridge, close enough now for me to see the detail on their shields: sea serpent, pentagon of spears, the face of a giant with the shield boss its roaring mouth . . . The fatal wounds Snorri had dealt out now glistened in the red and dying light—a man split from collarbone to opposite hip, another headless and led on a tether, more behind. Somewhere in that crowd Edris Dean watched us from behind a Viking face guard. Was the necromancer there too, in furs, a shield on her arm? Or did she spy from some remove, set apart, as so often before? Suddenly my bladder declared itself beyond full.

"Do you think there's time—" I began, but those bastard Red Vikings cut me off with their battle cries and started to charge.

It turned out there was time. I drew my knife and with wet legs prepared to face the onslaught of nearly two dozen Norsemen.

Something changed.

Although it made no sound the archway drew my gaze from the charging axemen. The whole of it lay black and darkness spilled from it, streaming cold about my ankles, thickening the shade before us.

"Jalan." Aslaug rose from the shadowed ground as a woman might rise beneath her bed sheets, shrouded at first, her form uncertain, then drawing them about her, tighter and more tight, until at last she stands framed before you. She faced me, her back to the enemy, and I stood filled with her power, seeing the world with perfect clarity, darkness smoking from my skin. "This is no place for you, my prince." She smiled, eyes gleaming, black with madness.

The first of the Hardassa, a fleet-footed young reaver, sprinted toward Aslaug, ready to bury his axe between her shoulder blades. Instead he came to a jerking halt, impaled on a sharp-ended black leg, thin as an insect's and seemingly emerging from Aslaug's back, though I couldn't see from where or how. This was new—she was actually *here* in the flesh. "Shall we go?" she asked as the man died, choking on his blood. She gestured toward the arch with her eyes.

Snorri met the next wave of men, carving through the first one's face with exquisite timing, long arms at full stretch. He leapt clear of the man a half pace behind, rotating to hack into the small of his back as momentum carried the fellow past. Tuttugu—already backed against the other side of the arch—slipped sideways with commendable skill and let the first of his foes hew stone so that his weapon was shaken from his grip. Tuttugu answered by burying the wedge of his blade in the man's sternum.

More men came from Tuttugu's left, keeping away from the yawning oblivion within the archway. Kara threw her runes at them, hurling a meagre handful. Each became a spear of ice, thrown with more force than even Snorri could manage. The shafts pierced shields, mail, flesh and bone, leaving the enemy staring in confusion at the holes punched through them.

"Jalan?" Aslaug asked me, drawing my attention back from the melee.

Small hands gripped my leg. The boy. God knows why he chose me for protection . . . Another two Hardassa reached us, trying to swerve around Aslaug. Both fell, sprawling forward, snared in web-like strands of darkness. "You need to leave," she said. Behind her, the man transfixed on her insect leg lifted his head and eyed me with the consuming hunger of those returned from death. From his wide-open mouth came that wordless roar that dead men keep in place of language. Aslaug flicked him off in a crimson shower as he started to struggle. "Mine is not the only magic here."

Snorri caught an axe just below the blade as it blurred toward him. He twisted into the attacker, a powerfully built redbeard, until his back pressed the other man's chest, with the back of his head pressed against the other man's nose guard. Arms outstretched, still trapping the axe, his own blade free on the other side, Snorri rotated into more attackers. Their blows thudded into the back of the redbeard Viking that he now wore as a cloak. Snorri let the man fall, dragging his Hardassa axes with him. Unencumbered once more, he hacked across his two closest foes.

A tearing sound behind me, and the archway pulsed with sudden light, like a bright wound in the darkness. From the resulting maelstrom of swirling blackness shot with motes of brilliance, Baraqel emerged, golden-winged, a silver sword in his hand—too bright to look upon, advancing on Aslaug. At the same time the ground about us began to boil, bones rising to the surface like bits of meat in a soup set above the flame. Bones and more bones, skulls here and there. The peaty soil vomited forth arm bones, leg bones, one piece finding another, and joining, linking with old gristle and stained sinew that had withstood the rot.

"This is a place of death!" Kara, yelling from the opposite spar of the arch. "The necromancer—" She broke off to apply her knife to a skeletal hand gripping her leg, more Hardassa closed upon her swiftly.

The dead men strewn in Snorri's wake also started to rise. Bony hands began to claw at Baraqel's feet, even reaching for Aslaug. The avatars of dark and light, rather than rushing at each other as Snorri and I had done, had to pause in order to deal with the necromancy reaching up to bring them down.

"Run!" Kara shouted, and free of the bones' grip, she dived headfirst into the archway.

I hesitated for a moment. It looked a lot like a wider version of the crack that had pursued me in Vermillion. The archway seethed with darkness and light making war, a mixture I'd seen reduce people to bloody and widely scattered chunks. For all I knew small pieces of Kara now decorated the grass on the far side of the arch.

"Don't!" hissed Aslaug, more limbs springing from her torso to pin Norsemen to the ground before they could reach me. Long, thin, hairy limbs. "Stay!" While the arch had been dark she'd been urging me through, but now she wanted me to stay?

That convinced me. I ran toward the swirling dark-light.

"Wait!" Aslaug's shriek a mix of rage and anguish. "The völva lied to you, she's a—"

I leapt through. The weight on my leg told me that the boy had come too. All the sounds behind me cut off in an instant and I started to fall.

The best thing I can say about what followed is that it probably hurt less than being butchered with an axe.

FOURTEEN

I'm falling. I stepped through an archway and now I'm falling, punching a me-shaped hole through endless night until it finally does end, falling through a white blindness, no kinder than the dark, through sharpness and thorns, through pain so fierce it steals time, and at last into dream. Cool, enfolding dream-stuff, grey as clouds . . .

I fall screaming through the cloud base, forgetting in my terror that this is dreaming, and plummet at last into the midst of the seven-towered castle of Ameroth wherein my grandmother stands besieged by an army of fifty thousand. An army wielded like a blade by the warlord Kerwcjz. The Harrow of Slov they call him—the iron fist of Czar Keljon who dwells upon the eastern steppes but would rather sit in Vyene, emperor by right of war.

We stand once more upon the outer walls atop the broad expanse of one of the seven towers. High as we are, smoke wreathes us, blotting out the sky, so thick that had I not fallen from heaven's vault and down through the burning I would be unsure whether morning had yet taken flight.

Grandmother is there again, Alica Kendeth—princess of the Red March, not yet twenty, broadsword in hand, her armour battered, the gilding worn, enamel splintering away where blows have dented her breastplate. The same iron look in her eyes as when she loosed an arrow into her sister's heart. She stands taller than me, and yet Ullamere Contaph towers above her in his demon-black Turkman plate, a livid wound scored from the bridge of his nose past the corner of his mouth.

Shattered rock and pieces of the battlements strew the tower top. Soldiers man the walls, less thickly than before. Dead are heaped beside the stairway down into the tower. Dead in two mounds, one pile flecked with the crimson of the March, the other more varied. Men of Slov lie there, entwined with warriors of the Mayar. There a knight of Sudriech, sprawled across him two Zagre axemen, faces tattooed in the blue wards those peoples favour. There has been an assault, recently turned. I wonder how many more of the foe lie heaped and broken at the tower base among the wreckage of their ladders, coiled amid their ropes . . .

"We have to fall back to the second wall." Contaph's wound gapes as he speaks. I see teeth through the gory mess of his cheek.

"No," says Alica.

"We're spread too thin, princess." There's no heat in his voice, just weariness. "This castle was built to be held by more men."

"I'm not interested in holding this castle. I mean to destroy Kerwcjz and let the Czar know he has overreached himself this time."

"Princess!" Exasperation now. "Attack was never an option. It—"

"It was the only option we ever had." She starts toward the stairs. She calls to Contaph over her shoulder. "Bring five hundred of the very best to the keep. Choose by skill, not blood. I want warriors. Father can make more nobles easier than he can make more warriors."

"The keep, highness?" Exasperation turning to confusion. "We can hold the second wall. At least for a few weeks. The keep should be our last—"

Alica Kendeth turns at the top of the stairs and looks back at him. "We can't allow them to gain the outer towers. Bring me five hundred and order that the towers be held. If that means surrendering the walls between—so be it."

Contaph pales, as if the edge of a terrible thought has sliced him, and more deeply than the blade that ruined his face.

I follow my grandmother down the steps that coil through the heart of the tower, a thick-bodied construction, packed with many floors. Down past staterooms, barracks chambers, armouries, storerooms, down through a second skin, this of poured stone, a smaller and more ancient tower housed within the thickness of the newer construction. The spiral stair broadens to a zig-zag flight arching on poured buttresses. Seemingly insubstantial, even as a ghost I am nervous to test my weight against it. Each stair is just a slab—you can see beneath them, through the stairway to the flight beneath . . . Even so, it has stood a thousand years and more and does not now crumble beneath the weight of my imagination. We descend through the Builder-tower, past iron doors, past doors of timber bound with steel, past a trio of Red March palace guards, and come to a chamber, a plain cube, in which sits a machine larger than a royal carriage, cast in silver steel, alive with dim light, and trembling with a faint but undeniable vibration as if deep within it some great beast draws breath in slumber.

Alica sets a hand to the silver metal. She bends, as if allowing herself to be weary in the solitude of this place, her forehead pressed to the coldness of the Builder-steel, hair, dark and red, falling about her face, eyes closed.

A moment later and she strides with purpose out of the chamber, a nod to the guards who set to sealing the door. A long corridor leads us to the main tower gates.

I follow her out through the exit. Men bow on every side. A detachment of six soldiers leave their duty at the tower to escort her. We take a broad thoroughfare through the town that crowds between the outer and inner wall of the castle. These are the homes of the castle folk, the labour force that keeps this castle running, that keeps food on the table, clothes on the defenders' backs, mortar between the stones, oil on the cogs of the war-engines. Here and there I see damage caused by the rocks thrown from without, but this place is built to last. Sturdy. Obstinate. The people show these characteristics too. There is no despair here, not yet. Thin cheers go up as Princess Alica passes by. At one point market stalls line the street and we slow to pass through the crowd. Some instinct turns the castle-dwellers aside when our paths cross. They can't see or hear me, but a sixth sense prevents them from contact.

The gatehouse at the second wall is pierced by a tunnel that can be sealed with four portcullises. All of them stand open. The escort is exchanged and we enter the killing-ground between the keep and the second wall. The bare flagstones echo beneath our feet. Well, not mine, I'm just dreaming.

The keep door stands on the side opposite to the four-fold gate in the inner wall, tall enough for a mounted man but small enough to be strong as the walls themselves. We pass through a smaller iron door set to one side. This is the Tower of Ameroth, reaching for the sky just as it did on my childhood visit. Though it stands now without the strange scars that lay etched into the Builder-stone when I saw it as a boy—and of course surrounded by a castle. I'm starting to wonder how I could be ignorant of whatever story explains how fifty years later no stone of that castle remained in place. Did it simply get hauled away block by block, stolen by locals decades after the war to build a castle elsewhere, or homes? There's enough stone here for a city.

We pass by more palace guards, elite soldiers from the personal guard of Gholloth, second of that name. Why these men aren't with my great-grandfather in his palace in Vermillion I can't guess.

Alica pauses before a captain who stands beside an inner door. "Bring the chosen within the second wall, John."

"Yes, princess." Heels click together, a curt bow of the head.

"Artisans only, John. Skilled labour. Allow them their children if it eases progress. Pack them tight."

"Yes, princess." No emotion in his voice.

We pass through the door he guarded and a man seals it behind us. A short corridor leads to a domed chamber. A spiral staircase penetrates a remarkable thickness of Builder-stone. The ends of reinforcing iron bars gleam with a dull light where they protrude into the stairwell that has been cut down through them. This stairway must have consumed years of labour. The lamps flicker as Alica sweeps past, her armour clanking at each step.

We emerge into a room maybe ten yards square. A silver-steel ring, three yards across, is set into the stone floor and rises to about waist height, the upper surface sloping toward us. Dim lights glow there, the pattern shifting slowly between three configurations. In the middle of the ring a strange blue star burns, without heat but with a light that captures the eye. It rests a man's height above the stone, as unsupported as any other star. I find myself staring at the thing, losing all sense of passing time. They say time is the fire in which we burn. Now I know what time looks like when *it* burns.

Alica walks through me—an unpleasant sensation but one that breaks me free of the star's entrancement. Without my grandmother's intervention I doubt I would ever have looked away. I'm careful not to look at it again. I have no idea if moments have passed, or hours.

The lights on the slanted top of the steel wall that forms a ring below the star now shine with a brightness that owes nothing to fire. The patterns have become more complex, more numerous, and shorter lived. Alica moves quickly here and there, touching one light as it glows, then another. I become aware that we are not alone. The room has few shadows but what shadows there are seem to gather in the far corner. A woman stands there, clad in grey, her robe wrinkled around her. She is almost as tall as Alica, but with a slight stoop, and looks no more than thirty-five but her hair is grey, falling lank about her face. She lifts her gaze—and finds me.

"How?" Any further questions die upon my lips. The woman's left eye has a pearly cast to it. She raises a pale finger to her lips as if to shush me. When she lowers her hand the slightest of smiles lies behind it.

"I'm ready," says Alica. "Are the people in place? The soldiers assembled?"

There's nobody here but me and her silent sister, and neither of us answer.

She raises her voice. "I said—"

"Optics indicate the stasis zone fully occupied."

Surprise nearly tears me from the dream. There's a ghost standing before my grandmother. It wasn't there a moment ago. A pale, see-through, honest-to-God ghost. A damned odd-looking ghost it has to be said—its face like a Greek marble, statued perfection that couldn't ever be mistaken for life.

Alica bows her head. "Begin the event."

"I have explained that stasis is not possible. Extensive repairs would be required before the generators could provide a sufficient pulse of energy. Generators seven and three are functioning at thirty percent, the remainder at less than ten percent. A failed stasis will result in a quickening. All that might be achieved is a bubble of quick-time, and at a peak ratio of thirty to one."

"And I have acknowledged this. You will run the reactors beyond failsafe."

"You do not understand the consequences of such action. The generators will fail catastrophically. Estimates place the devastation radius at—"

"Even so, you will do it." Alica keeps her gaze on the pulsing lights.

The ghost shows no expression, its tone unwavering. It seems even less human than Captain John at the keep door, and the palace guard practise hard at looking impassive.

"I am afraid User that as a Guest you do not have such authority. This algorithm will—"

"My sister has seen beyond you, Root. She has seen past the years, though the sight of it burned her eye. You are a dance of numbers, without soul. Cleverness without wit. You will do what I say."

"User you may not—"

"Security override Alpha-six-gamma-phi-twelve-omega."

"Compliance. Energy pulse in three minutes. Quick-time core ratio of thirty-two to one predicted."

We wait while the ghost counts away the seconds. Summoned by some unseen signal, Contaph descends the stairs leading a mix of palace guards, common soldiers, knights, and even a lord or two. Many of them carry the filth and stink of battle with them. Hard men, warriors born.

"Fifteen."

The chamber is packed and more men push down the stairs. Alica vaults the steel ring and stands on the other side looking out, the blue star just behind her head, making a silhouette of it.

"Clear the stairs!" Alica shouts, urgency in her tone now. "Clear the path to the gates."

"Fourteen."

The shout is echoed up the stairway and beyond.

"It's already done, princess," Contaph says. "As you instructed."

"Eleven."

"Contaph, you others there. Join me."

"Ten. Nine. Eight. Seven."

Men pack in close. I join them, hunched beneath the star itself.

"Six."

A faint whine can be heard rising through the clatter of arms and shuffling of feet.

"Five."

There's something in the air. A brittle buzzing that puts my teeth on edge even though I'm not really there.

"Four." I risk a glance at the Silent Sister, finding her through a momentary gap. She's watching me from her corner into which nobody wished to push.

"Three."

"You know me don't you?" I don't want to talk to her. I feel like that small boy again, just turned five and presented to the Red Queen for the first time. I remember the dry touch of her, that moment when the Silent Sister first laid her hand on mine and I fell into some hot dark place.

"Two."

She isn't going to answer. She only smiles.

"One."

"Yes," she says.

"Zero."

The blue star expands, its cold fire engulfs us and passes on through the walls of the chamber. And that's it. Nothing has changed. We all stand frozen, waiting, waiting for whatever magic was supposed to save the castle.

"Quickly now." Alica vaults back across the wall. It's not something I could do in full armour. Her strength is prodigious.

The men immediately before me are swift to follow her and I scramble after them, the contact with the steel a strange greasy thing as dream-flesh seeks purchase on the real. We've hurried along the cleared passage through the tight-packed warriors, and are nearly at the stairs before I realize that only the men closest to the ring have made any effort to follow us, and even they've been damned slow about it. Alica isn't waiting, though, and so I hasten after her.

At the top of the stairs I realize something is wrong. The soldiers here stand like statues, not even following us with their eyes. Has the Builder-magic frozen them? There's no time to consider the matter— Alica clanks along at a flat run, aiming for the great door.

I'm amazed to see the door standing wide open, as if we weren't at war. Glancing back, I see men from the chamber stretched out behind us, the ones farthest back moving as if they were running through thick mud. It takes a moment but I think I understand. The star's light has sped us up. Those of us closest to it have gained the greatest speed. Quick-time, it said? Has the Builders' engine made our seconds pass faster? Our hearts beat swifter than hummingbird wings?

Emerging from the keep, I think I must be dreaming. Then I recall that I am indeed dreaming but that these purport to be the memories of my line, bound into my blood and revealed by Kara's magics. The inner wall has been shattered, standing in places, reduced to heaps of rubble in others. Bodies lie crushed beneath tumbled debris—waiting to scream. Where the wall has fallen the flames have reached to the keep, patterning its walls with geometric scorch-marks, and reducing all the people in their path to burning pillars.

The sky is crowded with smoke and fire and falling rock. A chunk of masonry bigger than a horse descends along an arc that will end where I stand. It tumbles as it falls, slower than an autumn leaf. I step aside and move to follow Alica. Behind me the missile strikes the wall of the keep and breaks apart with a sound that is both indescribably deep and overwritten by the high scream of stone fracturing.

Through the breaches in the walls I see only boiling fire. No sign of the town, no hint of the great outer walls and the seven vast towers. The air is full of pieces. Rocks, tiles, masonry . . . There are bodies too: I see them dropping from on high as if sinking through water.

Alica runs beneath the gatehouse, under the four portcullises, still raised. Contaph and I can't keep up with her and she opens a lead. We emerge beneath the fourth gate and step into hell. Fire still billows here. Not the flames above logs in a hearth, or the blaze of a burning house, but clouds of inferno—a living, liquid thing. It seems to be thinning as we watch, spiralling skyward to reveal a scorched wasteland where no building survives. Alica has not waited. Her passage is recorded as a hole punched through the fire. We follow, praying that our swiftness will preserve us.

Alica weaves a path past craters, fire-pits, trenches gouged by unimaginable force. She dodges around stubborn foundations jutting up in our path. She skirts the most intense knots of flame, sidesteps falling debris and jumps the blazing rubble of the outer walls in three huge leaps. I follow, finding like Contaph in his platemail that I can jump distances that would put the athletes of ancient Greece to shame. I see that we are close to the place where one of the seven towers stood—now a column of white-hot flame spiralling above a vast crater. The pieces of stonework that still hang in the air about us, called to the ground along gravity's rainbow, all radiate from this spot.

Beyond the wall, back past bowshot, the many thousands arrayed against the Castle of Ameroth burn. We race after my grandmother across the dead ground between besiegers and besieged. The engines of war lie in flaming pieces. Chunks of flying masonry from the great walls have carved broad avenues through the ranks of the foe, torn bloody thoroughfares through their camps. Those men closest to the walls lie burning, turned by the heat into blazing fat, pooled amid charred bone. Further back, the soldiers are caught in their agony, their screams deep-throated and low to our ears. Further still and they remain standing, shields raised and smouldering, tents afire. If it is like this all around the seven towers then thousands upon thousands have died—many times more outside the walls than within them.

Alica seems to know exactly where she is going. We follow, with others from the chamber beneath Ameroth Keep strung out behind us, slower than we are but still far faster than any man should be.

We penetrate deep into the warlord's army, past the major harm done by the exploding towers, into the heart of his host where the pavilions fly the standards of noble houses. Even here great stones have landed, crushing men, horses, tents—but nine in every ten survive. We swerve around soldiers who stand almost frozen, their eyes too slow to track us, hands starting a slow crawl toward their sword hilts.

At last we sight the tight-packed standards of Slov, the pavilions growing larger and more resplendent. Anar Kerwcjz, the Czar's western fist, is emerging from his great canvas pavilion as we arrive, a magnificent spear in his hand. Cloth-of-gold decorates the entrance and the banners of his vassals hang on standard poles to make an avenue for his exit. The Last Blades stand thick about his residence, resplendent in their black chain mail, faces masked in jet and ivory, a feared elite whose reputation has echoed down the years so loudly that even I have heard of them.

We are slower now, as if our speed is like something gleaned from Maeres Allus's poppies, a drug that bleeds from our veins, returning us in time to the mortal world. Even so the Last Blades have barely flinched before Alica has slid her blade along Kerwcjz's throat. She wastes no time in decapitation—perhaps her blade would break if forced through a man's neck at such speed. She spares the storied warlord no second glance but simply moves to the nearest soldier and repeats the act before the spray of blood from Kerwcjz's wound is quarter way to the ground.

His spear hangs in the air, seeming somehow more real than everything around it, brighter than blood, more alive than the guards on every side. It's a dark wood, sheathed in a tracery of silversteel, blades flaring out six inches behind the point. It calls to me, and without thinking I reach for it. My hand closes on the shaft and I feel it, there, solid beneath my fingers.

"Kill everyone!" she shouts.

And Ullamere Contaph obeys. More of her chosen arrive as the butchery begins, and set to their own bloody work. I tug the warlord's spear into motion and follow Alica, wincing as the crimson deluge sprays over and through me.

She cuts twenty throats before the warlord hits the ground. She cuts a hundred before she has to duck beneath a sword. In places she moves through a clump of ten or twenty Slovian infantry and is on to the next concentration before the men start to fall.

It lasts for what seems an age but what must be only minutes to the army around us. Alica has killed several hundred men before she needs to parry a blow. She stands scarlet head to toe, blood arcing from her blade, flying from her hair as she turns. Blood paints her trail through the camp. Even now she must seem a blur, moving with inhuman speed and leaving dead men toppling in her wake.

The army of Red March, those few hundred survivors from Ameroth Keep, start to regroup as the Builders' magic fades. Alica and Ullamere lead them, aiming for any strong formations still holding station about the ruined castle, and slicing them apart as they make a circuit.

In the last battle my grandmother leads her four hundred survivors against an army of two thousand Zagre axemen, who have been held back in reserve. The men of Red March are still a touch faster than men should be, a handful of them twice or three times the speed of normal humans, all of them blood-soaked and gore-stained. The Zagrans break early and scatter. It's the last resistance. The siege is broken.

Grandmother's troops stand crimson, silent save for the patter of blood dripping from them. She paces a few yards away, ahead of the men, climbing some fallen chunk of wall stone in two steps. She stands there, panting, her breath slowly returning to her, her armour running scarlet as she surveys her warriors. The burning ruins of her castle form her background, with the defiance of Ameroth Keep tall among the collapse of the second wall.

Ullamere Contaph steps forward. He looks up at her, raises his broadsword, and although she is only a princess it is "Red Queen!" that he roars.

"Red Queen!" The army take up the shout. "Red Queen." Weapons raised. "Red Queen." Their voices are thick with emotion, though whether sorrow, triumph, or both and more, I cannot say.

FIFTEEN

"Wake up!"

"What?"

"Wake up!" Kara's voice.

"No," I told her. "It's still dark and I'm comfortable." Well, almost. Something I was lying on kept digging into my back.

A hand shook me. Hard.

I yawned and sat up. "I know why they call my grandmother the Red Queen."

"Because she's Queen of Red March." Tuttugu, somewhere behind me.

"You'd think so. But no." I touched the ground around me. Unyielding, damp, gritty. "Why does it smell so bad?" I rubbed my aching spine and patted the ground behind me, finding the long hard object I'd been lying on. "What the hell is this thing—"

A sudden light showed me Kara's face, Tuttugu's hinted at dimly, further back, and some larger shape in the deep shadow that must be Snorri. The light came from Kara's hand—a glowing bead of silvery metal.

"Orichalcum," I said, shaping my mouth around the word. Suddenly I remembered. "The arch!" I glanced around and saw nothing but darkness. "Where the hell are we?"

"I don't know," Kara said, which was disheartening, given that she was the one who is supposed to know things.

"Nowhere good," Tuttugu offered. Spoken in the dark it sounded true. "Where did you get the spear?"

I looked down and found that the object I'd been lying on was indeed

a spear. Kerwcjz's spear. I'd taken it from the warlord in my dream . . .
or in Grandmother's memories. "How the hell did I—"

"I don't know where we are. The works of the wrong-mages are
beyond me," Kara said. "But without guidance we should have come out
as close as possible—we've fallen back somewhere where the world grows
thin. Somewhere cracked by recent magic. Powerful magic."

"Isn't that going to take us closer to the Wheel?" Recent powerful
magic didn't sound good. "Why isn't it ever 'somewhere with cheap booze,
expensive women, a race track, and good views of the river'?"

"The arch is designed to serve the will of the user. I led the way and
I was trying to get us out of there . . ."

"Where's the boy?" I remembered him as the last dregs of dreaming
left me and the fear started to settle on my shoulders. "Snorri! Have you
seen . . ." The name escaped me. ". . . the boy?"

"Snorri's not here either," Tuttugu again—closer to my ear than I'd
expected. "I hope he's with Hennan."

"But . . ." I was sure I'd seen him. I shook my head, decided the dream
must still have had its claws in me. "What *is* that smell?"

"Trolls," said Tuttugu quickly.

"You smell trolls every time the wind changes—Snorri told me you've
never even seen one." *Please don't let it be trolls.* I'd never met one either
and didn't want to. The scars Snorri had showed me from his own encounter told all the story I needed to hear.

Kara moved in closer and we huddled over the glow of the orichalcum,
three pale faces illuminated in a sea of darkness. "It sounds as if we're
in a cave," she said.

"We should get out." I hoped somebody else would supply the how.

"Before the trolls eat us," said Tuttugu.

"Shut up about the damn trolls!" Fear raising my voice. The darkness
seethed with the bastards now, put there by my imagination—which took
some doing since I didn't know what the things looked like. "Snorri says
you wouldn't know a troll if one—"

"He's right this time!" Snorri's voice, a way off but coming closer.

"Snorri!" I tried hard not to sound too much like a damsel in distress.

"Is Hennan with you?" Kara asked. I could see she was relieved too, though she kept it from her voice.

"Yes." Snorri came close enough for the glow to catch him, a smaller figure just behind.

Hennan hurried across and attached himself to Kara's side. I can't say the same idea hadn't occurred to me. "Don't suppose you've got a tinderbox in that sa— Wait. Tuttugu's right? Is that what you just said?"

"Yes." Even Snorri didn't sound pleased about it.

"No tinderbox," Tuttugu said, rummaging as if he might find one even now.

"Let's have a little more light," Snorri said, holding out his hand.

"He just said we didn't h—" I broke off as Kara dropped the orichalcum into Snorri's palm. "Oh."

The glow became fiercer, pushing back the shadows to the margins of the cavern. The floor beneath us lay level, hard-packed mud left by some underground river. Lower down, the walls had been smoothed by ancient currents; higher up they became rough, the ceiling studded with stony icicles like so many of Damocles's swords depending above our heads. Some of these had already fallen and lay in pieces across the floor. They had a blackened look to them. In fact so did the walls . . . and the ground beneath our feet . . . as if a great fire had burned here, filling the place wall to wall.

"There," said Snorri, gesturing with his axe to a clot of darkness that resisted the orichalcum's glow. "And there." He indicated another further around the cavern wall.

"There what?" I squinted at them.

"Trolls."

An oath, sharp with terror, escaped Tuttugu before he mastered himself. I retreated toward Kara, gripping the spear tightly and wondering if I would ever be safe again.

"You beat a troll, right, Snorri?" I asked, mouth suddenly dry, cracking my voice.

"One," he said. "I got lucky." He nodded to a dark passage leading off from the far end of the cavern. "Two more there. The only thing I don't understand is why we're still alive."

One of the creatures detached itself from the wall and moved a few paces closer. Even so it remained hard to see, its hide swallowing any light that fell upon it. A black creature, taller and more powerfully built than Sven Broke-Oar who had hardly been a man at all. Long inky limbs, a face so black as to deny all features. Another step closer and I saw the gleam of its eyes, dark as Aslaug's, and a wide mouth opening to black teeth, black tongue, now stretched in what should be a roar though only a hissing reached me, running along the edge of hearing.

Snorri held his axe ready for the swing. He and Tuttugu wore other men's blood. The scent must be calling more of the things and driving those before us wild. I considered dropping my spear.

"Who are you, truce-breakers?" A voice rolled out behind us, the kind of deep voice that sounded at home here among the roots of mountains.

We turned to see the speaker. With so many enemies it became impossible not to aim your back toward at least one of them. Not that my front would help fend off a troll. The spear was a magnificent weapon but I had the feeling these trolls might just bite the end off. As I turned I saw for a heartbeat that small smile the Silent Sister offered me in the dream. Had she seen this moment with her blind eye? Was this the source of her amusement?

The thing that regarded us through eyes slitted against our light might once have been a troll but something had twisted it. I doubted God would touch such creatures so that left a darker hand altogether, reaching up from the brimstone to warp the beast. His rib bones erupted from his chest like long black fingers, almost coming together above his heart. An image of Aslaug and unfolding spider legs skittered across my mind and I shuddered. This one stood maybe seven foot, perhaps a little more, a foot shorter than the others, but considerably more solid, and clad in a hide that the shadows whispered might be red. Cat's eyes, teeth a direwolf might envy, and in place of the other trolls' long fingers ending in black claws, his fingers were thick as a child's arm, three to each hand, ending in blunt red nails. Also, unlike the others, he wore a robe of some sort, more of a toga really, of dark highland tartan. I had plenty of time to drink in his details while waiting for one of our number to overcome their astonishment and answer his question.

"We've broken no truce." It was Kara who at last found the wit to answer him.

"You may not have intended to break it, you might be wholly ignorant of its existence, but you most certainly have broken the truce." The monster troll spoke with remarkable calmness for a savage beast, and with a degree of culture that wouldn't be out of place at court if it weren't spoken in a voice deep enough to cause nosebleeds.

"A great magic was worked in this cavern," Kara said. "It called us here. What happened?"

"Two fire-sworn disagreed." A terse reply as if the memory pained him.

"What place is this? And what is your name?" Kara asked, perhaps hoping to keep the conversation from the topic of broken truces.

The monster smiled, a broad thing revealing many sharp teeth but not unfriendly. "You stand beneath Halradra, a fire-mountain within the Heimrift. These caverns were gifted to my brothers here by Alaric, Duke of Maladon."

"Maladon!" I couldn't keep it in. "Thank God." If it weren't for all the trolls watching I'd have sunk to my knees and kissed the mud.

"And I," the beast continued, "am Gorgoth."

"You rule here?" Snorri asked.

The monster shrugged and I could swear he looked embarrassed. "They call me their king, but—"

"Prince Jalan Kendeth, grandson to the Red Queen of the March." I thrust out a hand. "Pleased to meet you."

Gorgoth looked down at my hand, as if uncertain what to do with it. I was about to pull it back in case he might snap it off or take a bite, but he folded it in his three-fingered grip, and for a moment I felt a hint of his strength.

"So," I said, reclaiming my hand and making it into a fist to keep the ache at bay. "So, I hope as King of Hal . . . uh . . ."

"Radra," Snorri supplied.

"Yes, Halradra." I shot Snorri a sour glance. "As King of . . . beneath this mountain . . . I hope you'll extend the courtesy due to another Empire royal and have us escorted to the borders of your land."

Gorgoth made no indication that he'd heard me. Instead he sunk to one knee and extended his open hand toward Hennan. "How is it that you have a child with you, and blood upon your axes?" Then focusing those cat's eyes of his upon the boy, "Come."

I'll give the little bastard credit, he showed as much courage or fool-hardiness by dark as by day. We met him racing back into the teeth of a Hardassa raiding party and now he came forward on steady feet and put his small hand into the palm of the king of the trolls.

"Your name, child?"

"Hennan . . . sir."

"I had a little brother," the monster said. "He would be about your age now . . ." He released the boy and stood. "My new brothers are pre-paring to march to a new home, seven hundred miles to the southwest. It lies in the Renar Highlands. You may travel with us for any part of your journey that takes you in that direction."

"That would be gr—" I mastered my enthusiasm. "That seems accept-able." I couldn't bring myself to call him sire. But it did sound great. As long as they didn't eat us I could think of no bodyguards better suited to keeping the Dead King's servants off our backs. Men tend to stay dead if you eat them! "When do you plan to depart?"

"The Duke of Maladon is providing an escort to prevent any misun-derstandings with his people. They should be here within a week. The truce states we are to travel after the feast of Heimdal. And that no human is to set foot upon Halradra until that time . . . The duke's men patrol to ensure no one wanders this way."

"We came by paths beyond the duke's ability to guard," Kara said. "Can we impose upon your hospitality, King Gorgoth, now that we are here, and stay until you're ready to depart?"

I bristled at this—enduring the stink of trolls and staying in a dark damp cave when I could be supping ale at the duke's table. I saw the Undoreth frown too. But in the end I hadn't it in me to slog through mountains and forests to reach the duke and his halls, not even if the ale were nectar served by naked goddesses: I just needed to lie down and sleep, wet floor or not.

"You may stay," Gorgoth said. And that was that.

SIXTEEN

They gave us a cave opening onto the dreary slopes of Halradra, with views of unrelenting pine forest. I lay down exhausted and tried to get comfortable and fell asleep within moments.

"This spear you found in the cavern . . ." Kara's voice.

I jerked awake, disoriented, discovering that it had grown dark. Kara had lit a fire at the cave entrance and sat close to the flames, examining one of the last rune tablets still depending from her braids. "I didn't find it in the cavern."

"You were lying on it, you said."

"I found it in my dream. I took it from the warlord." It sounded foolish even to me. It must have been on the floor, discarded as inedible by the troll that killed its previous owner. Only it hadn't been. I'd seen it in Grandmother's memories, down to the last detail.

"It's hard to believe it was just left there," Snorri said, moving from the gloom, his face now lit by the fire.

"It wasn't. It was in my—"

"Show it to me again." Kara held out her hand.

I drew in a great sigh and rolled into a sitting position, drawing the spear from beneath me.

"Gungnir!" Tuttugu said, eyes wide, as I held it up.

"Gungnir to you too." I yawned and rubbed my face.

"Odin had such a spear. Thor had Mjölnir, his hammer. His father held the spear, Gungnir."

"Oh," I said. "Well, I doubt it's that one."

"It *is* a hell of a spear, though." Snorri leaned forward and took it from me.

"Keep it." I warmed my hands. "I haven't entirely trusted a dream since I met the Ancraths' pet mage, Sageous."

"It doesn't make sense for a Slov warlord to be carrying a Norseman's spear." Kara frowned at the weapon as Snorri turned it around, examining the overlay.

"The gods sent it to us." Tuttugu nodded, as if this were a serious suggestion. "Perhaps Odin himself."

"Gods know we need a weapon," Kara said. "If Snorri's set on leading us into Kelem's lair . . . What do you plan to do if Kelem says no? What if he just turns you into a column of salt and takes what you've brought him?"

Snorri narrowed his eyes and tapped the axe beside him.

"Kelem wouldn't be able to count Skilfar young if all it took to detach him from life was a sharp edge." Kara held her hands out and Snorri passed her the spear across the flames.

"And a spear will do the job better than an axe?" he asked.

"Myths cast shadows." Kara held the spear before her and the fire played its shadow across her face. "All the treasures of the sagas cast many shadows and even their shadows can be a deadly weapon. And to cast the darkest, sharpest shadow you need the brightest light. Darkness and light bound together can be a potent force." She glanced briefly between Snorri and me. "A spear like this . . . with a bright enough light, could cast a shadow of Gungnir. A thing like that would make even Kelem pause!"

"Great, let's go back to Skilfar and ask her if—"

"I could do it." Kara cut across me. "If I do it now, before the Wheel's touch has left me and my magic fades to what it was."

"Would the shadow-spear last any longer than whatever Osheim did to us?" Snorri asked.

The völva nodded. "It will be anchored by more than my spell."

"The gods didn't send that thing." I snorted and bit off the rest. It wouldn't do well to tell them their gods were heathen nonsense.

Kara ignored me and stood, still holding the spear. "Best be done quickly. Take hold each end." She nodded at me and Snorri.

We did as we were bidden. I made sure I got the blunt end. It looked every bit as fearsome a weapon here, with the firelight playing over the silver-steel runes cladding its dark timber, as it had in the warlord's hand.

Kara took a step back and brought out the chunk of orichalcum, driving the shadows back as it lit in her hand.

"Hold the spear steady, so the shadow falls between you." She raised the orichalcum. "Keep it close to the ground . . . Turn your heads away and don't move."

And without warning the metal in her grasp ignited into a white incandescence turning the whole world blind. The last thing I saw was the spear's shadow on the floor between us, a black line amid the brilliance all around. I gripped the spear for all I was worth and found it crumbling away beneath my fingers as if the light had burned out its vitality leaving only ash.

"Christ, woman!" I pressed the heels of my palms to my eyes. "I can't see."

"Shush. Wait. You'll see again soon enough."

My sight returned slowly, blurs at the edge first, light and shade, then colour. I could see the fire, and the glow in Kara's hand. The blurs resolved into edges and I saw that of the fist-sized ball of orichalcum she'd been holding only a fraction remained, a shining bead no bigger than an eyeball, as if the rest had burned away.

"Now, that's a spear worthy of a god!" Snorri straightened up having taken from the place where the shadow fell a new spear, seemingly taller than the old, the design similar but with something fierce added to the mix so that the runes about it seemed to shout their message, the wood between them darker than sin, the silver-steel burning with its own light.

We sat awhile, watching Snorri hold the spear. It grew darker. I fell asleep.

The week Gorgoth said it would take the duke's men to arrive turned out to be four days. Four days turned out to be three days too long—and I spent the first day sleeping.

Our beds were heaps of bracken, heather, and the occasional spiky sprig of gorse, all looking to have been yanked up, roots and all, still with the earth fresh upon them. Dinner predictably was goat, presented raw, and still eyeing us with that faintly surprised expression it wore when the troll ripped its head off. Breakfast was goat too. Also lunch.

I woke before daybreak on the second day and lay unmoving as the predawn began to reach in, blunt-fingered and finding only edges. Time passed and I saw, or thought I saw, amid the greyness, a deeper shadow, sliding toward the lump I took to be Snorri. The gloom seemed to knot about . . . something, concealing it, but leaving enough of a hint to draw my eye. Perhaps if I weren't dark-sworn I'd have seen nothing. The something, or the nothing, gathered itself as it drew close to Snorri and rose above him, and still I lay, paralysed, not with fear but with the moment, held by it in the way that a waking dream can sometimes trap a man.

Dawn broke, no rays of sun reaching into our cave, only a different quality to the light.

"Knocking." Snorri sat up, muttering. "I hear knocking."

And just like that the strangeness left me and I could see nothing more sinister than Snorri, rubbing the sleep from his face, and Kara leaning over him.

"I don't hear anything." She shrugged, perhaps a flicker of irritation on her brow. "I need to check those wounds. Today I'll make a poultice."

The morning of that second day Kara trekked down the ashy shoulder of the mountain to a level where plants dared to grow and returned hours later carrying a linen pouch stuffed with various herbs, barks, flowers, and what looked suspiciously like mud. With these she proceeded to treat the wounds our Vikings had sustained, the slice above Snorri's hip proving the most serious. All I could plead was skinned knees of the sort little boys endure. I probably sustained the injury falling to my knees to plead for mercy or praying to an uncaring God, but to be honest I had no recollection of it. Either way I got no sympathy from Kara who fussed around Snorri's over-muscled side instead.

Aslaug didn't return to me that second night either. The first night

I'd fallen asleep before sunset and lain so dead to the world it would have taken a full-blown necromancer to have roused me. The second sunset though, when Aslaug didn't appear, I wondered if Loki's daughter were still angry about me diving through the wrong-mages' arch. Since the alternatives had all appeared to end in gruesome death it seemed unreasonable of her to object, but she had been set against it at the time. Temper or no temper it struck me as odd. Aslaug had been so eager to return that first day ashore after being denied my ear for so long by the magics set around Kara's boat. I chalked it up to "women" and told myself she'd come round in the end. They always do.

In the gloom and boredom of our cave I replayed those memories of my grandmother at Ameroth Castle more than once. In truth, when my mind turned toward the events of the siege's last day I couldn't stop the carnage playing out behind my eyes. I wondered once more how I could have managed to avoid the story for so long. But then again I have been accused in the past of being a little self-centred and my only interest in the family's glorious history was to know where they'd buried the loot. Come to think of it, there was a song about the Red Queen of Ameroth but I'd never paid any real attention to the words . . .

I thought of Grandmother with her long-laid plans, her strange and creeping sister who ran her spell through me and Snorri, and of Skilfar, ice cold and old beyond the lives of men.

"Kara?"

"Yes?"

I tried to find the right words for my question and, failing, settled for using the wrong ones. "Why did you decide to become a witch? You know they all end up weird, yes? Living in caves and talking gibberish while they gut toads . . . scaring honest folk. When did you decide, yes, toad-gutting, that's the life for me!"

"What would you have done if you hadn't been born a prince?" She looked up at me, eyes catching the light.

"Well . . . I was . . . destined to be—"

"Forget divine right or whatever excuse your people use—what if you weren't?"

"I . . . I don't know. Maybe run a tavern, or raise horses. Something to do with horses." It seemed a silly question. I *was* a prince. If I wasn't then I wouldn't be me.

"You wouldn't pick up your sword and carve yourself a throne then? Regardless of your birth?"

"Well, yes of course. That. Obviously. Like I said, I was destined to be a prince." I'd rather be destined to be a king though. But she had me right—I *wouldn't* cut myself out a kingdom, I'd work with horses. Hopefully riding the beasts rather than shovelling their dung. But better wielding a shovel than a sword.

"I was born to peasant stock, thralls to the Thorgil, the Ice Vikings. I could tell you that I had a hunger to know things, to understand what lies behind what we see, to unlock the secrets that hold one thing to the next. A lot of the young völva apprentices will tell you that kind of thing, and a lot of them mean it. Curiosity. It's killed more cats than dogs have. But the real reason? For me at least—I'll tell you honestly, because you should never lie on a mountain. Power, Prince Jalan of Red March. I want to take my own share of what you had given to you with your mother's milk. There are bad times coming. For all of us. Times when it would be better to be a völva, even if it means being a scary witch in a cave. Better that than a peasant working to scrape a life from the ground, head down, as ignorant of what's coming as a spring kid is of the farmer's knife."

"Ah." I hadn't an answer for that. Every royal understands the value of ambitious men, and the danger inherent in them. The courts of the Broken Empire are packed with such. I had half-imagined that different forces drove those who toyed with the fabric of the world and dreamed of strange and frightening futures . . . but perhaps I shouldn't have been surprised to find ambition, the simple greed for power, at the bottom of that too.

By day three I got so bored that I let Snorri talk me into trekking up to the crater a thousand feet above us. He brought the spear, using it as a staff to lean on, and limped along favouring his good hip, setting a pace that I could match for once. The boy came with us, scampering ahead over the rocks.

"A good kid." Snorri jerked his head toward Hennan, waiting for us up the trail.

"Don't let the trolls hear you call him a kid. They'll gobble him up in two bites without even wanting to know who's trip-trapping over the bridge." I looked at the boy, hunched and windblown. I supposed he was a good kid. I'd never really had occasion to think of children as good or otherwise, just small and in the way, and remarking loudly about where I was touching their big sister.

We came up through gullies, deep-scored in the black rock. Up between the serrated teeth of the crater rim, and gazed down at a wide and unexpected lake.

"Where's the fire?" I asked. The lack of smoke rising overhead during our climb had already made me suspicious. I'd missed out on looking down into Beerentoppen's crater when Edris Dean force-marched me up the damn thing, and frankly I'd been grateful not to have to climb the last hundred yards to the rim. I remembered though that smoke had escaped Beerentoppen, to be scraped away by the wind, trailing south like a bald man's last wisps of hair. Labouring up Halradra I expected to be rewarded with some fire and brimstone at the very least.

"Long gone." Snorri found a seat out of the wind. "This old man has slept for centuries, perhaps a thousand years or more."

"The water's not deep." Hennan from further down the inner slope— the first thing he'd had to say all day. Odd when I considered that the defining characteristic of children for me had been how seldom they shut up. He was right though, it looked to be little more than an inch or two of water spread across a huge ice sheet.

"There's a hole out near the middle." Snorri pointed.

The reflected light had disguised it but once seen it was hard to know how I'd missed it. A carriage and four horses could have fallen through it.

I remembered Gorgoth's words. *Two fire-sworn disagreed.* "Perhaps that's how the trolls ended the fire-sworns' argument." A bucket of cold water to separate two fighting dogs—an entire lakeful to end a battle that cracked the world deeply enough to let us spill out into it from wherever the wrong-mages' arch had sent us.

The boy started to throw stones out into the water, as boys do. I half wanted to join him, and would have if it had involved less effort. There's a simple joy in casting a rock into still waters and watching the ripples spread. It's the thrill of destruction combined with the surety that all will be well again—everything as it was. A stone had fallen into my comfortable existence at court, so large that the waves washed me to the ends of the earth, but perhaps on my return I would find it as before, unchanged and waiting to receive me. Much of what men do in later life is just throwing stones, albeit bigger stones into different ponds.

Snorri sat silent, the blue of his eyes a shade lighter with the reflection of the sky in the lake. He watched the waters, watched the boy, arms folded. The wind reached around the rock he'd set his back to and threw his hair across his face, hiding his expression. I'd seen him step away from Hennan, more than once, leaving his care and safety to Kara or to Tuttugu. But he watched him, every time he thought himself unobserved, he watched him. Perhaps a family man like Snorri couldn't help but be concerned for an orphan child. Perhaps he thought his care a betrayal of his own lost children. I'd never really seen how family works—not out in the world, without nannies and nurses paid to do the job in place of parents, so I couldn't say. If I was right it seemed damned inconvenient though and an expensive vulnerability. All those years spent training, all that skill at arms, just to let a little boy get under your guard and weigh you down with his wants.

A few moments later I picked up a loose stone and lobbed it over Hannan's head, out across the lake. The question was never if I would throw a stone, just when.

We stayed up on the crater rim until the sun began to fall and the wind grew chill. I had to call the boy back from whatever silly games were occupying him at the lakeshore. He'd found a twig somewhere and set it to sail where new melt water had gathered on the ice.

He came running up between us, Snorri staring into the distance across the valleys choked with forest, and me huddled in the blanket that was serving me as a cloak.

"We're going down already?" He looked disappointed. "I want to stay."

"We don't always get what we want," I said, remembering as the words left my mouth that he didn't need advice on hardship from me. He'd watched the man who raised him die within moments of our acquaintance. "Here." I held out a silver crown between two fingers to take his mind off it. "You can have this coin, *or* you can have the most valuable piece of advice I own, something a wise man once told me and I've never shared."

Snorri looked around at that, taking in the two of us with a raised eyebrow.

"Well?" I asked.

Hennan furrowed his brow, staring at the coin, then at me, then at the coin. "I'll . . ." He reached out, then pulled his hand back. "I'll . . . the advice." He blurted it out as if the words pained him.

I nodded sagely. "Always take the money."

Hennan looked at me uncomprehending as I stood, pocketing the coin and pulling my blanket tight. Snorri snorted.

"Wait . . . what?" Hennan's confusion giving way to anger.

Snorri led the way and I followed.

"Always take the money, kid. Bankable advice, that."

By the time Gorgoth finally reported that the Danes had been spotted entering the forest we were all eager to be on the road again.

We left on a dreary late afternoon with a north wind raking rain across the slopes. The plan was to travel by night on our long journey but the earliest part of the route, down from the Heimrift, lay through lands so sparsely populated that the Danes said that there was no need for concealment. My bet was that our escort just didn't want their first meeting with a horde of trolls to be in the dark.

Still wearing what we'd escaped the wreck of the *Errensa* in we wound our way down the black flanks of Halradra toward the pine forests in the valleys below. Snorri kept us at the rear of the column and we counted one hundred and forty of the beasts as they left the caves, hissing at the light. An eerie thing to follow a hundred and more trolls, creatures few men have ever glimpsed even in ones or twos, and fewer men have lived to speak of. We five made more noise than they did, with barely a sound passing between the lot of them. And yet the exodus proved orderly and swift. Kara maintained the creatures must speak together in some manner beyond our hearing, without the need for words. I offered that sheep will form an orderly queue to leave their pen and they're just dumb animals. A troll at the rear turned his head at that and fixed those wholly black eyes of his upon me. I shut up then.

Once within the shelter of the trees Gorgoth called a halt and the trolls spread themselves about, breaking noisy paths through the dense thickets of old dry branches.

"We will wait here, as agreed," Gorgoth said.

How he knew where to wait I couldn't say. It looked like a random piece of forest to me, indistinguishable from any other, but I was content to wait now that we were out of the worst of the wind and rain. I sat against a tree, my wet shirt sticking unpleasantly to me. If it weren't for the presence of a hundred trolls I would have been fretting about pine-men and other horrors that might lurk in the shadows. Snorri and I hadn't had good experiences with the region's forests on our journey north. Even so I leaned back and relaxed, not caring how bad the troll stink got. A price well worth paying for peace of mind.

". . . man in charge . . ." Tuttugu chatting with Gorgoth a short distance from me. The two of them seemed to get on well despite one being a vast devil wrapped in a red hide, and the other a fat ginger Norseman not reaching up much past his elbow. ". . . duke's nephew . . ."

A ripple of unease ran through me, as if a stone had dropped into the recently calmed pool of my peace.

"The duke's nephew what?" I called out.

"The duke's nephew is leading our escort, Jal, they should be here soon," Tuttugu called back.

"Hmmm." It seemed fair enough. Only fitting that a Prince of Red March should have a noble in charge of escorting him safely home. Albeit a minor noble. Duke's nephew . . . somewhere a bell was ringing.

I shrugged off my unease and sat watching Kara watching Hennan while the rain dripped on me through the dense needles above. After a while I spotted the troll-stone that must be the reason for the place having been chosen as our rendezvous. An ancient and weathered chunk of rock, moss-covered and bedded in the ground at a slight angle. I could tell it was a troll-stone by the way it bore not the slightest resemblance to the trolls to either side of it.

"Horses! They're coming." Snorri stood, spear in hand, his axe now secured across his back with an arrangement of goat-hide thongs he'd fashioned during our stay in the cave.

Seconds later I could hear them too, branches snapping as they forced a passage through the trees. A short while later the first of them came into view.

"Hail, Gorgoth." The man sounded uneasy. I could see three of them in total, all mounted, pressed close together by more than just the trees. All around us black shapes moved in the shadows. The horses seemed even more nervous than their riders, the scent of troll making them roll their eyes.

They came closer, all of them in wolf-skin cloaks, round shields on their arms, helms not dissimilar to the Red Vikings', close-fitting, bound with riveted bands of bronze, eye guards and nose-piece reaching below the rim and elaborately worked.

"Good to meet again." Gorgoth lifted one of his huge hands in welcome. "How many are you?"

"Twenty riders. My men are down on the forest road. Are you ready to go?"

"We are." Gorgoth inclined his head.

The riders tugged on their reins but, as they turned, their leader caught sight of Snorri, pushing from the trees.

"Who are your guests . . . Gorgoth?" I heard the hesitation as he fought to give the monster some honorific, but failed.

My unease returned. The man looked to be young, of medium build. His golden mane spread across his shoulders. That struck a sour chord.

In my moment of hesitation Snorri came to the fore, grinning, showing his teeth in that way of his that mysteriously turns strangers into
friends in such short order.

"I'm Snorri ver Snagason, of the clan Undoreth from the shores of
the Uulisk fjord. This is my kinsman Olaf Arnsson, called Tuttugu." He
spread a hand toward Tuttugu who stepped from behind Gorgoth, picking twigs from his beard.

Kara came forward, as ignorant of protocol as the rest of them. A
prince should take precedent and be introduced before commoners. I'd
thought even commoners knew that!

"Kara ver Huran, of Reckja in the Land of Ice and Fire."

That was new! I'd assumed she came from one of the Norseheim
jarldoms. I'd met the occasional sailor in Trond who'd been to the Land
of Ice and Fire, but very few. They called the crossing treacherous, and
when a Viking says treacherous you know it means suicidal. Little wonder she seemed so at home living in caves on volcanoes.

I cleared my throat and stepped forward, wishing that I could make
my introduction from horseback and at least look the fellow in the eyes,
or better still look down at him.

"Prince Jalan Kendeth of Red March at your service. Grandson to
the Red Queen." I normally don't mention Grandmother, but having seen
how she took her name I thought it might add a little weight to my own.

The slightest nod of the head and the duke's nephew reached up to
remove his helm. He shook out his hair, sitting the helm upon the pommel
of his saddle and turning to fix me with his blue-eyed stare. "We've met
before, prince. My name is Hakon, Duke Alaric of Maladon is my uncle."

Shit. I forced myself not to say it out loud. I'd met him at the Three
Axes on my first day in Trond. In the space of ten minutes I'd managed
to slam a door in his face, break his nose, and have him harried from the
tavern as a charlatan.

"Delighted," I said, hoping that my role in his disgrace still remained
vague in his mind. I'd shown him up for a liar seeking to make himself out
the hero. At the time I'd been very pleased with myself, using Baraqel's

power to heal Hakon's injured hand and give the lie to his claim of being bitten by a dog whilst saving a baby. After all, he *was* showing off. Any fool can get bitten by a dog. Besides, it had looked as if he might steal Astrid and Edda away from me before my charms had had a chance to work.

Hakon narrowed his eyes at me, two furrows appearing amid his brow, but he said nothing more and turned his horse away, and off we set, following the Danes down to the road.

"Handsome fellow," said Kara as she stepped after Gorgoth.

Snorri and I swapped a glance at that. Mine said, "See, this is why I had to mess with him in the first place."

We didn't see much of Maladon beyond what lay illuminated by torchlight during our journey or the isolated moorland where we made camp by day. I counted it no great loss. I'd seen all I wanted to of the Danelands on our flight north the previous year. A dour land full of dour people, all wishing they were proper Vikings. The Thurtans weren't any better. Worse if possible. My *Nobles' Guide to the Broken Empire* entry for East Thurtan would be "Similar to Maladon but flatter." And for West Thurtan, "See entry for East Thurtan. Boggy."

Aslaug did not return though I waited for her appearance each sunset. Twice I heard a faint knocking as if far off someone were pounding on a heavy door, but it seemed that somehow our flight from Osheim had finally broken the bond the Silent Sister had forged between us. Perhaps Aslaug and Baraqel emerging like that to battle the Hardassa had torn them from me and Snorri, both of us emptied, or free, depending how you viewed it.

In truth I missed her. She'd been the only one of them to see my true worth. On our second night out from the forests of Maladon I lay huddled beneath my cloak, plagued by a thin rain, and imagined what Aslaug would say if she found me there.

"Prince Jalan, sleeping on the ground among these men of the north. Don't they realize that a man of your worth should be hosted in the finest halls this land has to offer?"

◆ ◆ ◆

As much as I missed Aslaug it was good that Baraqel had been banished from Snorri. "Watch him, Jalan," Aslaug had said. "Watch the light-sworn. Baraqel knows that key will open more doors than just the one Snorri seeks. Kelem's mines hold many doors. Behind one such door Baraqel and a host just like him, just as righteous and quick to judge, wait their chance. Come dawn he'll be whispering again in Snorri's ear, slowly turning him, until he sets Loki's key in that lock and Baraqel's kind come pouring out—not offering advice any more, but issuing sentence and execution."

I eyed the largest of the sleeping lumps. Aslaug had made it all sound very convincing but Snorri was a difficult man to steer along any path other than his own—I knew that from personal experience. Still—it pleased me that Baraqel was gone.

Somewhere the sun set and the distant knocking faded to nothing. I looked over at Kara and found Hennan looking back at me, snuggled up against the völva in her bedroll. He watched me with his unreadable stare and after a while I shrugged and went off to water a tree.

Night by night we crossed first Maladon and then the Thurtans. Duke Alaric's close alliance with the Thurtan lords meant he considered him-self responsible for the safe passage of Gorgoth and his brethren through those lands—a matter of honour and one that Lord Hakon repeated to Gorgoth on more than one occasion.

"If so much as a goat or sheep goes missing from a herdsman's flock it would be as if Duke Alaric himself had stolen it," Hakon said.

Gorgoth had simply inclined his great head and assured him that there would be order. "Trolls were bred for war, Lord Hakon, not theft."

Hennan came into his own on the march, uncomplaining about the miles, still with enough energy to run around camp come dawn, badger-ing the Norsemen for stories. He spent time with Gorgoth too. At first the monster's interest sparked my suspicions but it seemed he just liked the boy, telling him tales of his own, of the mysteries and wonders to be found in the dark places beneath mountains.

As the march continued I concentrated my resources on seducing Kara. Even though she made not the slightest effort to make herself alluring, still she managed to torment me. Even though she was as grubby and unkempt as the rest of us, lean, hard-muscled, shrewd eyed, I still found myself wanting her.

Despite the obvious negatives—being scary clever, knowing far too many things, seeing through me on almost every occasion, and being more than happy to skewer straying hands—I found her excellent company. This proved to be a new and rather confusing experience for me. Having Kara entertain twenty Danes with bawdy tales around the fire felt rather as if on a boar hunt in the Kings Wood outside Vermillion our quarry stopped running, sat down, and, pulling out a pipe, proceeded to discuss the merits of veal over venison with us, opining about the best wine to serve with swan.

Snorri, who until Hakon's arrival I had counted my rival in Kara's affections, seemed strangely guarded around the woman. I wondered if he were still bound by Freja's memory, faithful to a dead wife. He slept apart from us, and often his hand strayed to pat his chest where the key hung beneath his jerkin. On the rare occasions I rose before Snorri I sometimes saw him wince, stretching his side as if the poisoned wound that Baraqel had diminished in Osheim were returning to plague him.

The nights of marching passed slowly. East Thurtan turned into West with only an increase in dampness to mark the change. We walked, my feet grew sore, and more and more I wanted a horse to carry me.

We'd spent our first night crossing West Thurtan and had little to show for it save for muddy boots. I'd had about as much of Lord Hakon's antics for Kara's benefit as I could stomach—he was holding forth on classic literature now as if he were some shrivelled dame let out for the day from her book tower—so I sought distraction with the only one of our monsters that could speak.

"What waits for you and your subjects in the Highlands, King Gorgoth? I don't recall hearing that the Count Renar has a reputation for hospitality . . ."

"I'm no king, Prince Jalan. It's just a word that proves useful for the moment." Gorgoth held his hand out to the fire, so close it seemed impossible the skin wasn't bubbling off his fingers. The three digits, stark against the blaze, made something alien of him. "It's King Jorg who rules in the Highlands now. He has offered us sanctuary."

"Trolls need sanctuary? I— Wait, Jorg? Surely not that Ancrath boy?"

Gorgoth inclined his head. "He took the throne from his uncle by force. I came north with him to the Heimrift."

"Oh." For a moment words escaped me. I'd imagined Gorgoth born among the trolls, though I'd given no thought to how he came to language among them, nor to his knowing the ways of men sufficient to negotiate with dukes and lords.

"And yes, trolls need sanctuary. Men are many and take strength as a challenge, difference as a crime. They say there were once dragons in the world. Now they are gone."

"Hmmm." I couldn't find it in myself to be sorry for the plight of the persecuted troll. Maybe if they were more fluffy . . . "This Jorg of yours, I've heard tales of him. Queen Sareth wanted me to put the scamp over my knee and tan his hide. I would have too—very persuasive woman, Queen Sareth." I raised my voice, just a notch, nice and subtle, so Kara wouldn't miss my talk of queens and princes. "Beautiful with it. Have you ever . . . well maybe not." I remembered Gorgoth wasn't the type to be getting invitations to court, unless perhaps it was in a cage, as the entertainment. "I would have taught the boy a lesson but I had more urgent business in the north. Necromancers and unborn to put in their place, don't you know." My adventures may have been an unrelenting misery but at least I could now pull "necromancers" out to trump my opposition in any story of daring and adversity. Gorgoth might be a monstrous king of trolls, but what would a cave-dweller like him know of necromancers!

Gorgoth rumbled, deep in his chest. "Jorg Ancrath is wild, unprin-
cipled and dangerous. My advice would be to steer well clear of him."

"Jorg Ancrath?" Hakon, catching the name, broke off from his dis-
cussion of the finer points of some tedious verse from the *Iliad*. "My uncle
says the same of him, Gorgoth. I think he likes him! Cousin Sindri was
impressed with the man too. I'll have to take his measure myself one of
these days." The Dane stepped over from the fire—all golden hair, square
chin, and shadows. "And you thought to put him over your knee, Prince
Jalan?" I heard Snorri snort in the background, probably remembering
the truth of the matter and our hasty exit from Crath City. "That might
be difficult. The man put an end to Ferrakind . . ."

"Ferrakind?"

Kara answered. "The fire-mage who ruled in the Heimrift, Jal. The
volcanoes fell silent at his death." She watched me from the shadows,
just the lines of her face caught in firelight. I could see her smile echoed
on the faces of many of the Danes.

"Ah." *Damn them all.* I stood up, blustered about needing a stretch
and stalked off, leaving them with a defiant, "Well, Queen Sareth didn't
seem to think much of the boy."

As the nights stacked up one upon the next and we drew ever closer to
the Gelleth border I seemed to be making slow progress on my other
journey—the one toward Kara's furs—though unsettlingly I had the
feeling of being the one steadily reeled in rather than having hooked my
prey with the old Jalan charm and being the one to draw her to me.

To add to my vexation, whilst Kara mysteriously began to look my way
and offer me the kind of smiles that warm a man right through . . . she also
seemed to see right past my normal patter, laughing off my lies concerning
devotion and honour. Often she would ask me about Snorri and the key: the
circumstances by which we acquired it, the ill-advised nature of his quest,
and my thoughts on how he might be deflected from it. As much as it irked
to be talking about Snorri with a woman yet again, I enjoyed the fact that
she was seeking my opinions and advice on the matter of Loki's key.

"A thing like that can't be taken by force," she said. "Not without great risk."

"Well of course not—this is Snorri we're talking about . . ."

"More than that." She moved closer, lowering her voice to a delicious husk beside my ear. Memories of Aslaug stirred somewhere low down. "This is Loki's work. The trickster. The liar. The thief. Such a one would not let his work fall to the strongest."

"Well, to be fair, we weren't exactly gentle when we took it!" I puffed out my chest and tried to look nonchalant.

"The unborn captain attacked *you* though, Jalan. Snorri merely took the key from his ruin. It wasn't his purpose—he didn't attack the unborn for the key."

"Well . . . no."

"Trickery or theft. Those are the only two safe options." She held my gaze.

"If you think those are safe," I said, "you don't know Snorri."

At the same time that I felt my connection with Kara strengthening, she seemed more charmed each passing day by the annoyingly handsome Lord Hakon. Every night the bastard would demonstrate some new virtue, with consummate skill, and make it seem a natural revelation rather than showing off. One evening it would be his deep tenor, perfect pitch, and command of all the great songs of the north. The next it would be defeating everyone but Snorri, and some ogre of a man called Hurn, in an arm-wrestling contest that he had to be coaxed into joining. Another night he treated us to a great show of concern for a man of his who fell prey to sudden head pains—debating herb-lore with Kara as if he were an old-wife called to treat the invalid. And tonight Hakon prepared a venison stew for us which I choked down and forced myself to call "passable" whilst only iron will prevented me demanding a third helping . . . the best damn venison I ever ate.

For the duration of our penultimate night of escort Kara walked at the head of the column with Lord Hakon who came off his high horse to stroll beside her. The night proved warm, the going easy, nightingales serenaded us, and before long the pair of them were arm in arm, laughing and joking. I did my best to break up their little head to head of course, but there's a kind of cold shoulder that a couple can offer a fellow that's hard to get around, particularly with twenty mounted Danes staring at the back of your head.

On our final day we rose in the late afternoon, our camp a meadow beside a stream, the day warm and sunny, new blossom on the trees. Less than ten miles lay before us to the Gelleth border where Lord Hakon and his Danes would take their leave, and I was going to be heartily glad to see the back of them. Snorri and Tuttugu no doubt would happily have walked to Florence with the heathens, having spent the whole journey so far swapping battle tales. The Danes had a great love of sea stories and the old sagas. Snorri provided the former from personal experience and Kara the latter from her vast store of such trivia. I half thought some of the duke's men would volunteer to join the Undoreth and travel with the Vikings, such was the level of worship on display . . . Even Tuttugu got made out to be some kind of hero, beaching on the shores of the Drowned Isles one season, battling dead men on the Bitter Ice the next, making his last stand against the Hardassa by the Wheel of Osheim . . .

I yawned, stretched, yawned again. The Danes lay around the ashes of the morning's fire, horses tethered to stakes a little higher up the gentle slope, the trolls mostly hidden, sprawled in the long grass closer to the water. The day had been almost hot compared to those before it—a first touch of summer, albeit a pallid northern excuse for one.

An evening "breakfast" was prepared at leisurely pace, with nobody seeming in a hurry to depart. Tuttugu brought me over a bowl of porridge from the communal cauldron and a fellow named Argurh led his horse across from the herd for me to look at. That was the one thing the men of Maladon conceded I might know something about—horseflesh.

"Favouring his left he is, Jalan." The man manoeuvred his grey around me, bending to tap the suspect fetlock. I suppressed the urge to say "*Prince* Jalan." The further south we got the more the tolerance for such failings fell away from me. In the Three Axes I'd suffered the Norsemen's

"Jal"'s just as I'd suffered the winter, a natural phenomenon that nothing could be done about. But now . . . now we were closing on Red March and the summer had found us. Things would change.

"See? There, did it again," Argurh said. The horse took a half step.

From the corner of my eye I spotted Kara on the move, the bedroll she'd been given tucked under one arm, walking off into the long grass down toward the stream, wildflowers all about her, butterflies rising—

"And he's somewhat windy in his bowels." Argurh, in my face again, wittering on about his nag and closing off my view.

"Well." With a sigh I turned my attention to the horse—better to get a look before the light failed. "Walk him around over there. Let's see him move."

Argurh led him off. It looked as though the gelding might have a thorn just above the hoof or taken some knock that had left it tender. I motioned him back. I could sense the sun lowering behind me and needed to get the horse sorted before it set. Although Aslaug had not returned, and even the knocking had ceased, I always felt a hint of her presence as the sun fell and any animals around me became skittish.

"Hold him." I kneeled down to check the foot. From under the beast's belly I spied Hakon brushing himself down. He'd tied back his hair and washed his face. Highly suspicious in my view. When a man out in the wilds bothers to wash his face he's clearly up to something. I manipulated the joint, muttering the sort of nothings that calm a horse, fingers gentle. A moment later I found the end of the spine just below the skin. A scrape of my nail, a quick pinch and I had the thing out. A vicious thing, over an inch long and slick with blood.

"Let it bleed," I said, passing the thorn to Argurh. "Easy to miss. The problem's above the hoof often as not."

I stood quickly, ignoring his thanks, and moved away from the camp, crouching to shred a poppy through my fingers.

"Aslaug!" The sun hadn't touched the horizon yet but the sky lay crimson above the Gelleth hills rising to the west. "Aslaug!" I needed her then and there. "It's an emergency."

Kara hadn't just wandered off into the meadow with her bedding. Hakon wasn't just prettying himself up in case we met some Gelleth border guards, and the Danes weren't being painfully slow to get ready just out of laziness. If there's one thing I can't stand about licentious behaviour, it's when I'm not involved.

I glanced toward the west. The sun's torturous descent continued, with it now standing a fraction above the hills.

"What?" Not the word, not even a whisper of it, but faint unmistakable sound of inquiry, deep inside my ear.

"I need to stop Hakon . . ." I hesitated, not wanting to have to spell it out. The devil's supposed to know your mind, I always thought.

"Lies." So faint I might have imagined it.

"Yes, yes, you're the daughter of lies . . . what about them?"

"Lies." Aslaug's voice came on the very edge of hearing, the shadows reaching all around me. I wondered what had left her so mute and distant . . . It wasn't temper that kept her from me—she had been shut out somehow . . . "Lies." They have a saying in Trond—"lie as the light fails"—those lies were supposed to be the ones most likely to be believed.

"But what lie should I—"

"Look." The word seemed to take all her strength, fading into nothing at the end. For a moment it seemed the shadows flowed, coming together with a singular direction. A direction that led my eyes to a lone and stunted willow growing beside the stream some two hundred yards from where Kara had been headed. Though I could see no sign of her—the hussy would be lying out of sight . . .

"There's just trolls sleeping down there though." Hakon wasn't stupid and it would take more than stupid to go poking a troll.

No reply but I recalled not so long ago what Aslaug had said, crouching beside me, mouth beside my ear as the sun went through its death throes. "You would be surprised what I can weave from shadow." I wondered if she were planning to do some weaving tonight. Some trickery perhaps? She could want for no better canvas than the black hide of a troll . . . A sense of urgency stole over me. It seemed as if Aslaug had warmed to the task. It was, after all, a wicked one.

I lurched to my feet. Hakon was already on the move, passing by the outermost of his men, pausing to swap a joke. Heart hammering, I hurried to intercept him whilst doing my best not to look as though I were hurrying. That's pretty difficult. I don't think I pulled it off. I caught him just beyond the camp.

"Yes?" Hakon gave me a distant look. He'd never accused me of malice over the affair at the Three Axes, or indeed acknowledged that the incident ever took place, but I could tell he had suspicions. Even now, with Kara waiting for him, he didn't relax enough to gloat but regarded me with caution—once unbitten, twice shy, I guess.

"Just came to congratulate you, best man won and all that, spoils to the victor. She's waiting for you over yonder." I waved a hand toward the willow. As I spoke the words I felt Aslaug repeat them, wrapping the dark luxury of her voice about each syllable. It sounded as though she stood closer to him than I did—as though she whispered the last word into his ear.

For a moment Hakon just frowned. "You have very strange ideas about what is and what isn't a game, prince. And no human should be referred to as spoils." For a moment I worried he was going to hit me, but he stalked away toward the willow without sparing me another glance.

"A good night for walking!" Snorri hefted his pack. The Danes had purchased clothing, equipment and provisions for us in the last town we passed by. Using my money of course. "Across Gelleth and we'll be back in Rhone before you know it. Jal loves Rhone, Tutt, just loves it." Hennan looked up brightly from his bedding. "It's good there?"

"If ever a country needed stabbing, Rhone is it." I spat out a flying insect that decided to commit suicide in my mouth, possibly two, midges rising with the evening. Snorri seemed unaccountably cheerful. At least Tuttugu eyed me with a touch of sympathy.

"You're not worried for our völva's safety out there all alone with the night falling?" I poked at Snorri, wanting him to share my misery.

Snorri shot me a look under his brows. "She's hardly alone, Jal. And it's the things in the dark that should be scared of a völva, not the other way around."

Young Hennan watched us from beneath his blanket, still not having bothered to rise. He shifted his gaze as we spoke, as though he were weighing us up and deciding what path to choose.

Somewhere out in the gathering gloom a shriek pierced the evening calm.

"I rest my case!" I said, spreading my hands. Snorri was already past me, axe in fist, Tuttugu hurrying along in his wake. For my part I was less keen to follow. The night holds all manner of terrors—and besides, the scream came from the direction of the willow. Hennan made to follow but I stuck a leg out in his path. "Best not."

I have difficulty imagining the scene but all I can conclude is that Aslaug wove the shadow well. Very well indeed if she could make a reclining she-troll look like Kara's inviting silhouette. Quite in what manner Lord Hakon offended the she-troll was never made entirely clear but it seems his advances were sufficiently impertinent to occasion the troll's sticking of a sizeable willow branch into one of his orifices. Again the detail was never laid bare for us but suffice it to say that the escort ended in that meadow and Hakon was not riding when he left, but walking very carefully.

In the uproar immediately following the incident I took the opportunity to suggest to Gorgoth that he lead his people west rather than wait for the Danes' outrage to reach boiling point. Gorgoth took the advice and I went with them, thereby avoiding having to hear all the names Hakon might call me, and of course avoiding the effort of trying not to smirk while he did it.

SEVENTEEN

Snorri and the others caught us up on the side of some desolate Gelleth hill, moon-washed and covered with low scrub. Quite how they'd followed our trail in the dark I didn't know—I'd been expecting them to catch up by day. The old bond that used to bind the northman and me still gave a sense of discomfort and a gist of direction once we had a mile or two between us, but hardly enough to navigate through the night across treacherous country.

"You did that!" Snorri's first words to me.

"I did indeed get Gorgoth and his pungent friends out of a potentially violent confrontation, yes." Snorri opened his mouth again, wide enough this time to presage a shout, but I forestalled him with a lifted hand. "No need to thank me. The Red Queen raised the princes of her house to keep a cool head in a crisis."

"I just want to know how you did it!" Tuttugu pressed past Snorri, a hint of a grin in the thicket of his beard. "Poor Hakon didn't look like he'd be sitting in the saddle any time soon."

The sight of Kara's face in the orichalcum glow stopped the laugh in my throat. The funny side of the situation didn't appear to be pointing her way, and going by her murderous looks I'd be safer sleeping with the trolls.

Up at the head of the column Gorgoth issued some silent command and once more his subjects began to move. Grateful for the excuse, I turned my back on Kara and, after repositioning my pack, set off walking. I'd already petitioned Gorgoth to have a troll carry my gear, but he held some odd kind of reservation about the matter as if he thought it beneath a troll to carry the baggage of a prince of Red March. I guess that's the sort of madness that sets in when you spend your life living in a dark cave. In any event he finally excused them on the basis they were apt to eat my rations, and then the pack and my spare cloak.

I grumbled to Snorri about it but he just laughed. "Does a man good to carry his own weight in the world, Jal. It'll harden you up a bit too."

I shook my head. "Seems the concept of nobility ends north of Ancrath. That one," I nodded to the front of the column, "probably wouldn't bend the knee if they made a new emperor and brought him a-visiting. Reminds me of a beggar in Vermillion, Fussy Jack they called him, or at least Barras Jon used to call him that . . . anyhow, he'd hang out on Silk Street round the back of the opera house with his tin cup, showing off the stumps of his legs and shouting out for money at the honest folk passing by. Tossed him a coin or two myself. Probably. Barras told me he'd seen the man empty his cup on a cloth and clean each copper piece with a bit of felt, careful as all hell not to touch a single one of them until he'd wiped the stink off them. Barras said he tossed him a silver crown once, just to get him to catch it. Ol' Fussy Jack, he let it fall, picked it up with his cloth and wiped it clean. Silver from the son of the Vyene ambassador just wasn't good enough for him."

Snorri shrugged. "They say all money's dirty, one way or another. Seems this Jack might have had it right. We'll find out for ourselves soon enough, headed for Florence."

"Hmmm." I decided to cover the fact I was going no further than Vermillion with a non-committal noise.

"All the money of Empire flows into Florence, sits a while in the vaults of some or other Florentine banker, then flows out again. I've never quite fathomed the reason why, but if money is dirty then Florence must be the most filthy corner of the Broken Empire."

I considered educating Snorri on the finer points of banking, then realized I didn't have a clue what they were, even though I'd spent a desperately dire year studying at the Mathema in Hamada—another torture heaped upon all the princes of Red March by the ruthless old witch who claims to be our grandmother.

And so we trudged on. The trolls might not have missed the Danes and their torches, and I didn't much miss the Danes, but I did like it better when I could see where I was going. Kara gave the orichalcum to Snorri so we wouldn't break our ankles, but even in his hands the light made little impression on the dark and empty spaces around us.

After many miles wending our way through wooded uplands, around villages with their barking dogs and hedgerows, and down through tangled valleys, we stopped in the predawn grey to settle ourselves in an isolated dell.

I went across to Kara to make some pleasantry but astonishingly she still seemed to be holding a grudge, turning on me so sharply I took a pace back.

"And what *did* you do to Hakon?" she demanded. Just like that, no circling around the subject, no insinuations. Most unsettling.

"Me?" I tried for injured innocence.

"You! He said you'd told him where I was."

"You didn't want him to know?" A little bitterness might have slipped into that one.

I should have stepped back two paces. The retort of her hand striking my cheek set a dozen trolls hissing at the night, taloned hands raised to strike. "Ah." I touched fingers to my stinging face and tasted blood.

Discretion is the better part of . . . something. In any event I took myself out of arm's reach and spread my bedroll down on the far side of camp, muttering something about the anti-witch laws I'd be passing when I became king. I set myself down and stared angrily at the sky, not even taking a moment to be thankful that it wasn't raining. I lay there with the copper taste of blood in my mouth and thought it would be a long time before sleep found me. I was wrong. It dragged me down in moments.

Sleep pulled me down and I kept falling, into a dream with no bottom to it. I fell through the stuff of imagination and into the empty spaces we all keep within us. On the very edge of some larger void I managed to catch hold of something—I caught hold of the idea that a terrible thing waited for me at the base of this endless drop and that I might yet escape it. I clung to the idea, dangling from it by a single hand. And then I remembered the needle, Kara's needle driven through my palm, and the blood glistening along its length. I remembered the taste of it as they had set the needle to my tongue and the völva's spell wrapped me, that taste filled my mouth again. The pain of the old wound stabbed through my palm once more, fresh as the moment it first came, and with a despairing yell I lost my grip and fell again into memories—and this time they were my own.

"We'll get Fuella to put some salve on that cut." A woman's voice—my mother's.

I taste blood. My blood. My mouth still stings from where Martus's forehead struck me. Martus makes no concessions to my age in our play-fights. At eleven he would happily flatten me or any other seven-year-old and declare it a great victory. My middle brother, Darin, is only nine but has a touch more grace and merely overpowers me, or uses me as a distraction while he creeps up on our eldest brother.

"I've told you not to get involved in their battles, Jally, they're too rough." My hand in hers as she leads me along the Long Gallery, the backbone of Roma Hall.

"Oh," she says, and tugs me, changing course, back along the gallery.

I struggle to free myself from the boy's concerns, the sting of his swollen lip, the fury at Martus for heaping yet another defeat on him, the hot certainty that in the next battle he will give better than he gets.

It takes an effort to untangle my thoughts from the boy's but doing so offers considerable relief. I wonder for a moment if I've fallen into some other child's mind for nothing here is familiar or comfortable: he's got no caution in him, this one, no fear, no guile. Just a raw sense of injustice and a fierce hunger to throw himself back into the fray. Not me at all. This boy could grow into Snorri!

Mother turns from the gallery, leading me along the west corridor. The Roma Hall, our home within the compound of the Crimson Palace, seems unchanged by the passage of years that have redesigned me root and stem.

I wipe my mouth, or rather the boy wipes his, and his hand comes away bloody. The action is none of mine—I share his vision and his pain but have no say in what course he takes. This seems reasonable, if not fair, for these things are happening fifteen years ago, and technically I have already exercised my will in the matter.

In fact, as events unfold before me I remember them. For the first time in an age I properly remember the long dark sweep of my mother's hair, the feel of her hand around mine, and what that feeling meant to me at age seven . . . what an unbreakable bond of trust it was, my small hand in her larger one, an anchor in a sea of confusion and surprise.

We think that we don't grow. But that's because growth happens so slowly that it's invisible to us. I've heard old men say they feel twenty inside, or that the boy who once ran wild, and with the recklessness of youth, still lives within them, bound only by the constraints of old bones and expectation. But when you've shared the skull of your child self you know this to be untrue—a romance, a self-deception. The child carrying my name around Vermillion's palace sees the world through the same eyes as me, but notices different things, picks up on different opportunities, and reaches his own conclusions. We share little, this Jalan Kendeth and me, we're separated by more than a gulf of years. He lives more fully, unburdened by experience, not yet crippled by cynicism. His world is larger than mine, though he has barely left the palace walls and I've trekked to the ends of the earth.

We turn off the west corridor, passing a suit of armour that reminds me of the battle for Ameroth Keep, and reminds Jally of a stag beetle he found two days ago behind the messenger stables.

"Where are we going?" The boy's mind had been so caught up with the fight—with Martus's forehead swinging down into his face . . . my face . . . that he hasn't noticed until now that we aren't heading toward the nursery and Fuella with her salve at all.

"To the palace, Jally. That will be nice won't it?" Her voice holds a brittle tone, the cheerfulness forced past something so awkward that even a child couldn't fail to see through it.

"Why?"

"Your grandmother asked us to visit."

"Me too?" His first pang of anxiety at that, a cold finger of fear along the spine.

"Yes."

I hadn't heard my grandmother ask. The boy, whose thoughts I experience as a torrent of childish whispers playing behind my own narrative, thinks that maybe grown-ups have better ears than children and that when he's grown he too may be able to hear his grandmother's call across acres of palace compound, past a score of doors and through as many high walls. My own thoughts turn to the first moment of this dream, that "oh," the tug of Mother's hand, the sudden retreading of our steps. Had she in that instant remembered that the Queen of Red March wished to see her? That's not the kind of fact a person misplaces. I wonder if instead she hadn't heard a silent call of the type adults do not in general notice? I know my grandmother has a sister who likely can issue such summonses, but even so it probably requires a certain kind of person to hear them.

We are let out through the main doors of Roma Hall by the doormen, Raplo and Alphons. Raplo gives me a wink as I pass. I remember it now, clear and crystal, the wrinkling of his skin around the wink of that green eye. He died five years later—choked on a partridge bone, they said. A silly way for an old man to end a long life.

In the courtyard the sun dazzles on pale paving slabs, the heat enfolding—a Red March summer, golden and endless. I listen to the whirr of the boy's thoughts, struck by how at odds his desires for the season are to mine. He sees exploration, battle, discovery, mischief. My vision is of indolence, dozing beneath the olive trees, drinking watered wine and waiting for the night. Waiting to scatter my silver across the hot dark streets of Vermillion, spilling from one pool of light and decadence to the next. Fight-pits, bordellos, card halls, and any social gathering that will have me, so long as the hosts are of sufficiently high rank, and the noble ladies broad-minded.

We walk across the plaza beneath the watchful gaze of sentries on the walls of the Marsail keep. Guards look down from the turrets of Milano House too, the stone pavilion where the heir sits among his luxuries, waiting for Grandmother to die. Uncle Hertet rarely leaves Milano House, and when he does the sun paints him as old as the Red Queen, and less hale.

Heat suffuses the boy and I bathe in it, remembering what it's like to be truly warm. My hand grows sweaty within Mother's grasp, but neither the boy nor I wish to let go. She's new to me again, this lost mother of mine with her skin the colour of tea and her talent for hearing silent voices. I may be older, changed by the years into something very different from the boy trailing in her wake—but I have no intention of letting go.

Jally's thinking of the blind-eye woman and that touch of hers which stole his senses and left him dark for so long. The fear she puts in him is like pollution in a clear spring. It's wrong and it makes me angry, an unconflicted rage of a kind I've not felt in a long time—perhaps since I last knew my mother's hand was there for the taking. The shadow of the Inner Palace falls across us and I realize that I've lost all recollection of this visit that now unfolds before me. The story I've told myself so often is that after presentation to the Red Queen at the age of five it wasn't until the age of thirteen that I came before her again, a formal introduction at the Saturnalia feast with my brothers and cousins whispering at the margins of the great hall, Martus seeking takers for his bet that I would faint again.

We pass the looming facade of the Inner Palace and keep going.

"Grandmother lives in *there* . . ." Jally points back to the golden portals of the Red Queen's palace.

"We're seeing her in the Julian Palace."

The building in question rises before us across the broad square dedicated to our nation's many victories. The Poor Palace everyone calls it. A foolish number of years ago it was the seat of kings, then some name I've forgotten decided it wasn't good enough for him and built a better roof over his throne. So now it houses impoverished aristocrats who've thrown themselves upon the Red Queen's mercy. Lords who've fallen on hard times and are too old or too inbred to mend their fortunes, generals who've grown ancient while putting young men in the ground, even a duke ruined by gambling debts—a cautionary tale to be sure.

We climb the steps to the great doors, Mother waiting patiently as Jally labours up them, his legs—my legs—a touch too short to take them in his stride, though mostly it's reluctance that holds him back. The doors themselves tower into the shadowed heights beneath the portico, huge slabs of rosewood depicting, in inlaid brass, the long march of our people from the east to claim the promised lands as the shadows of a thousand suns retreated. The red march that gave our kingdom its name.

Two guards, half-plate gleaming, elaborate poleaxes held to the side, blades skyward, affect not to notice us, though Mother has married a son of the queen. They're Grandmother's personal guard, loath to show deference to anyone but her. They're also a sign that she might truly be waiting for us in the Poor Palace.

The left door opens on noiseless hinges as we approach, just wide enough for us to slip within, a grudging acknowledgment of our right to enter. Inside we pause, sun-blind in the comparative gloom of the reception hall. As my vision clears I see at the far end of the foyer an old man, bent by age but very tall. He shambles toward us from the bank of votive candles by the opposite wall. His tunic is mis-tied and grey from too many washes, the stubble of his beard white against dark red skin. He seems uncertain.

"Come away, Ullamere." A young woman, a nurse maybe, comes from the far doorway and steers the ancient out of sight. As he turns a pale scar is revealed, so broad I can see it even at this distance, running from the bridge of his nose past the corner of his mouth.

Mother turns from the aisle of marble columns, from the mosaiced splendour of the floor, and takes a small, unguarded arch leading onto a tight spiral of steps. Winding our way up the stairs makes me dizzy. Jally counts them to keep his fear at bay, but the Silent Sister's colourless face keeps surfacing between the numbers. I hate her on his account with an intensity I've never quite managed on my own.

"A hundred and seven!" And we're there, a small landing, a heavy oak door, a narrow window showing only sky. I know it for the tower room atop the western spire, one of two rising spear-like above the entrance to the Poor Palace. This is deduction rather than experience for I've never climbed these steps—or at least I had thought that I hadn't until this moment of recollection.

"Wait here, Jalan." Mother directs me to one of the two high-backed chairs to the side of the entrance. I clamber into the seat, too nervous to complain, and the door opens. Just like the grand portals this door opens narrowly—few doors it seems are flung wide in royal circles—this one reveals the angular features of Nanna Willow. Mother slips through and the old woman closes the door behind her, shooting me a hard look through the thinning gap. *Clunk*—and I'm alone on the landing.

I say the boy and I share nothing save a name . . . but he's off that chair and crouched with his ear to the door fast enough. I would perhaps have been slower, more scared of being caught, but I'd have listened even so!

"—why make me bring Jalan? You know how badly he reacted when—"

"That was . . . unfortunate. But he must be tested again." An old voice, deeper, and more stern even than Nanna Willow's but still a woman's. My grandmother then.

"Why?" Mother asks. A pause, perhaps remembering herself. "Why must he be, your highness?"

"I didn't have you brought all the way from the Indus to question me, Nia. I bartered dynasties with your cantankerous raja to make a match for my fool of a son in the hope that if I bred eastern wolf with Red March ass the promise of my line might out once more in a third generation."

"But you tested him, your highness. He doesn't have what you hoped for. He's a sensitive boy and it took so long for him to recover . . . Is it really necessary for him—"

"The Lady Blue has thought him important enough to send assassins after. Perhaps she has seen in her crystals and mirrors something that my sister missed in her own examination."

"Assassins?"

"Three so far, two this month. My sister saw them coming, and they were stopped. Not without cost though. The Lady Blue has dangerous individuals in her employ."

"But—"

"This is the long game, Nia. The future burns and those who might save us are children or have yet to be born. In many futures the Ancraths are the key. Either the emperor comes from their line or finds his throne because of the deeds of that house. They carry change with them, these Ancraths, and change is needed. The future-sworn agree that two Ancraths are required—working together. The rest is harder to see."

"I know nothing of Ancrath. And my son isn't some piece to move on your gaming board!" Mother's anger surfaces now. If the Red Queen scares her she isn't letting it show. She is the daughter of a king. At night she sings me old songs from her homeland, of marble palaces set with jewels, where peacocks strut and beyond the gates lie tigers and spice. "Jalan is not your toy, any more than I'm some broodmare you bought at market. My father is—"

"That's exactly what you are, my dear. Your royal father sold you west. Raja Varma took my rubies and silver rather than pay your weight in gold as dowry to some local satrap in order that he might overlook the taint in you that I so value. And I paid the price because in many futures your child stands at the right hand of the emperor, laying waste his enemies and restoring him to the throne."

"You—" I take my ear from the door and the thickness of timber reduces the rest to angry but indistinct denial. Some cold dread pulls me from my eavesdropping. Now it turns me toward the archway and the stairs beyond, just as if a hand had settled upon my neck and steered me, icy fingered.

She stands upon the topmost step, bone-thin, bone-white, the dead skin around her mouth wrinkled into some awful smile. I can't tell what colour her eyes might be, only that one is blind and the other a drowning pool. The sun splashes across the floor, the wall, the chairs, but the archway where she stands is so deep in shadow she might almost be a trick of the light.

I run. In this we are in accord, the boy and I. One swift kick sends the chair skittering across the flagstones. I chase it and when it stops I'm up and climbing, fear boosting me so that I gain the seat in one stride, the back in the next, and as it topples I launch toward the window. I've not been in the west spire before but I've been in the east. The young Jalan assumes they are the same. I pray it.

I've learned to fear a lot of things as I grew. Most things perhaps. Heights though, they still thrill me. I hang on to the stonework as I swing through the window, feet searching for the ledge that should be down and to the left. The boy doesn't look to check but slides lower, letting the window's edge slip through his hands. He lets go and a moment later his boots find purchase. We stand flattened to the outer wall, the windowsill above our head, arms wide to embrace the stones, a three-inch ledge supporting us.

By degrees I circle round to the gargoyle, twin to the ugly demon that watches the realm from the side of the east spire, just below the highest window. There are a series of such demons set in a descending spiral on both spires, all of the same design but as individual as people, each with its twin in the corresponding spot on the other spire. I know their faces better than I know those of my small tribe of cousins. My fingers tremble but it's the fear of the blind-eye woman that puts the tremor there rather than of the fall beneath me.

I drop from ledge to gargoyle, slide around horns and barbs to reach the supporting ledge, circle to the next, drop again. This is how I discovered the old man in the tower—only then I was climbing upward, and nearly a year younger. It's a wonder I didn't die.

Great-uncle Garyus lives, or is kept, in the east spire. When I first climbed there I was too young to understand the danger. And besides, the spires were made for climbing. There can be few towers in the empire with so many handholds, so much ornamentation placed at convenient intervals. It had seemed like an invitation. And even at an early age escape obsessed me. If the guards and nurses at the Roma Hall took their eye off me for more than a second I was off, running, hiding, climbing, learning all the ways out, all the ways in. Any high window drew me. Except the one in the west spire—that always looked like a devouring mouth, just waiting for me to clamber in.

I reach the palace roof and scamper up the tiled slope, over the serrations of the crest, and down toward the east spire. The dark slates are burning hot, scorching my hands. I try to keep my arms and legs clear, sliding on my arse, feeling the heat even through my trousers. Sweat-slick palms lose traction on the slate. I slide faster with nothing to grip, jolting my spine. A misjudged effort to slow myself turns me sideways and in a heartbeat I'm tumbling, rolling down the roof toward the drop. Arms flail, the world blurs, I'm screaming.

Thump. Something hard stopped my tumble, taking away in one painful crunch all the momentum the slope thrust upon me. The impact wrapped me around the immovable object that arrested my fall, and I lay there moaning. Somehow I'd become entangled in an old blanket—a damp old blanket—and it seemed to be raining.

"Jal!" A man shouting.

"Jal!" Another man, closer.

I moaned a little louder, though not much. My lungs had yet to refill after being so rudely emptied of air. Seconds later hands found me, pulling the wrappings from around my head. I found myself staring up at Snorri's face, framed by dripping black hair, with trees rising on all sides, terrifyingly tall and stark against a grey sky that seemed too bright.

"Whu," I managed. It seemed sufficient to convey my feelings.

"The trolls dropped you." Tuttugu, head thrusting into view, obscuring the sky, wet ginger hair dripping around a concerned expression. "Luckily you hit a tree."

I puzzled this new definition of "lucky."

"Did I fall off the roof?" I still wasn't really following the conversation. Tuttugu looked confused. "You've lost weight," I told him. Perhaps not relevant to the situation, but it was certainly true that the road's hardships had stripped a few pounds from the man.

The Vikings exchanged a glance. "Let's get him back up," Snorri said.

With a distinct lack of tenderness they unwrapped me from the tree. A tall conifer with sparse branches—others like it dotted the slope. Snorri hefted me to my feet, gasping as he straightened, as if it pained him. He looped my arm over his shoulder and helped me up toward a ridge maybe fifty feet above us. The troll column stood there, black and watching, Gorgoth at the front, Kara to the rear where Snorri angled me. It looked to be late evening with the shadows thickening toward night. Hennan watched from the back of a troll as we drew close. It seemed they had taken to passing him about their number. It hadn't struck me before that although there were both he-trolls and she-trolls in our merry band they hadn't a child amongst them.

The cold rain started to clear my head and I remembered the slap Kara had given me. By the time we reached her I felt exhausted. "What happened?" I asked, aiming the question at anyone listening.

"Hit a bump and you tumbled out." Tuttugu gestured toward what appeared to be a crude travois laid down on the trail.

"Can't see a bump myself," Snorri said. "Trolls dragged you for four days. Probably thought they could tip you out and nobody would notice."

Kara stepped closer and started to squeeze bits of me through my tunic. They all hurt. "You're fine," she said, looking slightly apologetic. She wiped at some graze on my cheek with a piece of cloth smelling of lemons.

"Ouch!" I tried to push her hand away but she proved persistent. "I was dreaming again . . . What the hell kind of spell did you put on me, völva?"

Kara frowned and put her cloth away, stuffing it into a little leather pouch. "It's a simple enough working. I've never seen it have this much effect on someone. I . . . I don't know." Her frown deepened and she shook her head. "I guess the Silent Sister had her reasons for choosing you as Snorri's partner to hold her magic. You must have an affinity for it, or a susceptibility. I could test you tonight . . ."

"You can keep that orichalcum stuff away from me is what you can do." I flomped down on the heap of bracken covering the network of bark strips that joined the travois poles. "I've had enough of witches. North, south, young, old, I don't care. I'm swearing off them." I put my head back, spitting out the rain. "Let's go!" I saw the smallest smile twitch across Kara's lips at that, in defiance of her will, and to my surprise the trolls bent to their task, dragging me along as the whole column resumed its trek.

For a few minutes I lay with eyes closed, struggling to recapture the dream. The word "assassin" had been in the air, perhaps the key took that memory from me and unlocked a might-have-been, perhaps Taproot's condolences for my mother had been balanced on rumours of the three visiting murderers that the Red Queen buried. Dreams though, like sleep, are elusive when you're hunting them, and sneak upon you when you're not. After a while the rain splattering my face became irksome and I sat up, wiping my face.

"Four days?" I looked from Snorri to Tuttugu, tramping along behind the trolls. "How come I didn't soil my—" Glancing down I discovered I wasn't wearing my old trousers but instead some sort of rough kilt. "Oh."

"Hungry?" Snorri fished out some strips of dried meat and held them toward me.

I rubbed my stomach. "Not for that." But I took them anyway and started to chew, discovering within moments that "hungry" was too small a word to cover it. It takes a lot of chewing to get through dried meat, so that kept me busy for a while. I call it meat rather than beef or pork or venison, because once it's been adulterated against decay it's really not possible to say what animal died to put it in your hand. Probably a donkey. The taste is similar to leather, of the kind that's been worn as a shoe for several hot weeks. The texture is too. "Any more?"

"So where are we?"

I'd feigned weakness all night and planned to carry on doing so as long as the trolls would drag me. The travois was hardly a royal carriage but it beat walking. Now though as dawn broke, and the trolls spread out through the forest to hunt, and Snorri hung an oiled cloth between the branches to keep off the worst of the weather, I started to take more of an interest in proceedings.

"Central Gelleth." Kara squatted down beside me. Tuttugu was sitting on a log nearby, tending a small fire above which a cauldron of stew simmered, hanging from an iron tripod. "According to Gorgoth you can plot a path from one side of the country to the other that never leaves the forests. A good thing too. The land's in uproar, marauding army units everywhere, levies summoned by a dozen nobles all battling away. There's been some kind of disaster around Mount Honas—they say the duke's dead and all his armies burned . . ."

"Mount Honas?" I'd never heard of it. But I knew the duke was a relative of mine, albeit distant. "Burned, you say? Damn fool of him to go poking around a volcano!"

"It's not a volcano. His castle was built on it. Some kind of ancient weapon blew the mountain apart. Huge areas of forest to the north have been incinerated and miles beyond that trees are dying. While you were sleeping we spent two days walking through dead trees. Gorgoth said it's Jorg Ancrath's work."

"Christ." I remembered when Queen Sareth set me up to challenge the little bastard to a duel. Only he wasn't so little after all, a six-foot stone-cold murderer, fourteen going on forty. "How long until we reach Rhone?"

"Less than a week. The town of Deedorf's just ten miles off. We're making good progress."

"Mmm." In truth I wasn't that interested in where we were, what really concerned me was how far we had to go to reach civilization. One wet forest was very much like the next, be it haunted by Thurtan peasants hunting truffles, Gelleth charcoal men, Rhone loggers, or the charmingly rustic Red March foresters. They could all go hang as far as I was concerned. "This curse you put on me—"

"This enchantment you begged me to work," interrupted Kara. "Yes. What about it?"

"I was close. Very close. Just before those trolls tried to kill me . . ." I lowered my voice and became serious. "I dreamed of things I didn't remember, but now I do. And I got close to the day she died. The summer when I turned eight. I might even have been dreaming of the actual day." I took Kara's hand, she flinched but let me hold her. "How do I get back to it? I need to finish this." I can't deny that the thought that I might sleep my way across the whole of Gelleth had occurred. Even better, I might then slumber another two weeks as Snorri and Tuttugu dragged me south through Rhone, and not wake until the Norsemen delivered me to the gates of Vermillion. With luck I might pass the entire excursion off as a nightmare and never think of it again. But those hopes aside—the desire to know the truth about my mother's death drove me, the need to lay to rest the lies Loki's key had infected me with. The thing had set a curse upon me and I would know no peace until the itch had been scratched—the boil lanced.

Kara bit her lip, vertical furrows appearing between her eyebrows. It made her look much younger. "Blood is the trigger."

I lifted a hand to ward her off. "You don't have to hit me again!"

"Bite your tongue."

"What?"

"Bite your tongue."

I tried but it's not easy to deliberately hurt yourself. "I canth geth any bluth," I told her, tongue trapped painfully between my teeth.

"Bite it!" Kara shook her head, despairing of me. Without warning she reached up and knocked my chin.

"Jesu that hurt!" I had a hand to my mouth, fingers reaching in to check my tongue was still attached. They came away scarlet and I could do nothing but stare at them, the colour filling my vision and my mind.

For a moment I don't know where I am or why my mouth aches. I crashed into the eastern spire feet first and everything went grey. My mouth hurts and when I take my hand from it crimson drips from my fingers. I must have bitten my tongue in the impact—an ungentle arrival but a kinder greeting than I would have got from the ground had I gone over the edge of the roof.

The need to get away from the blind-eye woman proves more pressing than the need to moan and groan, so I wipe my hands off and get to my feet. Sweaty, tired, and too hot I begin the climb to Garyus's window. In later years I often took the stairs, particularly if the weather proved inclement. But even in the months before I left the city with Snorri, when I found time between rising in the afternoon and setting out into Vermillion with my band of reprobates in search of sin, I'd scale the spire once in a while. Old habits are hard to break and in any event I like to keep my hand in. When a lady invites you from her bedroom window it's good to know how to climb.

Arms trembling with fatigue, tunic sweat-soaked and torn, I haul myself through the window to Garyus's landing. Sometimes an attendant waits there but today it lies deserted, the door to his chamber standing ajar. My ungainly collapse through the window has not gone without notice. I hear Garyus's cough and then,

"A young prince or an incompetent assassin? Best show yourself in either way." Words from a thick tongue, hard to understand at first but I've learned the knack.

I step in through the narrow gap, nose wrinkling at the faint stink. There's always an air of bedpans here though the breeze thins it. Over the years I came to understand it as more honest than the perfumes of court. Lies smell sweet—the truth often stinks.

Garyus is propped up in his bed, lit by sunlight through a small high window, a jug and goblet on the table beside him. He turns his misshapen head toward me. It looks as if it were pumped too full of brains, his skull a tuberous root vegetable, swelling above his brow, thin hair seeking purchase on shiny slopes.

"Why Prince Jalan!" He fakes surprise. Garyus has never once objected to me climbing his tower, though juggling scorpions would be a safer pastime. I think perhaps a man who has never walked, never held control over his own ups and downs, doesn't understand the danger of the fall in the same visceral way that grips any watcher seeing another hanging by fingertips.

"I'm running away," Jally announces.

Garyus raises a brow at that. "I'm afraid you've come to a dead end, my prince."

"The Red Queen is after me," Jally says, glancing back at the doorway. He half expects to see the dead white face of blind-eye woman peering through the gap.

"Hmmm." Garyus struggles a little further up his pillows, arms too thin and too twisted to make the job easy. "A subject shouldn't run from his queen, Jalan." He regards me for a moment, eyes wide and watery, each iris a deep and calming brown. He fixes me with a shrewd look, as if he's seen past the child to the man lurking inside. "And perhaps you do too much running away? Hey now?"

"She made Mother bring me to the other tower. The one where the witch lives. Said she was going to let her touch me again." Jally shudders and I flinch inside him—we both remember the Sister's hand settling upon ours. Paper and bones.

A frown, upon the deformity of Garyus's forehead, quick then gone. The smile returns to his lips. "I'm honoured that you should seek sanctuary with me, my prince, but I'm just an old man, bound to his bed in the Poor Palace. I've no say in the doings of the queen or of witches in towers . . ."

Jally opens his mouth and finds no suitable words. Somehow, deep down, his opinion and expectations of the man before him are totally at odds with the facts clearly on display. In the years that follow this, although I call on Garyus most months, that faith in him erodes into pity, until by the time I reach twenty I consider my visits a kindness, some secret duty that a last shred of decency binds me to. By the end it was the act of visiting that made me feel better about myself. At the start it was Garyus himself. Somewhere along the way I stopped listening to what he said and started listening to my pride. Even so, it was only ever in his presence, as now, that I saw myself unfiltered by self-deception. As I grew older the effect wore off more quickly, so that at the end any epiphany would have faded to vague discomfort before I'd made it back across the plaza to the Roma Hall. Even so, perhaps it was those moments of clarity, more than anything, that kept drawing me there.

"You should go back, Prince Jalan. The queen may be a scary old lady but she won't allow harm to come to her grandson, will she now? And the Silent Sister . . . well, neither of us please the eye, so don't judge our hearts by our hide. She sees too much and perhaps it twists her way of understanding what you and I see, but there's a purpose to her, and—"

"Is she good?" Jally asks. I've felt the question building behind his lips. He knows she isn't and wants to hear if Garyus will lie.

"Well, don't children ask the most complicated questions?" Lips wetted with a thick tongue. "She's better than the alternative. Does that make sense? The word 'good' is like the word 'big.' Is a rock big? Who knows. Is *this particular* rock big? Ask the ant, ask the whale, both have different answers, both are right."

"Is Grandmother good?" A whisper. Jally is too young for these answers. He listens to the tone of Garyus's voice, watches his eyes.

"Your grandmother is fighting a war, Jalan. She's been fighting it all her life."

"Who against?" Jally's noticed no war. He watches the soldiers drill and march, parade on high days and holy days. He knows Scorron is the enemy but we don't fight them any more . . .

"A thousand years ago the Builders put a slope under us all, Jalan." A woman's voice behind me, old but strong. "The world's sliding toward a fall. Some of us have been enjoying the ride too much to worry about that drop, or they think there will be something for them at the bottom of it. Others want to undo the deed that set us sliding in the first place. That's the war."

For a moment I think of that hot roof slipping beneath me, the desperate scrabbling at the tiles as the edge rushed toward me, the relief when I managed to steer into the east spire. Had she seen all that? I don't want to ask if she plans for us all to fall.

I make a slow turn. The Red Queen fills the doorway, her gown a deep crimson, bone spars rising above her shoulders to spread a fan of the material behind her. A necklace of jet sets stark black shapes across her chest, diamonds and rectangles. She looks old, but tough, like a rock that has weathered countless storms. There's no kindness in her eyes. I can see Mother behind her, winded by the stairs, tiny in comparison, and Nanna Willow with her.

"Come, Jalan." My grandmother beckons me, turning to leave. She doesn't offer her hand.

"Use a lighter touch," Garyus says. He coughs, thick with phlegm, tries to rise, then flails an arm at a shelf on the wall opposite. "The copper box."

Grandmother steps into the room. "It's a crude measure at best."

I stand gaping, amazed that the Red Queen would let an old cripple in the Poor Palace address her so.

"It says enough to tell you if the boy needs closer inspection." Garyus waves at the shelf again.

Grandmother gives a curt nod and Nanna Willow hurries to the box.

It's small, only just big enough to fit my fist in, no lock or latch, embossed with thorn patterns.

"Only what's inside," Garyus directs.

Nanna Willow opens it—*schnick*—it makes a satisfying sound as the lid comes free. She stands without motion for a moment, her back to us, and when she turns her eyes are bright, almost as if she were on the edge of tears, perhaps struck by some old memory at once both bitter and sweet. In her hands the box is open and a glow escapes, visible as her body casts it into shadow.

"The blinds, if you wouldn't mind." Garyus looks toward my mother who seems more surprised than the queen at being set tasks by this stranger, but after a moment's hesitation she goes to use the long stick beside the shelf to draw the cloth across the high window. The room is plunged into a half-light. Nanna Willow tips the contents of the box into her hand, closes the lid, and replaces it on the shelf. In her palm is some piece of shaped silver, a solid cone with little runes incised around it. The whole thing glows like a coal from the fire but with a whiter light, and the runes burn.

"If you could let your son hold the orichalcum, Princess Nia," Garyus asks. In the shifting glow of the metal cone his face becomes something monstrous, but no worse than the gargoyles that supported me in my climb.

Mother takes the orichalcum from Nanna Willow's hand and immediately the glow becomes brighter, more white, though shifting as if waves were rippling through it. She holds it at arm's length as if it might explode and brings it to me, passing Garyus in his bed. The glow becomes momentarily stronger still as she nears him. Grandmother steps back when Mother approaches us.

"Here, Jally. It won't hurt you." Mother holds the cone out to me, her thumb on the base, the point against her forefinger. I'm not convinced. The way she keeps it from her body suggests it might bite.

I take it despite my misgivings, and as I do the thing ignites, too bright to look at. I turn my head away, almost dropping the cone, and in my effort not to look I stab myself with the sharp end behind the knuckle. Keeping my gaze averted I now see the cone's illumination as light and shadow on the walls. When Nanna Willow held it the glow was a steady thing but now it's as if I hold a hooded lantern spinning on a cord, sweeping a beam of brilliance across the walls, throwing first the queen's face into sharp relief, then Mother's, leaving Grandmother in darkness.

"Set it on the table, Jalan," Garyus says. "On this plate." And so I do.

The light dies from it immediately, leaving only a faint glow, and the runes still burning bright as if carved through onto some hot place where the sun dazzles on desert sands.

"Unstable." Grandmother steps closer, bending in to see. Despite their interest both she and Garyus are careful not to touch the orichalcum. "Conflicted."

Unbidden, Nanna Willow comes to turn the plate, rotating the orichalcum so the queen can see all the runes, seven in total.

"Brave. Cowardly. Generous. Selfish. It's almost as if he were two people . . ." Grandmother shakes her head, turning to look at me as if I were some unsatisfactory meal set before her.

"His character is not the issue," Garyus tells her. "Jalan lacks the stability needed for training, and yes he's strong, but to fill the role my sister saw for Nia's child would require an extraordinary talent, something that might be pitted against the likes of Corion, or Sageous, Kelem or Skilfar. The Blue Lady is simply misled. Perhaps she has lost too many reflections and her mind has broken."

Mother comes and sets her hand to my hair, a brief touch as she takes the cone and returns it to the box on the shelf.

"Perhaps you're right." A low rumble from the Red Queen that sounds more like a threat than an admission. "Take the boy, Nia. Keep close guard on him though."

And as easily as that we're dismissed.

"What's an assassin?" Jally asks before reaching the stairs.

For a moment I glimpsed branches, lattice-worked across a bright sky, sliding past. A sense of bodies moving around me, a face leaning in, indistinct.

● ● ◆

"Bite your tongue."

I look up from the crimson carpet. "Sorry, Mama."

"Queen Alica is your sovereign and you must never speak ill of her,
Jally." Mother kneels to be on a level with me.

"She's mean," I say. Or rather, I said it fifteen years ago and now I
remember the moment, the feeling of the word, my mother still above
me though kneeling, disapproval painted on her face, trying not to smile.

"Sometimes a queen has to be . . . hard, Jally. Ruling a land is difficult.
The gods know I have a trouble enough getting three young boys through
each day." *The gods.* Sometimes Mother forgets herself. Father says there
is only one God, but then that's his job. Grandmother must have staked
a lot by the bloodlines to match her cardinal to a heathen, converted from
her many gods, glorious in their variety of form and virtue, to our singular
invisible deity. How much did that dispensation from Roma cost the
treasury I wonder? Father may have a cathedral and a fat book full of
God's own wisdom, but Jally likes Mother's stories better, told in a soft
voice by his bedside. She places a kiss on my forehead and stands again.

We're back in the Roma Hall, in one of the galleries on the first floor.
The north gallery, by the slant of the sun through its tall windows. These
have glass, dozens of small panes of Attar glass leaded together, each with
a faint green hue. When I was very young I called it the Green Sky Room.

"What's wrong with your hand, Mama?" She's standing with her right
hand in her own shadow and it looks wrong . . . a touch too bright. She
looks down and quickly folds her arms, a guilty motion. Jally stares up
at her and I watch. She's the same woman that I see in my locket. Not
much more than thirty and seeming younger, long dark hair, dark eyes,
beautiful. The picture I have is by a very skilled artist but somehow it
doesn't capture her. It's only when these memories flow through me that
I remember how far she travelled to be my mother, how alone she must
have felt in a strange land. Grandmother may have picked Mother for
her blood but whatever heritage she carried in her veins it made little

impact on my appearance or that of my brothers. She may have darkened the gold of our hair but to look at us there's nothing of the Indus to see. The blond comes from Gabron, Grandmother's third husband, or from her father or grandfather, Gholloths one and two, passed down to our father—though he hides it beneath a cardinal's hat often as not, along with his bald spot—and on down to us. "Your hand looks . . . different."

"Nothing's wrong with it, Jally. Let's get you back to Nanna Odette."

Where her fingers can be glimpsed behind the other arm I can see the glow, more pronounced now.

"Stealing is bad," Jally says. I suppose it's true—though I wouldn't let it stop me—but I can't see the relevance.

"It's borrowing." Mother brings her hand out and opens it. The orichalcum is glowing in her palm, brighter than it was in Garyus's room, the light more steady. "But you're right, Jally, it was wrong not to ask." She leans forward. "Can you give it back to him and not say where you got it? He won't be cross with you." She looks worried and that makes Jally afraid. He nods slowly, reaching out to take it.

"I won't say, Mama." He says it in a solemn tone, confusion filling him. He's sad but he doesn't know why. I could tell him that he's seen for the first time his mother do wrong, his mother be afraid and without certainty. It's a hurt every child must suffer as they grow.

Mother shakes her head, keeping the orichalcum in her grasp. "A moment." She turns away from me, goes toward the doorway that opens onto a chamber I call the Star Room, and steps inside. I follow to the threshold, peering through the crack in the door that she failed to close properly. She has her back to me. From the motion of her arm I can see she is moving her hand down from her chest to her belly. The glow gets brighter, throwing black shadows in all directions, brighter still, and suddenly it's a glare, like a flash of lightning, painting the whole room with an intensity that allows no colour. Mother drops the orichalcum cone with a shriek and I burst in through the door after her. As I run around her to discover what she's hiding I see she has both hands folded over her stomach, one atop the other. Tears are running from eyes screwed tight.

I stop, the orichalcum forgotten. "What is it . . . ?" Jally hasn't the slightest idea. I know though. She's pregnant and the child has a thousand times more talent in the womb than Kara has after all her years of training as a völva.

We stand there in the drawing room beneath a ceiling studded with star-shaped roundels, and watch one another.

"It will be all right, Jally." A lie, whispered as if even Mother doesn't believe it enough to say out loud. She smiles, pushing aside her hair and bends toward me. But I'm looking over her shoulder at the face of a man looming behind her. No smile there. I half recognize him but with the light streaming through the doorway to his rear his features are shadowed, offered only in rumour, hair so black as to be almost the blue of a magpie's wing, with grey spreading up from the temples.

"J—" The rest of my name comes out bloody. Both of us look down at the blade that has emerged from her belly. In the next second she has fallen forward, pulling clear of the sword, now dripping in the man's hand. Blood flows along the curves of the script set into the steel.

"Ssssh," he says, and sets the cutting edge against the side of Mother's neck where she lies bleeding on the Indus rugs. The man stands revealed now in his uniform, the tunic and breastplate of the general palace guard. His face is somehow blurred, for a broken second it wants to look like Alphons—the younger of the doormen—and when I refuse that it shifts toward old Raplo who winked at me that morning. I shake both away and see him clear, just for a moment. It's Edris Dean, without the scar along his cheekbone, and too young for the grey, but greying even so.

Jally's thoughts, that have for so long bubbled behind my own, childish and wide-roaming, have now fallen silent. He looks at Mother, at the sword, at Edris, and his mind is a smooth void.

"I knew you were coming . . ." I say it with Jally's mouth.

"No you didn't." Edris pulls back his blade, slicing Mother's throat. She starts to thrash, trying to rise. "No one ever does. That's my talent, sure enough. Given by God Almighty himself. The future-sworn can't see me, boy." He holds the point of his sword toward me. "I cast no shadow on the days to come. Bedevils the fortune-tellers no end, to be sure. Keep telling me I won't live to see the morning."

"I'll kill you myself," I say, and I mean it. A strange sense of calm enfolds me.

"Do you say so?" Edris smiles. "Maybe. But first you have to die." And he thrusts his sword into my chest. Some deeper part of Jally had us moving already, throwing himself backward, and a last twitch of Mother's leg, either by accident or design, puts Edris off his attack. Even so, the point of his blade cuts between my ribs and I hit the ground screaming, blood soaking my tunic. Even as I scream the thrust of the blade toward my chest is replayed across the darkness behind eyes screwed tight. I glimpse runes, half-visible on the steel beneath my mother's blood.

I hear a distant cry and as my head rolls to the side I see a huge guardsman tumble past Edris, his arm spurting blood where the assassin's blade has cut him as he sidestepped. It's Robbin, one of Mother's favourites, a veteran of wars before I was born—perhaps before she was born. Edris moves to finish him but the man sweeps the blow aside with his longsword, bellowing, and launches his own attack. The sound is terrifying, the crash of blades, staccato footsteps thudding, harsh breaths rasped in. I can't track the flickering swords. It's growing dim, the sounds more faint. I meet Mother's eyes. They're dark and glassy. She doesn't see me. Her hand is open, reaching for me in her last moment, the orichalcum cone sent spinning by a kick as the men fight and vanishing beneath a long couch against the far wall.

Over Mother's head I see Edris is already carrying a wound in his side, something he earned on the way in. Now the tip of Robbin's blade opens his cheek to the bone, painting his face scarlet. Edris repays the wild blow with a chop deep into the meat of Robbin's thigh, just above the knee. The man staggers but doesn't fall. Hop-stepping to stand between Edris on one side and my mother and me on the other, though we must both look dead. In fact I think we are. I hear faint shouts in the distance. Edris spits blood and shoots a disgusted look at Robbin, his glance falls quickly to the bodies on the floor. Decided, he spins on a heel and is out of the door with remarkable swiftness.

It's dark now. Cold. Big hands lift me up but it's all so far away.

◆ ◆ ◆

It's dark now. Cold. Big hands lifted me.

"I'll kill him myself!" It came out as a whisper though I'd tried to shout it.

"Kara! He's waking up!" Snorri's voice.

I opened my eyes. They felt sore. The sky above us lay deepest purple, shading into night.

"I'll kill the fucker." Someone must have given me acid to drink—each word hurt.

"Who are you and what have you done with Jalan Kendeth?" Snorri loomed across me grinning, thrusting a water flask at me.

I would have hit him but my arms had no strength, none of me did.

"H-how long?" I asked.

"More than a week." Kara moved in looking concerned, holding the orichalcum up to inspect my face. She stared into each eye, lifting my brows with her thumb to make them wide.

"Give me that!" I managed to get my hand on hers and with a frown she let me take the metal bead.

"Odin!" Tuttugu just arriving with an armload of deadfall dropped it to shield his eyes. Hennan hid behind him. The orichalcum pulsed and guttered in my grip, lancing brilliant beams out into the night and sweeping them randomly across the nearby tree-line, sending strange bright shapes sliding across the grass. I dropped it and let my arm fall.

"It was true . . ." Something reached up along the rawness of my throat and choked me so I could say no more. Instead I rolled to the side, face to the ground, buried in my arm. Young Jally's emotion still filled me—the little boy I didn't know any more—he still watched Mother's eyes, glazed and unseeing, and the sorrow of it, the red hurt, just flooded me, bursting my chest, so much misery I hadn't anywhere to hide it. I couldn't remember ever knowing a feeling so deep and so terrible, leaving no room for air.

Kara's hands found my shoulders. "Get more wood, Tutt. Snorri help him. Take the boy."

"But—" Snorri began.

"Do it!"

At last I could draw breath and hauled it in with a shuddering sob. Snorri and Tuttugu hurried away, Hennan trailing after.

"Jesus!" I hit the ground hard as my strength allowed. "Make this stop."

Kara demonstrated a völva's wisdom by not saying anything for the longest time.

Great emotion, it turns out, is a fire, and like a fire it needs fuel. Unfed it dies down to a hot and banked glow, ready to ignite again but leaving space for other matters. When Snorri and Tuttugu finally returned with half the forest piled in their arms, the night lay dark enough to hide the shame of my red eyes.

I found myself painfully thirsty and drained the water flask I'd been given. Snorri and Tuttugu set to work on the fire and preparing food. I saw Snorri anew now, understanding perhaps for the first time the kind of hurts he must have been carrying within him the whole time that we'd journeyed together. I understood in part what lay behind the man I'd looked down on in the blood-pits, what lay behind his "bring a bigger bear."

I drew a deep breath. "Where are the trolls?" I noticed the absence of that pungent fox-stink of theirs rather than the lack of menacing giants looming on all sides.

"Renar Highlands." Snorri broke a branch and fed it into the fire. "We said good-bye to Gorgoth two nights back."

"Which puts us in . . . ?"

"Rhone. The province of Aperleon, ten miles south of the ruins of Compere."

I sniffed, imagining I could smell the ashes of that city. "I've got to kill him."

Snorri and Tuttugu looked up, faces painted with firelight. "Who?"

"Edris Dean," I said, aware that a desire for revenge—a need—would prove a great inconvenience to a professional coward like myself. An inconvenience on the scale of a poker player afflicted by the compulsion to grin broadly every time he turns up an ace.

"Edris Dean needs killing right enough. I'm with you there." Snorri turned to face me, hidden in shadow now with his back to the fire. "But did it take two weeks of sleeping on the matter to reach that conclusion? He's tried to kill you twice already. And me."

Snorri knew I'd learned something in my dreaming—this was him asking how much I'd tell him. I rubbed my nose on my sleeve and sniffed again. The aroma of Tuttugu's stew reached me along with the realization of just how ravenous I was. They must have fed me something while I was dragged along all those days, but whatever it was it wasn't enough. Even so, I pushed the hunger aside, met Snorri's gaze.

Tuttugu spoke first. "Dean's only tried to kill me the once and I'd be happy to push him off a cliff." He stirred the stew. "Why does Jal need a new reason to be angry? The man's already attacked him two times."

"Three times." I lifted up my shirt. And there, just below the left pectoral muscle, a white scar an inch and a half long. I used to say that Martus cut me with a kitchen knife—and I believed it. More recently I claimed it as a war wound from the Aral Pass. I knew that one to be a lie. Now I knew it for Edris's, the thrust of the same sword that ran my mother through, her and my unborn sister both. And cut her throat. Sister? I couldn't say how I knew the child would have been my sister . . . but I did. A sorceress to play the role that the Silent Sister foresaw for her, a key piece to put into play on the board of Empire, sitting between the Red Queen and the Lady Blue.

I touched my fingers to the scar, remembering the pain and the shock of it. How long they had tended young Jally on his deathbed I couldn't say, but I'm sure a different boy left it. A boy who either had no memory of the past weeks or who set whatever wild talent that lay within him to burning out all trace of the events. I had sympathy with that choice, if it was a choice he'd made. I would make the same decision even now if I knew how. Or at least be tempted to.

"And the first time? When he gave you that scar, who else did Edris cut?" Snorri asked, Tuttugu and Hennan moving in behind him, stew forgotten.

"My mother." I gritted my jaw to say it but a breath hitched in as I saw her fall again and the word cracked.

"I'll kill him for my grandfather." Hennan sat cross-legged, looking down. The child had never sounded so serious.

Snorri looked down too and shook his head. A moment later he patted his chest where the key lay beneath his jerkin. "He'll come for me soon enough. Then I'll kill him for all of us, Jal."

EIGHTEEN

Nearly six months spent north of Rhone had improved my opinion of the country considerably. For one thing they knew what summer was about here. We walked south through long hot days and I basked in the sunshine whilst the others turned red and burned. Tuttugu proved the worst of them with the sun. At one point it seemed as though most of his exposed skin was attempting to peel off, and he moaned about it nonstop, crying out at the slightest slap on the arm—even going so far as to suggest some of them weren't entirely accidental.

The sun also burned off the dark mood that had enfolded me for days after I woke. It didn't reach the cold core of certainty that I would have to kill Edris Dean, but it rolled back the shadows the memory cast and left me with recollections of my mother that would have been lost forever if not for Kara's magics. Whilst we kept moving it seemed that the past was content to trail behind me, not forgotten but not getting in the way of each moment. For the first day or two I thought the dream's discoveries would drive me mad, but oddly with the passing of a week I felt more at ease in my own darkening skin than I had for years. Almost a form of contentment. I attributed it to the ever-narrowing gap between me and home.

Perhaps it was spending time trapped in my own head with the younger me but I seemed to have more of a rapport with Hennan on the last weeks of our journey. We started to pass through actual towns and I taught the lad a few tricks with a pack of cards I picked up. Just simple finesses, enough to bilk Snorri and Tuttugu out of their few coppers and some chore duties around camp.

"I'm sure one of you is cheating . . ." Snorri rumbled that evening when saddled with an extra night watch and the task of gathering firewood for the fifth time in a row.

"That's a common misconception among losers," I told him. "If you call the application of intelligence and a shrewd assessment of the statistical odds cheating then yes, both I and Hennan are cheating." In fact if you called "not playing in accordance with the rules" cheating, then we would both have to raise our hands to that also. "The rules of poker, Snorri, have outlasted the most basic information about the society and age in which they were constituted," I continued. The important thing when denying cheating is to continue—to not stop speaking until the conversation has travelled so far from its roots that none of the listeners can remember what the original point of contention was. "What a civilization manages to keep from that which went before says as much about it as what it leaves to the next age."

Snorri furrowed his brow. "Why is there an ace up your sleeve?"

"There isn't." It was a king, and there was no way he could have known it was there—just a lucky guess.

Continuation is a good policy, but sometimes it turns out that a barbarian is too stubborn to be led and you end up doing two night watches and gathering firewood all week. Snorri asked me what sort of lesson I thought my behaviour might provide Hennan with—a rather better one than would be taught by seeing a prince of Red March reduced to manual labour I thought, but at least I took satisfaction in the fact that my pupil's cheating went undetected, a credit to my teaching.

Another benefit of a return to sun and civilization was that the summer once more restored the gold to my hair, bleaching out the drab brown. Additionally the reappearance of people helped me remember at last that there were women other than Kara in the world. I purchased new clothes in the town of Amele and spruced myself up. I considered a horse but unless I bought at least four steeds then having a saddle under my arse wouldn't get me home any quicker. I did consider just riding on ahead by myself, but even in Rhone travelling alone can be a risky business, and even if our enemies were focused on finding the key I didn't like the idea of having to explain to them on some country lane isolated in the middle of a thousand acres of Rhonish cornfields that I didn't have it. I toyed with the idea of getting a nag for Snorri, Tuttugu, and Kara, with Hennan up behind me, but Mother's locket had started to look threadbare and I wasn't sure I could stand all the moaning and falling off the Norse were likely to do.

I visited a barber and had my beard shaved off—a ritual shedding of the north if you like. The fellow with the razor and snips declared it an unholy tangle and charged me an extra crown for the job. With it gone I felt strangely naked, my chin tender, and when he showed me the result in his mirror it took me a moment to accept that the man looking back out was me. He looked a lot younger, and vaguely surprised.

Walking through Amele in my new outfit—nothing fancy, just outdoors clothes that a country squire might wear—and my chin still stinging at the slightest breeze, I will admit to turning a few heads. I smiled at a buxom peasant girl off about whatever business it is that occupies peasants, and she smiled back. The world was good. And getting better by the mile.

"Bonjour," Hennan greeted me when I returned to the tavern where I left the others—the King's Leg, sporting a wooden stump above the door.

"Bon-what?"

"Snorri's been teaching me the language the locals speak." He looked up at Snorri to see if he'd got it right. "It means good day."

"The locals all speak the Empire tongue well enough." I sat down beside Tuttugu and stole a chicken wing from his plate. "Sometimes you have to wave a coin at them before they'll admit it. Don't waste your time, boy. Awful language." I stopped talking in order to chew. Whatever Rhone's failings—and they are many—I'll call any man a liar who says they can't cook. The lowliest Rhoneman can make a better meal than all the north put together. "Mmmm. That's worth the trip south on its own, hey, Tuttugu?" Tuttugu nodded, mouth stuffed, beard full of grease. "Where was I now? Yes, Rhonish. Don't bother. You know what the literal translation of the Rhonish word for defence is? The-gap-before-running-away. It's a hard language to lie in, I'll give you that."

Snorri made a warning face and Tuttugu became still more interested in the rest of his chicken. I noticed a few locals aiming hard stares in my direction.

"A wonderful brave people though," I added, loudly enough for the eavesdroppers to choke on.

"You look different," Snorri said.

"I think 'even more handsome' was the phrase you were looking for." I filched another piece of Tuttugu's chicken. He tried to stab my hand as I pulled it back.

"More like a girl." Snorri picked up his flagon and drained it.

"Well, I'll have to strain the bits out of my beer by hand now the moustache is gone . . . but otherwise it's all good. You should try it."

Tuttugu snorted at that. "My beard's the only thing that keeps my chin from burning in this furnace you call home." He sucked the meat off a leg bone. "I think the reason your chickens taste so good is that they're all half-cooked before you slaughter them."

Snorri rubbed his own beard but said nothing. He had trimmed it close, against the northern style: compared to most Vikings he merely looked as though he'd forgotten to shave that morning.

Kara watched me closely as if making a study. "You're changing your skin, Jalan, casting off the north. By the time we reach the gates of your city you'll be a southern prince once more. What will you keep from your journey, I wonder?"

And it was my turn to keep silent. Most of it I would gladly lose, though I'd learned a lesson about that. Throw away too much of your past and you abandon the person who walked those days. When you pare away at yourself you can reinvent, that's true enough, but such whittling always seems to reveal a lesser man, and promises to leave you with nothing at the end.

Two things I would keep beyond doubt. The ache to know that Edris Dean had died and died hard was one of them. The other—the memory of the Northern Lights—the aurora borealis Kara told me they are called—that ghostly show which lit up the sky on the longest night of my short life when we camped on the Bitter Ice at the end of our endurance.

The trek continued under blue skies. Despite our fears no agents of the Dead King intercepted us, no monsters clawed from their graves to put us in ours, and we passed over the border into Red March without incident. Even so, Snorri pushed us hard, more urgency in him now than at any point since the Hardassa were on our heels. I could tell his wound hurt him—there was a stiffness about the way he moved. I wondered what we would see if he lifted his shirt to show the mark Kelem had put upon him. Perhaps though, the memory of Kelem in that cave, holding Snorri's dead child, drove the northman forward more than the hooks in his wound drew him on. That had been a mistake on the mage's part. He could have blocked that particular route to death's door without that. I don't care what magics you command—putting that kind of fury into a man like Snorri is always a bad idea.

In the town of Genova, two days out from Vermillion, I weakened and spent the last of my gold on a decent horse and tack, together with a fine riding cloak and a gilded neck chain. A prince of the realm can't turn up looking like a footsore beggar however far he's travelled and however many enemies he's vanquished. I know Genova well enough and there's fun to be had there, but with home so close I pressed on without further delay.

"Damn but even the air tastes better here!" I slapped the pommel of my saddle and took a deep breath—savouring the heady musk of wild onions among the oak and beech of the hill forests.

Snorri, Tuttugu, and Kara, sunburned and tramping along in my wake had fewer good things to say about my homeland, but Hennan, perched behind me on the gelding, tended to agree.

It felt wonderful to be back in the saddle again, a touch unfamiliar but far better than walking. My new steed looked rather nice too, a deep black coat and a crooked flash of white down his face, almost a lightning bolt jagging its way from between his eyes to his nose. If he'd been a seventeen-hand stallion rather than a squat gelding barely reaching fourteen hands I'd have been all the happier with him—though of course considerably poorer. In any event, he ate up the miles nicely and provided a good vantage point to watch Red March pass me by. My only regret was that the Norse had strapped their baggage to the beast as if he were a packhorse. Even "Gungnir" was there, wrapped in old rags to keep it from prying eyes, with just the spear tip gleaming where it pierced the wrappings.

I flashed my smile at Kara from on high a time or two but had little response. The woman seemed to be getting moodier by the mile. Probably thinking about how much she'd miss me. She was clever enough not to believe that I was coming with them to Florence and the nightmare Snorri had his sights on.

I bought us a room at an inn that night and after supper Kara found me alone on the porch. I'd been sitting there a while, watching the last traffic hurrying along the Appan Way as the day dwindled into gloom. She came to me as I always knew she would, reeled in eventually by that good old Jalan charm after the longest courtship I'd ever undertaken.

"Have you decided how you'll stop him?" she asked without preamble.

I sat up at that, having expected some small talk before we began the old dance I'd been leading her up to. The dance that would see my passions requited at last in the hired bed awaiting us on the second floor.

"Stop who?"

"Snorri." She sat in the wicker seat opposite, unconsciously rubbing her wrist. A lantern hung between us, moths battering against its glass while mosquitoes whined unseen in the dark. "How will you get the key from him?"

"Me?" I blinked at her. "I can't change his mind."

Kara massaged her wrist, rubbing at dark marks there. It was hard to tell in the lamplight among all the shadows . . . "Are those bruises?"

She folded her arms—a guilty motion, hiding the hand, and kept silent under my stare until at last: "I tried to lift it from him two nights ago as he slept."

"You . . . were going to *steal* the key?"

"Don't look at me like that." She scowled. "I was trying to save Snorri's life. Which is what you and Tuttugu should be doing, and would be if you were any kind of friends to him. Why do you think Skilfar pointed him at Kelem? It seemed a long enough journey for me to stop him—either by talking him out of it, or if needed, by stealing the key." She got up and came to sit on the step beside me, composing herself and offering a sweet smile that looked good but most unlike her. "You could ask him for the key again and—"

"You! You were trying to steal the key off him in the cave that morning! He swapped it onto a chain because of you, not me! He's been wise to you all along!" I realized I was pointing at her and lowered my hand.

"Taking the key would save his life!" She looked at me, exasperated. "Changing his mind would too."

"It can't be done, Kara. You should know that by now. You *would* know it if you'd seen him heading north. He can't be stopped. He's a grown man. It's his life and if he wants—"

"It's not just his life he's throwing away, Jal." Soft-voiced again. She set her hand to my arm. It gave me thrills, I'll admit it. She had something about her, perhaps just built up after all those months of anticipation, but more than that I think. "Snorri could do untold damage. If Loki's key falls into the Dead King's hands . . ."

"It will be a bloody mess." Suddenly the moment had passed, the mood soured, the darkness around us full of undead threat instead of romantic possibility. "But I still can't do anything about it." And besides, I'd be safe in the palace in the heart of Vermillion, in the heart of Red March, and if the Dead King's evil could reach me there then we were all fucked. But I felt safer putting my trust in Grandmother's walls and her armies than in my ability to part Snorri from that key. I shook Kara off and stood abruptly, bidding her good night. I was so close to home I could taste it, practically reach out and set my fingers to it and I wasn't messing things up now, not for anything, not even the promise in Kara's touch. No man likes to be a last resort in any event, and on top of that, despite the wide eyes, the promise, the hint of desperation, I still couldn't shake the feeling that somehow the woman was playing me.

That was a long night. My room hot, airless, and refusing to let me sleep.

Another day, more endless stretches of the Appan Way, another inn. And then one glorious summer morning, after trailing through mile upon mile of cultivated fields golden with wheat and green with squash, we crested a ridge and there on the horizon beneath a faint haze stood Vermillion, walls glowing with the early light. I'll admit to a manly tear in my eye at the sight of it.

We made an early lunch at one of the many farmhouses close to the Appan Way that open their doors to passing travellers. We sat outside around a table in the shade of a huge cork tree. Chickens pecked their way about the dusty yard, watched by an old yellow dog too lazy to twitch when the flies landed on him. The farmer's wife brought out fresh bread, butter, black olives, Milano cheese, and wine in a large earthenware amphora.

I had a cup or three of that good red before I gathered up the resolve to try one last time to talk Snorri out of his plan. Not for Kara, well, perhaps a little in the hope of Kara's good opinion, but mostly just to save the big ox from his own stupidity.

"Snorri . . ." I said it with enough seriousness that he put down his clay cup and gave me his attention. "I, uh." Kara looked up at me from her bread and olives, encouraging me with the slightest of nods.

Even with a loosened tongue I found it hard to say. "This taking Loki's key to death's door business . . ." Tuttugu shot me a warning look, gesturing down with the flat of his hand. "How about *not* doing it instead." Tuttugu rolled his eyes. I scowled at him. Dammit, I was trying to help the man! "Give this up. It's madness. You know it. I know it. Dead is dead. Except when it's not. And we've seen how ugly that is. Even if the Dead King's creatures don't catch you on the road and take the key. Even if you reach Kelem and *he* doesn't just kill you and take the key . . . Even then . . . you *can't* win."

Snorri stared at me, unspeaking, unreadable, unnerving. I drank deeply from my cup and, finding I'd reached the bottom, tried again.

"You're not the first man to lose his wife . . ."

Snorri didn't explode to his feet as I thought he might with me touching his rawest nerve, in fact for the best part of a minute he said nothing, just looked out at the road and the people passing by.

"The years ahead scare me." Snorri didn't turn to face me. He spoke his words into distance. "I'm not scared of the pain, though in truth the ache inside is more than I can bear. Much more.

"She lit me up. My wife, Freja. Like I was one of those windows I've seen in the house of the White Christ. Dull and without meaning by night and then the light comes and they're aglow with colour and story. Have you known that, Prince of the Red March? Not a woman you would die for, but a woman you'd live for?

"What terrifies me, Jal, is that time will blunt the wound. That in six months or six years I will wake one morning and realize I can't see Freja's face any more. Discover that my arms no longer remember little Emy's weight, my hands her softness. I'll forget my boys, Jal." And his voice broke and suddenly I wanted nothing more than to take back my words. "I'll forget them. I'll mix one memory with another. I'll forget how they sounded, the times we spent on the fjord fishing, the times they chased me when they were little. All those days, all those moments, gone. Without me to remember them . . . what are they, Jal? My brave Karl, my Egil, what were they?" I saw the shudder in his shoulders, the hitch as he drew breath.

"I don't say it's right, or brave, but I'll carry my father's axe into Hel and I'll search for them until I'm done."

None of us spoke for an age after that. I drank steadily instead, seeking the courage that lies in the bottom of the barrel, though the wine seemed sour now.

Finally, with the shadows lengthening and all our plates long since empty, I told them.

"I'm stopping at Vermillion." Another swig, running it over my teeth. "It's been a pleasure, Snorri, but my journey ends here." I didn't even think I would have to do anything about the Sister's curse. It had worn so thin that I'd not heard as much as a whisper from Aslaug since waking from the last of Kara's dreams. Sunsets passed almost unnoticed now, with just a prickling of skin and a heightening of senses as the moment came and went. "I'm done."

Kara shot me a shocked look at that but Snorri just pursed his lips and nodded. A man like Snorri could understand the hold that home and family have on a person. In truth though, I disliked pretty much every surviving member of my family, and the fear of being murdered by agents of the Dead King ranked at the top of the list of reasons I wasn't continuing with Snorri's mad quest. The plain fact of it was, however, that even reason number 6 "travelling is an awful bore" would have been sufficient on its own. My family might not have much hold on me, but the prestige of their name, the comfort of their palace, and the hedonistic pleasures to be found in their city all keep a vice-like grip on my heart.

"You should take Hennan with you," Tuttugu said.

"Uh." I hadn't anticipated that. "I . . ." It made sense. None of what was to follow was anything a child should endure. It wasn't anything a grown man should endure come to that. "Of course . . ." My mind was already racing through the list of places where I might palm the boy off. Madam Rose on Rossoli Street might be able to use him for running messages and clearing tables in the foyer. The Countess of Palamo staffed her mansion with very young men . . . she might want a red-haired one . . . Or the palace kitchens could use him. I was sure I'd seen urchins in there turning the meat spits and whatnot.

Hennan himself didn't complain but chewed his heel of bread furiously and stared out at the road.

"I, uh . . ." I swallowed some more wine. "I should make my good-byes here and be off."

"We're not good enough to be seen with in your city?" Kara arched an eyebrow at me. She'd taken her braids out, having lost all her runes, and grown her hair longer. It was so bleached by the sun it looked almost like silver where it flowed around her bare shoulders, now freckled with the summer.

"Snorri is a wanted criminal," I said. A total lie of course, and even if he was I could probably argue his case for a pardon. The truth was that I didn't want the facts muddying the waters of any lie I felt like telling about my adventures in the ice and snow. And besides, when I made my triumphant return to high society I wanted all eyes on me, not wandering up and down the muscular length of the intriguingly handsome barbarian towering over me.

Snorri met my gaze across the table and, before I could look away, stuck out his hand for the warrior clasp. Somewhat awkwardly, I took it. A bone-creaking squeeze and he let me go. Tuttugu held out his more reasonably sized hand for the same.

"Fair seas, Prince Jalan, and many fish." As we clasped.

"You too, Tuttugu. Try to keep this one out of trouble." I nodded to Snorri. "And that one." A nod to Kara. I wanted to say something to her but couldn't find any useful words. I stood unsteadily. "No point drawing these things out . . . as the actress said to the bishop . . ." My horse stood at the trough on the other side of the yard and since the world appeared to be revolving around me somewhat faster than normal I waited a moment for things to steady. "You take my advice and throw that key in a lake . . ." I fluttered my fingers at Hennan to get him out of his seat. "C'mon, boy." And with that I plotted as steady a path as I could to my gelding who I decided in that moment I would name Nor, in memory of Ron, the beast that bore me much of the way north. Nor would carry me in the opposite direction and so should bear the opposite name.

I mounted without too much difficulty and reached down a hand to swing Hennan up behind me. The spear, Gungnir, knocked against my leg, tied there across Nor's side, still in its wrappings. It occurred to me I could ride off with it. Hope is always dangerous, and this spear, this false hope, was what Tuttugu, and maybe Kara, clung to. It made presenting themselves before Kelem seem less like suicide. Without it they might refuse at the last mile and perhaps even turn Snorri from his path.

"Gungnir!" Tuttugu started forward. I almost set my heels to Nor's ribs, but in the end I reached down to pull loose the ties and took the spear in hand. The thing shivered in my grip as if half-alive, much heavier than it had a right to be.

I tossed it to Tuttugu. "Careful with that. I've a feeling it's sharp both ends."

That done and their bags removed, I saluted the table and set off at a trot along the gravelled road to Vermillion.

"We should have gone with them." Hennan, his voice jolting to the beat of Nor's gait.

"He's going to ask some madman in a salt mine to show him the doorway into death so that he can unlock it. A madman who sent assassins after him. Does that sound like something anyone should be doing?"

"But they're your friends."

"I can't afford friends like that, boy." The words came out angry. "That's an important lesson right there—learning how to let go of people. Friends are useful. When they stop having something you want—brush them off."

"I thought we . . ." Hurt in his voice.

"That's different," I said. "Don't be ridiculous. *We're* still friends. Who else am I going to pass my card tricks on to?"

NINETEEN

Hennan and I rode without conversation after parting with Snorri, Tut-tugu, and Kara. I steered Nor through the thickening traffic converging on the Appan Way to enter the great city. The roadside houses were fully fledged taverns now, or shop fronts offering all a man might want for the highway. In the distance a glittering curve of the Seleen caught the sunlight and fractured it. My head had started to pound in the heat, and the stink of the capital reached out to us on the slightest of breezes.

The gates to Vermillion stand open year on year. By the time the Appan Way meets the great walls it has already passed through a quarter mile of the outer town, slum dwellings on the fringes, set back from the road, more gentrified homes further in, some two and three storeys intermixed with open tree-lined squares and public buildings. Grandmother regularly has notices posted reminding the inhabitants of these houses that the land will be cleared with fire should the city ever need to be defended— but each year the outer town spreads a little more, reaches a little further out along the five roads that feed Vermillion.

A scattering of guards endured the heat on the great gatehouse over-looking the Appan's course north, more lurked in the shadow of the wall at ground level, but these would seldom stir for anything less than a laden cart. Hennan and I passed through on Nor's back without challenge. Within moments we were clattering along Victory Street, past the Grand Old Stables, now given over to public use, and beside the cool delights of Fountain Square where cherry trees line the avenue to the new cathedral.

It seemed unreal—almost a dream—all this had been waiting here for me the whole time. While I shivered on the Bitter Ice, as close to death as a man can come, people strolled these streets, buying sweetmeats, watching the acrobats, letting the Seleen slip past, gambling, loving, getting drunk . . . I'd covered three thousand miles and here, here in this small patch of stonework, this terracotta encrustation, lay my whole life.

I let the horse move with the pace of the city's traffic and watched the buildings as we passed, at once familiar and strange.

A dark-faced man in the shadowed entrance to Massim's marked my progress along the street with rather too much interest. Maeres Allus, so long an abstract worry, almost forgotten, suddenly loomed large once more in my thinking. I shook the reins and made Nor pick up his feet.

"We'll go straight to the palace." I'd thought perhaps to look in on a few places, drop the boy off, get the lay of the land, but now decided it was better first to learn whatever could be learned in the safety of the palace. Better to make my presence known to my family so that Maeres couldn't have me dragged off to some lonely warehouse without anyone ever knowing I'd survived the fire at the opera.

Behind me Hennan said nothing. Eking a life from the wasteland around the Wheel of Osheim might prepare you for many things, but the city of Vermillion was not one of them. I felt his head turn this way and that, trying to take it all in. To me it seemed smaller than in my memory—to Hennan probably larger than in my tales. We build our expectations out of what we know already. I hoped he wasn't going to prove clingy. A prince of Red March can hardly be expected to shepherd a beggar boy around the corridors of power . . .

Passing along the grand streets around the palace we drew a few curious looks. Guards at the gates of mansion grounds narrowed their eyes and threw out their chests. Servant girls out on errands stared in surprise. In my country squire's garb I cut a rather different figure to the kinds of visitors these houses were used to, and the pale beggar boy behind me added a further pinch of the exotic.

We clipped and clopped along the Kings Way, across the broad plaza before the palace, and at last came up to the Errik Gate, where once my thrice-great-grandfather Errik the Fourth came back in procession from the port of Imperia carrying the heads of Tibor Charl, Elias Gregor, and Robert the Black, the worst pirate lords the Corsair Isles spawned since the Suns. I remember their names because Martus once put three artistically decorated cabbages under my bed and claimed they were the severed heads of the trio, taken from the spikes on the Errik Gate, and that if I told or tried to move them they would come alive again. Bastard.

The guards before the Errik Gate came forward sharp enough, two of them ready to see me off, one standing further back with his pike lowered. On the gate towers archers paid an interest. The Errik Gate is for the highest of visiting dignitaries, for royal households, and it is seldom opened.

"Be off. If you've business at the palace you'll want the Scullion Door, round past the old castle. See?" He aimed a finger at the Marsail keep.

At that point it occurred to me I should have bought a hood so I could have thrown it back dramatically and announced myself. As things stood I was starting from the position of having already gone unrecognized.

"I'm Prince Jalan Kendeth returned from the Utter North and I'll have the head of any man who denies me entrance to my grandmother's palace." I let it come out with an air of weary irritation while praying none of them would call my bluff.

"Uh." The younger of the pair, proclaimed the senior in rank by the star upon the shoulder of his tunic, sucked in his lips in consideration. I guessed that nobody had ever ridden up to the gates falsely declaring themselves related to the Red Queen. Perhaps some drunk too deep in his cups for self-preservation may have, but not a sober young man on a horse. A moment's more cogitation and he frowned up at me. "I'll go and check. If you could wait here, sir. Cogan, let them rest in the shade."

And so we waited in the shadow of the walls, in silence save for Nor guzzling water from the trough. Not quite the entrance I'd hoped to make but Vermillion had a goodly number of princes and these weren't my household guards.

It took longer than I felt it should but eventually the sub-captain returned with a familiar figure.

"Fat Ned!" I shouted, striding toward the man, arms spread.

Fat Ned, looking skinnier than ever, took one step back, then another. Overhead I heard the creak of bowstrings.

"It's me, Ned." I spread the fingers of both hands toward my face and gave him my winning smile.

"No?" Ned shook his head, loose skin flapping around his bones. "But you're dead, Prince Jalan . . . is it . . . is it really you?" He tilted his gaze, looking more closely with those tired old eyes of his.

I lowered my arms. I hadn't been intending to hug the man in any event. "Really, truly. And not risen from the grave either." I thumped my chest. "Hale and hearty. Reports of my death have been much exaggerated!"

"Prince Jalan!" Fat Ned shook his head in amazement, drawing his hands down across his face. "How—"

The gate captain emerged now from the postern gate, hastening across to us, sword rattling in its scabbard. "Prince Jalan! My apologies! We were told that you'd died. There was a day of mourning . . ."

"A day?" *One lousy day . . .*

"By order of the queen for all the victims of the great opera house fire. Many highborn died that day—"

"One day?" And not even just for me. "Wait—did my brothers survive?"

"You were the only member of the royal family in attendance, my prince. Your brothers are well." The man bowed his head and took a step back, gesturing to the postern gate, inviting me to precede him.

"A prince of Red March doesn't return from the dead to re-enter the palace after six months by a side gate, captain." I waved to the Errik Gate, my voice imperious. "Open it."

The guardsmen exchanged a glance or two at that. The captain, looking somewhat uncomfortable, cleared his throat. "The key to the Errik Gate is kept in the treasury, Prince Jalan. It has to be released by special order of her majesty, and—"

"Well run to my grandmother and let her know that I am waiting!" Somehow I was digging myself into a hole before even getting inside the palace but I was damned if I'd have some jumped-up gate captain and his men sniggering at my back as I squeezed in through the postern gate.

"—and the gate is currently closed for maintenance in any case. Several hundredweight of gravel would have to be moved and one of the hinges replaced before the gate could be opened . . ."

Curse the man. "Don't they open out?" I only had the vaguest of recollections of anyone using it. The Florentine duke, Abrasmus, visited when I was ten but I was busy causing mischief at the back of the royal stands when he rode through . . .

"My apologies, highness." He didn't look apologetic enough though, not by half.

"All right, dammit. Lead me in through your mouse-hole." I dismounted and, with a shake of my head, started off toward the postern. "You." I pointed to the sub-captain. "See that my horse is delivered to the Roma Hall. Ned you go along and make sure they don't get lost."

Hennan stood from crouching beside the wall and made to follow me.

"Take the boy, too." I waved Ned at him. "Tell Ballessa to give him a meal."

Hennan shot me a betrayed look at that and followed on behind the men and Nor, head down. I raised my hands toward the captain in exasperation. What the hell did the boy expect? I was hardly going to introduce him around the palace. Cardinal Kendeth, Hennan, Hennan, the cardinal. Prince Martus, Prince Darin, this is Hennan, he tends goats . . . Madness. The captain just gave me the same impenetrably bland look he'd shown ever since I arrived, nodded and turned away to lead me through the door. And so at long last I returned to the palace, squeezing my way through the narrow and doglegged passage from the postern gate. We emerged into the dazzle of sunlight on the far side and squinting against it I looked about, getting my bearings. I supposed I should present myself to Father and find something suitable to wear before making the rounds. Everyone would want to hear my story and whilst telling it in my unkempt road clothes would lend a certain something to the imagery of it all, I preferred the comfort and splendour of my court dress. A bath wouldn't go amiss either. And maybe a housemaid to pour for me and recover the soap when I dropped it.

"I will escort you to your father, highness." The captain waved a couple of his men to join the guard. I would have preferred to be asked where I intended to go rather than be told, but I nodded my permission.

"First, if I'm dead, show me my grave." I was interested to see what lasting memorial they had erected to the hero of the Aral Pass.

The captain made a short bow and we set off across the palace compound. With the sun blazing there were few people on the move. Small black-clad figures made leisurely progress along the shadowed sides of the Poor Palace, Milano House, and the Marsail keep, servants bound on various errands. Apart from that our audience consisted of scattered wall guards and a small contingent of crows, moulting feathers in the heat and looking distinctly ragged.

We came through the furnace of the West Courtyard to the palace church, actually the south wing of the Roma Hall. Father might be inside, though he spent less time in the halls of Christly worship than some pagans—which for a cardinal was no mean feat.

We approached the doors to the church foyer, the twin spires rising on high to either side of a peaked roof. A wall of saints looked down upon us, their disapproval set in stone. I started up the steps.

"Here, highness," the captain called out before I reached the top stair.

I turned. The man was indicating a plaque set in the outer wall, amid a host of others, markers for lords and generals of yesteryear, some weathered beyond reading. I re-trod my path, outrage building. The royal family were always laid to rest inside the church, our tombs crowding the margins of the aisles to either side of the nave, princes and princesses of the realm buried beneath black slabs of marble set into the floor, more renowned figures in their own sepulchres beneath their likenesses idealized in alabaster. For kings and queens they found space in the chancel. The slow tide of years moved forgotten royals down into the catacombs, freeing space for more recent departures . . . but even the most lowly prince got to have the church roof keep the rain off his title. My plaque was set between two other newish ones, on the left General Ullamere Contaph, Hero of Ameroth Keep, 17–97 year of Interregnum, on the right Lord Quentin DeVeer, 38–98 year of Interregnum. I set a hand to my own.

"In memoriam: Jalan Kendeth, third son of Cardinal Reymond, 76–98 year of Interregnum." I read the words aloud. "That's it? Cardinal's third son?" No prince? No hero of Aral Pass? Bastards. "I'll see the cardinal now. If he's sober and not abed with some choirboy." I found my hand resting on my knife, palm to pommel. "Now!"

The guardsmen snapped erect at that last barked command. The captain, standing to attention, gestured at the church doors with his eyes.

"I very much doubt I'll find him in there, captain!" But I returned up the steps in any case and set both hands to the left door, pushing through with a measure of violence.

For a while I stood blind, waiting for my eyes to adjust from the brilliance of the day to the softness of candles and the muted spectrum of stained glass. Dim shapes resolved and I stepped in. Three old ladies kneeling at the pews, an ancient bent over the bank of votive candles, and a stooped grey figure standing facing the wall about halfway along the north aisle. I hadn't really expected to find my father among them. At the far end beneath the mandala window a black-frocked priest stood turning a page at the lectern. I took another step forward. There wouldn't be any point asking if Father was hidden away in the transepts, but even so something drew me in. Perhaps just the coolness. The day outside was starting to get hellish hot. Maybe my time in Norseheim had lowered my tolerance for Red March summers because it proved a blessed relief to get out of the glare for a moment.

It wasn't until I made my way along the north aisle that I realized the stooping man was facing my mother's stone—a plaque bearing her name and lineage, and behind it, buried in the thickness of the walls, her remains. And—as I now remembered and perhaps no one else knew—those of my unborn sister.

"Prince Jalan?" The man looked up at me, grey and old before his time, lined with pain. He took a step toward me, hobbling, his right leg ruined. For some reason I matched his advance with a step back.

"Robbin?" One of my father's retainers, though at first I hadn't been sure of it in the gloom. He stood with his head bathed in green light. It streamed down through the serpent in the high window where Saint George battled the dragon. Now though I saw past his stoop and his old man's hair, I looked beyond one decade and half of another. "Robbin?" Once more, for a moment, I couldn't see him properly—damned incense in these churches stings your eyes something rotten. I squeezed my eyes against the tears and saw Robbin as he'd been fifteen years before, battling Edris Dean, putting himself between the assassin and Mother and me. The wound that crippled him he took in my service. I pressed fingers to my eyes to clear them, wondering how many times I'd mocked or cursed him for his slowness over the years as he hobbled about on errands for my father.

"Yes, highness." He started struggling to go down on one knee like men do before the throne. "Th-they said you were dead."

I grabbed him and hauled him up before he fell on his face or did something more embarrassing. "I don't feel dead." I let him go and took a step back. "Now, unless my father is lurking in here I'll go off and look for him somewhere he's likely to be. Our good cardinal should be able to settle the matter of whether I'm dead or not once and for all."

I straightened the front of Robbin's jerkin where I'd grabbed it to pull him to his feet, and with a curt nod I left him standing there, still half-stunned. My footsteps echoed loud among the pillars and the old widows amid the pews watched my departure, judgement written in every wrinkle.

"He's not there. Let's try the house." I waved the captain and his men after me and led the way to the grand entrance of Roma Hall. A carriage and four stood in front of the steps, the driver head down as if he'd been waiting a while. I ignored it and hurried up to the doorway.

I didn't recognize the flunky who opened the doors in response to my pounding, but I knew the two guards behind him, squinting against the brightness of the day in their house uniforms.

"Alphons! Double! Good to see you. Where's my father?" I pushed past the butler and on into the hall, its niches filled with those Indus statues the cardinal still collects to the vexation of his priests. The doormen fell in with me sputtering all the "but you're dead" nonsense that I could tell was going to become quite tiresome over the next few days.

"Jalan!" My brother Darin striding toward me, dressed for travel, a man beside him heaving a chest. "I knew you'd jump out of that fire into some frying pan!" He looked pleased, not overjoyed, but pleased. "There was a rumour running in the wine halls that you'd joined the circus!" Darin opened his arms to embrace me, handsome face split by a wide and apparently genuine grin.

"Fucker!" I punched him in the mouth, hard enough to knock him on his arse and to cut my knuckles on his teeth.

"What?" Darin stayed where he was, sitting on the floor and spitting blood. He shook his head clear and looked up at me. "What was that for?"

"Father expects you at this opera of his tonight," I mimicked the deep and condescending voice he had used when instructing me to go and burn to death. "No showing up late, or drunk, or pretending nobody told you!"

"Ah." Darin held up a hand to his bagman who hauled him to his feet. He wiped his mouth. "Well obviously I didn't know—"

"*You* didn't go!" I roared, remembering the screams. The fierceness of my anger took me by surprise. "Martus wasn't there! Dear Father forgot his own opera? Not a single one of Grandmother's brood in attendance?" I raised my fist again and Darin, though two inches taller and always the better brawler, stepped back.

"It was *opera* for God's sake. I didn't expect you to go! If you hadn't vanished the night of the fire I would have put money against you being there . . . and I was right, you weren't!" He wiggled his jaw with his hand, wincing. "I was just doing my duty by telling you yours. Father drank too much that evening and had to excuse himself. Martus turned up for the second half and found the place in flames . . ."

"Well I *did* go, and I damn near burned!" I lowered my hands a touch. "And someone's to blame!"

"Someone is. Just not me." He wiped at his mouth with a red hand. "Quite a punch there, little brother." He grinned. "It's good to see you!" And somehow he still managed to look as if he meant it.

"You—" I remembered Lisa and bit off the accusation. "Were the DeVeers there that night?"

Darin wiped away his smile. "Alain DeVeer was. The shock of it killed his father, Lord Quentin—died abed later that week. Fortunately there was some kind of scandal at the house the day of the performance and the sisters were kept in. Very fortunate in fact as I've married Micha, the youngest of them. Just off to our country house now as it happens."

I kept my face blank. Too blank in fact.

"Micha! You know her, surely? You must have met her?" Darin said.

"Ah, yes . . . Micha." A good half-dozen times. Most of them in her bedroom after a difficult scramble up an ivy-clad colonnade. Little Micha, a beauty whose face shone with the innocence of an angel and whose tricks I'd had to teach the ladies down at the Silken Glove and at Madam LaPenda's. "I remember the girl. Congratulations, brother. I wish you joy of each other."

"Thank you. Micha will be glad to learn you survived. She was always anxious to hear the rumours about you. Perhaps you'll come to visit when you're settled? Especially if you've any words of comfort to offer about poor Alain's last night . . ."

"Of course. I'll make a point of it," I lied. Micha was probably checking I was dead to set her mind at ease regarding any tales I might tell her new husband. And I doubted she wanted to hear that her brother died in a toilet after I kicked him in the face while he hauled my trousers down. "I'll visit first chance I get."

"Do!" Darin grinned again. "Oh! I forgot, you won't know. You're going to be an uncle."

"What? How?" The words made sense individually but didn't add up into anything comprehensible.

Darin threw an arm over my shoulder and put on a mock-serious voice. "Well . . . when a daddy and a mummy love each other very much—"

"She's pregnant?"

"Either that or she swallowed something very big and round."

"Christ!"

"Congratulations is what most people say."

"Well . . . that too." Me an uncle? My Micha? I felt a sudden need to sit down. "I've always thought I'd make a great uncle. Terrible. But great."

"You should come with me, Jalan. Recover from your ordeal and all that."

"Maybe." Watching Darin and Micha play happy families was not how I anticipated spending my first few days back in civilization. "But right now I need to see Father."

"Back on your travels so soon, Jal?" Darin cocked his head, puzzled.

"No . . . why?" He wasn't making sense.

"Father's in Roma. The pope summoned him for an audience and Grandmother said he had to go."

"Hell and fire." I had questions that wanted answers and I might have squeezed them out of Father more easily than elsewhere. "Well . . . look, I'm going to get cleaned up and—wait, you didn't throw out my clothes, did you?"

"Me?" Darin laughed. "Why would I go touching your peacock feathers? It's all there as far as I know. Unless Ballessa took it upon herself to clear your rooms out. Father certainly won't have got around to giving any instructions. Anyhow, I'd best go. I'm late as it is." He motioned for his man to start hauling the chest again. "Visit us when you get the chance—and don't rile Martus, he's in a foul mood. Grandmother appointed Micha and Alain's elder brother, the new Lord DeVeer, to captain the infantry army that's been put together these past few months. And Martus had already decided the post was his. Then a few days ago some other calamity or indignity. I wasn't really paying attention . . . something about a huge bill from a merchant. Ollus I think the name was."

"Maeres Allus?"

"Could be." Darin turned at the doorway. "Good to see you alive, little brother." A wave of his hand and he was off and gone. I stood, watching, until the carriage took them from sight. He hadn't even asked where I'd been . . .

Alphons kept his gaze front and centre at the door. The less ancient guard, Double, a dark fellow with bags beneath his eyes, watched me with undisguised curiosity. I let the insolence slip. It was good to see that at least one person found the returned adventurer fascinating.

TWENTY

With Father gone to Roma, Darin shacked up in his country retreat with *my* sweet little Micha, and Martus on the warpath over being presented with my posthumous gambling debts, I had no immediate family to regale with the saga of my accidental exile.

In the hope that Martus might actually pay Maeres what I owed before he discovered I wasn't dead I kept a low profile in the house. I reinstalled myself in my rooms and called a couple of the housemaids to scrub my back and incidentals while I had a much needed bath. The water soon turned black, so I had Mary go heat up some more while Jayne helped me select an outfit for court. All in all it had proved a disappointing homecoming so far and even the maids didn't seem as pleased to see me as they should be. I gave Jayne a little squeeze and you'd think she was a princess for all the offence she took! And that set me thinking about the last princess I met, the striking Katherine ap Scorron, owner of a particularly tempting behind and a vicious left knee. Memory of how she'd deployed that left knee put me right off my game and I sent Jayne off back to her duties, telling her I'd manage to dress myself.

Nothing felt quite right, as if the palace were another man's boots I'd pulled on by mistake. I went to the Glass Chamber, a room where some previous cardinal had gathered a collection of glassware from the sunken cities of Venice and Atlantis, all displayed in tall cabinets. I'd avoided the room for years since the incident with the egg fight where somehow Martus and Darin escaped scot free and conspired to have me take the blame. Now, though, I paced among the old cabinets and their forgotten contents gleaming in all the colours between red and violet, led on by some old memory and the taste of blood.

Crouching in a corner, I pulled away a piece of loose skirting board, and there, glowing in a small hole in the plaster sat the rune-set cone of orichalcum that had fallen from Mother's hand as Edris Dean killed her. When they released me from the care of the surgeon and his nurses, and when at last I had my first opportunity to be alone, I went to the Star Room, retrieved the cone from beneath the couch where it had been kicked, and came here to hide it. The thought that Garyus might want it back never troubled me, and he never asked after it—perhaps because to do so would mean accusing me or my mother of theft. I had hidden it away, and pushed all thought of the murder from my mind: the cone, its hiding place, the whole terrible business. Until Kara's blood magic woke those memories.

"Mine." I snatched the thing up, cold in my fist. The light pulsed through my hand, making the flesh rosy and the bones of my fingers into dark bars. I wrapped it in a handkerchief and thrust it deep into a pocket.

I stood, but kept my place, staring sightless into the corner. I say Kara's magic, because it was her spell that brought those dead recollections back to life, her work that disturbed their peace and set them playing over and over upon the inside of my skull like some monstrous shadow play . . . but the key had started it. Truly it had been Loki's key that unlocked all this—against advice I'd used the key and opened a door onto the past that I couldn't close. I wondered then just how hard it might be to close the door Snorri had it in mind to open.

I replaced the skirting board and for the next hour paced the corridors of the Roma Hall. Sleep did not come easy that night.

I needed to speak to someone who might understand what had happened to me. I considered going to Garyus but seeking advice from a man who hadn't left his room in sixty years and had never been outside the palace walls seemed foolish. Besides, the power lay with his sisters. After half a day reflecting on the matter I decided to confront the non-silent one.

I strapped on my dress sword before going. The door guard would take if off me but Grandmother would notice the scabbard and she liked to see her spawn go armed.

The walk to the Inner Palace was nearly long enough to erode my store of courage to the point where I turned back. Another hundred yards or so would have done it, but instead I found myself climbing the steps to the grand doors.

Ten of the queen's personal guard flanked the topmost steps, enduring the heat in their half-plate. The knight at the door towered over me, made taller by his high helm and crimson plume. "Prince Jalan." He bowed his head a fraction.

I waited for the "but you're dead," ready to be irritated, and found myself disappointed when it didn't come. "I wish to see my grandmother." She always held a noon court on Sunday after church. I'd gone to the Roma mass hoping to see her there, but she must have attended her private chapel, or skipped the whole tedious business as I normally do. Bishop James had conducted the mass at the Hall and offered thanks for the return of a lost sheep to the fold. I would have preferred "conquering lion to the pride" but at least it made my return official and meant Maeres couldn't have me quietly murdered.

"Court is in session, my prince." And the knight struck the door for admittance, stepping aside to let me past.

The Red Queen's court is unlike others in the region. King Yollar of Rhone holds a sumptuous court where aristocrats gather in their hundreds to slight and bicker and display the latest fashions. In our protectorate of Adora the duke hosts philosophers and musicians in his halls, with lords and ladies attending from across his realm to hear them. In Cantanlona the earl is famed for debauched court parties that last for a week and more, draining the towns around his capital of wine. Grandmother's court is more dour. A businesslike affair where fools are suffered only briefly and the sparkle of a new gown is seldom seen, there being no audience for such.

"Prince Jalan Kendeth." The court officer, Mantal Drews announced me, clad in the same sombre greys he wore the day I left.

The dozen or so attendees turned my way, heavily outnumbered by the royal guard hulking around the margins in their fire-bronze mail. These latter spared me not a glance. No surprise showed on the faces pointed in my direction, not even a whisper of it muttered behind fans— news travels fast in the palace. The word would have rippled out through guards and servants overnight, confirmed that morning by the highborn who saw me at the service.

The queen herself did not look up, her attention occupied by a fellow in a purple robe too heavy for the season, hunkered before the throne and making some or other impassioned plea. Two of Grandmother's sour old retainers flanked her, one a bony stick of a woman and the other a stout, grey-haired matron in her fifties, both in drab black shawls. I glanced around for the Silent Sister but saw no sign of her.

Gathering my resolve, I strode into the midst of the throne room, old anxieties queuing at my shoulder. I did my best to present the mask that had served me so well for so long: bluff Prince Jal, hero of the pass, a devil-may-care man's man. I lie as well with my expression and body language as I do with my tongue and like to think I carry off the deception rather nicely. The courtiers, or rather I should call them today's supplicants, for none of the aristocracy kept at court past the completion of their business, gave me space. I recognized a few of them: minor lords, the Baron of Strombol down from the shadow of the Scorron Aups, a gem merchant from Norrow whose daughter I'd known rather well for a night or two . . . the usual.

"And there he is!" The man before the throne concluded his petition by raising his voice past the point of decorum and pointing his finger directly at me.

"You have me at a disadvantage, sir." I offered him a tolerant smile, pretty sure we'd not met before, though something about him looked familiar.

"You'll get no advantage from me, Prince Jalan!" He looked to be about thirty, a solid fellow, shorter than me but wider, somewhat brutal in the cheekbones, and red-faced with anger. "I heard of your return and left my regiments immediately to discover the truth." He started to unbuckle his empty scabbard—which caused the guard to settle hands upon hilts. "I demand satisfaction. I demand it now." He threw his scabbard at my feet in the old way, making his challenge. "Fight me, and your reappearance can be a brief but swiftly corrected error on your obituary."

"Have a care, Lord Gregori." Grandmother from the throne, her voice low with warning.

The fellow swung round and offered a deep bow. "Meaning no disrespect, your majesty."

Fortunately I've had plenty of experience in avoiding duels and Grandmother had just handed me the key to exit this one.

"I don't pretend to know you, sirrah." I let mild outrage colour my tone. "But since you appear to know me then you will also understand that I am a prince of Red March, a man whom if ill fortune befell this royal house might one day have to carry the burden of the crown." I didn't mention quite how many other heirs would have to die to make *that* happen. "As a veteran of the Scorron campaigns my heart compels me to meet any challenge to my honour with cold steel." I saw him rise at that. "However, duty is a higher calling, and directs me to draw your attention to Gholloth's Edict of Year Six. No prince of the realm shall lower themselves to meet the challenge of mere aristocrats." I paraphrased the original and added in the "mere" to rub salt in the wound, but I knew my royal decrees in this area better than any lesson my tutors ever tried to teach me. In short he was beneath me—of insufficient rank to challenge a prince to combat.

For a moment I let him seethe, blood darkening his face until I thought he must either attack me or start bleeding from the eyes. I would have been happy to have him jump me and be cut down by the guard for his impudence, but sadly he drew a deep and shuddering breath before turning his back on me.

The pounding of my heart subsided to a point where I could hear myself talk and, now angry at being confronted in front of the court, I kicked his scabbard back at him.

"Your name, sir, and line!" I knew of no Lord Gregori.

He made a slow turn, empty hands flexing. "Lord DeVeer of Carnth, commander in chief of the Seventh Infantry. And you . . . prince, you deflowered my sister Lisa DeVeer, an act of unconscionable violation that drew my younger brother, Alain, to his death."

"Ah . . ." I understood where the familiarity came from. He had his brother's looks. The same overly hard skull too, no doubt. "Deflowered you say? Hardly, sir! They deflowered me if anything! I've never known sisters with such appetite!"

Again Gregori seemed on the very edge of throwing himself upon me, his rage so hot it left him unable to form words—then suddenly he lowered his hands.

"They? *They* you say? They! Your own brother's wife . . . my little Micha?"

"No!" I yelped the word before regaining control. "No, don't be more of a fool than you have to be, Lord DeVeer. Sharal of course." A man shouldn't name names but there were only three sisters in question. I couldn't help looking away for a moment to picture the lovely Sharal, hair reaching her hips, tallest of the three, always wanting to be on top . . .

"Sharal . . ." He said it with a tone of satisfaction that drew my attention back to him. Of the reactions I expected, "pleased" was very far down the list.

I flicked my fingers at the man, shooing him toward the bronze doors. "If your business is complete, DeVeer . . ."

"Oh don't worry, Prince Jalan. My business is complete. I shall retire." He bowed to Grandmother. "With your permission, highness." And receiving the nod he bent to scoop up his scabbard—a nice piece of work decorated with plates of black iron. "I will however pause at the city home of Count Isen. You may know the man?"

I didn't grace him with a reply. Everyone knew of Count Isen, the reputation he'd cut for himself down south had spread even beyond Red March's borders. In the lands he held for the crown his private army harassed smugglers and even pursued pirates across the sea to the very shores of the Corsair Isles.

Gregori offered me a curt bow. "Sharal is now engaged to be married to the good count. I'm sure when he hears how you pressed your lechery upon my sister, leaving her no options for resistance, that he too will wish for satisfaction of his honour . . . and I think you'll find that when a count comes knocking you will no longer be able to hide behind the late King Gholloth's skirts."

Gregori made a final bow to the throne and strode out.

It was only Gregori's departure that led my eyes to the Silent Sister, standing in the deepest shadow to the left of the great bronze doors, bone-pale and wrapped in cloths that looked to have been applied wet and dried in place like a wrinkled second skin.

"So, Reymond's boy." My grandmother's voice turned me back to the throne. "Where have you been?"

I looked up at her, a yard above me on the dais, and met her gaze. Alica sat there—the same girl from the Castle of Ameroth, who opened the siege with what she called the mercy killing of her youngest sister and ended it bathed in blood amid the ruin of her enemy—with a little help from her eldest sister of course. True, the passage of five decades and more beneath the Red March sun had sunk her flesh about her bones, scorched her skin into tight wrinkles, but the same ruthless calculation lay behind her eyes. I would get nothing from her if she thought me weak. Nothing if she caught scent of my fear.

"Lost your tongue again, child?" Grandmother narrowed her eyes, thin lips thinning still further into a line of disapproval.

I swallowed and tried to remember every hurt I'd suffered since the night I left the city, each hardship, each unnecessary moment of terror.

"I've been where my great aunt sent me." I swung round to point at the Silent Sister by the entrance. She raised her brows at that and offered me a mirthless grin, her blind eye almost glowing in the shadows of her face.

"Hmmm." A rumble deep in the Red Queen's throat. "Out." She waved at the people behind me.

Lord, lady, merchant, or baron, they knew well enough not to protest or delay but shuffled out, meek beneath her stare.

The doors closed behind them, the clang like a funeral bell.

"You have good eyes, boy." She stared into the palm of her hand, resting it on the throne's arm.

I had spent a lifetime dreading the throne room, keen on every occasion I attended the place to be gone from it as soon as possible and with as little fuss as could be managed. But now, though every nerve clamoured for a chance to run, I had come of my own volition and provoked the Red Queen to private audience. I'd pointed out the Silent Sister and spoken her secret. Sweat poured off me, trickling down across my ribs, but I remembered how Mother had stood up to the old woman, and how she died an hour or two later, not through Grandmother's wrath, but through her failure.

"Yes. I have good eyes." I looked at her but she kept her gaze upon her palm as if reading something there among the lines. "Good enough to have watched you in the castle of Ameroth, with Ullamere."

The queen raised her eyebrows as if taken aback by my boldness, then snorted. "That story is sung in taverns across the land. They even sing it in Slov!"

"I saw you in the chamber beneath the keep," I said. "Among the best of your troops."

She shrugged. "The keep is all that stands. Any fool could tell you the survivors gathered there."

"I saw the machine and heard it speak. I saw the time-star burning blue."

She closed her hand into a fist. "And who showed you these things? Skilfar perhaps? Mirrored in ice?"

"*I* showed them to me. They are written in my blood." I turned to glance back at the old witch by the door. She hadn't moved but her smile had left her. "And I saw my sister die. She had all the magic you were hunting for in me . . . but the Lady Blue stole that chance from you. Edris Dean stole it. Why haven't you killed him for that? He works for the Dead King now . . . why don't you reach out and . . ." I made a twisting motion with my hands. "Why doesn't *she*?" I pointed to the Silent Sister, only to find her gone.

"Edris Dean still works for the Blue Lady," the queen said. "As do many others."

"But the Dead King—"

"The Dead King is like a forest fire—the Lady Blue encourages the flames this way or that for her own purposes. The Hundred think this war is being fought for Empire but those of us who stand behind it know there are greater things at stake."

I tried to consider larger stakes than the whole of Empire. And failed. I wasn't even interested in the empire, broken or unbroken. All I wanted was for the world to roll on its merry way just as it had been doing for my entire life, and to provide me with a careless middle age and comfortable dotage which I could continue to misspend just as I'd been misspending my youth. I didn't even want to be king of Red March despite my moaning. Just give me fifty thousand in gold, a mansion of my own, and some racehorses and I wouldn't bother anyone. I would graduate from a rich lecherous young man to a stinking-rich lecherous old man, with a pretty and accommodating young wife and perhaps a handful of blond sons to occupy some pretty and accommodating young nursemaids. And when age claimed me I'd climb into the bottle just like dear Papa. I had only one stain on the glowing imaginary horizon of my future . . .

"I want Edris Dean dead."

"The man is hard to find." The queen's face showed a hint of the murder she wore at Ameroth. "My sister cannot see him and his service to the Blue Lady has taken him far beyond our borders. Patience is the key. In the end your enemies always come to you."

I thought then of Snorri. The key was the key—Edris would come for that. And Snorri would kill him.

"Your sister—my great aunt . . ." It made me uncomfortable to state our relationship so plainly but I'd discovered on my journeys that knowledge—a thing I'd always avoided as a tedious obstacle to having fun—could prove handy in the business of staying alive. Since I had so little of it I decided to lay out what I had in the hopes Grandmother might fill in the gaps. If there's one thing I know about people, from fool to sage, it's that they have a hard time not showing that they know more than you do—and of course by doing so they close that gap a little. "My great aunt tried to kill me. In fact she killed hundreds of people . . . and she's done it before!" Suddenly out of nowhere I saw Ameral Contaph, his round face, his eyes narrow with suspicion. Just one of many palace function-aries and a pain in my royal arse, but a man who I spoke to that day and who died in the fire. I saw him against a background of violet flames, lit by their glow. "Wait—Ameral Contaph . . . he wasn't . . ."

"Ullamere's grandson." The Red Queen inclined her head. "One of eight. The apple that fell furthest from the tree." She fixed her gaze upon me, eyes grave. I wondered if she knew quite how far I'd fallen from her tree . . . if we were talking apples then Jalan Kendeth had dropped from the Red Queen's boughs, rolled down a hill, into a stream, and been carried out to sea to beach on the shores of a whole other country.

"And the mass murder?" I got back to my point, glancing around for the Silent Sister once more, to find with a start that she now stood behind the throne, her seeing eye hard as a stone. I remembered how she looked that night in her rags, painting her curse on the walls of the opera house.

"This is a war that started before I was born, boy." Grandmother's voice came low and threatening. "It isn't about who wears what crown. It's not for the survival of a city, a country, a way of life, or an ideal. Troy burned for a pretty face. This is about more than that."

"Name it then! All this grand talk is very well, but what I saw were people burning." The words escaped me, unstoppable as a sneeze. I had no idea why I was goading the woman. All I really wanted was to be out of there, back to my old pursuits, working the Jalan charm on the ladies of Vermillion. And yet here I was criticizing the second most powerful woman in the world as if I were her tutor. I quickly started to apologize. "I—"

"Good to see you've grown, Jalan. Garyus said the north would make or break you." I swear I saw her lips twitch with the faintest suggestion of approval. "If we fail in this. If the change that the Builders set in motion is not arrested, or more likely reversed, if magic runs wild and the worlds crack open, each bleeding into the next . . . then everything is at stake. The rocks themselves will burn. There will be no countries, no people, no life. That's what the long war is about. That is what is at stake."

I drew a breath at that. "Even so . . ." I started, mind whirling. War is a game, games take two players, the other side have their own goals.

"The Lady Blue and all those working for her . . . they're not looking to destroy the world. Or if they are then there's something in it for them. Everyone's got an angle."

The Red Queen looked over her shoulder at that, eye to eye with her elder sister. "Not completely stupid then."

The Silent Sister smiled, her teeth narrow, yellow, each set apart from the next. She extended her hand, reaching past the queen's shoulder, and I flinched, remembering her touch. Fingers uncurled and somehow in her palm lay a poppy, so red that for an instant I thought it a wound.

"Smoking the poppy is an addiction that steps around people's sense, a hunger that reduces proud men and clever women to crawling in the mire in search of more." The Red Queen took the flower from her sister's hand and in her fingers it became smoke, a crimson mist, lifting and fading. "Magic is a worse drug, its hooks sink deeper. And it is magic that fractures the world, magic that will drag us to our end. The world is broken—each enchantment tears the cracks a little wider."

"The Lady Blue wants to doom everyone because she can't bear to give up her spells?" Even as I asked it my tone changed from disbelief to credulity. The old whores on Mud Lane would sell more than their bodies for the coin to buy another hit of the resin Maeres squeezed from his poppies. They'd sell more than their souls if they had more to barter.

"In part," Grandmother agreed. "I doubt she could give up her power. But more than that, she believes there is a place for a self-selected few, beyond the conjunction of the spheres. The Lady Blue thinks that those steeped deeply enough in their magic will survive the end and find new forms in a new existence, just as some among the Builders survived their Day of a Thousand Suns. Perhaps she sees herself as the first god to be born into what will come. Her followers she views as an elite, chosen to found a very different world."

"And you . . . don't believe?" With a start I realized I'd been addressing her without formality all this time and added in a belated, "Your majesty."

"What I think would follow such an ending is of no matter," she said. "I have a duty to my people. I will not allow this to happen."

And in the end, whatever Alica Kendeth said about the stakes, here was a queen defending her lands, her cities, and those subject to her rule. "And the burnings? The whole damn opera house?" I saw her eyes narrow and added, "Your majesty."

"The world may be wearing thin but still there are very few places where the unborn may return. The opportunities are seldom, and short-lived, hard to predict. A certain spot in a certain hour. If it is missed there may not be another window through which they may pass for months, and it might lie a thousand miles away. To bring an unborn through the veil at any other juncture requires an enormous expenditure of resource.

"The size of this city's population and the magics that are worked here make Vermillion a spawning ground for the unborn. My sister can give no warning, only detect and destroy the things as they emerge. The people around these events are food for the new unborn—it would use their flesh to repair itself, to build larger and more terrifying forms, and to feed its power. The only way to ensure the unborn's destruction is to burn out the nest before it realizes that it is under attack."

"But I saw it—at the opera house I saw the unborn. It escaped and pursued us north. That thing wasn't like the others. At the circus an unborn came for us, miscarried from womb to grave and bursting from the ground in the dead of night. And in the Black Fort Snorri's son, and then the captain of them . . ."

The Red Queen pursed her lips. I might almost think her impressed that I'd seen four separate unborn and yet stood before her with my insides on the inside.

"The creature you saw first was not newly returned but there to seed the event, one of two. Each unborn starts with a child killed in the womb. The longer that child stays in the deadlands the harder it is to birth into the living world, but the more it will be able to meet whatever potential lay in its blood. This was to be a very special unborn, perhaps the greatest of all of their kind. The two worst of the Dead King's servants were there to ease this one into the world: the Unborn Prince and Captain. The passage is made less difficult by the death of a close relative. It is likely the relative they needed was among the audience. It was a rare chance to test my sister's magics against the key figures in the ranks of those armed against us and to block the arrival of a powerful new servant for the Dead King."

I swallowed, remembering again the eyes that had regarded me through the slit of a porcelain mask. Then, realizing that my role in the failure of the curse was a bad place to let the conversation rest, I carried on. "And the Unborn Prince escaped and tracked us north to stop—"

"The Unborn Prince went south," Grandmother said. "The Unborn Captain to the north. They informed the Dead King of events, no doubt, and sent agents against you, but the prince went south, to Florence, where he works against us even now."

"Ah."

"When you broke her spell my sister glimpsed a possibility. The crack you put into her working allowed the two elder unborn to escape but she saw a way for the main investment of her power to be carried between two unusual men, and that the tides of chance would bear you to our foe in the north."

"Tides of chance?" That wasn't mere chance. I've bet on some long odds at the gambling table when drunk but I've never thrown the dice at quite so slim an opportunity.

"She may have moved some of the pieces into place. Hers is an art rather than a science, and even if she were not silent I doubt she could explain more than half of what she does. Her motives are unlikely to fit within words."

"But once she interfered, once she acted on what she knew would happen to me . . . she could see no more." I paraphrased Kara. "She reached into a clear pool to change the future and left it muddy."

Grandmother cocked her head to the side at that, as if seeking a new angle to view me from. I'd seen her offer the same look in the still-smoking ruins of Ameroth Castle fifty years before.

"We felt the curse released. We felt the unborn ended. Out in the wilds they are weaker, away from people on which to feed . . . So tell me, did Snorri ver Snagason find what he sought after he'd laid his enemies low?"

I paused. Always a bad idea if you plan to lie. Did she know what the

Dead King was hunting beneath the Bitter Ice? Did she know that we found it? The important thing was not to get myself into trouble . . . and trouble could come from being caught in a lie, but also from earning myself some kind of further task. "His family were all killed," I said. True though perhaps not what she wanted to know. Snorri wasn't seeking the key in any event—neither of us were.

The Silent Sister held out her hand again, closed about something. I held my breath and refused to meet her eyes. Slowly her fingers unfolded, revealing a long black key, Loki's key.

"Ah, yes, he found that." I didn't feel safe enough to lie. A damned unpleasant feeling. They say that the truth will set you free, but I find it normally hems me into a corner. "Snorri has the key." This time however an immediate sense of relief flooded me. I'd told them. It wasn't my problem any more. Grandmother had armies, assassins, agents, cunning and fearless men and women who would sort things out.

"And?" the Red Queen prompted, her face tight. The Sister's copy of Loki's key faded to a stain across the whiteness of her palm.

"He's taking it to a mage named Kelem, in his mines. Has some crazy idea to unlock a door the old man can show him . . . and . . . uh . . . get his family back."

"What?" A boom of disbelief that had me scuttling backward so quickly I stepped on my cloak and went crashing down on my arse. As the reverberations echoed through the throne room I swear I heard a hiss issue from Silent Sister's dark mouth. "Where . . ."

Grandmother rose from her throne, looking more terrible than Skilfar ever had. She seemed to be struggling with the question, struggling to draw in air and frame her outrage. "Where is Snorri ver Snagason now?"

"Uh . . ." I shuffled further back, not feeling it safe to get back on my feet. "H-he should be about twenty miles down the road to Florence. I left him outside Vermillion yesterday noon."

Grandmother clasped her hand to her face, reaching for the arm of her throne with the other. "The key was on my doorstep? Why—"

She broke off her question and I didn't feel it a good moment to volunteer that nobody had ever mentioned that she wanted the damn key.

"Marth." The Red Queen lowered her hand and looked to the grey-haired woman to the right of her throne. "Organize a hundred riders. Send them out to bring the Norseman back here. He shouldn't be hard to miss, about six foot eight, black hair and beard, pale-skinned. Is that right, boy?"

I'd been demoted to "boy" again. I picked myself up and dusted down my cloak. "Yes. He's travelling with a fat ginger Viking and a blond völva from the Utter North."

"Even better. Spread the net wide. Don't lose him."

TWENTY-ONE

Grandmother dismissed me from her throne room with no more ceremony than she had afforded the courtiers. A short walk, three sets of doors closing at my heels, and I stood once more in the blazing sun of a hot Red March afternoon. No duties, no calls on my time, no responsibilities—"Hennan!" I remembered the boy and with surprise found that it gave me a sense of purpose I welcomed.

"Ballessa!" Back in the slightly cooler confines of Roma Hall I set to finding Hennan, and that meant finding Ballessa first. The doughty mistress of my father's household knew where each pin lay. "Ballessa!" I'd been striding through the ground floor rooms shouting for a while now and, tired, I flomped down in one of the leather armchairs in Father's study. Innumerable worthy tomes on theology crowded the shelves. The books held no interest for me, excepting that I knew Father had hollowed out the twelve-volume works of St. Proctor-Mahler to hide whisky, two long salt-glazed earthenware jugs of it, stoppered tight. Also the legends on the top row may read "The path to Heaven" and "Saving the fallen, one soul at a time" and the like, but the etchings within were perhaps the most pornographic to be found in the city.

"Jayne!" I saw the housemaid trying to sneak past unobserved.

"Yes, Prince Jalan?" She straightened up and faced me.

"Ballessa—bring her here would you? I need to find out about the boy."

"You mean, Hennan, sir?"

"That's the one. Little fellow. Dirty. Where is he?"

"He ran off, sir. Ballessa put him to work in the kitchen garden and an hour later he was gone."

"Gone?" I stood up out of the chair. "Gone where?"

Jayne raised her shoulders, almost insolent. "I don't know, sir."

"Dammit all! Tell Fat Ned I want the boy found. He can't have got far!" Though in truth he could have got quite far. The palace was hard to get into. Getting out was much less difficult, providing you weren't carrying an armful of valuables.

Jayne went off to find Ned—in no great hurry it should be added. A sigh escaped me and I pulled a book from Father's desk to distract me. Hennan would probably have gone in pursuit of Snorri, heading southwest along the Appan Way where it exited the River Gate. With any luck he would see Grandmother's riders bringing the others back and follow them in. I didn't fancy explaining the boy's absence to Snorri. Especially not after Grandmother had taken the key off him.

I stared at the book spines for an empty moment, sighed again, and moved to check the strong-box in the corner, hoping to find a few coins. It was locked of course but I'd figured how to jig the mechanism long ago. All it took was a bent nail and some patience. It turned out that my reserves of patience weren't equal to the task but that a bent nail and some frustrated cursing would also do the job.

"Crap." The box proved disappointingly coin-free, though lifting a spare cardinal's cape I found unexpected treasure. Father's fone and holy stone lay wrapped in velvet. Two symbols of his office, second only to the cardinal's seal. The fone was a thin and battered tablet of plasteek and glass that would fit easily in the hand. A tracery of silver wire held the thing together, preventing the dark and fractured glass escaping. The priesthood told it that the Builders could speak to anyone they chose through such devices, and draw on the knowledge of the great and ancient libraries of the world. The clergy themselves put their fones to more pious use, speeding their prayers to God and, so they claimed, hearing his replies. I'd listened myself on several occasions but sensed no connection.

The holy stone looked for all the world like a small iron pineapple, its surface divided into squares by deep grooves, a tarnished silver-steel handle or lever held tight to the side. In ancient times the pineapple was ever the symbol of welcome, though the church used the objects in a different way. Apparently, each theological student of good family and destined for high office was given one on beginning their training and forbidden from pulling the lever on pain of excommunication. A test of obedience they called it. A test of curiosity I called it. Clearly the church wanted bishops who lacked the imagination for exploration and questioning.

I toyed with the thing. *Let he that is without sin cast the first stone . . .* and set it aside, knowing Father would disinherit me if I broke it. Treasures, but sadly too valuable and too difficult to pawn. I wondered briefly at their significance. As a rule, Father never let them from his sight. Perhaps he feared if he took them to Roma with him the pope might strip them from him by way of chastisement for his failings in office.

I closed the box and returned to my seat, plucking a book at random from the shelves. *The Prodigal Son.* Bible stories aren't my strong point but I had a feeling the prodigal son had been feasted and celebrated on his return, despite being a waste of space. Here I was, with actual accomplishments to my name and all I'd got was a plaque on the outside of the family church, and a telling off for not wresting from a giant Norse killing-machine something that I didn't know Grandmother wanted in the first place. Add to that Micha married to an undeserving Darin, Sharal promised away to a man who looked set to carve me up for sport, and Hennan running off to the road as if trudging through the dust was better than life in the palace of Vermillion.

"I'm going out." I tossed the book down. My life in Vermillion had always centred on its less salubrious spots, its flesh-pits and hellholes, the racetrack, the bordellos . . .

First to my rooms to find something suitable to wear for town. I found the place in a terrible mess and pursed my lips. It was entirely possible I'd left my gear scattered when I left—but I expected it tidied away by . . . someone. I wasn't sure who did such things, but they happened. Always. I made a note to complain to Ballessa about it. It almost looked as if someone had rummaged through my belongings . . . With a shrug I selected a fine waistcoat, pantaloons with slashed velvet revealing a scarlet silk liner, a dark and expensive cape with a silver clasp. A glance in the mirror. Ravishing. Time to go.

Down in the guardhouse I rousted out the two old men Father assigned to my personal protection: Ronar and Todd, both veterans of some war not worth a song. I'd never enquired after their family names. They got up, grumbling, and clattered along after me as if it were some great imposition after spending the last six months on their arses playing battamon in the barracks.

From Roma Hall I led off aiming for the guest range to gather up some of my old cronies. I cut through the Field, a poorly named courtyard where in my youth I spent many unhappy hours being drilled in all the military arts. I passed Uncle Hertet, almost lost amid his retinue. Into his fifties and wearing his years poorly he cut a gaudy figure in a high-necked tunic sewn with enough gold thread to found an orphanage. I spotted cousins Roland and Rotus in the mix but none of them so much as spared me a glance. They seemed to be coming from the direction of the Inner Palace—perhaps another formal visit where the heir-apparently-not checked in to see if his mother had had the decency to die yet.

From the Field I led my two layabout bodyguards to the guest range, a sprawling arm of the Inner Palace, secured from the royal quarters and home to a fluid population of visiting nobility, diplomats, trade delegations and the like. Barras Jon's father, the ambassador from Vyene, held a suite of chambers on the second floor. Vyene might be the capital of a broken empire but the memory of its former glory lent its ambassadors a certain gravitas—further bolstered by the quality of the Gilden Guard who once served the last emperor and now protected the dynasty of officials he left behind.

Quite why Grand Jon had been at court for three years now nobody seemed to know. The empire had a hundred fragments as large as Red March and while the Vyenese ambassadors would certainly call in at each of them from time to time, few stayed to take up residence. Barras only said that his father, having negotiated a truce between Scorron and the March, now refused to leave for fear it would fall apart the moment his back turned.

I led the way through several long corridors, stairs up, stairs down, and stairs up. At last we reached the correct doors and I hammered for admission.

"Barras!" He came to the chamber doors half-dressed, though it took an age after I'd sent the doorman to get him. Rollas came up behind him, a hefty fellow, competent with fists and blade, good company but you never forgot he was there to protect the ambassador's son from the consequences of his own recklessness.

"Jalan! It's true! We thought the opera killed you." He grinned, though with a nervy air. He'd buttoned his shirt wrong and had what looked like bite marks on his neck.

"It was touch and go for a while," I said. "But I got out during the intermission. Had a bit of an adventure up north, but I'm back and ready for trouble. We're hitting the town tonight."

"Sounds good . . . Who is 'we'?" He rubbed at his neck, eyes flicking to Rollas who'd come to crowd the doorway, giving me a friendly nod.

"We'll get the Greyjars, winkle Omar out of his studies, head down to Davmar Gardens and spill a little wine . . . see where the night leads us." A flicker of satin skirts caught my eye and I peered past Barras to the corner at the end of the hallway behind him. "Entertaining a young lady in there, Barras? What would the Grand Jon say?"

"He, ah . . . he'd give me his blessing." Barras looked at his feet, frowning. "I, um."

"He got married," Rollas said. "When you 'died' it shook him up a bit. Started thinking about what his plans were, what he might leave behind him if something cut him short too." He gave a shrug as if this were a stage all men went through.

"You old dog!" I tried to sound cheerful about it. Though it's hard to cheer the loss of a good man. "Who is she? Someone rich I hope!"

Barras still couldn't look me in the eye. Rollas cleared his throat.

"Oh for Christsake . . . not Lisa?" My voice came out louder than intended. "You married Lisa DeVeer?"

Barras looked up sheepishly. "She was very upset when you . . . when she thought you'd died with Alain. I thought it my duty to comfort her."

"The hell you did." I could see him "comforting" her right now. "Poor

Jalan. I expect he's in a better place now . . ." shuffling closer to her on the chaise longue, "There, there!" arm creeping around her shoulders. "Dammit all." I turned on my heel and started to stride away.

"Where are you going?" Barras called after me.

"To find Roust and Lon. I expect you'll try and tell me the Greyjars are married now?"

"Gone back to Arrow," he shouted as the distance between us grew. "Their cousin has taken the country to war. They're part of the invasion of Conaught now!"

"Omar then!" I roared back.

"Returned to Hamada to study at the mathema!"

"Shit on it all!" And I was past earshot, taking the stairs three at a time. I paused for breath at the main doors and let the injustice of it all sink in. I had definitely been going to ask Lisa to marry me. Lisa, whose memory sustained me in the icy wastes, kept me going despite pain, hardship and the suicidal nature of our quest. Lisa, who my mind kept returning to in the empty wilderness. Married! To my *friend* Barras! I gave the doorpost a vicious kick and hobbled out into the blazing sun. I made the Poor Palace my next stop. I hadn't intended to but with things at a low ebb I set out across Victory Plaza and went up to see what old Garyus had to say for himself. I used the stairs, it being too hot for climbing. In any case such activities were beneath the dignity of a prince returning from staring death in the eye on margins of the Bitter Ice.

"Hello?" Nobody stood in attendance and the door lay half-open.

No answer.

"Hello?" I leaned in. "It's me. Jalan."

The lump on the bed turned ponderously. With a sigh and an effort that set him trembling Garyus raised his head, as ugly and misshapen as I recalled, but older and more tired.

"Young Jalan."

"I'm back." I took the chair by the bed and sat down uninvited. With the curtain drawn I could make out little save for the furniture.

"I'm glad of it." He smiled, his lips wet, a trail of drool drying on his chin, but a genuine smile.

"You're the only one." I bent to rub my toes, still smarting from kicking the wall. "Grandmother just roared me out of the throne room over some key . . ."

"Loki's key." It didn't seem to be a question. Garyus watched me with mild eyes.

"Probably going to be Kelem's key soon enough." A silence stretched. "Kelem is—"

"I know who he is," Garyus said. "Anyone with business interests knows old Kelem. Not so many years ago it might just as well have been his face on every coin of Empire."

"And now? I thought he owned every bank in Florence." What was it Snorri had said? Something about the beating heart of commerce.

"They call him the father of the banking clans, but if a father lives too long his children are apt to turn on him." With effort Garyus waved his arm at correspondence piled on the desk behind his bed. "There's trouble brewing in Umbertide. Finance houses seeking new partners. Some have even looked as far as the Drowned Isles. These are interesting times, Jalan, interesting times."

"The Drowned Isles? The Dead King is interested in gold as well as corpses?"

Garyus shrugged. "One often follows the other." He lay back, rasping in a breath, apparently exhausted.

"Are you . . ." I hunted for the right word, obviously he wasn't "well." "Can I get someone for you?"

"Tired, Jalan. Old and tired and broken. I . . . should sleep." He closed his eyes. There were a thousand questions I'd wanted to ask him on my journey. But now, seeing him frail and ancient none of them seemed so pressing. Quite how we ended up talking about banks I wasn't entirely sure but I hadn't the heart to challenge him over any of my suspicions— they seemed silly now I sat here before him.

"Sleep then, Uncle." Almost a whisper. I turned to go.

He spoke once more as I stepped through the door, voice thick with dreams. "I *am* glad . . . to see you, Jalan . . . knew you had it in you, boy."

◆ ◆ ◆

"Just you and me for the now, boys."

Ronar and Todd waited for me, lounging in the shade, at ease in the way only old soldiers can manage. They seemed neither excited nor disappointed by the news, simply straightening themselves up and preparing to move out. They didn't look much, both grey, grizzled and carrying pot bellies, and I didn't expect much of them either, remembering how quickly they faded away that last time in the Blood Holes when Maeres Allus came over for a word.

Off we set, through the Surgeons Gate out into the sullen heat of late afternoon, a dirty haze above the city's roofs and a threat of distant thunderheads clustering above the Gonella Hills to the south. I felt somewhat deflated, but there's nothing like a skin-full of wine to reflate a man's ego, so I led my guards out along the Corelli Line which mirrors the curves of the Seleen, set back on a ridge from where the waters can be glimpsed between the houses. Merchant dwellings and the town houses of minor aristocracy give way in time to the squares and plazas of Little Venice, divided and bracketed by innumerable canals. We crossed a few of the many humped bridges and came to the Grapes of Roth, a wine-house I knew well. Old Roth had died years ago but his sons inherited his flair for selecting good vintages and keeping the hoi polloi out.

"Prince Jalan!" The elder son danced between the tables, graceful despite the swing and sway of his belly. "We thought you had abandoned us!"

"Never!" I let him guide me in and draw out a chair for me at one of the reserved tables near the centre beneath high awnings. "Not even death could keep me from your hospitality, Marco!"

"What can I bring you, my prince?" A genial smile on fat and pockmarked cheeks. The man generated a miasma of good humour, his ugliness somehow charming, and if the fact that I owed him the best part of fifty crowns in gold bothered him . . . well none of it showed on the surface.

"A good Rhonish red," I said.

"Ah, your tastes have broadened, Prince Jalan! But all Rhonish reds are good. Which to choose? Bayern? Ilar Valley? Chamy-Nix? Don P—"

"Chamy-Nix."

"As you say." And with a bow he was off. Soon a boy would be scurrying to the cellars in search of my wine.

I leaned back. Todd and Ronar had taken themselves to the shade of a large maple not far outside the part of the plaza roped off for Roth's customers. The slow ebb and flow of the world passed by as shadows lengthened. My wine came and I sipped it, washing the flavour over my tongue. Relaxed, warm, safe, respected. It should have felt better than it did. After a while the wine began to erode my sense of discontent but from time to time I would see some or other long and rolling horizon from my travels, stretching away, full of secrets waiting to unfold. I tried to shake off the sensation and remind myself how awful it had been from beginning to end.

"Prince Jalan! How are you? You must tell us about your adventures." A man, catching my eye from a neighbouring table. I frowned a moment taking him in, thin, weasel-like, balding, a port-wine stain beneath his eye as if he'd been crying blood . . . Bonarti Poe! A dreadful social climber and a fellow I would normally cut dead, but lacking company, and remembering how pretty his sister was, I gave him the slightest nod and with a twitch of my finger beckoned him and his cronies over.

Before Roth's sons had the lamps lit I was in my cups, a bottle and a half to the good, and lying my way through the first leg of my trek north. I steered clear of unsettling detail and made no mention of the Dead King, but even so surprised myself by discovering that for once the lies were merely window-dressing and the truth provided a decent backbone to the tale.

"Two dozen of the brigands, pursuing us up into mountains as steep as any you'll find around the Aral Pass!" I drained my goblet, shaping the mountains in question with my spare hand. "Edris Dean at their head— as foul a murderer as ever—"

The conversation waned around me, not dying as if a man had walked in carrying a severed head, but fading as if every person there suddenly didn't want to be noticed. From the looks on the faces around me, all aimed my way, I thought for a moment that perhaps Edris Dean was standing behind me exactly as I had described him.

"Prince Jalan, how good to see you." A soft voice, slightly nasal, one might almost call it boring.

I turned, having to crane my neck awkwardly. "Maeres Allus." I managed not to stammer, though immediately I felt as though I were tied to that table of his, waiting for Cutter John to redesign my face with a sharp little knife.

"Don't let me disturb you, my prince." Maeres laid one of his small and neatly manicured hands upon my shoulder. "I just wanted to welcome you back from your travels. I believe that Count Isen is to pay a call to the Roma Hall tomorrow, but if you are available after that then it would be a pleasure to see you at the Blood Holes again and discuss matters of business."

The gentle pressure lifted and Maeres moved away without waiting for a reply. He left me feeling uncomfortably sober and all of a sudden wishing for the security of the palace walls.

"Damn fellow." I stood up, brushing at my shoulder where he'd touched me. "Remembered I've a thing at the palace. Royal . . . reception." I didn't feel drunk but my lying was below par. I have on occasion placated wronged husbands with the most ridiculous of excuses—the art is in the delivery. Said with enough conviction even "I dropped my cufflink down her bodice, gift from my mother don't you know, and she needed help getting it out," can be made to sound temporarily plausible. Nobody at this table however thought for one moment that I was leaving for any reason other than Maeres Allus.

I hastened away through the tables, making a waiter stumble to avoid disaster, and veering away as Marco hoved into view, no doubt to discuss his own matters of business and the purchase of four fine bottles of Chamy-Nix '96.

"Get up. Quick about it!" I snapped my fingers at Todd and Ronar dozing beneath the maple. Martus's guard would have stood all night, not sat down with their backs to a tree trunk. "We're going back." I could have been talking to the tree itself for all the response I got. I kicked Ronar's foot, hard. "Wake up! If you're drunk I'll have your—"

He slumped over, head hitting the paving slabs with a dull thud. Somewhere behind me a woman laughed.

"Shit."

I nudged Ronar over with my foot. His head lolled, eyes glassy, a line of red drool running from his mouth. Maeres had had them both killed. It was the only explanation. He'd had them murdered as a warning. I set off at a sprint.

It took me about two hundred yards to run out of puff and I stood gasping for air, doubled over, one hand against the gatepost of a large house. Sweat soaked me and dripped from my hair. Once I'd stopped running and let common sense catch up with me I realized I had no reason to run. If Maeres wanted me dead I'd be dead already. I knew from my time in his warehouse that madness lurked behind his calm and reasonable exterior. He didn't get to run half the criminals in the city by gentle persuasion, I'd always known that, but I had mistakenly thought him just another form of businessman, a pragmatist who would roll with the punches. The man I'd seen unmasked in that warehouse though— that man would consider my escape an injury to his pride and how much gold might be required to heal such an injury I couldn't say. Except that it would be more than I had.

TWENTY-TWO

The messenger brought two scrolls to the Roma Hall and though a hangover had been driven through my head like a huge metal spike I was awake and ready to receive them at the breakfast table. Outside grey dawn had started to tiptoe along the Kings Way toward the palace. I sat looking at the scramble of my eggs, the black scroll-case, and the copper-worked one, all with equal mistrust. My stomach's protests led me to push the plate away first. The black case bore an ivory cartouche displaying a wrecked ship in silhouette, the Isen crest. Inside would be formal announcement of his planned visit. The only question in my mind was where I was going to run to and whether to read the other message first. I had no funds to speak of, nowhere to run, and no excuse for running, but there wasn't any question of me staying to duel the Count of Isen. It would take more than Grandmother's disapproval to have me ready to face a lunatic like Isen in combat.

Pressing the heel of one hand to my forehead in an attempt to squeeze out the self-inflicted pain I reached, groaning, for the copper scroll-case. It bore no legend. I tried to pry the end off one-handed, cautious in case Maeres had sent me an asp. I ended up fumbling the thing to the floor and having to use two hands—both of them trembling with the aftermath of too much wine, stress, and the certainty that if there were an asp in there it would now be a decidedly pissed off one. The end cap unscrewed rather than pulled. I shook out the scroll within then smoothed it across the table. At first I had trouble focusing bleary eyes sufficiently to read the calligraphy set across the vellum. Some sort of official letter or warrant.

I fixated on a line near the top: "Davario Romano Evenaline of the House Gold, Mercantile Derivatives." Then one near the bottom. "Bearer

Prince Jalan Kendeth deputized to represent the interests of Gholloth in Afrique trade—specifically the RMS *Jupiter*, *Mars*, and *Mercury*." I blinked, lifted the scroll before my face and squinted at it. "House Gold, Umbertide, Florence."

It seemed to be a document both authorizing and dispatching me to conduct some kind of commercial negotiations in Umbertide, the banking capital of Florence. I ran my finger across the hard blob of sealing wax impressed with a complex sigil. It took me a moment to remember where I knew it from. Eight interlocking fingers.

"Garyus!" I said it out loud. Too loud. And wished I hadn't. For a moment the piercing agony of my hangover left no room for thought. "Garyus." A whisper. He had this symbol tattooed across the veins of his left wrist. And Gholloth must be his true name, after his father, King Gholloth II, Garyus being a diminutive, perhaps even "Gharyus"—I'd never seen it written. I looked more closely and saw that the "Jalan" appeared to overwrite some other name that had been scraped away, with another seal-mark to notarize the change.

I rolled the scroll up and tapped it into the case, then clutched it tight, hauling in a sigh of relief. I had my excuse for leaving and a place to go. Dear old Great-uncle Garyus had heard of my predicament and swapped me in for the duty. If I hurried I could be out of the palace before they dragged Snorri in, before the count turned up waving his sword and bleating about satisfaction, and before Maeres Allus knew anything about it. Better still, I was bound for Umbertide, where all the world's money washes up sooner or later: what better place for an impoverished prince to line his pockets? I could come back laden with gold, pay off Allus and the other vultures, and hopefully find that Sharal DeVeer had talked sense into her new husband by then.

"Saddle my horse!" And, hoping that someone would convey the order to the stablemaster, I plotted an unsteady path back to my rooms, determined to pack for the journey this time. The first thing I did was to swap my old campaign blade for the dress sword at my side. The queen's peace held on the roads to Florence but even so the old adage also held—the more used your sword looks, the less likely you'll have to use it.

• • •

Horse-riding is a kill-or-cure treatment for hangovers and I managed to stay on the right side of the divide, whilst wishing not a few times for the merciful embrace of death. I cantered out of Vermillion with over-full saddlebags bouncing against Nor's flanks and the morning sun beginning to heat the cobbles all around us.

I slowed Nor to a walk as soon as distance had diminished the city behind me to something I could block out with an outstretched thumb. It felt good to be on the move again, this time with a safe destination, a letter of authority in my pack, plenty of provisions, spare clothes, a horse, a handful of coppers, and six silver crowns. I'd left instructions for the count to be told I'd been called away on official royal business. It pleased me to think of him kicking his heels in the heat outside the Roma Hall then stomping back home. Maerus Allus could go hang too. I rode on in good spirits. There's something remarkably uplifting about moving on and leaving your troubles behind.

I rode a day, slept at a decent inn, enjoyed an enormous breakfast of mushroom omelette and fried potatoes, and set off again. Travelling incognito through my homeland proved a liberating experience, and whilst I missed the company the Norse had provided it did give me time to think my own thoughts and watch the world go by. It turns out that's highly over-rated.

Two thoughts started to gain prominence among all my speculation about events back in Vermillion. Namely, where were Grandmother's riders, with Snorri a prisoner in their midst, and why the hell hadn't I caught up with Hennan yet? How had an urchin on foot with just a day's start on me managed to stay ahead this long? Another day of clip-clopping down the Appan Way didn't answer either question. The sun set behind me bringing the faintest whisper of Aslaug's presence and throwing all the valley of Edmar into shadow. The white flash down Nor's face seemed to catch the last of the light and point the way. Warm air, the chirp of crickets rising among the vineyards lining the slopes to either side, the odd wagon or laden cart hauled by a sway-backed donkey . . . as peaceful an evening as a man could wish for. Instead I found myself wishing for the drunken riot of an evening at the Follies, followed by a drunken tumble with one of the more flexible performers (they liked to call themselves actresses) or perhaps two of them, or three. I rolled comfortably in Nor's saddle pondering how Vermillion called to me the moment I left it despite having proved something of a disappointment after my long absence.

I wasn't aware of the horsemen coming up behind me until the last moment—that's another disadvantage of getting lost in your thoughts. On my left a man leaned from his saddle and drew my sword, on my right another pulled his horse across Nor's path and grabbed the reins from me.

"If you'd be so kind as to dismount, Prince Jalan." A voice from behind me.

Leaning around, I saw three more men on horseback, the middle one a solid fellow, well-dressed in a high-collared cloak, the latest fashion, fastened with a thick gold chain. He looked to be about fifty, with close-cropped grey hair, dark eyes, and a grim smile. Cold hands contracted around my stomach and bladder with the realization that this was likely Count Isen. To his left a slighter figure hooded in grey, holding his reins in a single hand, to his right an ugly dark-haired bruiser much like those flanking me, only this one had a heavy crossbow levelled at my back.

I raised my hands, mind racing. "I'm on the queen's business. I've no time for games—especially not for being waylaid on the highway. This is common criminality! My grandmother has men nailed to trees for this kind of thing." I kept my voice as even as I could, choosing my words to remind the count of his duties and of mine. Challenging a man to a duel is one thing. Forcing him off the road at crossbow point is a very different matter.

"I asked you to dismount, Prince Jalan. I won't be asking again." The count seemed unmoved.

Slowly, so as to give no excuse to the fellow with the crossbow, I dismounted. It would just take one nervous twitch from the man, or even from his horse, and I could be staring at the hole a crossbow bolt had punched through me. I'd seen men hit by crossbow bolts at short range and very much wished that I hadn't.

"Easy now. This is madness! You only had to wait—"

"Свяжите его руках." The count waved at the two men who had dismounted as I did. I shook my head but couldn't make sense of the words.

"Hey now!" They grabbed my hands and secured them behind me with disturbing swiftness, having a rope noose already prepared to loop around both wrists.

The count glanced back down the road then stood in his stirrups to look ahead. Satisfied we weren't about to be disturbed in the next minute or two he sat back. "And the mask." Neither man shifted. The count placed his palm over his mouth, "слепок!"

A rustling behind me and hands reached around me to press something heavy across my mouth.

"No!" I started struggling but the man in front, tall as me and thick with muscle, punched me in the stomach, right in that spot that tells all the air to leave your lungs fast as it can.

While I doubled up they secured the gag, forcing the leather bit between my teeth as I gasped for breath. The thick leather straps reached out across my face and round the back of my head like the fingers of a hand, partly blocking my nose and half-covering my eyes. A common liar's mask of the sort used to transport seditionists and madmen. I would have smiled if I could. Count Isen had gone far too far. Grandmother wouldn't stand for anyone bearing her name to endure such humiliation. Dragging me through Vermillion like this might sully my reputation somewhat but the count would be lucky to escape with his lands and title, certainly there would be no question of me having to duel him.

"Up!" The count waved his hand at the pair manhandling me and with distressing ease they lifted me back onto Nor. I slipped my boots into the stirrups and held on tight with my knees. Falling off a horse with your hands tied behind your back is a quick way to break your neck.

The third of the Slavic men lowered his crossbow and removed the bolt. I guess the trio didn't speak the Empire tongue, though why the count would employ such men I couldn't—

"No!" Is what I would have said. Instead I made a muffled scream around the gag. The man on Isen's other side had raised his hood. He released his reins to do it since he only had the one arm. The hood slipped from a bald white skull, pale eyes stared into mine from a fleshless face that somehow, despite seeming nothing but skin stretched over bone, managed to look pleased to see me. How the hell did Maeres Allus's head torturer, Cutter John, come to be riding with Count Isen? I tried to urge Nor into a trot but the bully beside me had tight hold of the reins and the other punched me in the leg, hard enough for me to lose feeling in it.

"Steady now!" The count raised a hand. "You left it a little late to run, Prince Jalan." He smiled without humour. "I see you've recognized John. I'm Alber Marks, and my associates' names are unimportant. What is important is that they won't understand anything you say to them and have no idea who you are. I mention this only to save you breath when trying to bribe them or otherwise sway them from their purpose."

Shit. Shit. Shit. Maeres Allus had sent one of his best lieutenants after me. Alber Marks had a reputation for ruthless efficiency. Here I'd been thinking that only social niceties and royal duty stood between me and being run through with the count's longsword. But the real threat had been re-acquaintance with Cutter John's pincers—and anything that stood between me and being tied to a table in one of Maeres's warehouses had slipped away when I stopped paying attention. I should have known it wasn't the count. Isen was said to be a small man and even on a horse, dwarfed by henchmen, Alber Marks hadn't fit the bill.

"Come." Alber tilted his head and led off toward a gap in the verge where a tiny track angled away from the highway. The Slavs rode two in front, one behind, corralling me. They led me after Alber and Cutter John at an unhurried pace. It took a minute or two to get out of sight of the road among the vine rows and the dividing hawthorn hedges.

The men lifted me from Nor's back again and Cutter John came over to check my bonds, running a cold and long-fingered hand over each of the five straps about my head—an intimate touch that made me shiver with revulsion. A moment's fiddling at the back of my head and I heard the snap of a lock. Cutter John came back into view, dangling a small key before dropping it into his pocket. He smiled, displaying narrow teeth and pulled open his cloak to show the stump of his arm, ending in an ugly mass of pale scar just above the elbow. The last time I'd seen Cutter John blood had been pulsing from the wound—Snorri having sliced the arm off just moments before—and I'd given him several good kicks in the head while he lay unconscious, and I rather hoped, dying. I wished now I'd staved his skull in with a table leg.

Rummaging somewhat awkwardly in an inner pocket Cutter John drew out a pair of iron pincers. "Remember?" he asked.

I hadn't forgotten, though Lord knows I'd wanted to. The damn things had featured regularly in my nightmares for the past six months.

"I'll be waiting," he said, and moving behind me he caught the tip of one of my fingers in the pincers, squeezing hard. I roared behind the gag and threw myself about in the Slavs' grip and somehow my finger came free though with so much pain I couldn't tell if he'd snipped off the fingertip or not. The whole hand pulsed with agony and I hauled air in and out through my nose, slobber escaping the gag.

Alber Marks rode closer and leaned in. "John and I will be leaving now. It wouldn't be sensible to risk getting caught with you in our possession. We'll arrange a discreet entrance into the city for you and if I don't meet you again . . . well, I'm sure that John will." He straightened up. "Safe journey, Prince Jalan." And with that they both rode off at a trot, Cutter John bouncing along like a man unused to the saddle.

I sat struggling to draw breath past the mask, eyes swimming with tears, and with my finger ablaze with agony as if it had been dipped into hot acid. Even so my heart hammered slightly less frantically with each yard that opened up between us. It might seem small comfort but however dire my circumstances were the fact that Cutter John was riding away just made everything that bit better.

The relief proved short-lived. With a grunt one of the three Slavs tugged Nor's reins and we started back toward the Appan Way. I blinked a few times to clear my eyes and glanced around at the guards as we rode. They shared the same coarse features, their faces each comprising a set of broad planes: heavy brow above a small nose, prominent cheekbones from which sallow skin stretched down to a square jaw. I judged them to be brothers, possibly even triplets, for there was little to tell them apart. Without the mask and the language barrier I might stand a chance of talking my way out of it, but something about their eyes—that flat and unimaginative look they all had—told me they would be hard to turn from their course even then.

The first three times we passed people on the road I immediately started struggling and trying to call out. It earned me looks of disgust and jeers of derision from the travellers as they passed by, and cuffs around the head from the Slavs once they were out of sight. The fourth time I tried the carter's mate threw a rock at me and the largest of the Slavs punched me in the kidneys hard enough that I'd be pissing blood come morning. I gave up after that. The liar's mask made me near impossible to recognize even if our household servants were to walk on past. Moreover it marked me as an enemy of Red March whose untruths were poison. Most would assume I was being taken to trial and would probably lose my tongue once found guilty, or perhaps if the judge were lenient merely have it split to the root.

We made camp at the side of the road, far enough back into a field of maize to hide us from view. The relief I'd felt at being separated from Cutter John once more had quickly eroded as we reduced the gap again, making steady progress toward Vermillion. I hadn't any ideas about how to escape and being ridden through my own kingdom past dozens of loyal subjects, unrecognized and unable to ask for help was maddening.

Squatted in a flattened circle of maize and hemmed in on all sides by the tall green legion of undamaged crop, we were well hidden. Even the horses wouldn't be seen, heads bowed and crunching away on the nearly ripe cobs. One of the Slav brothers hammered a wooden stake into the ground and attached the back of my mask to it with a length of chain already bolted to the stake. This done, the brothers broke out cold rations and settled to eat—black bread, a tub of greyish butter, and a length of dark red sausage mottled with white lumps of fat and gristle. They devoured it in silence save for the constant chewing and occasional unintelligible word as they exchanged foodstuffs. None of them paid me the slightest attention. I tried to think of an escape plan whilst trying not to think how much I needed to piss. Neither attempt proved successful and it began to seem like the only way to alert the bastards to my toileting needs would be to wet myself.

It turns out that wetting yourself is quite difficult, going against a number of key instincts as it does. Even so, with enough time you'll get there. I was on the point of soiling myself when one of the Slavs got up and took a peculiar metal hook from his pocket. Without warning he grabbed the back of my head with one arm and forced the hook past the gag, snagging me by the corner of the mouth like a fish. Then, preventing my struggles simply by holding the hook, he took out a funnel and jammed its point into the end of the hook—which turned out to be a hollow tube.

"воды." He reached for a water skin and started to fill the funnel. From that point, until he stopped, the business of not choking to death kept me fully occupied. The incident made two things clear—firstly that they didn't have the key to the mask, and secondly if I were ever going to be fed again it would be after we reached Vermillion.

The "watering" solved the other problem I'd been having, my bladder losing all its shyness as I choked. The effect was at first a not-unpleasant warmth, fading fairly quickly to the less pleasant sensation of cold wet trousers.

The sun set and though I imagined Aslaug whispering amongst the dry voices of the corn I couldn't make out the words and she offered no help. In fact, it sounded almost like laughter.

Two brothers settled down to sleeping, leaving the third to watch me, and eventually I lay down on the bed of flattened maize stalks to try to sleep. My finger, or what I imagined might be left of it, pulsed with hurt, and without being able to bring my arms forward I could find no position in which they didn't ache, the mask was a misery and bugs emerged in the darkness to explore every inch of me. Even so, at some point in the night I passed out, and ten seconds later, or so it seemed, my captors were shaking me awake with the sky hinting grey above us.

I watched them break their fast, choked down more water, and was hoisted onto Nor's back once more. We resumed our journey toward Vermillion, clattering along at a gentle pace past the day-to-day traffic of wagons, messengers, carriages bound for distant destinations, and peasants making shorter visits on laden carts or leading over-burdened mules along behind them. The road rose among some stony ridge of hills that I didn't recall from my outward journey, and farmland gave over to a dry forest of cork oaks, beech, and loose-limbed conifers. The morning haze burned away and the sun beat down again, seemingly harder than before, raising a stink from the manure piles punctuating the Appan cobbles and making me yearn unexpectedly for the cool clean winds of a Norseheim spring. I lolled in the saddle, sweating, thirsty, and wretched, wondering how many flies were clustered around the aching ruin of my finger and laying their eggs in the glistening wound.

"That's him!" A man's voice, strident and triumphant. "Or at least it's his horse. Certain of that. Look at the flash."

I unglued my eyes and tried to focus. Four men on horseback had moved to block our way.

"It can't be him." A different man, dismissive. "A prince of Red March wouldn't—"

"Check him, Bonarti." This from the man on the largest horse, a real monster.

The last of them urged his steed toward me. The Slav brothers tensed but made no move to prevent his advance.

"Definitely his horse." The first man, daring anyone to disagree with him.

Relief flooded me. If I'd not been gagged I would have shouted for joy. Every ache vanished in the instant. Grandmother, Martus . . . someone . . . had learned of Maeres's intentions and sent out a rescue party. A rescue party including a man who'd taken note of Nor's peculiar markings—that jagged white flash down the velvety blackness of his nose. His distinctiveness had drawn me to buying him—I'd wanted to look good riding back into my hometown and, even though a connoisseur of horseflesh like myself shouldn't be guided by such frippery, I had let it guide me. And it must have guided Maeres's men too. If I'd only chosen a plain dun nag and worn a hood I would have been crossing the border into Florence instead of a day's hard ride from Vermillion and neck deep in the mire.

The thin man closing in on me leaned forward in his saddle to peer at me, his eyes narrow, one with the red stain of a birthmark just below it. It was Bonarti Poe! I'd last seen him at the Grapes of Roth just before Maeres showed up to ruin the evening. He might be an oily fellow with a pointy face that seemed to beg for slapping, but at that moment I'd never been so pleased to see anyone I knew. I didn't even begrudge him all the Rhonish red he'd swigged at my expense that night.

"Prince Jalan?"

I nodded vigorously making gurgling noises that I hoped sounded affirmative. Bonarti continued to peer at me closely, shifting his head from side to side as though it might help him see past the straps across my face. "It's him all right!" Then in a quieter and puzzled voice. "Prince Jalan, why are you—"

"He's hiding, obviously! A ruse to smuggle himself back into the city unobserved." The man on the enormous horse cut across Bonarti's question. My attention though was on the Slav brothers—given half a chance they'd cut my saviours down and carry on to Vermillion as if nothing had happened. I gestured urgently toward them with my head making gurgling noises that I hoped sounded a strong note of warning.

"Stop this foolery! Get down from there, sir! And face me like a man! Face me as you should have had the decency to do when you first received my challenge!" The man on the big horse had my attention now, his face red with fury around a neat grey moustache and the narrow slit of his mouth.

"His hands are bound, Count Isen!" Bonarti, leaning around me.

"Prisoner!" the Slav brother closest to me declared.

"Nonsense!" Count Isen—the real article this time—was having none of it. "Enough of this farce. Cut him loose and get him down. I've no time for such foolishness. A day wasted on the road when I could have been doing something useful . . ."

Bonarti took his knife, a small bejewelled thing, and cut my wrists free.

"Prisoner!" the Slav repeated but with no small amount of the traffic having stopped to watch the entertainment the brothers would be fools to try anything.

I brought my hands forward, rubbing both wrists and making a close study of my mutilated finger. It proved less injured than I'd imagined, with only the nail ripped away and the exposed flesh crusted over with black scabs. Part of me was pleased the damage wasn't irreversible, the other part horrified that so much pain had come from so small an injury. Even with the Count of Isen ready to slice me into quivering chunks I managed a shiver at the thought of what Cutter John could achieve given his leisure with a man.

"Get down, sir! I mean to have my satisfaction without delay!" And Count Isen swung himself from the saddle of his vast horse, to vanish entirely behind it. He emerged from its shadow, hands on hips, glaring up at me. He was as small a man as I'd seen in my months on the road, with the exception of Dr. Taproot's dwarf, dressed in the finest possible travel attire and trailing a sword at his hip that might have scraped the floor even if it hung from my own.

I reached up to my mask and tugged at it, pointing at Bonarti then at the back of my head.

"Yes, I bought Bonarti as your second. Mine's Stevanas over there." Isen waved a hand at a solid warrior glowering toward me from his horse. Sir Kritchen here will adjudicate to ensure fair play. Now get down, sir, or so help me I'll have you dragged from the saddle."

I met Isen's stare for the first time. Beneath neatly barbered hair and well-manicured eyebrows the eyes of a maniac stared up at me. A small maniac, granted, but somehow scary as all hell even so. I got off Nor's back sharp enough, tugging at the mask and discovering the heavy lock at the rear. Dismounting wasn't an act of bravery. The thing about horses is that they're great for running away once you're actually running away, but they lack a touch of initial acceleration so if you're right next to a threat and looking to escape, you may well find you're better off on foot. By the time Nor got up to speed and broke clear of my various captors, enemies, and would-be murderers, a least one of them would likely have stuck a sword through some part of me that I'd rather keep. Instead I tugged meaningfully at the straps and pointed at my mouth.

"Enough of this mummery! Defend yourself!" Count Isen drew his over-long sword and pointed it my way.

I held out my empty hands. "I haven't even got a sword you tiny madman!" is what I tried to say, though it emerged as a long string of "ung" sounds.

"Sir Kritchen." Isen kept those little black beads of insanity fixed on my face. "Give the prince his sword. I see the fellow behind him has two blades."

And while I made further protests Sir Kritchen, a tall elderly fellow I remembered from somewhere, dismounted to retrieve my sword from one of the Slav brothers. With the gathered crowd growing by the minute the man had little option but to hand it over. He didn't look happy. Probably wondering if his homeland was far away enough to avoid Maeres's wrath if they didn't get me back to him in Vermillion as charged.

Sir Kritchen, immaculate despite his long and dusty ride from the city, wrapped my right hand about the sword's hilt. The last time I'd swung the weapon in earnest had been at the Aral Pass. The notches told a story that I'd largely forgotten and wasn't keen to relive. Somehow terror had pushed me into a berserker frenzy that day. Even if I could repeat the feat here on the Appan roadside it would do me little good. Battle madness doesn't make you the better swordsman, it just stops you caring whether the man you're facing is the better swordsman.

I stared stupidly at my blade a moment, dazzled by the sunlight flashing from it. Dehydration and hunger had left me slow-minded, not quite connecting with the events unfolding around me.

"Clear a space! Stevanas—make some room!" Isen swung his sword in wide and dangerous circles.

"Wait! Get this thing off me first!" I tugged ineffectually at the mask, the words emerging as gurgles. A moment later I realized I was holding a sharp edge and with great relief turned it against the straps. Unfortunately it didn't seem possible to hold the sword far enough away to get the point to my face. I tried instead to saw at the straps with the length of the blade but they were so tight I couldn't get fingers beneath them, and so bedded into my flesh that cutting away at them blind and clumsy would inflict horrible wounds. Seeing Isen turn my way and knowing he intended to inflict rather more fatal injuries on me I started to cut at the most prominent strap, albeit somewhat tentatively. It hurt.

The highborn, barking as highborn are trained to, made a hole in the crowd quick enough. The onlookers were eager to see a show in any event and keen to help.

"Defend yourself, man!" Isen stepped toward me, his sword leading the way, point held steady and level with my heart.

"Stop!" I yelled. "I'm being held prisoner!" Or more accurately, "Gogh! Mmm meen meld mimimer!" My fingers were slick with blood or sweat or both but the strap seemed to be giving.

"It's better I don't have to listen to your lies, Prince Jalan, and better you don't have to shame yourself before these witnesses with excuses for your cowardice." The count's eyes burned with an insanity I couldn't quite place . . . perhaps three parts homicide and two parts absolute certainty that every word ever to pass his lips was God's own truth. "Have at you!"

"I'm not going to fight you!"—"Mmm mot mowing moo migh moo!" I resolved to make no move to defend myself and to rely instead on the count's honour to save me, or at least his fear of having his honour called into question.

The first strap gave. And with that he lunged.

Despite my conviction that I wasn't going to react I found myself leaping back and swinging my sword to deflect his. Whether it had been an earnest attempt on my life or a ruse to goad me into action I couldn't tell, but my body had made the decision for me and now he attacked with a flurry of blows very definitely intended to disembowel me.

My sword arm moved instinctively, following the patterns beaten into it over the course of so many long and miserable hours training in the weaponmaster's halls at Grandmother's insistence. The clash of steel on steel is always frighteningly loud and a helpful hint of the agony that being hit will involve is transmitted through the hilt, driving shards of pain through palm and wrist and making you want nothing more than to drop the damn sword.

For the first . . . well it felt like an hour but must have been considerably less than a minute, the tempo of Isen's attack left no fragment of a second spare for thinking. Instinct and training actually served me pretty well. I defended well though made no counter-attacks. The idea of deliberately slicing my sword into flesh—even the flesh of an odious dwarf like Count Isen—turned my stomach. It's not any sort of compassion—I'm just squeamish. I couldn't even contemplate it. Like sticking a needle into my own eye I found it something I just couldn't bring myself to try. Besides—I was busy.

We clashed our way in mostly one direction, me backing, scattering the crowd. Isen advancing with a small grimace of satisfaction on his face as he cut and thrust. It felt like battling someone standing in a hole, an uncomfortable sensation that left me worrying about a different set of vital organs than usual. I left the road, nearly tripping in the ditch and retreated across uneven ground, scrub catching at my feet.

All this for Sharal DeVeer's honour? For bedroom antics that happened long before he'd laid an eye on her . . . or perhaps the old goat had laid both eyes on her years back and had simply been waiting for her hand to be old enough for his ring, or maybe he'd had to wait for her over-protective father to die before forging a marriage deal with the new and less scrupulous Lord DeVeer?

Instinct and training served me well and it wasn't until the raw terror of it all caught up with me that my mind started interjecting and causing mistakes. The tip of Isen's blade scored a hot red line across my shoulder. It wasn't pain so much as shock . . . and horror. I knocked his sword up, sprang back, turned on a heel and ran flat out for the trees.

The surprise of it gave me a good head-start. I'd opened a lead of twenty yards before Count Isen's roar of disbelief caught up with me. I could hear the pursuit begin before I made it halfway to the tree-line but few men are gifted with my particular turn of speed and none of those I'd venture to say stood eye to eye with little Isen.

I passed between the first two elms with what would have been a wild grin, but for the mask. I could lose myself in the forest, be rid of the gag, sort myself out a safe passage to Umbertide and damn their hides. The Slavs would swear it wasn't me and I would, in the fullness of time, deny the whole thing. "You must be mistaken. Me in a liar's mask? How can you even tell who the wretched traitors wearing those things are? You should have taken it off—then it would have been obvious. Lucky Isen didn't murder the poor fellow!"

Panting, scratched and sweaty I paused, lost among the trees, mostly tall copper beeches. The ground beneath them lay thick with the rustling remains of last year's leaves, overgrown with brambles. I set my back to the thickest trunk in sight and started to work on the leather straps around my head again. This time wedging my sword hilt between my feet and going at it with considerably more care.

Applying a sharp edge to your face with sufficient force to cut old leather whilst trying to preserve your boyish good looks is a tricky business. In fact the task took up so much of my concentration that I almost missed the faint crunch of dry leaves beneath approaching boots.

Somehow the need to be able to talk over-rode the sudden rising panic and I kept sawing just long enough to break through the last of the straps. I pulled the damn thing free, working my sore mouth but careful not to spit or make any other sound that might draw attention.

"Stevanas? Poe?" More rustling, a muttered oath. "Sir Kritchen?" Count Isen's voice booming out far deeper than might be expected from so small a man, and far closer at hand than I'd thought he was. "Jalan Kendeth! Show yourself!" He sounded rather hoarse, as if he'd been shouting quite a bit.

With agonizing slowness I set the mask down and started to turn my sword around so I could grasp the hilt. Despite the utmost concentration my hands, slippery with sweat and blood, managed to do the exact opposite of what I asked them to and dropped the weapon. It landed with a muffled crunch among the dry leaves.

"Ah ha!" Count Isen appeared, rounding the bole of the forest giant next to mine, arriving from a completely unexpected direction and turning out to be far closer than I thought he was—the tree he skirted stood so close to the one at my back that their lower branches interlocked above us like the fingers of praying hands.

We both froze for an instant, eyes fixed to each other's, me sat on my arse with my sword on the ground before me, the silent forest all about us, lit here and there by irregular patches of sunlight, golden in the dappled gloom. Without further warning Isen charged, some wordless and murderous battle cry on his lips. I dived for my sword, shrieking that I was unarmed.

Just two yards short, with me still rising from my roll, the count's foot snagged on some hidden root and his lunge, intended to skewer me, became an ungainly thing, jolting with those overlarge strides we take in such circumstances to avoid falling on our faces. He ended up impaling the beech tree, his blade buried two or three inches deep in the exact spot my head had been resting against the trunk.

To the little bastard's credit he reacted swiftly, whipping out a knife fit for gutting oxen, and spinning round to brandish it at me.

"See here, Isen . . . bit of a misunderstanding . . ." The words felt wrong in my mouth after so long biting on the mask's bit.

Still he came on, holding that hideous knife up high so I saw his eyes one to either side of it, their pupils tiny black dots of madness, mouth twitching.

"Wait!" I held my blade between us at arm's length to fend him off. I struggled to think of a good reason for him to wait and of its own accord my mouth said, "Free your sword, man. I won't have it said I beat you unfairly!"

Count Isen paused, frowned, and glanced back at his sword still jutting from the trunk. His frown deepened. "Well . . . knife fighting *is* beneath men of noble birth . . ." He shot me a look that showed some doubt on the question of whether I were truly sprung from royal loins, then backed toward the tree.

Genius! Years of habitual lying had left me with a tongue capable of invention without requiring any conscious input from my mind. I tensed up, preparing for the sprinting away stage as soon as he started tugging on that sword hilt. As I did so however, I noticed my right foot was resting on a sturdy-looking branch, about three foot in length—a splintered section broken from the tree in some recent storm.

Count Isen sheathed his knife and set both hands to his sword hilt, his back to me as he got ready to heave. I swapped my sword to my left hand, picked up the stick and advanced on stealthy feet. Slow steps brought me up behind the count, the gentle crump of leaf litter under my boots inaudible beneath his grunting as he strained to work the trapped blade free. I glanced at the stick. It had a good weight to it. I shrugged and—trusting to my longer legs to win me clear if anything should go wrong—I whacked him squarely around the side of the head. I'd had poor experience before pitting vases against the back of a man's head, so I thought I'd try the side this time.

For a trouser-soaking heartbeat I thought Isen was going to stay on his feet. He started to turn, then fell into a boneless heap about halfway through the move. I stood there for a few moments, staring down at the unconscious count, breathing hard. At last it occurred to me to toss away the stick and at the same time I became aware of distant shouts and the clash of swords. I paused, wondering what the source might be.

"Nothing good." Muttered to the forest. And with a shrug I set off. Left to my own devices I might have lightened the count's purse to pay for the inconvenience and a new horse, but the sounds of fighting were drawing closer.

I set off at a decent pace, blundering through bushes into the bed of a dry stream that I proceeded to follow. I'd gone no distance at all when with a crashing of branches someone cannoned into me from the side, sending both of us tumbling in a confusion of twisted limbs and sharp elbows. A confused period of terrified shrieking and wild punches followed, ending with me managing to use my superior weight and larger frame to get on top with my hands around a scrawny neck.

"Poe?" I found myself looking down into the narrow and purpling face of Bonarti Poe. With a modicum of reluctance I unwrapped my fingers from his throat.

"T—" He hauled in a huge breath. "T-They followed—" He turned to the side and retched noisily into the leaf-filled streambed.

"Who followed what?" I got off him and stepped back, distaste twitching on my lips.

"T-Those men . . ."

"The Slavs?" I spun around, imagining them advancing on us through the undergrowth. Poe hadn't the spine to try and stop me, but those three needed me back in their clutches if they wanted to keep their skins.

"They attacked Stevenas and Sir Kritchen." Poe nodded, clambering to his feet. "I ran." He looked a sorry affair now, his city finery torn and dusty. "To get help." A hasty addition. He had the grace to look guilty.

Away to my right leaves rustled, twigs snapped—something advanced unseen toward us.

"Oh God!" Bonarti clutched his chest. "They're coming!"

"Shut. Up!" I grabbed his arm and yanked him down with me as I crouched low. The main thing about panicking is to do it quietly. I clutched him tight, wondering how long he'd slow the Slavs down if swung into their path. Insects buzzed around us, dry pebbles ground beneath my boot heels, the urge to piss built relentlessly, and all the time the crashing in the undergrowth drew nearer. It didn't sound like a charge directly at us so much as a meandering search that just might uncover us.

"We should run," Bonarti hissed.

"Wait." Running is all well and good but it has to be balanced against hiding. "Wait."

The rustling and tearing grew suddenly louder and a small figure stumbled from the bushes into the streambed about thirty yards from us.

"Count Isen!" Bonarti sprung to his feet as if the count's presence solved all his problems.

I leapt up a split second later, or tried to, but wrong-footed by the count's sudden appearance, my feet lost purchase amid the pebbles and I went sprawling forward onto all fours.

"You!" Isen pointed his over-long sword at me.

"I can explain!" I couldn't.

"You just left me! You can't abandon a man you've defeated!" He sounded disapproving rather than murderous. Sticky trickles of blood striated the side of his face below the spot where the branch caught him.

"Prince Jalan beat you?" Bonarti glanced round at me, surprised.

Count Isen advanced, a touch unsteady on his feet. "Found him in the forest, made my challenge, and had at him. Can't remember much after that. Must have caught me on the head with the side of his sword." He touched crimson fingers to his wound.

"Yes! Yes I did!" I got to my knees and shuffled backward.

The count paused a couple of yards before Bonarti and executed a short bow in my direction. "Well fought, sir!" He touched his matted hair again. "But—but, didn't you run?" Confusion in those beady eyes of his, hardening toward anger.

"Of course I did! We were endangering honest citizens, swinging away on the queen's highway like common brawlers. Besides, I needed to get clear of my captors and lead them into the forest where I could kill them without risk to the peasants."

"Commoners! Pah." Count Isen made to spit.

"Have a care, Isen." I got to my feet. "Those are my grandmother's citizens. The Red Queen says how their lives are spent, and nobody else!" I sheathed my sword just in case he should take offence.

Isen waved the matter away. "But you left me lying there!"

"I had to draw the Slavs off." Sometimes my lies impressed the hell out of me. "I couldn't have them find you unable to defend yourself. I would have stayed and fought them over your body but I couldn't be sure enough of defeating all three of them if they all came at once . . . so I drew them off." I straightened up to my full height and with both hands tugged my tunic forward across my chest in what I hoped would seem an authoritative, manly, and self-righteous gesture.

"Well . . ." Isen didn't quite seem to know what to make of it all. I suspected his wits were still somewhat scrambled from the blow to the head. He narrowed his eyes at me, at Bonarti, at a nearby tree, puffed through his moustache, and at length sheathed his own sword.

"Right then!" I gave the smallest of bows. "Honour is served. Let's go kill some Slavs!" And I led off in the opposite direction to the one in which I'd heard the clash of swordplay.

◆ ◆ ◆

Forests, it turns out, are treacherous things. It's damned easy to get turned around in among all those trees, and each one looks pretty much the same as the next. Somehow, despite declaring myself sure of the way and ignoring all of Isen's advice about getting back to the road, we found the Slavs. Or at least two of them, sprawled inelegantly across the forest floor amid their own blood—thankfully face down. Sir Kritchen had been laid out with his arms folded across his chest, almost obscuring the wound that killed him. I spotted Stevenas last, sitting with his back to a fallen tree, legs stretched out before him, his sword across them, dark with drying blood. His arm and left side were crimson, the puncture wound in his shoulder bound about with strips of his torn shirt, the musculature of his torso on display.

"Where's the other?" Isen, looking around, all business.

"Ran for it." Stevenas nodded toward a dense thicket of saplings.

Isen gave a dissatisfied snort. "We'll hunt him down soon enough." A glance at Sir Kritchen then a wave toward Stevenas. "Get him up." He paused for a moment, finding himself in the unusual position of not being able to order everyone around. "Bonarti, do it!"

Quite how Bonarti Poe, skinny and effete, was to get a slab of muscle like Stevenas off the ground I had no idea, but I damn well wasn't going to help with a mere count watching on. Besides, the man had been brought along to ensure fair play as Isen carved me up so I had little sympathy for him. Though I did appreciate his work on the Slav triplets. That said, two out of three isn't bad in many circumstances but here I'd really rather Stevenas had got the full set.

Count Isen and I watched on while Bonarti struggled with the warrior. Fortunately, despite his blood loss, Stevenas had enough go left in him to help out and soon we were following him as he led us back to the road, demonstrating considerably more competence than the rest of us in the business of navigation.

We clambered back across the ditch and onto the Appan Way once more, all of us rather more dirty, battered, and bruised than we had been a hour earlier. The crowd had long since dispersed but fortunately a pedlar had taken it on himself to park his cart and watch over all the abandoned horses. He'd probably spent the time weighing the chance of a reward against the profit in horse theft and juggling the odds of being caught alongside the rather harsh justice horse thieves tend to meet in Red March.

"Good man." Isen tossed the fellow a coin and waved him on his way. "Wait!" The count held up a hand before the pedlar could climb back into his cart. "Poe, take this man into the forest and retrieve Sir Kritchen. We can put him in the cart and take him back to Vermillion." He shook his head as if the thought of a knight reduced to cargo in a pedlar's cart offended him.

Bonarti looked about to complain but thought better of it and trudged back toward the tree-line with the pedlar in tow. Stevenas meanwhile managed to get himself into the saddle where he sat, hunched about the pain of his wound.

"So . . ." Count Isen peered up at me, eyes hard and narrow as if searching for a memory.

I decided to bluster my way out of there as quickly as possible in case as Isen's head cleared and the detail of quite what had fogged it in the first place started to seep back in. "Can't say I appreciated this whole affair, Count. A man marrying as fine a woman as Sharal DeVeer should be focusing on the future rather than rummaging in her past to find offence." I held my hand up to forestall him as he stepped forward, something bitter on his tongue. "I'll thank you though for freeing me from those rogues. They were in the pay of a man named Maeres Allus, a distributor and producer of opium among other things. Probably has fingers in some of your pies too. I hear he has influence in the Corsair Isles. In any event, I shall be dealing with him on my return but for now I've business in Umbertide on the queen's behalf."

I set a foot into Nor's stirrup and stepped lively onto his back. Count Isen kept setting his fingers to his bloody scalp and I really didn't want to be on hand if he dug out a splinter and jogged back any of those lost memories. I leaned over and snagged the reins of first one, then two, finally all three of the Slavs' horses.

"Count Isen." I inclined my head some fraction of a degree. "Stevenas." And I set off awkwardly, leading the three nags alongside me. I planned to sell them at the next decent inn and my need for gold overrode any shame at such looting with Isen and his henchman watching on.

For the first hundred yards I could feel Isen's stare burning into the back of my neck. I may have got the drop on the little madman but he still scared the hell out of me. Men like him and Maeres deserved each other. I hoped Isen would take Sir Kritchen's death as a personal insult and take Master Allus to task over the matter.

Riding on in the noonday sun with the road ahead drowned beneath a shimmering heat haze a sudden rush of relief ran through me and left me shuddering. In the space of a day I'd been caught by both the nightmares that chased me out of my home so quickly after finally making it back. I'd jumped, or been pushed, from the fire into the frying pan and finally escaped, somewhat singed, to retrace steps I'd taken two days previously. "I hope the bastards eat each other alive," I told Nor, then kicked his ribs to break him into a canter. Standing in the stirrups I gave a whoop and urged him on. I couldn't leave that shit behind me quick enough!

TWENTY-THREE

Having escaped both Maeres Allus and Count Isen I rode on south buoyed up by the kind of good spirits I hadn't had since . . . well, since being on the road with Snorri. My good mood lasted until early evening when the sullen heat piled up a thunderhead of titanic proportions that proceeded to try and drown everyone on the Appan Way. I took shelter beneath a huge oak a hundred yards off the road in the midst of a tobacco field. Lightning began to fracture the sky, the thunder rolling back and forth. Nor nickered and pulled, skittish and threatening to bolt with each new crash from above. They do say it's foolish to stand beneath a tree when there's lightning all about, but getting soaked through when there's shelter to hand seemed more foolish so I decided it was probably an old wives' tale and ignored the advice. Soon enough a small crowd of travellers had joined me—a couple of old wives among them.

We stood waiting for the rain to slacken off, the commoners gossiping among themselves, me keeping a dignified silence and listening in surreptitiously.

". . . Nobby? Ain't seen Nobby in donkey's years. Had a flat head did Nobby—last time I saw him he had a flagon of beer balanced on his head and a beer in each hand . . . must've been twenty years ago . . ."

". . . two dozen palace riders! Going like the devil they were, headed south. More following behind, checking everyone . . ."

"Gelleth! No? Truly? . . . Must have been a judgment on them. A godless lot they are up north . . ."

Out on the road a tight pack of riders hastened north toward Vermillion. Through the rain, and with their cloaks sodden and dark, it was hard to make out the uniform but I could see that it *was* a uniform, which made it pretty certain they were some portion of the cavalry that Grandmother had sent out after Snorri. Probably the Undoreth and Kara were in the middle of the bunch, quite possibly each tied across a saddle.

When the ferocity of the downpour abated I took to the road again and pushed on at a decent pace. The sun re-emerged and the puddles began to steam. Two hours later the road ahead lay dusty and parched as if the rain had never happened. There's a lesson in that somewhere. The road forgets. Make your life a journey, keep moving toward what you want, leave behind anything that's too heavy to carry.

The miles passed easily enough. I took a room at a decent inn and got a quantity of lampblack with which I set to obscuring the distinctive flash of white along Nor's nose. Sometimes it's better to travel incognito than in style.

I pressed on, day after day, expecting to find Hennan on the road still hunting the good life with Snorri, not knowing the Norse had been captured and taken back to Vermillion with that damned key.

The further I rode the more impressed I was with Hennan's fortitude and pace. By the time I reached the Florence border I assumed I must have missed him along the way. That or some harm had come to him. The type of harm that grabs you from behind and buries your body in a shallow grave. The idea gave me a peculiar type of pain, deeper and different from the simple fear of what Snorri would say if he found out I'd let the boy run away and get himself killed. I shrugged the feeling off, attributing it to indigestion from the pastry I'd had off a roadside salesman some hours before. The nearer I got to Florence the less the local food seemed to agree with me.

Ten miles before the frontier between Red March and Florence the Appan Way joins the Roma Road and becomes subsumed by the larger route, our traffic lost in the to and fro of that great artery of Empire. For all of us heading south an air of anticipation grew. After Vyene, and Vermillion of course, there is no greater city than Roma in any fragment of the Broken Empire, and the taste of Roma lay thick in the air. The sight of papal messengers reminded us all how close the pope lay now. Scarcely an hour would pass without one of the pope's riders clattering by, flamboyant in their purple silks atop lean stallions, glossy black and bred for endurance. Monks traipsed the road in columns of ten or thirty, chanting prayers or calling the plainsong up and down their length, and priests of every shade and flavour beat their paths north and south. I recalled that my own father must have passed this way with his retinue scarcely a week earlier. I guessed the old man must be in Roma by now, presented before her holiness and perhaps having it explained to him what a cardinal should be and by just how wide a margin he had missed the mark.

My banking papers and obvious breeding got me through the border checkpoint, a pleasant enough inn with an attached barracks full of ornately armoured and overheated Florentine soldiers. The country on the other side of the frontier proved as dry and as hot as the southern stretches of Red March had. Where streams ran they grew olive groves, tobacco, chillies and oranges. Where there were no streams they farmed rocks, with the occasional goat watching on.

Sleepy whitewashed villages observed the Roma Road from the slopes of the arid foothills. In time the villages became towns and the foothills reached up toward mountains. The Roma Road, forced at last from its stubborn addiction to straightness, began to wind and turn, bending its will to that of the surrounding terrain. The air grew a touch fresher and the peaks' shadows filled the valleys, making each evening a blessed relief from the heat of the plains.

Umbertide revealed itself as the road wound down from a high pass into the broad and fertile valley of Umberto. The city, viewed from an elevation, lay white and splendid, surrounded by orderly farming districts and outlying villas of enviable size. The impression of wealth and peace only grew as the remaining distance shrank.

My papers won me swift passage through the city gates and soon I was trailing one of the urchins who wait by the entrance of every city, touting to lead you to the best example of whatever it is you're seeking, be it a bed for sleeping, a bed for fornication, or a hostelry to wash the road dust from your throat. The trick is to remind them that if it doesn't look like the best then they'll get your boot up their arse rather than a copper in hand.

I took a room at the boarding house the boy led me to and stabled Nor across the road. After cleaning myself up with a washbowl and rag I took my meal in the communal hall and waited out the noonday heat listening to the local chatter. The travellers in Mistress Joelli's house of good repute came from every corner of the empire and held little in common save for their business in Umbertide. There didn't seem to be a man among them who wasn't in search of a loan or finance for some or other venture. And they all carried the scent of money about them.

That afternoon found me in the cool marble vault of the reception hall at House Gold. Visitors paced, their footsteps echoing, clerks passed through, bound on definite courses, and receptionists scribbled behind marble counters, raising their heads only when some new arrival presented themself.

"Prince Jalan Kendeth to see Davario Romano Evenaline." I waved the papers at the small and pinch-faced man behind the counter, affecting that strain of boredom that my brother Darin uses so well on officials.

"Take a seat, please." The man nodded to a bank of chairs against the far wall and scribbled something in his ledger.

I held my ground, though tempted to lean over the counter and slam the fellow's head into it.

A long moment passed and the man looked up again, mildly surprised to see me still there.

"Yes?"

"*Prince* Jalan Kendeth to see Davario Romano Evenaline," I repeated.

"Take a seat please, *your highness.*"

It looked to be the best I'd get out of him without the application of a hammer and so I stalked off to view the street from one of the tall windows. Halfway across the foyer I spotted a familiar face and veered away. Some faces are hard to forget—this face, tattooed as thickly as any clerk's ledger with heathen script, was impossible to forget. I'd seen it last in Ancrath, in a peculiarly lucid dream, urging me to have Snorri killed. I found myself facing a row of chairs along the wall beside the counter and took a place beside a dark fellow in light robes. I kept my head down, hoping Sageous hadn't seen me, my eyes on his feet as he continued across the marble floor. I didn't draw another breath before the dream-witch exited into the street.

"He saw you."

I turned to look at the man beside me, a fellow of modest build in the kind of loose, flowing robe that keeps a body cool in places where the heat is even less tolerable than in Umbertide. I gave him a nod. My enemy's enemy is my friend, I always say, and we had both suffered at the hands of the jumped-up desk clerk. Perhaps we might also share an enemy in Sageous.

"He was depositing gold," the man said. "Maybe a fee from Kelem. He has spent time in the Crptipa Hills. It makes a body wonder what two such men might work at together."

"Do you know Sageous?" I tensed, wondering if I were in danger.

"I know of him. We've not met, but I doubt there are two such men wandering the world."

"Ah." I slumped back in my chair. I shouldn't have been surprised. Knowing everyone's business was everyone's business in Umbertide.

"I know you." The man watched me with dark eyes. He had the mocha tones of North Afrique, hair black, tight-curled, and tamed with ivory combs that bound it close to his skull.

"Unlikely." I raised a brow. "But possible. Prince Jalan Kendeth of Red March." Not knowing the man's station I omitted any promise of being at his service.

"Yusuf Malendra." He smiled, revealing jet-black teeth.

"Ah. From the Mathema!" All the mathmagicians of Liba blackened their teeth with some kind of wax. I'd always felt it a peculiarly superstitious practice for a sect otherwise so bound with logic.

"You've been to our tower in Hamada, Prince Jalan?"

"Uh. Yes. I spent my eighteenth year studying there. Can't say I learned much. Numbers and I agree only to a certain point."

"That will be where I know you from then." He nodded. "Many things escape me, but faces tend to stay."

"You're a teacher there?" He didn't look old enough to be a teacher, thirty maybe.

"I have a number of roles, my prince. Today I am an accountant, come to audit some of the caliph's financial affairs in Umbertide. Next week perhaps I'll find myself wearing a different hat."

A metallic whir turned our heads from the conversation. A sound halfway between that of a hand rooting in the cutlery drawer and that of a dozen angry flies. A shadow loomed across us, and looking up I saw the towering architecture of what could only be one of the banking clans' famous clockwork soldiers.

"Remarkable," I said. Mostly because it was. A man built of cogs and wheels, his motion born of meshing gears and interlocking steel teeth, one thing turning the next turning the next until an arm moved and fingers flexed.

"They are impressive." Yusuf nodded. "Not Builder-work though. Did you know that? The Mechanists made them over a century after the Day of a Thousand Suns. A marriage of clockwork that descends to scales smaller than your eye can perceive. It wouldn't have worked before the Builders turned their Wheel of course, but one wheel turns another as they say, and many things become possible."

"Jalan Kendeth." The thing's voice came out higher and more musical than I had been expecting. In truth I hadn't been expecting it to speak at all, but if I had I would have imagined something deep and final, like lead blocks falling from a height. "Come."

"Amazing." I stood to measure myself against the construction and found I didn't reach to its shoulder. The soldier unsettled me. A mechanism, lifeless and implacable, and yet it walked and spoke my name. Apart from there being something deeply unnatural and wrong about a heap of cogs aping life itself I felt most uncomfortable at the thought of something so dangerous, and so near, that lacked the usual levers by which I manipulated potential opponents, such as flattery, pride, envy, and lust. "And they can bend swords? Punch through shields like the stories tell?"

"I've not seen such," Yusuf said. "But I did see one carry a vault door into a bank being refurbished. The door could not have weighed less than fifty men."

"Come," the soldier repeated.

"I'm sure it can ask better than that, can't it? Or has its spring for manners unwound?" I grinned at Yusuf and rapped my knuckles on the soldier's breastplate. "Ask me again, properly." My knuckles stung so I rubbed them with my other hand. "Fifty men, you say? They should build more and take over the world." I walked around the thing, peering into the occasional chink in the filigreed plates of its armour. "I would."

"Men are cheaper to make, my prince." Again the black smile. "And besides, the art is lost. Look at the workmanship on the left arm." He pointed. The arm was larger than its counterpart, a thing of brass and iron, marvellously worked, but on closer inspection the gears, pulleys, cables and wheels, though ranging from tiny and intricate to large and chunky, never became smaller than something I might just about imagine a very skilled artisan producing.

"It's driven from the torso, and lacks any strength of its own," Yusuf said. "Most soldiers are part replacement these days, and the clock-springs that were wound to give them power are winding down—the knowledge required to rewind such mechanisms was lost before the clans took ownership of the Mechanists' legacy."

As Yusuf spoke my eyes fixed upon an indentation between the soldier's shoulders, a complex depression into which many metal teeth projected. Perhaps a winding point, though how one might work it I had no idea.

"Come, Prince Jalan." The soldier spoke again.

"There." I walked past it into the open space of the hall. "You see, you can address me properly if you try. I advise that you study the correct forms of address. Perhaps you might master them before you unwind completely and become an interesting drawing room ornament."

Iron fingers flexed and the soldier came toward me on heavy feet. It brushed past and led on through the crowd. I took some measure of comfort knowing the thing actually did appear to have attitude and that I'd managed to get beneath its metal skin.

I followed the mechanism up a flight of marble stairs, along a broad corridor with offices to either side in which a great number of clerks sat at desks checking through rolls of figures, tallying and accounting, and up a second flight to a polished mahogany door.

The office behind the door had that mix of Spartan design and money that the very richest aspire to. When you've moved past the stage of needing to show everyone how wealthy you are with gaudy displays of your purchasing power you reach a stage at which you return to simple and purposeful design. With cost being no object, each part of your environment will be constructed of the absolute best that money can buy—though it may require close inspection to determine it.

I of course still aspired to the stage at which I could afford my gaudy displays. I could however appreciate the utilitarian extravagance of the paperweight on the desk in front of me being a plain cube of gold.

"Prince Jalan, please take a seat." The man behind the desk didn't bow, didn't rise to greet me, in fact he barely glanced up from the parchment in front of him.

It's true that the niceties of courtly etiquette are rarely offered to me outside the confines of the palace, but it does pain me to have such conventions ignored by people who should know better. It's one thing for some peasant on the road to fail to recognize my station, but a damned banker with not a drop of royal blood in his veins and yet sitting on a pile of gold, metaphorically, that would dwarf the value of some entire countries . . . well that sort of injustice practically demands that the man smarm all over any person of breeding to make up for it. How else are they to persuade us not to damn their eyes, march our armies into their miserable little banks and empty the vaults out to serve some higher purpose? It's certainly what I plan to be doing when king!

I took the seat. A very expensive one and not the least bit comfortable.

He scratched something with his quill and looked up, eyes dark and neutral in a bland and ageless face. "You have a letter of deputization, I understand?"

I lifted the scroll Great-uncle Garyus had sent me, drawing it back a fraction as the man reached for it. "And you would be Davario Romano Evenaline of the House Gold, Mercantile Derivatives?" I let him chew the consequence of failing to introduce himself.

"I am." He tapped a little nameplate angled toward me on his desk.

I passed the scroll across, lips pursed, and waited, staring at the dark and thinning hair atop his head as he bent to read.

"Gholloth has placed a significant trust in your hands, Prince Jalan." He looked up with considerably more interest, a hint of hunger even.

"Well . . . I guess my great-uncle has always been very fond of me . . . but I'm not entirely clear how I'm to represent his interests. I mean they're just ships. And they're not even here. How far is it to the nearest port? Thirty miles?"

"To the nearest port of consequence it is closer to fifty miles, prince."

"And, between you and me, Davario, I'm not fond of boats of any kind, so if there's any setting sail involved . . ."

"I think you rather miss the point, Prince Jalan." He couldn't help that smug little smile that people get when they're correcting foolishness. "These vessels don't concern us except in the abstract. We've no interest here in ropes and barnacles, tar and sailcloth. These ships are assets of unknown value. There's nothing finance likes to speculate about more. Your great-uncle's ships are no common merchant ships hopping along coasts. His captains are adventurers bound for distant shores in ocean-going vessels. Each ship is as likely never to return, sunk on a reef or the crew eaten by savages, as it is to limp into an empire port groaning with silver, or amber, or rare spices and exotic treasures stolen from unknown peoples. We trade here in possibilities, options, futures. Your paper . . ." Here he held it aloft. ". . . once the seals are checked by an expert archivist against our proofs . . . gives you a position in the great game we play here in Umbertide."

I frowned. "Well, games of chance and I are no strangers. This trading in papers . . . is it a bit like gambling?"

"It's exactly like gambling, Prince Jalan." He fixed me with those dark eyes and I could imagine him sitting across a poker table in some shadowy corner rather than across his exquisite desk. "That's what we do here. Only with better odds and larger wagers than in any casino."

"Splendid!" I clapped my hands together. "Count me in."

"But first the authentication. It should be complete by tomorrow evening. I can give you a note of credit and have the soldier outside escort you back to your residence. The streets are safe enough but one shouldn't take unnecessary risks where money is concerned."

I didn't much like the idea of the clockwork soldier following me back to Madam Joelli's. A touch of caution I'd developed on the road made me want to let as few people as possible know where I lay my head, and besides, the thing made me uncomfortable.

"My thanks, but I can make my own way. I wouldn't want to have the thing wind down halfway there and have to carry it back."

Davario's turn to frown, an expression of annoyance, quickly gone. "I see you've been listening to gossip, Prince Jalan. It's true much of the city's clockwork is winding down, but we have our own solutions here in the House Gold. You'll find we're a progressive organization—the sort of place a keen young trader like yourself might fit in. Consider keeping your business in-house and we may have a good future together, prince." He pulled from just beneath the lip of the desk what looked like a drinking horn attached to some kind of flexible tube, and spoke into it. "Send in the beta-soldier." Davario nodded toward the door. "You'll see something special here, Prince Jalan."

The door swung open on noiseless hinges and a clockwork soldier walked in, smaller than the one that led me to the office in the first place, its gait smoother, a porcelain face instead of the side-on view of brass spacing plates and clockwork that lay behind the first soldier's copper eyes and voice grille. A man came in behind the soldier, presumably the technician responsible, a white-faced and humourless fellow in the tight-fitting blacks and peculiar headwear of a modern.

"Show our guest your hand, beta," Davario said.

The construct raised its arm with a whirr of meshing teeth and presented me with its left hand, a corpse-white thing, in every regard human save for its bloodless nature and the fact that brass rods slid into the flesh behind the knuckles and moved to flex and curl the fingers.

"The clockwork pokes around a dead hand? Did you buy some beggar's hand, or rob it from a grave?" The thing turned my stomach. It gave off no discernible aroma but somehow made my nose twitch with revulsion.

"Donated to clear a debt." Davario shrugged. "The bank will have its pound of flesh. But you're wrong, Prince Jalan. The rods don't drive the hand. The hand pulls on the rods and winds secondary springs within the torso. Not as efficient as the Mechanist clock springs, but something we can build and repair, and adequate for mobility if constantly rewound by flesh augmentation."

The white fingers before me curled into a fist and returned to the soldier's side.

"But the hand is . . ." The hand was dead. "This is necromancy!"

"This is necessity, prince. Necessity spawning invention from her ever-fertile womb. Need breeds strange bedfellows and those who trade in a free market find all manner of transactions coming to their door. And of course it doesn't stop with just a hand or a leg. The whole exoskeleton of a clockwork soldier can . . . potentially . . . be clothed in cadaverous flesh. So you see, Prince Jalan, you need have no fears for the security and vigour of House Gold. The last of the Mechanists' work may indeed be winding down, but we, we are winding up, gearing for a bright future. Your great-uncle's investments and trades are safe with us, as are those of the Red Queen."

"The Red Qu—"

"Of course, Red March has been at war or on a war footing these past thirty years. Some say west would be east by now if it weren't for the Red Queen sitting in between them and saying 'no' to all comers. And that's all well and good, but a war economy consumes rather than generates. Umbertide has financed your grandmother's war for decades. Half of Red March is mortgaged to the banks you can see from Remonti

Tower just across the plaza at the end of the street." Davario smiled as if
this were good news. "By the way, allow me to introduce Marco Onstantos Evenaline, Mercantile Derivatives South. Marco has recently been
appointed to help audit our Red March account."

The modern standing behind the abomination that Davario seemed
so proud of offered me the thinnest of smiles and watched me with dead
eyes.

"Charmed," I said. All of a sudden I wasn't sure which unnerved me
most, the monstrosity of corpse and metal before me, or the white-faced
man standing in its shadow. Something was seriously amiss with the
man. A coward knows these things, just as the cruel and violent have an
instinct for seeking out cowards.

Without further remark Marco led the clockwork soldier from the room.

"He's a banker then, this Marco?" I asked as the door shut behind
them.

"Among other things."

"A necromancer?" I had to ask. If the House Gold were extending
the use of their clockwork soldiers by means of such crimes against nature
then I had to wonder who was doing the work for them and if the Dead
King had his bony fingers in their pie.

"Ah." Davario smiled and showed his small white teeth, too many of
them, as if I'd made a witticism. "No. Not Marco. Though he has worked
closely with our practitioners. Necromancy is an unfortunate word with
overtones of skulls and graveyards. We're much more . . . scientific here,
our practitioners adhere to strict guidelines."

"And what of Kelem?" I asked.

The banker stiffened at that. A nerve touched.

"What of him?"

"Does he approve of these . . . innovations? Of your practitioners and
their arts?" I really wanted to ask if Kelem owned half of Red March but
perhaps I didn't want to hear the answer to that question.

"Kelem is a respected shareholder in many of Umbertide's institutions." Davario inclined his head. "But he does not control the House

Gold nor make our policy. We are a new breed here, Prince Jalan, with many profitable associations."

Davario took a piece of parchment from his drawer, heavy grade and cut into a neat rectangle. The thing had been marked all over with precise scrollwork and an exquisitely detailed crest of arms. He took his quill and wrote "100" in a clear space near the middle, signing his name below.

"This is a credit note for one hundred florins, Prince Jalan. I hope it will be sufficient for your needs until your great uncle's paperwork is certified." He slid it across the desk to me.

I picked it up by the corner, and shook it as I might a suspect letter. It hadn't any weight to it. "I do favour cold currency . . ." I turned the note over, the reverse decorated in more scrollwork. "Something more solid and real."

A small frown creased the flesh between Davario's eyes. "Your debts aren't currency, my prince, and yet they're every bit as real as your assets."

My turn to frown. "What do you know about my debts?"

The banker shrugged. "Little more than that they exist. But if you sought to borrow money from me I would know far more about them by sunset." His face became serious and despite our civilized surroundings I felt little doubt that in the matter of collecting what might be owed to the House Gold Davario Romano Evenaline would be no more inclined to show mercy than Maeres Allus. "But I wasn't talking about your debts: it's your Uncle Hertet's debts that are the stuff of legend. He's been borrowing against the promise of the throne since he came to his majority."

"He has." I managed to stop the words becoming a question. I knew the heir-apparently-not liked to spend and had several ventures on the go, including a theatre and a bathhouse, but I had assumed that the Red Queen indulged him in recompense for her failure to either be a doting mother or to die.

Davario returned to his theme. "Debts are very real—they're not hard currency but they *are* hard facts, my prince. This note is a promise: it carries the reputation of the House Gold. The whole of Umbertide, the whole of finance, runs on promises, a vast network of interlinked promises, each balanced on the next. And do you know what the difference is between a promise and a lie, Prince Jalan?"

I opened my mouth to tell him, paused, thought, thought some more, and said, "No." I'd uttered plenty of both and the only difference seemed to be the side you looked at them from.

"Well and good, if we ever found someone who did we might have to kill them. Ho ho ho." He spoke his laugh, not even pretending humour. "A lie may prove true in the end, a promise might be broken. The difference might be said to be that if a person breaks one promise then all their promises are suspect, worthless, but if a liar tells the truth by accident we don't feel inclined to treat all their other utterances as gospel. The promise of this note is as strong, or weak, as the promise of every bank in this broken empire of ours. If it breaks, we plunge into the abyss."

"But . . . but . . ." I grappled with the idea. I'm an easy man to put the fear of God into . . . unless it actually is *God* you're talking about, then I'm rather more relaxed, but this notion of kingdoms and nations standing or falling on the reputation of a collection of grubby bankers took more imagination than I could muster. "Any promise can be broken," I offered, trying to think of anyone whose promise I might actually stake something on. For a promise that benefited me rather than the other person I could only come up with Snorri. Tuttugu would try not to let you down, but that's not the same as actually not letting you down. "Most promises are broken." I set the note back upon the table. "Except mine of course."

Davario nodded. "True, just as every man has his price, every promise has a fault along which it might be fractured. Even the bank has its price, but fortunately nobody can afford to pay it, and so to all intents and purposes it is as incorruptible as the holy mother in Roma."

And that took my faith in the paper away again in a stroke. Even so I took it, and left with the necessary pleasantries, once more turning down the idea of an escort.

In the lengthening shadows and narrow alleys of Umbertide I almost regretted the decision not to have a mechanical monster walk me home. To find necromancy waiting for me in the city's innermost circles did nothing to settle my nerves after the narrowly avoided horrors of my journey. At each turn I felt hidden eyes upon me and picked up my pace a little more, until by the time I reached my lodgings I'd almost broken into a run and my clothes were soaked with sweat.

I wondered about Hennan too, lost on the road, and about Snorri; was he in Vermillion now, a broken man, the key taken from him?

TWENTY-FOUR

Despite my fears I settled into Umbertide life like a gambler taking his place at a card table. I hadn't come for the night life, to attend the balls, to savour the local wines, nor for the opportunities to climb the local social ladder, not even to find a rich wife—I'd come to take the money. Of a certainty I would be interested in many of those other things, wife-hunting excepted, in due course, not that a banking town like Umbertide had much of a seedy underbelly to explore, but I can be surprisingly focused when it comes to gambling. My ability to spend twenty hours a day at a poker table for seven days straight is one of the reasons I was able to pile up so prodigious a debt to Maeres Allus at such a tender age.

A number of major trading floors punctuate the map of Umbertide, some defined by the Houses that control them, others by the nature of the trades conducted there. I started on the House Gold floor so I could receive instruction on the basics from Davario's white-faced and humourless underling Marco Onstantos Evenaline.

"Stakes in business ventures of modest size are sold in twenty-fourths, shares in larger enterprises, even the banks themselves, can be purchased in ten thousandths. Though even a ten thousandth of a concern like the Central Bank will be beyond the pocket of many private traders." The man had a voice that could bore goats to death.

"I understand. So, I'm ready to play. I've got stakes to sell in three of the finest merchantmen beneath sail on any ocean anywhere, and an eye to buy." I looked out across the traders: a mixed bunch, House Gold men in the majority but interspersed with independents from many distant shores. The House Gold traders wore black with gold trim and smoked constantly, pipe and cigarillo, in such quantity that a pall of acrid smoke floated above the traders' heads. Can't abide the smell myself. Tobacco remains one of the few dirty habits that holds no appeal for me. "I think I can wing it from here."

"Stakes are purchased using the calendula paddle to attract the seller's attention," Marco continued as if I hadn't so much as twitched my lips. "Both parties then retire to one of the transaction booths after contracting a House Gold witness to officiate the paperwork. The sale must then be registered at—"

"Really, I understand. I just want to get start—"

"Prince Jalan." A prim and reprimanding tone, the first colour to enter his voice in my hearing. "It will be several days before you're ready to make any purchase on this or any other floor. Davario Romano Evenaline has charged me with your education and I cannot in good faith allow you to trade in ignorance. Your licence will not be forthcoming until I say you are ready to purchase." He clamped his pale lips together and craned his neck until it made the most unhealthy creak. "For sales greater than one thousand florins in value a senior witness, indicated by the green flashes on the lapels of the trading coat—"

"What about the clockwork soldiers?" I cut across him. "Is there a 'concern' that specializes in those? Could I buy a piece of that?" I didn't want to make any such purchase but the only time I'd seen a flicker in those blank banker eyes of his was when Davario was discussing his ghoulish pet project, dead flesh on metal bones.

"Ownership of the soldiers rests in the hands of many private individuals and business enterprises. There is no central regulation, though the state, in the name of Duke Umberto, hold the rights to the Mechanists' knowledge—"

"The rights to knowledge that nobody understands . . . I think I'll pass on that one. But tell me—how many ten thousandths of House Gold would I need to own before I got to have a say in what goes on in your laboratories? How much would I have to pay over to find out just how far the Dead King's hand reaches into the things that get built below Davario's office?"

If possible Marco's face grew even more stiff and more pale at my impertinence. "The utilization of cadaver material on our mechanical frames is perhaps . . . commercially sensitive in detail, but not a secret in general. We contract input from independent experts in the field. Again, their names are not classified information."

"Give me one then," I said, grinning as broadly as I could, trying unsuccessfully to spark an echo on lips so narrow and bloodless that I doubted they even had the ability to smile.

"I can give you three, one of them newly arrived in town." He hesitated. "But all information has value in Umbertide and nothing of value is given away."

"So would a thousand florins purchase the names of your specialists?"

"Yes." Marco reached into his tunic and drew forth a sale bill, no expression on his face but the speed with which he moved was enough to know that even the heart of a juiceless creature such as him beat a little faster at the thought of a thousand in gold. He placed the bill on the table and reached for a quill so I could sign.

"No," I said, holding out my hand. Marco studied it quizzically.

"Prince Jalan, why are you hold—"

"So you can give me my licence, Marco. You must consider me ready to make purchases since you just offered to sell to me."

I heard his jaw grind and click as he pulled the document from his tight black overcoat and handed it to me.

"Don't feel bad, Marco, old boy, I was born for places like this. Got an instinct for them, don't you know. This time next month I'll own the building." I slapped him on the shoulder, mostly because I thought it would annoy him, and walked off rubbing my hand. Despite appearances the man was built like a rock.

That night in my room at Madam Joelli's I dreamed of Hennan, running scared across a dark and stony field. It seemed I chased him, getting closer and closer until I could hear the ragged panting of his breath and see the flash of his bare feet in the moonlight, dark with blood. I chased him, hard on his heels but always out of reach—until I wasn't and I

reached forward. The hands I caught him with were hooks, black metal
hooks, cutting into his shoulders. He screamed and I woke, sweating in
the black night of my room, finding his scream my own.

I spent several days watching the ebb and flow of things across House
Gold's trading floor and made a few trades, small bets against the price
of olives and salt. Salt is traded on huge scales, a seasoning for the rich
but an essential preservative to everyone else, and despite Umbertide
having a salt mine in the hills that could be seen from its walls, the city
still imported significant amounts of the stuff from Afrique. Once I had
the feel for the mechanics of the business, I moved on.

I graduated to the Maritime Trading House, a large sandstone edifice
fashioned rather like a domed amphitheatre and situated on the edge of
an extravagantly green park near the middle of the city's financial quarter. I call it a quarter but it's closer to two-thirds.

Each day from first light to midnight crowds of the wealthiest men
in the Broken Empire gather within the airy confines of the Maritime
House and shout themselves hoarse while runners, normally young men
with quick minds and quicker feet who hope one day to be doing their
own shouting, carry trades back and forth. It's not so very different from
betting on fights back at the Blood Holes in Vermillion, except the fights
are just the differences of opinions about the value of cargoes being
brought into various ports by ships which the vast majority of the traders
will never see or care to see. Ships with the most distant destinations
and which have gone unsighted the longest time attract the largest odds.
Perhaps that ship will never be heard of again; perhaps it will turn up in
three weeks laden with nuggets of raw gold, or barrels of some spice so
exotic we don't have a name for it, just an appetite. Ships about which
some information is available—maybe a sighting a month back by another
captain, or some word that it was fully laden with amber and resin when
inventoried off the Indus coast in the spring—those ships are safer bets,
with lower odds. And you don't even need to wait until your ship comes
in to take your profit or endure your loss—any bet can be sold on, perhaps

at considerable gain or perhaps for far less than it was purchased, depending on what new information has come to light in the interim, and how trustworthy said information is.

For my first two weeks I bounced along, breaking even by the second. Despite my natural flair for gambling, good head for figures and excellent people skills, even swinging the sizeable financial stick that my great uncle's ships represented, I couldn't quite beat out a profit. Some might say that working the markets is a science, a trade that takes years to learn as you build your networks and develop understanding of the various trading domains. To my mind though it boiled down to wagering, albeit at the largest casino in the Broken Empire, and what I really needed was a system. Also more sleep. Between the long hours and the recurring dreams of Hennan meeting one grim end after another, I was wearing myself thin.

Week three found me nearly two thousand florins to the good and back at House Gold depositing my collection of certificates of sale. I still had to wait in line, intolerable on two counts, firstly no prince should have to stare at the sweaty back of another man's neck and wait his turn—unless of course that man is a king, and secondly I sincerely doubted any of those ahead of me would be bringing quite such wealth to the counter, and surely any sensible bank should give priority to the rich.

I'd made most of the money on an arrangement to buy harbour space in a Goghan port. By the complex magic of my system I wouldn't actually have to do the buying until much later on. Never, if I timed my exit from the city properly. A cough to my rear startled me from my contemplations.

"Prince Jalan, how are you enjoying your time in Umbertide?" The mathmagician I'd met on my first visit joined the queue behind me. He wore a striking robe of interlocking shapes, alternately black and white, a pattern that both fascinated the eye and told you the man's home lay very far from here.

"I . . ." The fellow's name escaped me but I covered it up pretty well. "Well, thank you. Profitable shall we say, and that's always enjoyable."

"Yusuf Malendra," he said, offering me the black smile of his caste and inclining his head. "So you're changing your skin I see." He ran an amused eye down the length of my attire.

I frowned at that. Kara had said something similar. I'd adopted some of the local fashion and spent fifty florins on fine silk shirts, brocaded pantaloons, high calfskin boots, and a good felt hat complete with ostrich feather.

"Style never goes out of fashion, Yusuf." I offered him a rich man's smile. A handsome fellow like me can carry off most looks, and although a prince is always in fashion it never hurts to put on the right display.

"You're a rich man now?"

"Richer," I said, not sure I liked the implication that I'd arrived as a beggar.

"Perhaps you'll be buying yourself some protection now that you're rich . . . er? A wealthy man cannot be too careful, and a man that makes his money so fast must be running risks. We have a saying in my homeland. *Taking risks is risky.*" He shrugged apologetically. "It doesn't translate well."

"Perhaps I should." The idea had occurred to me. I missed having over six and a half foot of Norse killing machine beside me. I had only to bump into the wrong person in the street and I could find myself at the sharp end of an argument that no amount of money in the bank could save me from. And besides, annoyingly, Yusuf had the right of it: my system wasn't exactly the sort that would please the authorities if it came to light, and some muscle at my side might buy me time to get away if things ever came to a crunch.

"You'll find no more capable defender than a clockwork soldier." Yusuf made a question of it, cocking his head. "With such a one at your side you'd be a proper Florentine and no mistake."

Six steps ahead an overly tall merchant from the Utter East concluded his transaction and we all shuffled closer to the counter.

"I've considered it," I said. Actually I hadn't. Something about the things rubbed me the wrong way and, despite the fact that a soldier would properly signify my status to the other traders on the floor and the unwashed beyond it, I had no intention of having one of the things follow me about. "I would be concerned over loyalty, though. How could I trust such a . . . mechanism?"

"How does one trust any man? Especially when his loyalty is purchased?" The mathmagician drew his robes about him as if cold, though Umbertide sizzled beyond House Gold's walls and the relative coolness within would be considered hot by any sane man. "The Mechanists' automata are 'reset' when sold. A machine, of which two working examples are known to exist, is used to form an impression of the new owner and creates a thin copper rod, no longer than my finger, in which striations may be seen, presumably encoding the new owner's particulars in some manner. This rod is inserted through a small hole in the soldier's head casing and the transfer of ownership is complete."

"Fascinating." Or at least marginally less dull than watching the back of the neck of the Nuban in front of me, a fat fellow smelling of unfamiliar spices. "Still, I'd prefer a man of flesh and blood as my bodyguard."

"A sword-son, Prince Jalan. Buy the contract of a sword-son. You'll find no finer protector. At least not one that bleeds."

I made a note to invest in the services of a sword-son. Given that my profits all depended upon a "system" for delaying the payment of taxes and transaction charges via a complex network of traders and sub-traders, all of whom existed only on the forms necessary for their part in my scheme, it seemed likely that I would soon need to turn my paper money into gold and leave the city unobserved. If my timing proved to be off then I might very well need someone to bleed for me—because I was damned sure I didn't want to do the bleeding myself.

TWENTY-FIVE

Summer rests upon Umbertide's rooftops, sizzling on the terracotta, dazzling across whitewashed walls where lizards cling, motionless, waiting as all of the city waits, for the sun to fall.

For three nights the same dream haunted me, making those that had recurred during the three weeks before seem mild in comparison. By day I felt a modicum of distress about Hennan—I'd liked the boy and hadn't wished any harm to him, but I hadn't signed on as his guardian or adopted him into the Kendeth family. The child had run off, as many children do, and it was hardly my duty to hunt him down amid the vastness of the Broken Empire.

Apparently my conscience disagreed—though only past midnight. Three mornings in a row I woke exhausted and harrowed by endless visions of Hennan in torment. Most often I saw him captured, many hands seizing him and dragging him screaming into the dark. I saw him curled about his misery on a filthy floor, ragged, little more than bones wrapped tight in a pale skin, the fire gone from his hair, eyes dull and seeing nothing.

On the first morning I hired an investigator to hunt for the boy. I had the money for it, money by the bucket-load.

On the second morning I paid a priest to say prayers and light candles for Hennan, though I was far from sure whether a few candles would induce God to watch out for a heathen.

On the third morning I decided that having a conscience was definitely over-rated and resolved to see a doctor in order to obtain some form of medication for my ailment. Worrying about other people, especially some peasant boy from the wilds, wasn't me at all.

Umbertide is a city of narrow alleys, whose cobbles are lit but briefly when at the zenith of each day the sun dips its fingers deep into each crevice and cranny. Along these shadowed ways men come and go about their business—their business being other people's business. These messengers bound on errands, bearing credit notes, invoices, transactions recorded and notarized, bring with them droplets of information, rumour, scandal and intrigue, and draw together to form a river, flowing from one archive to the next, filling and emptying vaults. You would think the blood of Umbertide gold but it runs ink-black: information holds more value and is easier to carry.

And today one among those many men was bound upon *my* business, carrying, I hoped, some small fact valuable to me.

The restaurant door opened and after some negotiations amid a huddle of waiters the maître d' led a tall thin man, still wrapped in the blackness of his street-cloak, to my table.

"Sit." I waved a hand at the chair opposite. He smelled of sweat and spice. "Try the quails' eggs, they're wonderfully . . . expensive." I'd been pushing an exquisite meal around three highly decorated Ling plates for some while now. Caviar from Steppes sturgeons, tiny anchovies in plum sauce, artistically spattered across the porcelain, mushrooms stuffed with garlic and chives, thin strips of cured ham . . . none of it appealed, though it would require a full piece of crown gold to pay the bill.

The man took his seat and turned a face, as long and angular as his body toward me, ignoring the eggs.

"I found him. Debtors' cells for Central, over on Piatzo."

"Excellent." Irritation wrestled relief. Damned if I knew why I'd wasted good money on an investigator—I could have guessed he'd end up behind bars somewhere. But a debtors' prison? "You're sure it's him?"

"We don't get many northerners in Umbertide—well, not pale-as-milk, godless heathen northerners anyway, and not like him." He pushed a small roll of parchment across the table. "The address and his case number. Let me know if I can be of further service." And with that he stood, a waiter swooping to escort him from the premises.

I uncoiled the parchment and stared at the number as if it might unravel the path that led a penniless child to a debtors' cell, or perhaps even answer the more vexing question—why I had wasted both time and money hunting him down? At least it had turned out to be surprisingly quick and easy to find him. The next thing to do was to set him up safe and secure somewhere he wouldn't run away from. Then perhaps I could recover from my inconvenient and thankfully rare attack of conscience.

The year I spent at the Mathema had armed me with the expectation that numbers held secrets, but had failed to give me the tools to reveal them. I'd been a poor student and the minor mathmagicians tasked with my training soon despaired of me. The only corner of numbers that I had any purchase on were odds—born from my love of gambling. Probability theory, the Libans called it, and managed to suck most of the joy out of that too.

"98-3-8-3-6-6-81632."

Just numbers. The Central Bank? I'd thought to find Hennan dead in a ditch or chained to a bench in some workshed . . . but not a guest of the Firenze Central Bank.

I stayed a while longer, watching the diners devour a small fortune, unable to tell how many of them were truly enjoying the over-salted delectables arranged in sparse displays across their platters.

I turned to signal for another glass of Ancrath red. There's a noise that coins make when they move across each other, not quite a chinking, not quite a rustle. Gold coins make a softer sound than copper or silver. In Florence they mint florins, heavier than the ducat or the crown gold of Red March, and in Umbertide they also mint the double florin, stamped not with the head of any king, not with Adam, third of his name and last of the emperors, nor yet with any symbol of Empire—just the cipher of the Central Bank. That soft chink of gold on gold, double florins sliding over double florins, accompanied my motion when signing for more wine, and, though it made no more than a whisper beneath the currents of conversation, several pairs of eyes turned my way. Gold always speaks loudly and nowhere are ears more tuned to its voice than in Umbertide.

Most of the people at their lunch were moderns, driven like all of Umbertide by the ebb and flow of fashions that changed with bewildering speed. Where fashion pertained to garments the only constants in Umbertide style were that it would be uncomfortable, expensive, and not resemble clothing.

I looked down at the number again. I should let him stew while I finished my meal. Under ideal circumstances I should let the ungrateful urchin spend another month on stale water and scraps. I munched a quail's egg, gazing out over the small sea of multi-tiered hats angled over plates. Apparently it was the fashion not to remove them to dine—at least for this week. I didn't have a month though. The time had come to leave town and delaying even a day could prove risky.

With a sigh I pushed myself away from the table, placed a cut florin beside the main plate, and left. The gold secreted all about my person chinked quietly to itself and the excess, stowed in the case in my hand, did its best to pull my arm off.

The moderns watched me leave, eyes drawn by some instinct to the departure of so much capital.

Ta-Nam waited for me outside the Fatted Goose, at ease in the shade but not dozing. I could have hired six guards for the price I paid the sword-son but I judged him more deadly, and certainly more loyal to his coin, loyalty being the credo of the caste. They bred and raised men like Ta-Nam to this one purpose on some hellish isle off the coast of Afrique, far, far to the south. I had taken the mathmagician's advice and secured the services of a sword-son as soon as I deposited my first thousand. The price of his contract left considerably less of it to guard, but even so I felt that Yusuf's advice had been sound—a prince should have the best and his protection should make a statement about the worth of what's being protected. In any event one of the beauties of Umbertide is the way that the magics of the market enable one coin to become many, floating on a network of credit, promises, and fiddly little calculations called "financial instruments." Perhaps for the first time in my life I was in credit and could afford the best.

"Walk with me," I said. "We're going to prison."

Ta-Nam made no reply, only followed. It took a lot to get an answer out of the man. Whatever their training entailed it took as much out of the sword-sons as it added, leaving them too bound to their task to waste time or thought on social niceties or smalltalk. I could afford to replace Ta-Nam with the city's ultimate accessory by now—should I want to. I'd made a middle-sized fortune staking ships of the line, merchant vessels under Grandmother's flag, against complex future options on cargo. With the wealth I'd accumulated I could afford most things. As poor a conversationalist as the man was, though, one of the region's famous clockwork soldiers would hardly improve things on that front. And besides, though there might be no guard more competent, the Mechanists' toys made me nervous. Just having one near me made my skin crawl. The constant whirring of all those cogs and wheels beneath their armour, grinding at every move, so many little teeth geared to each other, everything in motion . . . it unsettled me, and the copper gleam of their eyes promised nothing good.

Ta-Nam walked behind me as a guard that's for protection rather than show always will, keeping his charge in sight at all times. Every now and then I'd glance back to check he was still there, my silent shadow. I'd yet to see him in action but he certainly looked the part, and the prowess of the sword-sons had been a thing of legend for centuries. Muscled for strength but not past the point where a price is paid in quickness, impassive, solid, watching the world without judgment. Darker even than a Nuban, his head shaved and gleaming.

"I don't even know why we're going," I told Ta-Nam over my shoulder. "It's not like I owe him anything. And *he* left *me*! I mean, of all the ingratitude . . ."

We made slow but steady progress. I'd come to learn the layout of the city in the weeks I'd spent here—despite most of my hours passing in the gloom of the exchange, bilking traders, playing the percentages, and lying from the hip.

Umbertide's narrow streets and grand sun-baked plazas hold a mix of people hardly less unusual than its most upmarket restaurants. The ubiquitous black-cloaked messengers thread cosmopolitan crowds. The lure of the city's wealth draws visitors from every quarter of the known world, most of them rich already. There are perhaps no other places on the map where you might find a Ling merchant from the Utter East at table sipping java with a Liban mathmagician and with them a Nuban factor draped in gold chain. I've even seen a man from the Great Lands across the Atlantis Ocean striding the streets of Umbertide, a lighter brown than the tribes of northern Afrique and with blue eyes, his robe feathered and set with malachite beads in mosaiced profusion. What ship bore him across the wideness of that ocean I never did find out.

The alley broadened into what might almost be called a street, bracketed on each side by plaster-clad tenements reaching five and six storeys, all faded and shuttered, cracked and discoloured, though inside the luxury would shame many a mansion and the cost of such an abode would beggar most provincial lords. Ahead a fountain tinkled at the crossing of two streets, though I couldn't see it yet, just hear its music and sense the coolness.

"Prince Jalan." The flow of the crowd thinned around me.

"Corpus Armand." Formally I should name him to the House Iron but he'd already trampled protocol by not listing my family and domains. I glanced back at Ta-Nam—when a modern discards protocol you know it means trouble. A modern breaches etiquette the way an Ancrath murders your family, i.e. it's not unheard of but you know it means they're pissed off.

Corpus drew himself up to his full unimpressive height and stalked into my path. Behind him his soldier whirred into position, looming above its master. They made a curious pair, the modern clad in his close-fitting blacks, wholly unsuited to the heat, his skin a dead white where it showed, not a Norse pale, but an albino colouration achieved with bleaches and, if the rumours were true, no small amount of witchcraft. Behind him the soldier held almost trollish proportions, taller than any man, lean, long-limbed, glimpses of mechanism where the armour plates met, steel talons flexing as cables wound about their wheels or vanished down past the wrist-guard.

"Your note for the Goghan deal is void, prince. The Waylan and Butarni both refused it."

"Ah," I said. Being refused by any bank was bad enough. Having your credit voided by two of the oldest in Florence effectively ruled a man out of all the best games of finance that Umbertide had to offer. "Well, this is a grievous oversight! How dare mere banks impugn the name of Kendeth? They might as well call the Red Queen a whore!"

Ta-Nam moved to my side. Umbertide regulations prohibited the carrying of weapons larger than knives in the old town, but with the razored pieces of chrome steel at his hips the sword-son constituted mass murder on legs. Unfortunately the automaton behind Corpus was reputedly immune to stabbing.

Corpus narrowed his dark little eyes at me. "Nations stand or fall on finance, Prince Jalan. A fact I'm sure your grandmother is well aware of. And finance stands on trust—a trust cemented by the honouring of debts and of contracts." He held out the promissory notes in question, fine crisp documents on the thickest parchment, scroll-worked around the edges and signed by my good self along with three witnesses of certified standing. "Restore my trust, Prince Jalan." Somehow the white-faced little creep managed to slide an impressive level of threat around all his formality.

"This is all nonsense, Corpus, my dear fellow. My credit should be good." I meant it too. I'd taken great care when hollowing out my finances to leave a skeleton of assets sufficient to keep the edifice standing for at least a day or two after my departure. All I had to do was transform my overly heavy heap of gold into some still more portable form of wealth— one that didn't depend on bank vaults, trust, or any of that foolishness— and I'd be off on the fastest horse stolen money could buy. In fact, if not for my investigator finding me at luncheon, I would already be at the doors of a certain diamond merchant purchasing the largest gems in his collection. "My credit is as good as any—"

"Suspended over issues of taxation." Corpus offered a thin smile. "The Central will have its pound of flesh."

"Ah." Another long pause filled with furious excuse-creation. Bank taxes on each transaction make it very difficult to scrape a legitimate profit in Umbertide's markets. I discovered early on that the real key to success was to not pay them. This of course required an ever more elaborate scheme of deferred payments, scheduled payments, conditional payments, lies, and damn lies. I'd calculated it would be the end of the week before those particular large and potentially lethal chickens came home to roost. "Look, Corpus, old fellow, of the House Iron and all that." I took a step forward and would have flung an arm across his shoulders but for the fact he took a step back and his soldier looked ready to grab any arm that touched the man and fling it over the rooftops, with or without its owner still attached. "We'll deal with this the old way. Meet me at Yoolani's Java House first bell tomorrow and I'll have your payment ready for you in gold." I patted my ribs to make the coins bound under my tunic chink for him. "I'm heir to the throne of Red March, after all, and my word is my bond." I set my smile on the offer and let the honesty beam out.

Corpus took on that look of distaste that all of Umbertide's financiers do when something as common and dirty as raw gold is mentioned. They build their whole lives on the stuff and yet somehow consider the actual substance beneath them, preferring their papers and notes, rather than the weight of coin in hand. To my way of thinking an extra zero on a promissory note is far less exciting than a purse that weighs ten times what it might. Though right there, with the bulk of my assets packed into a case and conspiring with gravity to remove my shoulder from its socket, I had some sympathy with the idea.

"First bell . . . prince. The full sum. Or there will be sanctions." He turned his head, eyes flickering to the soldier, leaving little doubt that the sanctions would be rather worse than the revoking of my trading licence.

I stalked on past Corpus, not sparing him or his monstrosity another glance, and disguising my relief. I'd bought myself the best part of the day with a little bluster and a lot of lying. Cheap at twice the price! Falsehoods were a currency I was always willing to spend.

"There are two agents following us," Ta-Nam said behind me.

"What? Where?" I spun around. Nothing in the sea of heads around us stood out, save for Corpus's clockwork soldier, diminishing in the distance, nobody even reaching to its shoulders.

"It will be harder to evade them if you let them know you're aware of their presence." Ta-Nam managed not to make it a rebuke, not through servility but perhaps a reasonable expectation that everyone else was an amateur in this kind of game.

I turned back on our path and sped up a touch despite the heat. "Two of them?"

"There may be others more competent," Ta-Nam conceded. "The two I have noted must be private hires—bank agents would not be so clumsy."

"Unless they were sending a message . . ." Private hires? Investigators like the one who'd brought me news at lunch. Perhaps I was his next case and he was following me even now. Either way, the message was clear, Corpus of House Iron wasn't the only one with suspicions. They couldn't move on me until I defaulted but they sure as hell could watch me. All of which made my plan of skipping town rather more difficult. Fear reached out from that place nearby where it's always waiting and took me by the balls. "Damn them all."

TWENTY-SIX

When you emerge into Piatzo plaza you remember what summer is this far south. In the alleyways, shaded and angled to channel the breeze, you get just a hot breath of it, a reminder of the violence that waits for you, but step into Piatzo at noon in high summer and it hits you like a fist. Suddenly I wanted a hat, even one of those ridiculous confections the moderns sport. Head bowed against the onslaught from above, eyes narrowed against the glare reflected from broad and pale paving slabs, I strode out toward the Central Bank debtor prison on the far side.

From the front the place looks like a genteel residence, architecturally fit for its surroundings and meriting a place facing out into one of Umbertide's most famed plazas. They tell me that in winter the square becomes a place where well-heeled citizens gather to socialize, hawkers sell expensive tit-bits, and renowned orchestras put on performances. Little wonder then that debtors with sufficiently generous friends and family often choose to take up residence in the apartments at the front of the prison, waiting there the weeks, months, or perhaps decades required either for their fortunes to rally sufficiently to pay what's owed, and the interest upon it, or for their reserves to dwindle to the point where they begin the slow and inevitable migration toward the hidden rear of the building.

We came up to the front doors, palatial things, gilded and ornate. First you pay the doorman. Everything costs in the debtor cells and only the rent is added to the slate. If you want a bed, want to eat, want clean water, you pay. If you can't pay you sell what you have. The servants in the front apartments are selling their services. Further in they sell their clothes, their bodies, their hair, their children. And at the far end, emptied from tiny and cramped cells, come the corpses, skeletally thin, naked, sold to feed pigs, the credit removed from the final summation of their debt.

I knew these things because the debtors' prisons, and there are many in Umbertide, seemed my likely destination should my adventures on the commodities markets turn sour. It's not in my nature to over-investigate the downsides of any vice I entertain, and gambling has always been to the fore of my weaknesses. I do, however, like to explore all the escape routes, and that necessitated finding out more than a little about establishments like the one run by Firenze Central Bank. The conclusion of my study was—don't get caught.

That conclusion held me there on the steps, the sun pounding down on my head, my shadow puddled black about my feet, Ta-Nam impassive behind me. I'd come here to buy freedom—but what had led me here? A slip of parchment. A note given to me by a man whose services were for sale to anyone with coin or credit. Given to me on the day the banks had refused my paper.

"It would be an irony if I came here thinking to help an inmate and found I was handing myself into custody." I said it loud enough for Ta-Nam to hear but he made no answer. I found myself suddenly dry mouthed—the city rising about me like a grasping hand. Running was the only thing I wanted to do. Forget the plan. Forget the diamonds. Drop the damn gold if need be. Just run. The visions that had haunted me for three nights returned to swim before my eyes—Hennan wasting away, rotting like fruit left in the sun.

I turned to face Ta-Nam. He stood immobile, sweat gleaming on ebony arms, watching everything, even me.

"I've got a . . . a child under my care in there." Silence. "I should go in and see him released." Silence. "It . . . it could be dangerous." This wasn't me. Friends were ballast, to be cast overboard if you start riding low in the water. Not you, I'd told Hennan, not you, other friends—but of course I'd meant him too. And yet I couldn't quite turn away. Perhaps the dreams scared me.

Ta-Nam regarded me with the same eloquent silence, no hint of judgment in him, as if he'd carry me to the city limits in his arms if I ordered it, and set me on a fast horse without the least reproach. Damn him. I tried to focus on what Snorri would do to me if he discovered I'd left Hennan behind. Going in felt slightly more sensible when set against the background of the Norseman twisting my arms off.

In the prison foyer three heavyset but impeccably dressed men-in-waiting took the surrender of Ta-Nam's chrome-steel daggers and my own stiletto, its hilt tastefully decorated with blood-rubies from the Afrique interior. The largest of them then approached us with some plasteek device almost like a gaming racquet but without the catgut stringing required to hit the ball.

"What is it?" I stepped sharply behind Ta-Nam, prepared to let him earn his contract-price for once. The moderns are fearsome keen on their Builder artefacts, scavenged from time-vaults across the empire: it's hard to find a modern with any significant holdings who doesn't have some device from before the Day of a Thousand Suns, a fone perhaps so they can talk to God—probably to complain—or some nameless thing of wires and parts and glass. Corpus kept some strange machine of rustless silver-steel, two interlocking tear-drop cages that rotate each through the other when a handle higher up the device is turned. He would hold it up on the trade floor, spinning the cages when seeking to place an order. I peered at the approaching footman. "I don't want that . . . thing . . . near me!"

"It finds concealed weapons, sir." The thug smiled reassurance at me as if I were some country squire. He waved the device across Ta-Nam's thick arms and down across his front.

"Well, I don't like it!" And I didn't, but when he'd finished with the sword-son he came my way waving his bat. The thing started squealing the moment it drew near me, an unearthly tone, a pure note, higher than any castrato ever reached. That set all three of them advancing on me, grim as you like, and ready to manhandle me despite my station.

It soon transpired that the Builders' toy considered gold to be a weapon—which to be fair it is in many regards—and so, to the bemusement of the staff, I had to strip three hundred and eighty double florins from about my person and let them rifle with greedy fingers through the three thousand and twenty-six additional coins in my case.

"You're sure you wouldn't like to leave this with us during your visit, sir?" The thug seemed keen to take charge of my funds. "We've had riots here over a dropped silver. Taking this much money in there . . . it's not sensible."

"Not safe." The second thug, younger, his eyes unable to leave my case.

"Not sane." The last and smallest of them, though still a solid chunk of muscle, and seemingly angered by the sight of such riches in a place of debt.

"It's all well hidden." I frowned at the heap of ribbons between whose double layers the spare florins were sewn. "Well it was before you laid hands on me." I picked up a loose end and started to wrap the length of it, chinking, about my waist and torso. "Ta-Nam will be more than suffi-cient to protect my interests, with or without his knives." I dropped that last slowly, letting the words hammer in the fact that the sword-son could end them where they stood. Moreover he could do so with a clean con-science since Umbertide law lays the crime at the feet of any man who can be shown to have paid for its commission. By signing themselves over to contract the sword-sons were virtually immune to charges of criminal-ity, as much a device as a sword or clockwork soldier, and no more guilty.

Despite their avarice the guards made no attempt to take my gold. Ownership and debt were a religion in Umbertide and held in no place more sanctified than in the debtor prisons. The whole prison was essen-tially a device to bleed dry those that fell into its clutches—to bleed them in a highly structured and entirely legal manner. In the midst of such institutionalized theft on so grand a scale individual thievery could not be tolerated in any degree. Only by strict adherence to the rules of the theft could the illusion of it being lawful and civilized be maintained.

Our manicured thug took us through the more salubrious quarter of the prison and handed us over to a cell monkey who would lead us the rest of the way. I had to pay him too.

"98-3-8 . . . what was the rest?" He walked ahead of us swinging an unlit lantern.

"98-3-8-3-6," I said, squinting at my paper. We'd gone past the high windows, past the lantern-lit corridors—the wooden doors punctuating the walls had given way to barred gates and the oil lamps smoked so as to set you coughing. "What does it mean?"

"Means he came in this year, '98, not so long ago, less than a month, and that he's poor as shit 'cos he's about as far back as this place goes."

I glanced through the next set of bars into an empty cell, stone floor strewn with dirt, a bare bench, a heap of rags for a bed. An eye glittered amid the rags and I realized it wasn't a bed.

The stink intensified as we went on, a raw mix of sewage and rot. The passage became more tunnel than corridor and I had to bend to keep from scraping my head. Lone candle stubs, balanced amid pools of wax, broke the darkness here and there. Elsewhere things moaned and rustled in the blind and fetid spaces behind the bars and I was glad not to see. Our guide lit a taper at the last of these candles and we followed the glowing ember of it into hell.

"Here we are 3:6." The man lit his lantern, reintroducing us to the sweaty and lumpen topology of his naked torso. We stood in a square and low-roofed chamber from which eight arches gave onto largish cells, each arch walled with grimy rusting bars. The creatures within turned their faces from the light as if it hurt their eyes. Most were naked but I couldn't tell if they were men or women. They seemed uniformly grey, smeared with filth, and gaunt beyond the point that one might imagine a person could be reduced to and yet live. And the smell of the place . . . it held less of the sewer and more of rot . . . the kind of stink that wouldn't quit your nostrils for days after. The smell of death—death without hope.

"What's the last bit?"

"What?" I looked back at the jailer.

"The last bit. The case number."

"Oh." And I held up the roll of parchment to read it off.

We approached the arch that bore the legend "VI" upon its keystone.

"Get back!" The cell monkey ran his baton along the bars and the debtors shrank away, cowering like dogs accustomed to beating. "The new one! Show me the new one!"

The grey crowd parted, edging to the margins of their cell, bare feet shuffling through wet filth. The shadows retreated with them, the lantern revealing a stone floor strewn with litter.

"Where—" And then I saw him. Lying on his side, back toward us, his spine a series of bony knobs beneath pale skin stretched painfully across them. I'd seen dead beggars in the gutters of Vermillion with more meat on them after a night with the dogs chewing at their limbs.

"Eight-one-six-three-two!" the guard bellowed it as if he were on a parade ground. "On your feet!"

The harshness of that shout made me wince, me who would be walking out of here burdened with gold and with a meal whose price might buy one of these souls' freedom turning sour in my belly. I reached out a quick hand to the man's bicep. "Enough. Open it." Teeth gritted.

"Costs two hexes to unlock in the Dregs," he said without rancour.

I fished in my pocket for something as small as his fee, bringing up three of the six-sided coppers after an age of fumbling. "Do it." My hand trembled though I wasn't sure what I was angry about.

The cell monkey made a show of counting through his keys and eventually set the heaviest bit of iron on his ring into the lock before us. He beat the bars once more, setting my teeth on edge, and drew back the gate.

"You're sure that's him?" The figure held nothing familiar about it. Ribs standing out where they curved toward his spine, hair dark with grime. I could pick this thing of skin and bones up in my arms and stand without effort. All those miles we'd trekked south . . . bringing us out of the northern wastes had delivered him to this?

I handed my case to Ta-Nam and stepped inside, painfully aware of the debtors to either side, hands hooked into what seemed like talons. The stench of them made my eyes water and caught at my throat. Five paces brought me to the figure. I kicked a patch of flagstone cleaner and went to one knee.

"It's me . . . Prince J—It's me Jalan."

The slightest twitch, a hunching, as if the bones all squeezed that bit closer together beneath the skin.

"Are you—" I didn't know what to say. Was he all right? He didn't look all right.

I reached out a hand and turned him toward me. Bright eyes watched me from beneath matted hair.

"Hennan." I ran my arms under the boy and careless of the dirt drew him to me. He proved even lighter than he looked. I stood without effort and turned to the gate, and found it closing as I faced it.

"No!" I lurched forward, still carrying the boy, boots slipping on the muck, but the jailer turned the key before I made it halfway. He offered me a grin through the bars. My sword-son stood unmoving in the middle of the central chamber. I watched him, flabbergasted for a moment, before realizing that technically the jailer hadn't offered me any harm.

"Ta-Nam! Get me out of here!"

The sword-son stayed where he was. A heartbeat stretched into an age, and my stomach curled into a tight and heavy ball. Hennan started to feel like all the weight in the world.

"Ta-Nam! A sword-son never breaks his contract!" There aren't many truths in the world, and fewer certainties. Death, taxes, and not much else. But the loyalty of a sword-son was a thing of legend . . .

"*You* broke our contract, my prince." Ta-Nam bowed his head as though the deed sorrowed him. "You purchased me with paper. A man came to me a day ago and paid what was asked for my next contract though I told him I didn't know when you would release the option on my service. I further told him that I would have to report our conversation and agreement to my master. At that point he explained I had no master as the Butarni bank would no longer honour your script since the Central Bank suspended your credit over charges of tax evasion. Without a master the contract I had just agreed became active."

"What charges?" Corpus had said the same thing. "There haven't been any damn charges. And what bastard *do* you work for now?"

Ta-Nam lifted his head to meet my gaze. "I work for Corpus Armand of the House Iron." He reached into the small pack at his side and withdrew two wooden scroll cases. "The charges were delivered this morning. I received them in your name and kept them from you on Corpus's instruction."

"That's my money!" I gestured toward the case in his hand. It didn't seem to burden him as it did me.

"I told Corpus you had a case full of gold—"

"You can't tell! Sword-sons don't tell!" All around me heads lifted, turned toward the case in Ta-Nam's grip. Pale and dirty hands gripped the bars across the mouths of the seven other arches, bright eyes staring.

"We had no contract, my prince." Ta-Nam bowed his head once again and turned to go. Even in the depths of my despair I noted that he hadn't dragged me out to strip the double florins from my body. Corpus hadn't known about those and the sword-son had no more malice in him than any sharp edge that cuts both ways.

"Crap," I said.

Ta-Nam and the cell monkey turned to go, throwing us into deep shadow. Step by step the light left us, darkness stealing in from all sides, the debtors advancing with it.

"Crap." It bore repeating.

Hennan, who had seemed so light, grew heavier still in my arms. A sense of betrayal rose through me and the loss of Snorri settled on me suddenly and from nowhere. Friendship felt somehow more valuable than unbreakable contracts. Whatever his faults the northman would never have stood there and let this happen to me.

TWENTY-SEVEN

The saving grace of the Central Bank prison is that the inmates are not criminals. They're not murderers, addicts, and thieves, but instead they're the kind of people who could run up debts serious enough to warrant action and with sources reputable enough to make that action incarceration rather than a knife to the guts. Add to that the fact that the people surrounding me in my dark and stinking cell were three-quarters starved, weaker than a healthy child, and an utterly terrifying prospect became merely very grim.

The debtors around me proved so in awe of the handful of change in my pocket that I was able to establish order with the promise of a couple of copper halves. If they'd known I was wearing enough gold to buy out the debt of everyone in all eight of the cells facing into the central chamber then perhaps more base instincts would have taken over and the crowd would have become a monster. Hennan lay silent beside me while I fended off the more persistent of our cellmates with promises and shoves.

I watched the darkness and worried. My immediate fear of course was that the guards would come to take my remaining wealth but Umbertide was not like other places, and its debtor prisons were bizarre institutions, run on the strictest of rules. A debtor entering the prison could buy themselves out at any time if they had the means, but they were not compelled to do so. A debtor owned whatever assets they managed to keep and the hope was that many would be able to continue their enterprises from the comfortable front of the prison, earning sufficient coin to balance their ledgers. A portion of any coin spent maintaining life and limb in the prison went to the creditors in any case, so every day I survived I would be chiselling away at my mountainous bills.

After what seemed forever, and might have been less than an hour, the jailer returned. His tardiness and the relaxed slope of his shoulders told me that he'd not yet spoken with the boys at the entrance. Perhaps they didn't even know I'd been detained—but sooner or later news of the wealth about my person would spread. What had drawn the man back was the change he'd seen earlier when I paid him to unlock the cell. He knew I had copper hexes left and a handful of halves, and came not to steal but to sell. Such was the way of things in Umbertide.

He set his lantern on the floor and held out a candle, a fat thing as thick as his forearm and half as long, cheap yellow tallow that would smoke and sputter, but it'd burn a while.

"Some light, yer lordship?" He offered me that same grin he'd had when locking the gate. By rights it should be gap-toothed and off colour, in truth he had small even teeth all polished to a surprising whiteness.

"Your name, jailer?" Always good to make the personal connection.

"Racso, they call me." He glared around at the pale faces pressed to the bars on all sides. "And don't you lot forget it."

"Racso then." I knew without coin I'd be no more to him than the dying flesh clinging to bones on all sides. "How much for the candle?"

"Two halves. Or I can let you have a third of it for one. Lighting it is free." He smiled. "First time."

Although I had Umbertide's civilized ways to thank for not being robbed with violence and stabbed in my cell, "civilized" seemed the wrong word for it. A set of rules to die by. Clinging to life by pennies and halves until the money ran out. Somehow the beatings and shivs offered by the jailers and inmates of more usual prisons felt more honest at that moment, sat there bartering for the rudiments of life.

"How much to buy the boy out? What's he owe?" It couldn't be much. I was amazed he could have run up any official debt at all.

"Ah." Racso scratched his belly, an uneasy look on his face. "That's a puzzler that is."

"A puzzler? He's in debtors' prison. He's a debtor. How much does he owe?"

"Well . . ."

"It's just a number."

"Sixty-four thousand." A mutter rippled through the cells.

"Pennies?"

"Does it matter?" Racso asked.

"Well . . . no. Sixty-four thousand? That's not even a number."

"It is—"

"Nobody has sixty-four thousand!" I doubted even Grandmother could lay her claw on sixty-four thousand in crown gold without selling something holy or spilling some blood. "Who lent him that kind of money?"

"It's a code, see." More scratching and Racso bent his balding head as if the admission shamed a man who was paid to watch people starve. "Means the bank has them here for its own reasons. An abuse of the system is what it is. Puts honest men in a questionable position regarding the law is what it does." He shook his head and spat dolefully.

I took us back to the more immediate questions. "A penny for the candle then. And food, for me and the boy, bread, butter, apples?"

"A hex." Again the grin, pleased to be on more familiar ground. "Better hope you can eat fast though." An eye to the bodies behind me, a shiver of anticipation running through them.

"How much to get out of here, a private cell back up the corridor?"

"Ah." A slow shake of the head, almost regretful. "That'd take silver that would, yer lordship. Don't think I've ever seen the colour of it down in the dark cells. You got silver on you? Have you, yer lordship?" He seemed to think it unlikely.

"Just the food for now," I said. "And the candle." I fished in my pocket and brought out a hex and a penny.

Racso took my money on a flat wooden paddle hooked upon his belt. A device that meant he never had to come within grabbing range of the bars. "Done and dealt." He stowed the coins away, nodded to me, and handed me the cold end of my candle. Transaction complete, Racso wiped his hands across the sides of his trousers and sauntered away whistling some spring tune that remembered flowers and joy.

◆　◆　◆

When Racso returned he carried a reed basket containing three crusty loaves, a wedge of blue cheese, and half a dozen apples of a good size, bursting with the summer. He also brought with him a barrel on wheels from which he doled out ladles of water to those who could pay. Water exchanged hands for the clippings of a copper, for a left shoe, for one of the tin mugs into which he was pouring—that man took his ration in his cupped hands—and for promises of company from several of the younger women. I had to pay over a penny for two cups and their contents, my earlier order not having made mention of water.

"Give me two apples first," I said. And Racso rolled them over to the bars.

I tossed them to the two largest and least dead of our inmates, Artemis and Antonio, men I'd selected and negotiated with before. They cleared a space and kept the others back while I took the remaining food.

"Behave yourselves and there'll be crusts to share out. Give me any shit and jaws will get broken." It's easy enough to be the hard man when you're fit, fed, and hale and the foe are skin and bones.

Backs to the wall, bread between us, cups on the floor and the candle burning at our feet, Hennan and I began to eat. The boy dipped his bread in the water to ease it past his sore gums. I still couldn't pin an age on him and he'd never had a clear idea of it himself. Today I settled on twelve. He looked older starved. All of them did. Ancients with young men's fears. Old women with children like tiny old men. A mother with breasts as withered as any crone, the baby in her arms black with dirt and unmoving. I choked down what food I could and threw the rest at them, cursing the lot for beggars and thieves. Fear stole my appetite.

Hennan recovered faster than I thought possible, wrinkling his face at the cheese as he wolfed it down.

"Steady—you'll be sick." I say "recovered" . . . he remained a skeleton dressed in skin, but the light returned to his eyes, the words to his tongue.

"Why did you come?" he asked.

I'd been asking myself the same thing. "I'm an idiot."

"How come they locked you in? You've got money."

"I owe more than I've got." That had been the story of my adult life. A short enough tale but one that had never got me locked up in hell before. "In debtors' prisons you own what you carry in. They call it bankruptcy."

"How are we getting out?" He wiped his mouth with the back of his hand and reached for his water. Across the cell fights were breaking out over the loaf I'd thrown.

"I don't know." Honesty always pains me. Telling it to a child who considers you a hero puts any number of barbs on those words, making them harder than you'd expect to spit out. "You shouldn't have run." Recriminations are useless but it takes a better man than me not to kick someone close when they're down. "You were in the palace of Vermillion for God's sake! And now . . ."

"I wanted to be with the others . . ." He kept his eyes on the apple in his hand, red with his blood where he'd bitten it.

"Yes, but you didn't find them did you?" Snorri and the others were back in Vermillion enjoying my grandmother's hospitality—the second time for Snorri. There was no way they could have beaten the Red March riders to the border and I'd seen the riders returning, so they must have been captured.

"I did find them." So quiet I almost missed it.

"What? Where? I've been here weeks and not a whisper of them."

"Kara's here. In this prison."

"She is not!" I couldn't believe that. How could this place hold a völva? I imagined her watching from the bars of the cell opposite, one more grey face among the rest, and found I didn't want to pursue the thought. "Where?"

"She's serving at the front." Hennan put the bread down, a hand clutching the distended ache of his belly. "She doesn't know I'm here."

"But you know she's here?" I raised a sceptical brow.

"News travels front to back, not the other way. They say Lady Connagio has a heathen maid with white hair and white skin who can do charms that cure warts. Came in the same time as me."

"God's sake!" A thousand questions fought to exit my mouth at once, but the biggest one won. "Where's the key?"

Hennan shuffled closer and spoke lower, the bread wars were coming to an end with the victors pitting wobbly teeth against the crusts and the losers licking wounds.

"Can't talk about it. That's what we're in for."

TWENTY-EIGHT

True to his word Hennan wouldn't tell me about the key. Every question I hissed at him about it met with silence. I exhausted myself quizzing him but the child kept his lips clamped tight and in the end I fell into a doze, unsure whether the sun was still shining outside or not.

I dreamed of a book, surely for the first time ever. I've long maintained that nothing of interest ever took place between the covers of a book, excepting the cardinal's whisky and pornography of course, but here I was turning page after page in my dream. Even in my dream I didn't want to read the thing, but some compulsion kept me going as if hunting for a particular page. I tried focusing on the writing but the letters carried no meaning, sliding this way and that like spiders who've forgotten how to master so many legs.

One more page, one more page, one more and then I saw it, a word like any other, buried amid its fellows but anchoring my eyes. *Sageous.* And as I said it the dream-witch's face rose from the page, carrying the text with it so that the words lay across his skin, sinking in like tattoos. And his name—well that disappeared into the black slit of his mouth, now opening wider and wider to speak my own.

"Prince Jalan."

"You!" I leapt to my feet, letting the book tumble to the floor. I stood in the room where I first met him, a guest bedroom in the Tall Castle, Crath City, Ancrath. "What the hell?"

"You're dreaming, Prince Jalan."

"I . . . I knew that." I brushed myself down and glanced around. It didn't look like a dream. "Why are you here? Looking for Baraqel to skewer you again?" I didn't like the man one bit and wanted him out of my head quickly.

"I don't think either of your friends will trouble us tonight, Prince Jalan, light nor dark." He touched a word on his left arm then another on his right as he spoke of light and darkness. "And I am here to see if anything can be salvaged. You were supposed to free the boy and then be led to the Norsemen. With so much gold at your disposal it shouldn't have been beyond you to free them too. You could have hired an army with what you carried. Instead I find you locked with the child in a debtors' cell."

"I was . . . supposed to?" I stared at the heathen trying to make sense of his gibberish. "The dreams?" I put a hand to my face. "You sent the dreams. I thought I was going mad!" All those nights haunted by Hennan's fate. I knew that wasn't like me. "You bastard!" I took a step toward him, then finding my legs would no longer listen to me, I stopped.

"It seems I over-estimated you, Prince Jalan." Sageous shooed me back and my traitor legs obeyed. "A man who walks himself into a prison is unlikely to be able to walk himself out. I fear my employer will have to accept both your failure and his resulting losses."

"Employer?"

"Kelem wishes you to free your companions from the custody of House Gold so that they may continue their journey and bring Loki's key to him. I do not believe this will be possible however."

"But Kelem owns the banking clans . . ." Though now I said it I did recall talk of strife between them.

"The House Gold has its own ambitions and has grown close to other interests in recent years."

"The Dead King!" It made sense now. Or at least it was moving in that direction. "The clockwork soldiers and the corpse flesh . . ."

"Even so." Sageous nodded.

"So the bank captured Snorri hoping to find Loki's key? And when they get it they'll give it to the Dead King." That didn't sound good.

"Perhaps, perhaps not. They have, as I said, their own ambitions. However, the key has yet to be found. Your Norsemen must know where it lies and so Kelem wished you to free them."

"He could have asked!"

Sageous smiled as if we both knew the answer I would have given. He'd pointed me at Hennan, a gentle push that would normally be mis-construed as the nagging of a guilty conscience. It seemed important to Kelem that Snorri not feel pushed toward their encounter for fear of changing his mind. I took some small comfort in the fact that neither the dream-witch nor the door-mage seemed to understand either of us. Conscience would never compel me into harm's way, and nothing would ever turn Snorri from his path, certainly not the fact that Kelem so badly wanted him to pursue it.

Sageous's smile hung for a moment then fell away as if it had never been. "And to the purpose of my visit." Sageous advanced on me, intim-idating though he was the smaller man by more than a head. "Where is Loki's key?" His eyes became drowning pools and terror washed over me. I fell into darkness screaming only the truth. I don't know. I don't know. I don't know!

I woke sweat-soaked, screaming the words, Hennan shaking me and shouting for me to wake up.

After the dream-witch's visit I resolved never to sleep again.

It took a day's insistence and the privacy of another food riot to get Hen-nan to talk about the key. Once the food got into his system and he found a little energy the boy wanted to talk about everything under the sun, about Kara, about how Snorri got taken down, about what happened to Tuttugu. I wouldn't listen. I had one question—where is the key? In the end the need to talk about something, even if it was the one thing he'd promised not to talk about, was what broke Hennan's resolve.

"Kara hid it," he said.

"Snorri wouldn't trust her with the key."

"He watched her do it."

"Did they bury it somewhere?" I don't know what I'd been anticipating, but the idea of the key in a box under four foot of soil, or jammed in some remote crevice on a cliff face, didn't offer much hope. A thing like that wouldn't stay hidden. The unborn felt its pull and it seemed as though the necromancers could track it too. If the only thing the Central Bank wanted wasn't still there once I'd bargained our release for its exchange then we'd all leave the prison the same way and nobody would be happy but the pigs. And if I did find out where it was, Sageous would pick the fact from my mind the very next time I fell asleep. Kelem getting the key might be the lesser of two evils compared to the Dead King getting his claws on it, but it still seemed a pretty evil evil to me. The only hope would be to find out where it was and use that information to my advantage before I next fell asleep.

"Tell me they gave it to someone for safekeeping—someone we can trust." I couldn't think of anyone I could trust, but maybe Snorri had more friends and was less troubled by that particular problem.

"Snorri didn't give it away," Hennan said.

"Well where is it then?" I hissed, fending off an old man who'd stumbled past our guards after being elbowed in the face over the ownership of an apple core.

The boy scratched his head as if this were a difficult question.

"Hennan!" I tried to keep the exasperation from my voice.

He withdrew his hand and opened it. A small iron tablet lay in his palm, no bigger than the nail of my little finger, set with a single rune. Kara wore the same things in her hair, or had until she sewed the Hardassa's ruin with them close to the Wheel of Osheim. Hennan must have had it hidden in the matted filth of his own hair.

"How will this help?" I didn't say it wouldn't—I'd seen marvels spring from such runes.

Hennan frowned, trying to remember the exact words. "Let the shadow of a key fall upon it and it will unlock the truth and reveal the lie."

"It will . . . what?" He'd forgotten the spell. All we had was garbled nonsense. The death of a small hope hurts more than an age of despair. That constant fear swelled again from the pit of my stomach and tears stung my eyes.

"It *is* the key." Hennan kept his gaze on the rune. "But we can't see it or use it until the charm's taken off."

It sounded like madness. "With a shadow?"

"Yes."

"Of a key?"

"Yes."

"Christ." I lay back, shoulders to the roughness of the wall. "You think any of this lot have a key?" I leant to the side and grabbed the ankle of the old man who'd collapsed to the floor. "You! You got a key?" I started laughing, too loud, the kind of laughter that hurts your chest and isn't but a hair from sobbing.

There's one thing to be said for sitting in a cell with absolutely nothing to do but keep what's yours and nurse your hunger—it gives you time. Time to think, time to plan. Obviously to give the lie to this nonsense Kara had spun Hennan, or possibly prove it true, we needed someone with a key. The only someone likely to come down into the bowels of the prison was our friend Racso. So all we needed to do was to get the shadow of Racso's key to fall across it, and we'd have our opportunity when he next unlocked the cell.

Racso wouldn't be back until he felt like selling the debtors food and water, probably another twelve hours or so. I sat back against the wall and invited Hennan to tell me just how Snorri had managed to get them all locked up.

"And how the hell did you find them?"

And Hennan told me. The food supplies he had taken from the Roma Hall kitchens ran out after two days. Hungry and tired, he had managed to get a ride with an old couple visiting relatives in Hemero. The pair of ancients appeared to be taking all their worldly possessions with them in their cart but found room for the boy atop the heap. Hennan's part of the bargain was to fetch and carry water, gather kindling, take the horses to pasture, and carry out miscellaneous chores. To me it sounded as if the old folks had taken pity on a strangely pale beggar boy. In any event the arrangement got him safely to within ten miles of the Florentine border.

Back roads took Hennan across the invisible line between the two kingdoms at a point without any guards to turn him away. He arrived sunburned and hungry in Umbertide, exhausting the last of the provisions that his ageing benefactors had sent him off with. Getting into the city had been an adventure of sewers and climbing, Umbertide having enough street children of its own without the soldiers at its gates letting any more in.

It wasn't until Hennan had nearly finished the tale of his getting into Umbertide that I realized what the real problem was. The understanding struck as a cold contraction of the stomach and a sudden reluctance to ask the questions that needed answers.

I forced the words out. "How long ago did you get taken?"

Hennan frowned in the candle light. "I don't know. Everything feels like forever down here and there's no days."

"Guess."

"A couple of days before you came?"

That sinking feeling became something more savage as if some great hand were trying to pull me through the cell floor. I thought he'd been in the cell the whole time I'd been in Umbertide. "But you're so thin . . ."

"I've been living off rubbish and sleeping in the streets for . . . weeks. Snorri didn't come by road. Not at first. They took a boat down the river—"

"The Seleen?" The cunning bastards. They hadn't trusted me to keep quiet about the key and knew the Red Queen would come after them. They'd done what northmen do. Taken to sea.

"Yes, they got a merchant to take them down the coast on his ship. Only they had problems and it took them a long time. They put in at some port on the Florentine coast and walked to Umbertide. I saw them coming through the Echo Gates. I used to sleep by there, up on a roof."

"So you met up with them and . . ."

"Soldiers took us a few hours later."

"Soldiers?"

"Well, men in uniform anyway, with swords."

"And what had you done?"

"Nothing. Kara got us a room and we'd gone to a tavern and Snorri got me something to eat. They were talking about how they would find Kelem once they reached his mines—Kara said they weren't far off. And then the soldiers came. Snorri knocked some down and we barricaded ourselves into the room. And that's when Kara convinced Snorri to let her hide the key. Snorri said . . ." Hennan frowned again, as if trying to remember the exact words. "'Hide it with the boy. He needs something to give them.'"

"Shit." Not good. Not good at all.

"What? What's wrong?" Hennan said, as if there weren't already enough wrong for me to curse every time I opened my mouth.

"If they want the key they'll be coming here soon enough."

Hennan was all questions then, but for once I couldn't think of any plausible lies and the truth was too ugly to share. When I thought that House Gold had held Snorri for weeks without coming to the debtors' prison to question their other captives things had seemed less urgent. If they'll wait three weeks then chances are they'll wait another one, and another. My own questions spiraled in my skull, chased by inconvenient answers. Why would they capture Snorri if not for the key? What could be more dangerous in a city where locked vaults lay everywhere than a key that opened everything? Why would Snorri give the key to a child? Because when they came to question the boy Snorri needed to know Hennan had something to give them rather than be tortured for information he didn't have. And the biggest question was how long—how long would the northmen hold out once the bankers stopped asking nicely and got out the hot irons? If it were me I'd be babbling out every secret I ever knew before they'd even got past harsh language. They'd had them three days. If they were asking questions the hard way then nobody could hold out much longer than that, not even Snorri.

Common sense said the bank was after the key and they'd be coming to my cell once they'd broken Snorri. *Or*, and the thought only increased my panic, once they'd broken Tuttugu, which would take far less time. Without the key I wasn't ever getting out of this cell, except as a bag of bones destined for the back door. We needed to get out as soon as possible—now in fact. But until we had a key's shadow we didn't have a key, and without a key we could do nothing but hurry up and wait.

A whole day passed before Racso's return—a day and a sleepless night in which each hour crawled and I sweated through every minute. I couldn't imagine how either northman could be holding out so long under inter-rogation and each distant clunk of metal on metal had me sure that someone had come for Hennan. But in the end it was our jailer that came, with a new debtor in tow, fresh meat for the cells. Or rather a long-term debtor whose funds had finally run so low that she'd been judged ready for the final stop in her repayment plan. The gate should have been unlocked nearly a day earlier when a bag of bones named Artos Mantona died quietly in the middle of the floor, being too weak to keep his corner place. We shouted through the bars but if Racso heard he showed no inclination to remove the corpse, probably thinking a replacement would be along sooner or later and he'd kill two birds with one stone.

By the looks of some of the gaunt faces in the light of my flickering candle Artos might not be the only inmate waiting to be dragged away for the pigs by the time Racso deigned to unlock. One of the "heavies" I paid in apples to keep the starving masses off my back, a man bearing the unlikely name of Artemis Canoni, had taken a turn for the worse despite the improvement my arrival had wrought in his diet. I'd never seen a man go downhill so fast. He seemed to curl up about some hidden pain, growing smaller by the hour. Another fellow nursed a wet cough, not wet in the normal spluttery way, but in the ragged sound of his lungs and the bubbling corruption to be heard inside his straining chest. I kept away from him.

"Get back, you defaulting maggots!" Racso's bellow always made me flinch, each utterance of it scoring the hate I had for him a little deeper. The debtors moved back from the bars as Racso's baton rattled across them, the actual maggots stayed where they were, chewing on the ruins of Artos Mantona's eyeballs with tiny mouths. "Back!"

Hennan and I stayed where we were, sitting around our candle, the latest in a line of them, now burned down to its last few inches. We'd positioned ourselves as close to the bars as we thought would be tolerated.

Behind Racso stood a middle-aged woman in grey rags, regarding us with horror. She looked gaunt rather than starved, and once among the other inmates she would seem almost healthy.

"Move that debtor beside the gate." Racso nodded at Artos's remains. "You there, stay close and roll him through." He counted through his keys and approached the gate with the chunk of iron best suited to opening it. He held his lantern in the other hand, sending a confusion of shadows swinging this way and that, the pattern of the bars playing back and forth across the floor. I opened my hand to reveal the small rune in my palm, colder than it should be, heavier too.

"Come on, dammit." A desperate mutter as I chased shadows, trying to catch them in my hand. There wasn't any blasted shadow that looked like a key, just random blurs and the sweeping shadow of the bars.

"What you got there, yer worship?" Racso helped the woman in with a kindly shove between the shoulder blades. "Something to trade?" The old wreck he'd detailed to move Artos struggled to roll him through the gap. The rotten stink that went up made him retch over the body as he rolled it. "Something good?"

I stood up, holding my palm out toward him. The movement came too fast and, ever suspicious, he slammed the gate, turning the key in the lock. A few seconds earlier and Artos's dead legs would have kept the gate from closing, but the old man had pushed them through just in time.

What I would have done then I'm not sure. Certainly pitting my skull against Racso's baton did not appeal. He looked to have the sullen strength possessed by many fat men with slab-like arms. Not a showy, muscular strength, just the killing kind.

"Easy, emperor! Nothing sudden. Nothing sudden!" He squinted at my hand as he withdrew the key. "Don't look like much."

"Take a closer look!" I stepped forward and he stepped back, lantern waving, key jutting at me as if to ward off attack. I'd tried too hard though, unnerved him, let the need show.

"You want to settle yourself, emperor, take it easy. Don't let this place get to you. A little fasting will calm you down." He turned away, evidently not taking food orders today.

I punched the bars in frustration. It didn't help. Another night would see me falling asleep and spilling all my new secrets to Sageous.

"Wait!" Hennan's high voice. "A silver crown. Crown argent of Red March!" He nudged me in the ribs, hard. Racso swivelled with considerable grace, pirouetting on a heel.

"Silver? I don't think so. I'd've smelled out a silver." He tapped his nose.

Hennan nudged me again and with great reluctance I drew one of the three silvers from the depths of my pocket, not the promised crown argent but a silver florin from the Central Bank's own mint. A hungry gasp went up on all sides.

"Shut it!" Racso banged the bars, scowling at the inmates before returning his gaze to the florin. "Silver is it?" A peculiar greed stole over his face as if the coin were a pudding he were about to devour. "And what is it you'd be wanting, yer lordship? Meat? A good joint on the bone? Beef? A jug o' gravy with it?"

"Just hold your lantern like so." Hennan mimed the action. "And the door key, like so." He held the one hand before the other. "And let the shadow fall onto Jalan's palm."

Racso frowned, his hands moving to obey even as he considered his objections. "Witchcraft is it? Some heathen thing of yours, boy?" He unclasped the key hoop on his belt and worked the largest of them free.

"He says it will bring us luck." I shrugged, joining in. "Damned if I'm not tired enough of this place to want a bit of that. The key symbolizes freedom."

"You following the north gods now, yer lordship?" Racso picked absently at his nose with the hand holding the key. "Don't hardly seem Christian."

"Just taking a gamble, Racso, just a gamble. I've been praying hard to Jesu and the Father since I got here and it hasn't done a bit of good. Me the son of a cardinal and all! Thought I'd spread my bets."

And just like that Racso held out the door-key, his lantern behind it, close enough and still enough for the shadow to fall on the floor. As Hennan surmised, everything's for sale at the right price, and you won't find many shadows that will earn you a silver florin.

I reached out with the rune at the middle of my palm and caught the shadow from the air, closing my hand about it. In one moment fingers closed about empty space and in the next they held Loki's key, as cold, heavy, and solid as a lie.

In the same instant I tossed the florin between the bars and a hundred pairs of eyes followed its ringing progress. Racso scampered after it, dropping the door-key on the floor, beyond arm's reach though that didn't stop half a dozen of my cellmates stretching for it.

He tracked the coin down and stamped on it to halt its progress. "Now that weren't right, debtor." He called the ones closest to dying debtor, as if it excused everything happening to them. "Ain't right to send a man running after a coin like he's a street beggar. Not even for a silver." He straightened, bit the coin, and crossed back toward us, the florin in his meaty fist. He barked a laugh at the arms withdrawing between the bars. "Take more'n a key to get out of Central Prison. I could open all eight of these gates and wouldn't none of you maggots get halfway out. You'd need all these here." He patted the ring at his hip, making the keys hooked upon it jangle. "And a sword-son to get past the guard. There's close on a dozen standing between you lot and freedom." He frowned over the arithmetic. "Six or seven anyway."

Racso looked down at the coin in his palm, his face almost lit with the glow of it. "Easy money." He laughed and slapped his belly, shadows swinging. "I'll be back for the debtor." He toed Artos's corpse. "Got me some spending to do." And off he walked, whistling his song of cool breezes and open fields.

I sat in my island of light, the candle flame guttering around its wick, Loki's key in my hand, and in the thickness of the shadow on all sides desperate men muttered about silver coins.

TWENTY-NINE

We waited for Racso to come back. We didn't need his key but I needed light for my plan and before the light I'd needed darkness. We had to wait. I didn't want to wait. I didn't want the boredom or the misery or the sense of uncertainty, but most of all I didn't want to fall asleep and find Sageous waiting there for me.

It proved a long and miserable test of endurance, there in the unbroken night of the cells. I moaned and sighed about it, until I remembered Hennan had endured the place alone before I arrived, much of his time starving and parched. I kept quiet after that even though I thought it had probably been easier on him, raised as he was to the hardships of peasant life.

Artemis Canoni stopped answering my calls to have the inmates and their prying hands kept from my person, and took to moaning in a corner—whatever had been eating at his insides seeming now to have gained the upper hand. My other bodyguard, Antonio Gretchi, a former cobbler to Umbertide's moneyed classes, proved unequal to the task on his own, and so I indentured a new servant for the price of a wizened apple and set him to his duties—which meant stamping on any hand that he encountered creeping in my direction in the dark.

For hour stacked upon empty hour we sat on the hard ground, too hot, too thirsty, and listening, always listening for the rustle of any approach. My head kept nodding, imagination creeping in to paint pictures on the darkness, tempting me into dream. I jerked my head up with a curse, more desperate each time. Occasionally someone would start to speak, sometimes a muttered conversation with a confidant, sometimes a long slow litany uttered into the dark. In the anonymity of blindness people confessed their sins, spoke their desires, made their peace with the Almighty, or, in some cases, bored the arse off everyone with endless dreary recollections from profoundly dull lives. I wondered how long I would have to sit there before the company became acquainted with every detail of events at the Aral Pass and I progressed to a comprehensive reconstruction of all Vermillion's bordellos. Quite possibly another day would get me there.

The low mutter of conversation rose and fell in cycles, petering out to long silences then building again, sparked by a memory that built into a recounted moment and split into half a dozen threads running through our number. The thing had a natural rhythm to it, and when that rhythm broke it jarred me out of my reverie. The muttering of four or five people had stopped at once. Even the wet death rattle of Mr. Cough paused.

"What is it?" I asked. It clearly needed someone of royal blood to voice the important questions.

Silence, save for a scraping noise, something heavy being pulled across flagstones.

"I said—" The scraping noise came again and I realized with a start that whatever was making the sound was beyond the bars.

I held my breath. Silence. Fear kept that breath trapped in my lungs, only to burst out in a shriek when Mr. Cough suddenly started choking on his own held breath, hacking so hard I felt sure his lungs must be filling with blood. When he finally trailed off a couple of people started to mutter again, the tension broken. With a dull thud something fell against the bars—and everyone swallowed their words, the breath trapped in their chests once more. Inmates shuffled back further into the cell starting to curse and cry out in fear.

"What the hell?"

"How can—"

"There's no one out there . . ."

And then someone said it. "Artos?" The corpse that had been left sprawled just beyond the gate.

"Maybe he wasn't dead."

"He was dead. I checked him. He was my friend."

"Maggots were eating his eyes."

"Of course he was dea—" A second dull thud of meat against bars cut the conversation off.

"Oh shit."

"Sweet Jesu!"

"Artos? Is that you?"

The darkness seethed with possibilities—none of them good.

"It *is* Artos, isn't it?" Hennan's voice, closer to me than I'd imagined. I flinched.

"Yes."

"And he *is* dead, isn't he?" A small hand seeking mine.

"Yes." In my left hand I held the key, removed from its hiding place, the witch's spell undone . . . Loki's key ready for use once more, and once more free to draw the attention of any foul thing that might be seeking it.

The thud of meat on iron came again. I imagined what I couldn't see. Artos, staggering back from the impact on dead legs, face still crawling, ready to lunge forward once more, answering the call of what I held in my hand.

"Don't worry." I used my bluff hero-of-the-pass voice, loud enough for everyone but aiming the message at just one pair of ears. "Don't worry. He's out there, and we're in here. If he couldn't manage to get through those bars in all the months they held him trapped on this side, he's not going to manage to get back through them before Racso's next visit, now is he?"

I'd barely got the words out before Mr. Cough drew in another gurgling breath as if he were drowning in whatever filth was filling his lungs. On cue, after that chilling breath rattled into Mr. Cough, my former bodyguard Artemis Canoni loosed a soft cry of agony from his corner of the cell. Neither Hennan nor I said it, but from the sudden tension in his hand I think we came to the understanding in the same moment. Artos might be trapped out there—but if Mr. Cough or Artemis Canoni were to meet their maker within the next ten hours or so before Racso came back . . . the Dead King would have a new corpse to play with, and this time we'd be trapped in the cell with whatever he chose to stand back up again. Suddenly my concern for my fellow inmates reached new heights.

"Give that man with the cough some room, dammit! Don't crowd him. Someone give him some water—there's a copper in it for the man that does. And Artemis—where's my faithful Artemis got to? Water for him too. And here's a crust to dip into it."

It took a bit of organizing but I did my best for them. Not that I had much faith in the curative powers of stale water and staler bread. Our friend outside kept bumping against the bars, and our friends inside kept muttering about *why* he might be doing it, but in the end with nothing to see and nothing to be done about it, we settled back into an uneasy quiet.

The truth about sheer terror is that even for a world-class coward like me it's unsustainable. When the dreaded thing doesn't happen hour after hour it becomes something that whilst still terrible allows a little room around the edges through which other thoughts may slip. Thoughts came. Thoughts that seeded suspicions into the blindness of the cell. Suspicions, watered by darkness, growing, slowly but relentlessly. The Red Queen's war lay at the midst of my troubles. Her elder sister had sent me to the distant north to find the key I now held. And what was I doing in Umbertide? The Silent Sister's twin had sent me here. It had seemed a mercy at the time, an escape from the dangers at home . . . but was it? Red March mortgaged to the banks of Florence, a power struggle between House Gold and others against Kelem, the Broken Empire's unofficial master of coin, the Dead King sticking his bony fingers into the pie . . . the last staging post for Snorri before heading into the hills bearing Loki's key to seek the door-mage out . . . and young Prince Jalan thrust into the middle of it all by a man I'd come to understand more fully in Umbertide than I ever had in the palace—a man the traders here considered Red March's unofficial master of coin. I thought of Garyus slumped in his bed, looking two steps from death as he sent me on my way with the only kind words I heard on my return. I thought of him lying there and tried to square that image with the new ones being built behind my eyes. With a start I realized I was holding Loki's key tight to my chest. I lowered my hand, wondering if its lies were bleeding into me even now.

I sat pondering, clutching Loki's key, shifting position every few minutes to keep from getting sore against the flagstones, until every part of me was sore and it didn't matter any more. I would rather have set the key in a pocket but I couldn't risk losing it, and so I held it tight, that slick and treacherous surface seeming to slide beneath my fingers like melting ice.

To start with I'd gripped the thing as if it might bite me, remembering how at my first touch memories had pulsed through me, images from the day Edris Dean killed my mother. But the key didn't bite any more than old Artos found a way through the cell's bars. I sat with it cool in my fist for an hour or more, listening to the sounds of the dungeon. At one point I heard a knocking, as if someone were rapping on a door close by—though I knew we had only bars and gates, no door. The knocking grew louder, more insistent, though no one around me mentioned it, and the darkness around my ears seemed crowded with whispers just beyond the edge of hearing. It lasted a minute, another, and then no more.

The fear subsided into unease, disquiet fermented into boredom, and only the long battle against sleep remained as the blind hours passed. That was when the key struck. It felt as if the key were hauled sideways. I could let it go or be dragged along with it. Darkness melted into vision though I fought with all my strength to stay where I was, and struggled to see only what lay about me. My efforts blew away in a cold wind. I stood once more on the margins of the Wheel of Osheim. The archway, that empty arch through which we'd escaped from Edris and the Hardassa Vikings stood once more before me, a lone work of the wrong-mages in the bizarre wilderness through which Kara had guided us. Of the völva, of Snorri and Tuttugu, there was no sign. No sign of me either, just my disembodied point of view, watching, unblinking, waiting for the lie, waiting for the key's deception. And nothing came. I held a dim awareness of my body, somewhere else, in another place and time, the key a cold and heavy bar locked tight in my grip.

"It's an odd sort of vision that shows me nothing . . ." The words sounded only in my head. In Osheim the wind spoke and everything else lay silent. I stared at the arch, and at the strangely sculpted encrustations of black and glassy rock that punctuated the surrounding terrain. I looked up at the mauve wound of the sky. "What?"

Light reflecting from one of the nearer outcroppings drew my eye. Obsidian they called this stuff. I knew it not from the lecturing of some tutor but because there had been a fad back in Vermillion for jewellery made from the material. For several months one autumn everyone who was anyone was wearing it, and after Lisa DeVeer had dropped enough heavy hints on me from the considerable height of her balcony, I borrowed sufficient money to buy her a necklace fashioned from polished beads and discs of obsidian. She wore it once if I recall . . . The key burned cold in my hand and suddenly I knew what it had been made from and from whence it came.

"Ah hell." No story that begins "near the Wheel of Osheim" ends well. I looked down and saw that I'd arrived in body as well as spirit. In my hand, where the key should be was nothing but Hennan's iron rune tablet. A moment later it was the shadow of a key. Then the key. "Kara hid you in a shadow . . ." My eyes roamed up the sides of the arch, gaze sliding uncomfortably over the symbols set there in stone. "She's dark-sworn?" I remembered the ease with which she cast Aslaug from her boat. She hadn't opposed the spirit with light or fire, just ordered her gone . . . and Loki's daughter had fled.

I looked at the arch and remembered how Kara had prepared it with spells before getting Snorri to use the key. The arch had opened onto the dark and Aslaug had emerged, then Baraqel had broken through, setting light at war with darkness within the span of the portal, forming some kind of recreation of the powers at the heart of the Silent Sister's spell. Only then had the völva urged us through, leading the way. And from that moment to this I hadn't heard another word from Aslaug nor had Snorri mentioned Baraqel. Their voices suddenly silent and their influence fading to nothing in the space of a week. It hadn't seemed that odd until now. Everything about magic is strange and untrustworthy in any case . . . but . . . Kara had led us to that arch, she had worked enchantment upon it, and then as well as transporting us from danger it had stripped away our patrons, the strength given to us by my great-aunt. Granted, they were strange spirits we bore and not to be trusted, and granted my great-aunt was as mad a witch as might be found in the Broken Empire, but even so they had been a form of power, our only protection from the worst of what our enemies might bring to bear upon us . . . and Kara had taken them from us.

I walked through the arch and found myself on the other side, back on that same blasted heath. When Kara had activated it the arch had taken us to the darkness beneath Halradra . . . but I'd come from darkness this time and required light. For the longest moment I stood staring back at the archway, remembering the darkness of my cell and the darkness of the caves beneath the volcano. Light. That was why we were waiting. We needed light. And, as if a key had turned, pieces of memory aligned and I had my answer.

I closed my eyes, opened them again, and found it dark, just as it had always been. Near silence—the low muttering of two people across the width of the cell, the rattle of a dying man's breath, the scraping shuffle of a dead man beyond the bars. I patted my pockets and cursed myself for a fool.

I worked blind, breaking free double florins from the linen strips into which they'd been sewn, unwrapping the used lengths of cloth and stacking the coins between my knees. I took exquisite care not to let them chink.

"What're you doing?" Hennan close by.

"Nothing." I damned his keen ears.

"You're doing something."

"Just be ready."

The boy had the sense not to ask what for, where many grown men would not.

With even greater care I balanced a tin plate upside down atop the stacks of coins.

"I'm going to make a light," I said loud enough for everyone. "You should shield your eyes."

Loki's key opened a lot of things, memories not the least of them. I reached down into the depths of my back pocket, down among the fluff, the old handkerchief that needed cleaning, scraps of parchment, a locket with Lisa DeVeer's likeness inside, and found the small hard lump I'd been searching for, wrapped in cloth. I slid a finger past the covering to touch the cold metal. Immediately a glow broke through the handkerchief, through the questing fingers, and shone through the fabric of my trews. Had there been a wit among our number he might have commented that for once the sun did indeed appear to be shining out of my arse. I pulled Garyus's orichalcum cone out, hidden in my fist and yet still bright enough to light the room in the rosy hues of my blood, the illumination pulsing and erratic as a heartbeat. Gasps of awe and shock went up on all sides. Even muted by my hand the light was enough to make everyone there, me included, shield our eyes.

The awe turned to horror within moments. On all sides my fellow debtors were screaming and shuffling back from the bars. Being closest to the source, the light blinded me for longer than most so that I had to unscrew my eyes against the glare and blink helplessly to try to see what had caused the panic. When I finally focused on the thing beyond the bars a shriek nearly escaped me too and only my greatest resolve kept me from bundling back to bury myself in the crowd.

Artos had scraped off most of the maggoty flesh and the eyes that regarded us from that raw and glistening face were oozing sockets, night-dark with shadow. Even so a hunger seemed to stare from the darkness of those eye-pits, a hunger that felt horrifically familiar. Dead hands gripped the bars and a jaw full of broken teeth ground out still more fragments whilst gargling incoherent threats at us.

"In a moment I'm going to unlock the gate," I said.

A collective gasp and a chorus of "no"s went up.

"Even if you *could* open it I wouldn't go out there!" Antonio, my longest-serving bodyguard, looked from the dead man to me as if I were mad, his eyes watering from the light. "Hell, I wouldn't go out there even if that thing weren't standing there! The guards would just catch me in the next corridor and I'd be back here with a fine added to my debt and a beating for my troubles. We need to wait until Racso comes. He'll bring the guard to deal with . . . whatever the hell that thing is." He paused, squinting against the glow from my hand. "How the hell are you *doing* that?"

"In a moment I'm going to unlock the gate," I repeated more loudly, holding the black key before me. "The next person to die in here will end up like Artos out there—only he'll be locked inside with us." I looked around meaningfully at Mr. Cough, lying semi-conscious on his back, chest shuddering up, wheezing down, shuddering up. "Just think about that."

I went over to the gate and the thing that had been Artos moved to stand opposite me. As I approached the bars it stuck its arms through, reaching for me, the remains of its face pressing forward as if somehow it might squeeze its skull through the gap. I just about managed not to jump back. These people needed courage if they were going to get me out of here. They needed a good example, needed to see some bravery on display. I couldn't give them that but I could give them a passable impression of it.

"Not too clever are you?" I kept just out of range of the clutching fingers. There was an intelligence in those dark and gory sockets, that same awful one that had stared at me through the eyes of dead men back in the mountains with Snorri, but hunger dominated the thing's actions, a hunger to kill me at any cost. For what felt like an eternity I stood there, knowing I couldn't back down but without a clue what to do. Eventually I patted my pockets for inspiration. After all, Garyus's orichalcum cone had sat there forgotten ever since my return to the palace, something else useful might be down at the bottom of another pocket . . . I glanced down and discovered that the useful thing was right at the top. I pulled free a length of the linen strip that had until recently had double florins sewn into it. I made a wide noose from it—no simple task while still clutching the orichalum. With the noose complete I advanced on Artos, after a few tentative tries, I slipped it over his right wrist. Throwing my weight behind it I pulled the arm sharply to the side. The elbow joint gave with a vomit-making cracking sound, and the arm bent at an impossible angle, allowing me to bind it to the bars out of reach of Artos's left hand. I took another length of the linen and repeated the process with the other arm.

"There." Artos now glared at us, pinned to the gate by two broken arms, his tongue protruding and scraping over shattered teeth as if it too were trying to reach me. I set Loki's key in the lock. It fitted perfectly and turned without protest. Click. I took hold of the gate's outer edge and pushed it open, lending my weight to overcome the resistance as

Artos lunged at me. I held the gate open with one arm and beckoned the debtors with the hand clutching our light. At each of the seven other cells scores of faces pressed to the bars, watching on amazed.

The debtors, all terrified and confused, stayed where they were; some even shuffled further back, though giving Mr. Cough a wide berth.

I sighed, stepped back, thrust my hand into my pocket and pulled out all my smaller coins, two silver florins, three hexes, a dozen halves. A jerk of my hand scattered them into the room beyond the gate. As if scalded, half the cell's population launched themselves forward, most of the other half jumping to their feet. A number of them got jammed in the gateway, fighting each other, desperate to be the first through, right under Artos's nose, his hands twitching uselessly at them.

I moved quickly to Hennan's side and handed him the orichalcum. "Hold that."

In the resulting darkness I scooped up the pile of double florins from under my plate, some fifty in all, and tipped them into my shirt, folding it up over them.

"Give it back, now." I had to raise my voice over the cacophony rising from the riot beyond the gate. After a moment or two of fumbling we made the exchange and the place lit up once more, my hand glowing, brilliance lancing out between my fingers. "Come on." And I led the way out, Hennan at my heels, and others following, drawn by the departing light and fear of being left alone in the dark with dying men who might not die properly.

I would have given Hennan the key and let him open the other gates but it seemed cruel to let him touch it. I had to blink at that notion. A year ago the matter of my convenience would have outweighed any worry about cruelty to a child—in fact the cruelty might have been considered an added bonus . . .

I stepped over three men wrestling for ownership of a hex, and unlocked the first gate. A few of the more healthy and larger men hurried out to join the struggle for small change, most held back, almost as frightened of me with my glowing hand and black key as they had been of Artos and his half-eaten face.

By the time I reached the fifth cell people were slowly edging out of the already-open cells. I unlocked the gate and immediately a big fellow pushed through. He didn't join the struggle for the last coin out in the centre: instead he turned on me. I had to look up to meet his gaze. Belligerent dark eyes narrowed at me beneath a shock of black hair. The man had starved with the rest of the last-stage debtors but he'd been a bruiser in his day and he seemed far less impressed with me than his fellows did.

"Been watching you eat while the rest of us go without. Been watching you throwing your money about, northerner." His scowl deepened and he fell quiet as if he'd asked me a question.

"Northerner? Me?" That was a new one, though I guessed technically it was correct. I eyed him up, wondering if I could overpower him and definitely not wanting to have to try.

"Suppose you throw some of that money my way—in fact suppose you hand it over nicely, boy?"

The cells had fallen quiet behind me, the inmates in front of me all staring my way. All I had to defend myself was the key in my hand, clutched somewhat awkwardly because of the double florin hidden in my palm. My other hand held the orichalcum cone and I kept it tight to my stomach where it pinned up the fold of my shirt, pregnant with a modest fortune in gold.

"Uh." Panic seized me and my legs got ready to run away. The lout extended a raw-boned hand, reaching for my neck.

"Knock him flat, Jal!" Hennan piped up unhelpfully from behind me. He'd got that damned "Jal" habit from Snorri.

Inspiration struck before the bully did. "Look!" I said, and opened the hand with the key to reveal the gleaming gold disc in my grimy palm. For a second his face lit with reflected light while an amazed and stupid grin spread across his face. "Fetch!" And I tossed it through the bars into the cell behind him. A score of filthy grey bodies immediately threw themselves on top of the double florin and with a snarl my tormentor turned and charged into the fray roaring dire threats.

"Spend it in good health." I closed the gate behind him and locked it, slipping the key into my pocket.

I turned back, expecting my audience to be at least a little impressed but it turned out they hadn't gone quiet because of my little drama at gate number five. Racso stood in the mouth of the corridor, three guardsmen behind him, big men draped in chain-mail shirts with bare steel in their hands.

"Get. Back. In." Racso dropped each word like a stone. He'd replaced his usual baton for one ending in an ugly lump of black iron. The grey sea of bodies drew back toward the cells, the multitude of their shadows swaying and swelling across the walls as the orichalcum pulsed within my grip. A few more seconds and my chance would be gone entirely.

"Look!" I shouted, digging out a handful of gold from the fold of my shirt and holding it toward the ceiling.

That got their attention. Scores of heads turned on scores of scrawny necks. The peculiar nature of our incarceration meant that in my hands I held their freedom. Despite threats, sharp iron, or blunt instruments, there were few here who couldn't buy their way out the door even now with ten double florins. Many of them could purchase their release with just one or two coins and at the very least a single coin would give them a year of food and drink, another year between them and feeding the pigs.

I let the money do my talking. I threw the whole handful over the heads of Racso and the guardsmen and sent it rattling on down the corridor behind them.

The effect was immediate. The debtors surged forward without a moment's hesitation. Even Racso and the guards were looking in the direction of the departing florins. The debtors didn't so much attack the men in their way, but rather they flowed over them, and each other, a rolling tidal advance.

I grabbed Hennan and hurried on at the rear of the wave, setting a booted foot to the back of Racso's thick neck as he struggled to rise. Always kick a man when he's down, I say. It's the best chance you'll get.

The debtors who had collected the most gold, scrambling for it in the half-crazed melee with almost no light to see by, now pressed on through the prison, desperate to pay out their debt before their hard-stolen florins were taken from them in turn. Those who had done less well in the free-for-all gave chase, anxious to even the distribution of funds.

Unfortunately a few of the crowd paused to think about where the money had come from and were still paused as Hennan and I reached them. A shabby man of middling years stepped out into my path, an old woman at his shoulder naked but for smeared filth; to the side waited a young woman with straggling dirty-blond hair, heavyset and mean-eyed, wearing what seemed to have once been a sack. Three older men, small and similar enough to be relations, moved from the shadows to back them up.

"Cough up." The young woman held out her hand. "Three doubles will cure my ills. Heard you're a prince. Three doubles is the cheap way past me, lover-boy."

Immediately the rest of them started clamouring out their demands and crowding forward in a grimy rabble.

"Get back!" I boomed, and they stopped. Royal breeding will do that for you. The accent, the posture, and centuries of breeding the lower classes to obey, all combine to allow a prince's outrage to carry rather further than the common man's. "How dare you?" I drew myself up to my full height, puffing out my chest, and raised my hand to strike any of them who came near. The threat of violence must have been somewhat muted by the fact I kept my left arm clamped across my belly, holding thirty or forty more double florins tight against myself.

"Well?" I roared. The debtors seemed frozen by my reprimands, staring at me slack-jawed. I took a sharp pace forward and all of them bolted for it, a half dozen and more of them scampering away down the dark corridor. "Well!" I grinned down at Hennan, quite surprised how successful I'd been. "I think—" Two large hands clamped about my throat and cut me off. I whipped around in panic, scattering gold, before the grip fully tightened, and found myself facing what had really scared the other debtors off. My eyes met the dead gaze of a guard whose head flopped at a wholly unnatural angle. His neck must have been broken at some point during the exodus of debtors over his prone body.

Fear is marvellous stuff. Not only will it get you running considerably faster than you thought possible, it will lend you more strength than you should rightly own. Not enough strength, sadly, to break the hold a dead man has on your neck, since being dead seems to lend some men strength as well, but enough for me to drive my assailant back across the chamber. I slammed him into the bars of a cell. I think I also managed to knee Racso in the face on the way past as he sat up, groaning . . .

The charge took everything out of me and I hung in the dead man's grip, black spots crowding my vision and a feeling of distance sliding over me. The pain in my neck and lungs receded as the world drew away, shrinking to a single bright spot. I had time in that soft and enfolding darkness to reflect on two things. First, that being choked by corpses was becoming something of a habit, and second, that my only chance for survival depended upon the greed of the many and the quick thinking of a singular child.

As the last traces of my vision faded from me I saw a dozen hands reach out through the bars, pinning the dead man to them. And just before the pounding of my heart grew so loud as to drown out all other sound, I heard the grating of a sword being dragged across stone.

I woke suddenly, freezing and wet.

"Hold it!" Hennan's voice in the dark.

"W—" My throat hurt too much to say more.

"Take this." Something hard pressed into my palm and brilliance erupted, filling the space with razored white light. I closed my hand around the orichalcum and screwed my eyes shut. The boy had thrown water over me . . . I hoped it was water.

It then occurred to me that I appeared to be a lot more naked than I had been. My next question started off as a "Where are my clothes?" but changed swiftly into "Where the hell is my money?"

"They took it." Hennan pointed at the last few grey backs pressing on down the corridor, a very trampled Racso in their wake. The guardsman who had been choking me lay twitching close by, furious glare fixed on me, though lacking the limbs required to make good on the threat.

"I gave them the sword through the bars and they cut him into pieces." Hennan winced at the memory of it.

I levered myself up. The linen wraps my coins had been sewn into lay strewn around, stained by pooling blood. Unclenching my hand, I found Loki's key still in my grip, my flesh marked with its impression.

"How did they—" I rubbed my bruised throat. "Get out?"

"I got Racso's keys," Hennan said.

"You let them rob me!"

"They had you by the legs and were taking your gold anyway. The big one said if I let them out they wouldn't hurt you."

"Uh." I supposed he had an excuse. I levered myself up, pulled on my ripped trews—they'd been very thorough in their search for florins—and got unsteadily to my feet. "C'mon."

We hurried after the departed debtors.

As hoped, close on two hundred well-motivated debtors put quite a hole in the prison's security. Instead of following them toward the front entrance where they were either rioting or busy buying their way out, I found a passage leading further back. We came through three locked gates, past a deserted guard post, and out via a heavy door into a stinking high-walled yard. A full moon bathed the scene in a silvery light that disguised rather than revealed. I wrapped the orichalcum in a cloth and shoved it deep into my pocket.

"Come on." I led the way, stepping around the lime pits where they put the remains of debtors whose relatives had paid the body-price. Two rickety carts stood against the wall, one heaped with several skin and bone corpses bound for the pigs.

"But . . ." Hennan grabbed my hand and anchored me.

"What?" The anger at finding myself penniless broke out to colour my tone.

"They're dead," Hennan whispered.

"Well I'd hope so . . ." I frowned at him. He might only be a child but he'd seen plenty of dead bodies before. Then it dawned on me why we might have been better off chancing the rioting and the possibility of recapture in the front of the prison. "Shit."

A dry scraping sound came from the lime pits behind us and on the cart the three emaciated corpses started scrambling to untangle themselves. "Run!"

I'm only a little ashamed to say I outsprinted the boy. Old habits die hard. It's good to be faster than what's chasing you, but really the important thing in running away is to be faster than the slowest of those being pursued. Rule number one: be ahead of the next man. Or child.

The gates to the outside world towered above me, thick slabs of dry timber, iron studded, a heavy locking mechanism in the middle. I shoved in the key with an ecstasy of fumbling, turned it and pushed through with a strength born of desperation. Hennan shot through the narrow gap seconds later, a white figure hard on his heels, lime powder smoking its trail. Together we slammed the gate and Loki's key locked it just as the first body hammered into the timbers.

THIRTy

"Keep running!" I grabbed Hennan's hand and dragged him across the street that ran behind the prison. We took the first alleyway that presented itself. Dark alleys might be dangerous places but when you're on the run from a debtors' prison in a banking town, with dead inmates anxious to eat the soft parts of you, even the worst alley in Christendom is the frying pan not the fire.

The narrow passages shadowed the moon as effectively as the sun, and save for the odd chink of lamplight escaping from the buildings we ran near blind. At each corner I imagined some beggar's corpse might be standing there in the darkness, with arms wide-stretched and a hungry grin. Turn after turn proved me wrong: it was Hennan who stopped me, not some dead man hunting the key.

The boy's strength gave out within just a few minutes, at first he only needed a moment here and there to catch his breath, but the stops got longer and soon it was a choice of carry, drag, abandon, or stop. I felt pretty tired myself, so we stopped, hunkering down in a gated archway leading into somebody's walled garden. I could only hope that the dead saw no better without light than the living, and that the gate at our backs would at least stop attack from that direction.

"We just have to get past the city gates and head north. They might send riders up the Roma Road so we'll need to take another route. The border could be a problem . . . but that's days away." I paused to haul in some much-needed air. "It'd be a damn sight easier if we had some money." I allowed myself a moment's silence to remember my lovely gold, variously thrown, scattered, and stolen in that blasted prison. My eyes prickled with the injustice of it all. I'd had a king's ransom in that case and even when they took *that* I had enough tied about my person to ransom his favourite dog . . . I may even have shed a manly tear in the privacy of that darkness.

"We need to get Snorri and the others first," Hennan said.

"Kara will be fine: she probably got out in the rioting. Besides, she's a witch, I'm surprised she hasn't used her magic and escaped already. In fact . . ." In fact I was suddenly hit by the realization that her being in the debtors' prison at all was pretty odd. Wouldn't they be keen to put her to the question as well?

"We've got to get them out." Hennan's voice came insistent through the dark. "We can't leave them in there to die!"

"Well, yes, of course I *want* to rescue Snorri and Tuttugu, Hennan, it's just . . ." It's just I don't want to at all because we'll be captured or killed. "There's no way of doing it. Not with only one man. Not even if that man's a prince. No, what we need to do is get back to Vermillion as fast as possible and then send help."

"Send . . . help?" He might be just a kid but he wasn't buying it.

"Yes. I'll tell the Red Queen and—"

"They can't wait that long! They need us to get them out now!"

"They'll have to wait. I don't even know where they are for Christ's sake!" I did, though. They'd be in the Frauds' Tower. The grimmest of all Umbertide's prisons, a squat grey tower wherein all the plots and ploys used outside bank-law to steal money were unravelled and undone, using a variety of variously sharp or hot or crushing implements to ensure a thorough solution. Those who stole money inside bank-law of course were very well rewarded, and known as bankers. In Umbertide the fraudster got a rawer deal than the murderer, and murderers were laid beneath a wide plank called "the door" upon which rocks were piled one at a time until the criminal was judged to be dead.

I'd been lucky not to go straight to the Tower myself, and probably it would have been just a matter of time before I was transferred there once the full scope of my tax and tariff evasions became clear. Or perhaps my family connections had kept me out. Either way heading there now seemed like the worst idea ever.

"I'm not going without them." Hennan, his voice steely with determination.

"The world doesn't work like that, Hennan." I tried for a fatherly tone, firm but fair. Not that I really had much to go on by way of experience. "You can't always do something just because it's the right thing to do. You've got to be sensible about these matters. Think them through."

"You've got the key. It got us out of one prison. It could get us into another."

He had a point. A point I needed to counter. I mean, I could have just cuffed him to the floor and set off for the hills on my own. Lord knows a prince of Red March doesn't have to answer to a child, a common-born child at that . . . a common-born, foreign child! But the fact was that somewhere along the line something had changed, perhaps it was some lingering damage that Baraqel had inflicted on me . . . but, damn it, I knew if I just left him behind it would start to niggle at me and leave me no peace, or at least not enough peace to properly enjoy myself. So, it seemed in my best interest to convince the little bastard to come with me.

"It's not only a matter of keys, Hennan," I began in a consoling tone. "There are other considerations. It's not safe for a boy of your age. For a start the Dead King wants the key. We can't hang around here, there are too many corpses, there's too much for him to work with . . . cities are built on layer upon layer of dead people . . . it's all that holds them up. And even if we made it to the right jail—"

"There are guards. A key won't get you past the jailers." The speaker unhooded her lantern close by, dazzling me. I scrambled back, blocked by the gate. My hands found Hennan and held him in front of me as some kind of small and ineffectual shield.

"Uh . . . ah . . . you have me at a disadvantage, madam." I blinked and averted my gaze, trying to clear my eyes.

"You need to run, Jalan. Give me the key and the Dead King will follow it instead of you." The voice seemed familiar.

"Kara?" I squinted through screwed up eyes. But the figure in front of me was small, a girl no older than Hennan, blond and pale, holding the lantern before her, her dress a simple thing of white linen, a servant's garb.

"Give me the key and run. They're out to get you, Jalan. You need to be safe in Vermillion." The little girl held her hand out, palm up and open.

I blinked away tears, my eyes adjusting to the light. "What?" It didn't make sense.

"Hennan can come with me." She seemed frayed around the edges now, as if the shadows were nibbling at her. Frayed and . . . taller.

"No." I gripped his shoulders tighter and he gasped, trying to twist loose. Something kept me unwilling to relinquish the boy.

"Come on, Jalan, this isn't your place. You need to get away. You need to run." The words had a cadence to them, a rhythm that got under my skin. I did need to get away—I did need to run. No argument there.

The girl seemed more of a memory now—I could still imagine her there, see the blueness of her eyes, but if I blinked I saw Kara holding the lantern, ragged and dirt-smeared.

"It's just a glamour, a spell to fool the eye, shake it off, and look clear," she said, and there she was, Kara, as if she'd never been anything else. "A casting to keep me from the Frauds' Tower. Quick. We won't have long, the dead are moving." And still she kept her hand out.

Hennan wrenched free of my grip. I thought he would run into her arms. Hell, I would if I knew I'd get a nice protective hug. But he ran off into the night instead—the ungrateful bastard.

Kara glanced after him and shook her head in annoyance. "He'll have to catch us up. We need to go *now*! Give me the key."

"Can't you just hide it again?" I didn't want to give it up—it was the only thing of value I had left. Just maybe it might earn me enough credit with Grandmother to forgive the loss of Garyus's ships to my creditors. Besides, Kara wanted it too much. A poker player learns the signs— whatever else she said the only thing that mattered to her was that I hand her the key. "Turn it back into a rune again so the dead can't sense it."

Kara shook her head. "I'd been working on that enchantment for a long time and it doesn't last long if you keep moving. It's a static charm.

Besides, the glamour that's been hiding me has exhausted the best of my strength."

I blinked at her. "How do I even know you *are* Kara? You looked like a child a moment ago . . ." What might she look like in an hour? A sudden cold thought seized me. "You could be Skilfar! Maybe there never was a Kara."

She laughed at that, not a particularly pleasant laugh it must be said. "Skilfar would have throttled you in your sleep a month back. The ability to suffer fools is a rare trait in our line."

"Your line?"

"You're not the only person to be a disappointment to their grandmother, Jalan."

My eyes widened at that. The thought of that icy witch having spawned didn't fit easily into my imagination. "I—"

"Enough. No more games." She glanced over her shoulder as if worried about pursuit. "The key, Jalan, or I'll take it."

I hit her. I'm not one for hitting women . . . or anyone else for that matter. In fact I'm not one for hitting anything liable to hit back, but given the choice between a hefty man and a slightly built woman I'll punch out the woman every time. I'm not entirely clear why I hit her. Certainly I wanted to keep the key but I also didn't want the Dead King dogging my trail all the way home along with half of Umbertide's troops. So in many ways her offer was entirely reasonable. What was neither reasonable nor expected was the way she rolled with the blow and hit me back hard enough to break my nose and set me on my arse, my head clanging against the gate behind. She didn't even drop her lantern.

"Last chance to do this nicely, Jalan." She wiped blood from her split lip across the back of her hand. I wondered if prison time hadn't addled her mind—there seemed little resemblance to the Kara I knew from the boat . . . except the constant threat of violent retribution if her personal space was invaded of course . . . In any event I couldn't believe all those months of the old Jalan charm hadn't lit a spark in her somewhere.

"Come now, Kara dear." I said it nasally, wincing as I touched my nose.

Somehow that long thin knife of hers appeared in her hand. "It would have been better if you just—" And she slumped to the ground, folding up with a graceful economy and coming to rest in a swirl of skirts, somehow contriving to set the lantern gently beside her, the knife landing with a thump on the dusty road. Hennan stood revealed behind her, his expression hard to read, a sock that looked to be full of sand swinging from his fingers.

"Would you rescue Snorri for twenty double florins?" He glanced down at Kara but she showed no signs of rising.

"You don't have twenty double florins." I'd *say* I would do *anything* for twenty double florins right now.

"But would you?" he insisted.

"Hell yes."

Hennan took a step back, knelt down, and turned the neck of the sock my way. A heavy gold coin slid out onto the dirt, another gleaming behind it. The sock looked to be full of them!

"How the hell?" I remembered the coins I'd dropped on the floor when the dead man grabbed my neck in the cell.

"Always take the money," Hennan offered with a small grin.

THIRTY-ONE

Kara lay senseless in the dark alleyway. Senseless or dead. Snorri told me as often as not the head-struck die, or their wits are scrambled to the end of their days. Worse, like Alain DeVeer on the morning that started this long nightmare so many months ago, they might just turn around and try to kill you.

"She's not dead," Hennan said.

"How can you tell?" I stared hard, raising the lantern, looking for some small signs of breath being drawn.

"She hasn't got up and tried to bite your face off."

"Ah. True." I looked left then right down the alley. "Let's get out of here."

I led off and Hennan followed. Any small pang of guilt I felt at leaving Kara unconscious in the gutter washed away with the thought that if there were dead things stalking us in the dark then we were leading them away from her. The blood, continuing to run from my nose, dripped from my chin and left a pattering trail behind us. I could taste it running into the back of my throat, hot and coppery. I swallowed without thinking. Blood triggers the spell—the only thought I had time for before I pitched forward into my own darkness.

The night swallows me and I rush through it, blind and reckless, the wind tugging at my clothes. For some endless time there's nothing, no sound, no light, no ground beneath my feet though I'm running fast as I can, faster than is safe. A pin-prick of brightness pierces me, so thin and sharp I wonder that it doesn't hurt. I race toward it—there's no other direction here—and it grows, becoming larger and brighter and brighter and more large until it fills my vision and there's no rush, no running, no motion, just me at the window, leaning across the sill, looking out, out onto a sunlit city far below.

"Vermillion looks so small from here."

The voice comes from beside me, a boy's voice, though cracking with the rumours of the man to come. I turn, and flinch away. The child is deformed. A boy of maybe fourteen, his arms twisted into unnatural positions, straining and tight against his body, wrists bent at painful angles, hands clawed. His skull bulges out above his forehead as if over-burdened with brain . . . just like—

"What, Garyus?" A girl's voice on my right.

"The city looks so small from up here, like I could hold it in the palm of my hand," he says.

"It looks that way to me when I'm down there in the middle of it."

I turn and it's the Red Queen, just a girl, no more than eleven. Jaw set, staring out into the sun-bright distance.

Garyus seems unconcerned. "The world though, sister . . . now that looks big wherever you stand."

"I could conquer it," says Alica, still staring out across the palace walls into the streets of Vermillion. "I could lead my armies from one end to the other."

"When you're older," says Garyus with the superiority of a big brother, "you'll understand how the world works. You don't conquer it with the sword. Armies are the last thing you use, when the result is no longer at issue. Money is the lifeblood of Empire—"

"The empire is broken. It was broken before we were born. And merchants grub after gold—wars are won by soldiers. You're just obsessed with money because Father gave you those hundred crowns and you bred them into more. You only care because—"

"Because I was born broken, yes." Garyus's smile seems genuine. "Broken like the empire. Even so, I'm correct. Money is the lifeblood of Empire, and of each part of it, and of any kingdom, or nation where there exists sufficient industry to arm and equip a military of consequence. Money is the blood of nations and a person who understands that, who controls that, controls the future. Let the blood out of any country and it will collapse soon enough."

Both of them turn and look back into the room. I turn too, blinded for a moment by the change from the brightness of the day.

"I'm right. Tell her I'm right, ——." Garyus speaks a name but it slides past me as if it is deliberately evading my ears.

It's Alica who replies though. "He's not right. Wars decide, and when I'm queen I'll lead my armies to Vyene and remake the empire." Her scowl reminds me of the expression she will wear when she gazes out across Czar Keljon's forces from the walls of Ameroth, less than ten years from this day.

I can see who Grandmother and Great-uncle Garyus are addressing now. A pale girl, painfully slim, hair lank and colourless, of similar age to Garyus. She's not looking at them—she's looking at me. Her eyes are startling, one green, one blue, both unreal shades that seem to have been taken from some alien place.

"Don't be so sure you'll be queen, little sister," Garyus says, his tone light but hurt behind his smile. "When Father sees what I've made of his investment in me he'll—"

"He just gave you the money to give you something to do up here," Alica says, her scowl half-frown now as though the hard truth doesn't taste as good on her tongue as she thought it might.

"Father knows that a king needs to rule his economy as much as his people . . ." Garyus trails off and looks toward his twin. "I could be king . . ."

The Silent Sister gives him an unreadable look, those strange eyes fixing him for the longest time. At last she gives a slight shake of her head and looks away. Garyus's face stiffens in disappointment. He's almost handsome beneath the deformity of his brow.

"I will be king." He returns his stare to the city beyond the window. "You don't see *everything*!"

The three of them stand in silence in the dimness of that tower room where only the shape of the window, sun-blazed upon the floor, seems alive. Something nags at me, somewhere I should be, something I should be doing.

"Wake up."

I look around to see which of them said it, but they're all three bound in their own thoughts.

"Wake up."

I remember the dark street, the dead things creeping, the witch lying in the road.

"Wake. UP!"

I tried to wake, willing my eyes wide, trying with every ounce of my determination to spit the blood from my mouth and shake off the chains of Grandmother's memories.

"Wake." I opened my eyes and looked up at Hennan. "Up." We both closed our mouths on the word. Panic had me on my feet in moments, reeling from one side of the alley to the other, reaching for the wall of a house to support me. Half of me still felt as though it were in that tower room. "How long?"

"Ages!" Hennan looked up at me, face dirty and etched with worry. He'd rescued the lantern from my tumble, though it looked pretty battered.

I glanced up at the sky—still velvet and dusted with stars. "Couldn't have been more than an hour?" Kara's spell could have had me on my back for a week. Had she planned it that way? Perhaps I was growing less susceptible. "Two hours?"

Hennan shrugged.

"Come on." And I snatched the lantern before leading off. The voices of Garyus and the Red Queen followed me, sounding somewhere deep behind my imagination.

I hurried along, taking turnings at random, unhooding the lantern only when some or other obstacle presented itself—the damaged hood leaked enough illumination the rest of the time to stop me running into walls. I kept my eyes on the patch of light before me—whenever I glanced at the dark I saw the lines of Garyus's room written across it. He seemed less damaged back then but surely he knew no king so crooked as he ever sat upon a throne. Still, children hope in ways adults find hard to imagine. They carry their dreams before them, fragile, in both arms, waiting for the world to trip them.

I ran, trailing other people's lives and dreams, and each time I slowed they caught up, surging around me to fill the night so that I had to wade through the images, through scents, memories of a touch, struggling all the while not to be dragged down beneath them and cast into one of those endless sleeps that had plagued my journey south.

In time the visions lessened and we came to broader streets where the occasional person still came and went despite the hour. The morning couldn't be very far away and I felt I could ward off the memories that my blood had sparked, at least until I had to sleep—what dreams might come then I couldn't say. Sageous would have to fight Kara's magic if he wanted a place on stage. I pulled Hennan to the side of the road and sat with my back against the wall, slumped.

"We'll wait for dawn." I didn't say what we'd do at dawn. Run away probably, but at least it sounded like a plan.

I could have taken Hennan's twenty doubles off him. The fact that it was my gold in the first place only made it an easier thing to justify. I could have taken the boy's money, left Kara senseless in the alley, bought a horse and ridden for the hills. I should have done that. I should have taken him by the ankles and shaken my florins out of him. Instead dawn found me staring across the width of Patrician Street at the high bronze doors of the Frauds' Tower, and the silvered steel bulk of the clockwork soldier standing guard before it.

Morning made its slow advance down the street. I'm sure a tutor once told me that day breaks at a thousand miles an hour, but it always seems to creep when I'm watching. The high points on the soldier's armour caught the first light and seemed to burn with it.

"There. I told you. Nothing we can do." I took Hennan's shoulder and pulled him back into the shadows of the side street. He shot me a sour look. He still hadn't forgiven me for taking him by the ankles and trying to shake my florins out of him. I'd failed on two counts. Firstly, he'd proved heavier than I'd imagined and I got very little shaking done, and most of that with his head on the ground. Secondly, he'd had the foresight to hide all the gold. He'd probably stashed it when I fell into the vision-sleep. I explained to him how terribly mistrustful this was and how it wasn't only an insult to my royal person but by extension to the whole of Red March. The little bastard just clamped his mouth shut and ignored all reason. Some people might say I only had myself to blame, what with teaching him to cheat at cards, advising him to always take the money, and sharing with him my policy on disposable friends. It's not the kind of education that builds trust in the tutor. Of course I'd say to those people, "shut the hell up," and also that it was Snorri's fault for filling the boy's head with nonsense about never abandoning a comrade and for making that ridiculous last stand with Hennan's grandfather back in Osheim. In any event the boy'd hidden the money and I was hardly going to twist his arm until he told me where he'd put it. Well . . . I *did* twist his arm, but not far enough to get him to tell me where my gold was. Hennan had turned out to be tougher than I'd expected and whilst I might twist his arm, I didn't want to break it. Or at least not unless I was sure it'd get me my answer. And of that I wasn't sure.

In the end we'd come to a compromise. I agreed to take him to Frauds' Tower and show him just how impossible what he was asking would be. In exchange he would, when convinced, recover the money and we'd buy a horse then ride it to death getting to Vermillion in the hope of getting the Red Queen's aid in freeing Snorri and Tuttugu.

"Maybe there's a back way," Hennan hissed at me.

"If there is, you know what it will have?" I whispered my reply. I wasn't sure why we were whispering but it fitted the mood. "Guards. That's what prisons are about. Guards and doors."

"Let's go and see," he said. We had already watched for hours as the guards came and went, made their rounds carrying their lanterns, swords at their hips. It would look no better in the light of day or from a different angle.

I kept hold of his shoulder. "Look, Hennan. I want to help. I really do." I really didn't. "I want Snorri and Tuttugu out of there. But even if we had fifty men-at-arms I doubt we could do it. I don't even have a sword."

I felt the boy slump beneath my grip. Perhaps finally accepting in the light what I'd told him over and over in the dark. I felt sorry for him. And for me. And for Snorri and Tuttugu under the question in some torchlit room, but, in all truth, there really was nothing to be done. Snorri had sealed his own fate when he decided to keep the key and set off on this insane quest. The fact was that the day Sven Broke-Oar told Snorri his family were gone Snorri had stopped caring whether he lived or died. And the thing about people who don't care if they live or die . . . the thing is . . . they die.

"We can't stay long," I said. "If we don't keep moving the witch will find us."

"Don't call her that." Hennan scowled.

I touched fingers to my swollen nose. "Damnable witch, I say." I was sure she'd broken it.

"She just wants to take the key somewhere safe," he said. "She's no worse than you. At least she was ready to help Snorri while she could . . ."

"No worse than me? She's a witch and she wants to give the key to an even worse witch!" I started to think the only reason he'd brained her was he knew he could buy me.

"My grandda used to tell stories about Skilfar. She never sounded too bad. Helped as many people as she didn't." Hennan shrugged. "Who do you want to give the key to?"

"The Queen of Red March! You're not going to insult my grandmother I hope?"

The boy shot me a dark glance. "And the key will be safe from witches in your grandmother's hands will it?"

I opened my mouth, then closed it. Kara had obviously been telling the boy tales about the Silent Sister. I glanced over my shoulder. The shadows still lay thick enough to hide a multitude of sins—any manner of witch or dead man could be creeping up on us as we wasted time watching the prison.

Still, the fact that all the dry bones in the city hadn't converged on us during the night seemed to indicate that the Dead King couldn't track the key with any great accuracy. Perhaps he only knew its location when it came near a corpse. In most cities there would be enough fresh corpses in the gutters come morning to pose a problem if they started dragging themselves out. Umbertide has remarkably little violent crime though—I guess its citizens are all too busy with the more lucrative kind. I hoped that, barring someone dropping dead at our feet, we would be safe enough if we kept our eyes open, especially during the day. Kara, however, had found us pretty quickly after our escape. She'd placed one charm on the key to hide it—it seemed likely that she'd placed another on it to find it. Her magics couldn't be that potent though or she would have found a way to get to Hennan in the debtors' prison . . . unless of course her hiding charm hid the key from even her . . . my head began to spin with the possibilities and I found myself imagining the curve of her lips instead and feeling a deep sense of injustice and betrayal. None of the tales I'd told myself about Kara and me had ended like this . . .

I rubbed my sore eyes and sat back on my haunches. A yawn overwhelmed me. I felt more tired and in need of sleep than I had at any point in my life. All I really wanted to do was lie down and close my eyes . . .

"We have to do something!" Hennan tugged at my shirtsleeve with new resolve. "Snorri would never leave you in there!"

"I wouldn't be in there!" I bristled at the suggestion. "I'm no fraud—" I broke off, realizing that in the eyes of Umbertide's officialdom that was exactly what I was. Very likely only my family name had saved me the horrors of the Tower, or perhaps the paperwork just hadn't had time to go through. Considering Umbertide's addiction to bureaucracy, and the glacial pace with which they progressed things, the latter guess was possibly the true answer.

I looked up with a shudder at the granite walls of the Frauds' Tower. High above us the first rays of the sun were warming terracotta tiles on the conical roof. Snorri had held out against his jailers' questions for days now, how many I couldn't say, four? Five? And for what? Eventually they'd break him and, for all he knew, take the key. His pain was as pointless as his quest. Did he really think someone would save him? Who the hell was going to do that? Who did he even know? Certainly not anyone he could possibly expect to storm the jail and get him out . . .

"We could climb the . . ." Hennan trailed off, silencing himself—I didn't even have to tell him that we couldn't.

"God damn it, the big idiot can't think that . . . I? That's just not reasonable! I don't even—"

"Shhhh!" Hennan turned and pushed me back.

Two men passed our side street, deep in conversation. We crouched, hidden behind a flight of steps, me fighting a sudden urge to sneeze.

". . . the other one. The regulations though! Do this, do that, get this signed . . . ah Jesus! Ten forms, two courts, and five days just to set a hot iron to flesh!" A solid man, thick-necked, silhouetted against the brightening Patrician Street. Something familiar about him.

"Everything in its time, specialist, and in its turn. It is not as if the duress applied so far has been . . . gentle. The law requires that beating, the stick, and the flail are used before irons. A case must be made for each, along with the correct . . ." The second man's voice trailed off as they carried on down the street. A horse clattered by in the opposite direction, black-clad rider astride its back. Soon the streets would be full of errands as banking hours arrived.

I raised myself above the steps and looked down at Hennan. "There was something . . ." The second man had seemed familiar too, though I only saw him in silhouette, a smaller man, a modern to judge by the stupidity of his hat. Something about his gait, very precise, very measured. And the voice of the first . . . he'd had an accent. "Come on!"

I dragged Hennan to the corner and, crouching, peered after the pair. They'd crossed over to present themselves to the clockwork soldier at the Tower door and stood with their backs to us. The soldier dwarfed them both, taking the scroll offered by the taller of the two in a surprisingly delicate pincered grip. The modern turned a fraction so I caught his profile. Like all his kind, he had the white face of a man who avoided the sun with fanaticism, but this particular shade of fish-belly white went past even the pallor of a Norseman in winter. "Marco!"

"Who's—" I clamped a hand over Hennan's mouth and pulled him back.

"Marco," I said. "A banker. One of the least human humans I've ever met, and I've known some monsters." Also the last person I wanted to see since I owed his bank more than I owed Maeres Allus. But what was he doing here? Had it been the House Gold who put a sixty-four thousand florin debt on a beggar boy and set him to starve in debtors' prison? Was it House Gold that had turned the wheels and cogs of Umbertide justice to licence hot irons to loosen Snorri's tongue?

I risked another glance around the corner. Marco had already set off up the street. The soldier held the door of the Frauds' Tower ajar for the specialist and as the man slipped through the gap I caught a glimpse of him. Just a glimpse, a snatch of dark tunic, grey trews, dusty boots, and his hair—I saw that too—close-cropped to the skull, iron grey, with just a band of it yet untouched by age, running front to back, a crest so black as to almost be blue.

"Ow!" Hennan tore free of my grip where my fingers dug into his arm. "What was that for?"

"Edris Dean," I said. "Edris fucking Dean." And I stood and walked out into the new day.

THIRTY-TWO

I'm cursed with berserker blood. Perhaps it's the Red Queen's taint, her penchant for violence breaking out of me in rare but concentrated bursts. It's happened twice to my knowledge and I don't remember anything but fragments of the time that followed, just loose images of blood and dying, my blade cutting a red path through other men's flesh. That, and the screaming. Mostly mine. I can't remember the emotion of it, not anger, not hate, just those images as if seeing pieces of another man's nightmare.

Walking out into Patrician Street in the first light of what must be my last day I still had my fear but it seemed as though I'd put it in a small box somewhere at the back of my mind. I heard its shrieks of terror, its demands, its attempts at reasoning with me . . . but, like the boy's shouts at my back, it was just noise. Perhaps the lack of sleep had me dreaming on my feet. Nothing felt quite real. I didn't know what I would do except that Edris Dean would be dead at the end of it. As I approached the clockwork soldier I lifted a hand before me steady and sure, no sign of a tremor in it.

The thing took a step toward me, looking down to study my features, copper eyes burning. At each move it made a thousand gears hummed, a million teeth meshed, from the minute, through small to large, to cog-jaws big enough to eat me. "Yes?" A proper clockwork voice this time, a metallic rasping that somehow made sense.

The boy stood at my side now. I could see him reflected in the silver-steel of the soldier's armour, warped and distorted, but still Hennan. He'd tried to drag me back, tried to stop my advance, and found he couldn't. Strange, when this was what he'd been demanding all along. We're like that. Give us everything we ask for and suddenly it's too much.

The soldier's breastplate gleamed, bearing few scratches despite its age, but in one place, low in the side, a puncture wound spoiled the perfection, a dark, angular hole, driven through the thickness of the silver-steel, a gauge no man could support and a metal no smith could work. "You can be hurt then . . ." I turned and took the boy by the shoulder. "Go to the door, Hennan." I angled him and thrust him toward it.

"State the nature of your request." The soldier flexed its fingers, articulated in many places and each as long as my forearm. It put me in mind of the unborn monster built from the graves in Taproot's campsite. It had taken an elephant to put that down, and the soldier looked like an elephant might just bounce off it.

"I just came to see what the boy is doing," I said. "It looks as if he's breaking in."

The soldier pivoted about its spine, the upper half of it rotating toward the door behind it. A clockwork soldier doesn't worry about presenting its back to a potential enemy. All that slamming a battle-axe between its shoulders would do is ruin a good axe and remove any doubt concerning whether you were an enemy or not.

I had one hand in my pocket. It closed now about the key. Loki's key. The thing felt cold against my fingers, slick, as if it would slip from them at the first chance for treachery. I pulled it clear and a dark pulse of joy rang up my arm.

High above me, between silver shoulder plates, a circular depression edged with intricate teeth glittered in the light. Up close I could see not just one ring of teeth but a second set further back and narrower, then a third and fourth, and more, forming a cone-shaped indentation maybe two inches across. The key held the shape of the one whose shadow Racso set upon it, a crude and heavy thing, a notched rectangular plate on a thick shaft some six inches long.

Olaaf Rikeson had held this key before Snorri had. It had been taken from his frozen corpse, and before he died Rikeson had raised an army with it. An army that thought it could march on the gates of Jotenheim and face down the giants that even the gods feared. Olaaf had opened more than doors with this key—he had opened hearts, he had opened minds.

Reaching as high as I could, I lunged forward and slammed the key into the soldier's winding lock. The obsidian flowed beneath my grip, colder than ice, searing my skin, but I kept hold and in the moment it met the lock the key became a thick black rod ending in a cone pitted with an infinity of notches.

There's a rule for doing and undoing, a rule older than empires, even a word to go with it, clockwise, and the opposite, anti-clockwise. One direction to wind up, the opposite to wind down. In the heat of the moment, in the cold terror of the moment, I just guessed. I set every part of my strength behind the task. For three pulses of my heart, each seeming to boom out slower than the most solemn funeral beat, the bastard thing wouldn't move. Time congealed all about me. The soldier halted its own rotation with a shuddering clunk and began to turn back toward me, starting to drag the key from my hand. One arm reached for me, articulating against the elbow joint in a way that gave the lie to any pretence of humanity. Long metal fingers stretched wide to encircle my waist, each ending in talons razored to slice flesh from bone.

Maybe the additional fear lent me strength, or Loki had had his joke by that point, but without warning the lock surrendered and the key turned. It gave with a sharp jerk accompanied by a sound like something expensive breaking. A resonating metallic twang followed, and a multitonal whirring as a thousand wheels, flywheels, cogs and escapements spun free. The soldier ground to a halt just as the key wrenched from my grip and that metal face turned my way. The whole thing slumped, the strange light dying from those copper eyes, and within the span of a single second the entirety of that great steel behemoth stood inert before me, no hint of sound, and without rumour of motion.

The fingers of the soldier's hand nearly met around my chest, the point of the claw on the longest finger having sliced a three-inch tear into my shirt, a small crimson stain just beginning to spread through the fabric at the far end.

"Shit!" I took hold of the finger and tried to pry it back. Hennan rushed to help, glancing nervously at the soldier as he tugged. Despite the mechanism's apparently relaxed slump there wasn't any give in the thing, I might as well be caged in iron bars.

"Slip through," Hennan said.

"What?" The most emaciated corpse behind the debtors' prison couldn't slip through the gap between the fingers.

Hennan raised his arms above his head by way of answer and wriggled down onto his haunches.

"Ah." Undignified, but what the hell? I followed his example and a moment later was crawling out from beneath the soldier's hand with no additional injuries save for the brocaded epaulette torn from my shoulder.

"You stopped it!" Hennan stood gazing up at the soldier, showing a degree of awe now that he was close up that had proved lacking when we'd watched from the corner and he'd urged me to storm the place with nothing but my bare fists to defeat the guards.

"If I can't do better than that we're in trouble." Some large part of my mind had set itself screaming at me to run. But Edris Dean's face floated over that noise, not as he'd been on Beerentoppen this spring, but as he'd looked when Mother slipped bloody from his sword. The scarlet stain from the soldier's claw spread like a memory of the wound Edris's blade gave me that day. It grew slowly, blossoming from the site of the old injury that had nearly taken my life. For a moment the sight hypnotized me.

"Jal!" Hennan, urgent, tugging at my sleeve.

"Prince Jalan," I said. "Unhand me." I shook him off, recovered the key, and walked around to face the soldier head on. The street lay empty left and right. A messenger clattered through the cross-roads fifty yards further on, intent on his business. I reached up and took hold of the soldier's shoulder, stepping onto its knee and hauling myself up.

"Jal—Prince—we should . . ." Hennan gestured at the door.

"It's locked and there are men with swords on the other side," I said, staring at the soldier's gleaming metal skull.

On the smooth forehead where my face distorted in hideous reflection a small metal disc lay raised a hair above the surrounding. I banged the side of it with the base of the key and slid it aside to reveal a small circular hole no wider than the pupil of an eye. I pressed the cone-shaped point of the key to the hole and willed Loki's piece of trickery into action. It took a moment's concentration before the obsidian started to flow again, liquid night reforming beneath my fingers, cold with possibility, draining into the narrowness of the hole until all I held was the end of a thin black rod.

"You're mine." I whispered it, remembering Yusuf waiting with me in the House Gold, the blackness of his smile as he told me how the Mechanists' machine coded a rod to each new owner and that rod, inserted into the specified clockwork soldier's head, would transfer its loyalty to the person who had purchased it. I felt the rod change, felt it lock, and then, with a twist, I drew it slowly out, six obsidian inches of it. "Mine!" Louder now.

"But . . ." Hennan, frowning as I jumped down beside him. "You broke it . . ."

"I unwound it," I said. "There's a difference. And it was pretty much unwound in any case." I moved back around to the winding port. The key changed to fit the indentation as I reached toward it. "Let's . . ." I started to turn the key in the opposite direction to my first attempt. "See . . ." I put some muscle into it. "What . . ." Throughout the soldier's torso cogs began to whisper and whirr. "We . . ." I kept turning. "Can . . . Do."

I'm no scholar or artificer but I seem to recall that the physic of things is much like that of life. You don't get anything for nothing, and if you want a lot out you've got to put a lot in. I wanted a lot out of my newest possession and I didn't want to put a lot in. By rights I should have stood there winding for an hour just to get the thing to take a single step forward, but the key I held had its own rules. The key had been crafted to unlock, to remove obstacles, to allow the user to get where they wanted to. I wanted to get to a fully wound soldier. Its failure to work was the obstacle before me. I remembered how when I'd held the orichalcum I could, with enough focus and will, direct the wild pulsing of its illumination into a single brilliant beam and steer it forward until my concentration failed and it fell apart. I summoned that same focus and tried to will whatever potential I had in me into a single beam driven through the black rod in my hand and into the metal mass of the soldier.

With each turn of the key the noise from within the soldier grew, wheels rotating, springs groaning, cogs buzzing in a fury of motion, creaks and twangs as things deep within grew tighter, tighter, and tighter still. I thought of Edris Dean and turned the key though it resisted me and threatened to tear the very skin from my palm rather than rotate another degree. The soldier groaned, its armour flexed as deep inside the reservoirs of its power clenched into potent cores that might drive it on for another seven centuries. The great head above me turned on a neck of silver-steel collars, gears meshing, cricks giving with high pitched retorts. And the eyes that found me blazed even in the light of the new day.

"Jalan Kendeth," it said in a voice sharp with angles and twanging like lute strings wound too tight.

"Prince Jalan," I corrected it. "See this child." I pointed and waited for the head to swivel and fix upon Hennan. "Hennan Vale. We're going into this jail to extract two prisoners. You are to precede us and protect us from anyone trying to stop us."

The soldier's head rotated back toward me, a smooth and sudden motion, far more rapid than its movements prior to rewinding. "This will contravene numerous laws applying in the city of Umbertide."

"Duly noted. Let's go." And I waved it toward the formidable door that gave access into the Frauds' Tower.

The soldier strode smartly to the door and rapped four times. I heard rattling, someone mutter, and the door began to open. The soldier jerked it wide and the guardsman behind came sprawling out into the street, dragged by the door handle. He landed face first a short distance before me. I kicked him in the head as he got to all fours.

"Son of a bitch!" I'd been about to apologize for kicking the man while he was down but it hurt me more than him. I hobbled around his senseless form muttering more explicit curses under my breath, pausing only to slide his short sword from its scabbard.

The clockwork soldier had vanished inside by the time I reached the entrance. I managed to grab Hennan's shoulder and haul him back. "Fools rush in. And granted this whole exercise is deeply stupid, but let's not make it worse." I pushed him behind me and peered into the foyer. The soldier stood there with a guardsman in one metal hand and a clerk, plucked from behind the counter, in the other. Maybe they were gripped too tightly to holler for help or they were too scared of being ground to pulp, but either way they both held quiet.

"Well, done . . . erm . . . do you have a name?" I looked up at the soldier.

"Guardian."

"Well done, Guardian. Best not to kill anyone you don't have to. We can put these two in a cell if they behave themselves." *I should be terrified. I should be four blocks away and still sprinting,* but when I tried to reach for my fear all I found was Edris's face as it had been fifteen years ago, and Mother sliding off his sword for the thousandth time, with that same look of surprise. "You, clerk." I pointed unnecessarily at the balding man, his pot belly bulging through the gaps between Guardian's many-knuckled fingers, his face purpling. "What cell are the northmen in and how do we get there?"

The man gasped something, his eyes bulging, shot through with burst veins.

"Put him down so he can answer my question, Guardian."

The soldier opened his hand and the man fell with all the grace of a grain sack.

I came a few steps closer. Close enough to smell that the man had soiled himself. "Tell me again. And make sure you get it right or Guardian here will come back and pull your arms off."

"Cells ten and thirteen, level four." The clerk heaved in a wheezing breath. "Please don't hurt—" The soldier swept him in its grip again.

"Keep going then!" I shooed the soldier on. "Wait, stop!" It jerked to a halt, teetering mid-step. "Go back and get the guard from the street." Even if he didn't wake up in a hurry he would attract attention left lying in the road.

Guardian dutifully clunked outside and returned with the unconscious guard over one shoulder. I closed and bolted the door once the soldier was through.

"Stairs!" I waved the mechanism on and it moved past me, through the foyer, great feet clanking on stone until it reached the central spiral of steps. A large gate of crossed iron bars, a boss set with a rose symbol at each junction, sealed the stairs. Various doors led off into rooms or corridors around the stairwell and a thorough man, or at least a cautious man like me, should really have secured the ground floor first to ensure a clear escape and no attackers sneaking up from behind. On the other hand, Edris Dean had almost certainly gone straight up to Snorri's cell with his torture warrant. I set Loki's key into the gate's lock and turned it. "Level four! That's what the man said!"

On level one a jailer startled from his doze, nearly falling off his chair. He managed a brief and startled shout before Guardian clubbed him with the clerk. The familiar human stink told me they kept prisoners here and unlocking doors off the stairwell revealed the jailer's sleeping quarters, a storeroom, broom closet, and a corridor leading to a passage that paralleled the Tower's perimeter, running in a circle between two concentric rings of cells. Heavy doors, each set with a small barred window, lined the passage walls. Guardian deposited the door guard, ground floor guard, jailer, and clerk into the first of these, surprising the ragged and elderly man inside with this unexpected company.

Returning to the stairs behind Guardian, I could hear cries of alarm from the levels above us. Evidently the jailer's strangled squeak and subsequent flattening with a blunt instrument hadn't gone unnoticed.

"Up! Up!" I clapped my hands. "And you, stay close." I motioned Hennan to my side and held my short sword ready. The fear had started nipping at my heels now. Guardian led on. The jailer on the second level had kept his station, standing with brass-banded club in hand and flanked by two guardsmen, steel drawn. Guardian advanced on them, arms wide, as they stared in disbelief. The jailer dropped his club, one guardsman managed a half-hearted thrust that glanced off the soldier's armour, and all three were swept up into a metal embrace.

"We'll lock them up." I hurried past to unlock the door to the corridor and then the first door off the corridor. Guardian followed to toss its captives into what proved this time to be an empty cell. "Quickly!" I didn't know how much time we had, but I knew for sure it was running out fast.

Guardian set off up the stairs with me right behind. Almost before the soldier had taken its first step a prison guard hurtled down the spiral hollering the kind of battle cry that sounds mostly like terror, his short sword raised on high. The man had no time to register what he was up against before being backhanded into the wall. Guardian caught the guard's limp form in both hands on the rebound.

"Damn." The crimson smear along the stonework told an unpleasant story. "Careful! You don't need to hurt them!" I'm not perhaps the most generous of souls but generally there's no murder in me. It's not conscience so much as being squeamish, and also afraid of the repercussions. For Edris Dean though I would make an exception and call it justice.

Guardian took three more strides carrying the guardsman, clearing five steps a time and leaving them spattered with blood. Without warning the guardsman's head snapped back up revealing a gleam of fractured white skull in the scarlet mess where the left side of his head should be. His eyes found me and the appetite in them made my legs too weak for stair climbing. Hennan crashed into my back.

"He's dead!" Fear reduced my voice to a squeak. The guardsman started to struggle in Guardian's grip. "Quick! Make an end of him!" I found my shout.

Guardian carried out his instruction with gruesome efficiency, ramming the corpse's head into the wall with a steel palm and pressing until nothing remained but a splat of bloody porridge and bone shards dribbling down the wall. I vomited acidic yellow drool onto the step in front of me.

"Keep hold of the body and keep moving." I wiped my mouth on the back of my hand then looked for somewhere to wipe the back of my hand. I moved on past my own mess and the one on the wall, clutching at my nose which being sick had made throb like a bastard for some reason, and trying to shield my eyes so I didn't have to see the corpse still twitching in Guardian's grip.

"At least they're easier to deal with when you've got help." Hennan, close behind me, sounding less scared than I felt.

"One dead man isn't the problem," I said, still sounding nasal. "They know where we are now." If the Dead King had looked at us through those eyes he could be steering every dead body in the city our way. I wondered just what might be waiting for us outside when we came back down the stairs. Up until this point the worst my imagination had shown me was rank upon rank of city guard.

We stepped from the stairwell through the arch onto the third floor, keeping close to Guardian. It looked identical to the floor below, absent the jailer and guards. I could see down the short corridor into the passage that circled the Tower—something seemed off, but I couldn't put my finger on it.

"We've got to check for guards," I said. "Can't have them escaping to raise the alarm." Or creeping up behind us.

Guardian took three heavy steps into the room. Another heavy footstep and something huge loomed from the side where the column of the stairs had hidden it. It came out swinging—swinging a large iron door, which immediately resolved what had looked wrong about the place: the corridor to the cells should have been hidden behind a locked door.

The impact of the blow knocked Guardian off his feet and sent him slamming into the wall, reducing the jailer's desk to splinters on his way. For a moment Hennan and I stood horrified, gazing up into the gleaming red-copper eyes of a clockwork soldier both broader and taller than Guardian. The thing held the dented iron door over its head in a pincered grip, ready to squash us like flies. And, unlike flies, we were neither of us quick enough off the mark when the soldier began to swing the door down toward us. Cogs whirred as great brass and steel muscles contracted and the iron door came speeding down, on course to reduce us both to stains.

Guardian leapt to intervene, as if driven by a single huge and coiled spring he shot in beneath the blow, narrowly missing taking my head off, and drove into the newcomer's chest. Both went tumbling across the stone floor, their progress arrested by a crunching impact with the opposite wall. They rose, locked in combat, each gripping the other's hands and straining to break some vital part.

"We should help Guardian." Hennan said it with conviction but made no move to do anything.

"We should get to Snorri and Tuttugu while we still can," I said, although "we should run away while we still can" very nearly came out instead. I grabbed the boy and pushed him back onto the stairs. Behind us the two metal combatants thrashed around with no concern for bystanders. A wild kick from Guardian knocked a chunk of stone nearly as big as my head from the corner where the cell passage led off and sent it ricocheting off the walls. I couldn't tell who was winning but although the tower-soldier was the larger of the two, Guardian had been fully wound for the first time in centuries and the extra strength that bought him soon began to make itself told. Metal strained against metal, joints creaked, reinforcing bars groaned under the pressure, and gears ratcheted up through their cycles.

"Jal!" Hennan tugging at me.

A rivet from the tower-soldier's armour shot free and hit the arch above my head, pulverizing a small piece of the stonework. Taking my cue, I ducked back and hurried past the boy, off up the stairs.

The fourth floor had a different smell to it, a stench of blood and vomit. You couldn't miss it, not even with a broken nose. On the jailer's station downstairs a truncheon and lantern had hung; on this level manacles, ropes and gags depended from various pegs in addition to the usual tools of the trade. This floor had more to it than just wasting away people's lives in small stone boxes. Here they hurt people. Every piece of me wanted to run—it felt as though I were voluntarily putting myself into Cutter John's care. A sharp metallic retort echoed up the stairwell as some vital part of one of the soldiers surrendered to the pressures mounting against it.

"We should check the cells." Hennan, stepping forward. "Find Snorri and Tutt." He'd never seen the horrors I'd seen, never been tied to a table and visited by Maeres Allus. Also he wasn't a coward. The short sword trembled in my grip, feeling too heavy, and awkward. Every piece of me wanted to flee, but somehow the sum of them stepped forward on uncertain legs, pushing Hennan behind me. A small voice behind my eyes cut through the baying panic—without Snorri at my side I wouldn't get far out of the city, perhaps not even past the reach of the Tower's shadow. When I reasoned it as a more forward-looking version of running for the hills my legs seemed better prepared to play their role.

I went to the jailer's station and took the lantern from its hook. The jailers had left in a hurry, perhaps gathering together on the top floor to make a stand. If so I hoped they stayed there. If they found their courage and came down in a group I'd be sunk. I made a quick check for any sign of jailers or guardsmen then unlocked the door to the cell corridor. The stink lay thicker here, sharp with something new and unpleasant . . . a burnt smell.

Hennan tried to rush on ahead. I held him back. "No." And advanced, short sword out before me, lantern in the other hand, sending the blade's shadow dancing across the walls.

"Fifteen, fourteen, thirteen." Hennan read the numbers from above the doors. I didn't know if he could read but his grandfather had at least taught him the Roman number runes.

"Watch the corridor for me," I told him. I didn't know what waited beyond the door but it probably wasn't something he needed to see.

"It's dark!" Hennan waved an arm at the gloom.

"So watch for a light!" I turned from him, held my lantern up, out of my line of sight, and placed the key into the lock. It fitted perfectly as always, almost eager to turn. With the door unlocked I returned the key to my pocket and drew the short sword I'd stolen. Edris could be waiting on the other side. The door creaked as I pushed it and the stink hit me immediately, a sewer stench, laced with vomit and decay, together with smoke and an awful aroma of burned meat.

Tuttugu looked smaller in death than he had in life. The weight that he'd carried across frozen tundra and wild oceans despite meagre rations seemed to have dropped from him in less than a week in the Tower. They'd torn away his beard leaving just scraps of it here and there amid raw flesh. He lay upon the table they had tortured him on, still bound hand and foot, the marks of the iron on his arm, belly, thighs. The brazier still smoked, three irons with cloth-wrapped handles jutting from its small basket of coals. They'd been ready, waiting for the authorization, and set to work immediately.

I stood, looking around stupidly, not knowing what to do. The chamber was otherwise empty, a water jug on its side on the floor, broken, a bucket in the corner. And, seeming at odds with its surroundings, a mirror in a wooden frame hung from a chain-hook above the table, a cheap thing and tarnished, but out of place.

Blood from Tuttugu's cut throat pooled about his head. It had soaked into the red curls of his hair and dripped between the planks to the flagstones beneath. He must have been alive when we entered the Tower . . .

"Hennan!" I spun around.

Edris already had the boy, his sword at his neck, the other hand knotted in his hair. They stood opposite the doorway, against the corridor wall.

"You hid in one of the other cells . . ." I should have been terrified for myself, or angry for Tuttugu, or worried for the child, but somehow none of those emotions would come, as if the part of me that dealt with such things had had enough and gone home for the night.

"So I did." Edris nodded.

I hadn't seen a friend dead before. I'd seen dead men aplenty, and some of them I'd liked well enough. Arne Deadeye and the quins I'd liked. But Tuttugu, lowborn and foreign as he was, had become a friend. I could admit that now he was gone.

"Let the boy go." I lifted my short sword. The steel Edris held to Hennan's neck was rune-marked and stained with necromancy, its blade considerably longer than mine, but whether that would still prove an advantage in the confines of the corridor I couldn't say. "Let him go."

"I will," Edris nodded, that crooked smile of his on narrow lips, "to be sure. Only first give me this key everyone's talking about, hey?"

I watched his face, shadows twitching across it. The half-light caught his age, seamed with old scars, grey, but toughened by the years rather than diminished. I set the lantern down, keeping back out of his reach, and fished for the key in my pocket. In the moment my fingers made contact a younger face pulsed across Edris's, the one he'd worn when he killed my mother, killed my sister inside her, and driven the same blade he held now into my chest. Just for a beat of my heart. Only his eyes remaining unchanged.

I drew the key out, a piece of blackness like the shape of a key, cut through the world into night. The Norse called it Loki's key, in Christendom they'd name it the Devil's key, neither title offered anything but tricks, lies, and damnation. The Liar's key.

Edris's smile broadened to show teeth. "Give it to the boy. When we're safely past whatever's making that racket downstairs I'll take it from him and let him go."

To some men the desire for revenge can be a craving that will lead them on through one danger into another—it can consume them, a burning light outshining all others making them blind to danger, deaf to caution. Some call those men brave. I call them fools. I knew myself for a prince of fools to have let my anger lead me into the Tower in the first place, in defiance of all reason. Now, even with Tuttugu dead behind me and his murderer before me, all the anger in me blew out like a flame. The sharp edge at Hennan's throat captured the light, and my attention. Shadows outlined the tendons stretched taut beneath the skin, the veins, the swell of his neck. I knew what a ruin one quick draw of that steel would make of it. Edris had opened Mother's throat with the same economy a butcher uses when slaughtering pigs. With the same indifference. With the same edge.

"What's it to be, Prince Jalan?" Edris pressed the blade closer, hand to the back of the boy's head to help press him into the cut.

All I wanted was to be out of there, miles away on the back of a good horse, riding for home.

"Here." I walked toward them with the key held out. "Take it."

Hennan looked at me with furious eyes, giving me that same mad look Snorri was wont to offer up at the worst possible times.

"Take it!" I made a snarl of the order and stepped out through the doorway. Even so, and with Edris twisting his hand still tighter into the boy's hair, I didn't think Hennan was going to accept it. And then he did.

Hennan snatched the key from me and I slumped, relief washing over me. I saw that look come over the boy, eyes widening as the thing fed its poisons into him, opening doors in his mind, filling him with whatever visions and lies it had stored up for Hennan Vale.

"No!" And in one sharp motion Hennan tossed the key past me, into Tuttugu's cell.

I found myself lunging at Edris, the point of my blade driving at the place his smile had fallen from. He proved quick—damn quick—managing to raise his sword and deflect my thrust. I may have nicked the lobe of his ear as the blow slipped past. Hennan spun away, leaving plenty of hair in Edris's grip, but the boy slipped, struck his head against the wall and tumbled on to collapse boneless somewhere in the dark length of the corridor.

"Ah." I backed off into the doorway. All around me the sounds of movement in the cells, the occupants roused by the clash of steel, a muffled bellowing close at hand. "Sorr—"

Edris made to cut off my apology with his sword so I saved my breath for defending. Swordplay on the training ground is one thing, but when an evil bastard is trying to cut bits off you most of that goes out the window. Your mind, at least my mind, remembers almost nothing when soaked in the raw terror of someone doing their level best to kill you. Any memory is done by your muscles which, if they've been trained year in year out, with or without much enthusiasm on your part, will make the best they can of what they learned in order to keep you alive.

The sound of sword hammering into sword in close confines is deafening, terrifying. I turned one thrust after the next, backing slowly, yelping when they came too close.

"Take the damn key." I inserted the gasp into the melee.

Fifteen more years didn't weigh heavy on Edris. He showed the same quickness and skill that had got the better of my mother's guard, Robbin, back in the Star Room. It proved all I could do to fend him off. The reach of his long sword meant I'd no chance of getting to him even if I'd had a heartbeat to make any sort of attack.

"I don't want the damn thing!" I backed through the cell's doorway and Edris stepped up to it in pursuit, the lantern in the corridor silhouetting him. Mad thoughts yammered at me, rising amid the terror seething through my mind, an insane desire to throw myself on him and rip out his guts—the sorts of notions that get you killed.

There's a problem with continually stamping down on the least sensible instincts that drive men to recklessly endanger themselves. Even the most reasonable and level-headed of us have only limited space to store such unwanted emotion. You keep putting the stuff away, shoving it to the back of your mind but like an over-full cupboard there comes a point where you try to cram one more thing into it and all of a sudden something snaps, the catch gives, the door bursts open and everything inside spills out on top of you.

"Just let me live!" But even as I said it the red veil I'd been trying to hold back descended. A liquid and fiery joy rose through me and while a tiny voice deep inside me wailed "no" I launched myself at the man who killed my mother.

With the entrance between us Edris's long sword became a liability, confined between the door jambs. I swept his next thrust aside, pinning his blade to the side of the doorway with my own and smashing my forearm into his face. I felt his nose break. Spinning inside Edris's reach, keeping his sword pinned until the last moment, I set my back to him and brought the elbow of my sword arm around into the side of his head with all the force I could muster. Without turning, I took my blade in both hands, reversed the point, and stabbed it under my armpit into his chest, grating between his ribs.

I pulled away at Edris's roar of pain, stumbling into the cell, my sword caught on bone and torn from my grasp. His blade hit the flagstones behind me with a clatter. I stopped myself just short of sprawling over Tuttugu's remains on the table and turned, hopping on my lead foot, on the edge of balance. Edris Dean stood in the doorway, leaning against one side for support, both hands on the short sword I'd driven into him, low on his chest. Blood ran scarlet over the steel.

"Die, you bastard." It came out as a whisper. The battle madness had left me as quickly as it came. I coughed and found my voice, putting some royal authority into it. "You killed a princess of the March—you deserve worse than Tuttugu got." It seemed too easy for him to just die there and slip away. "Be thankful I'm a civilized man . . ." Unkind words might not amount to much after the driving in of a sword but they were all the salt I had to rub in his wound.

Edris watched his blood patter on the floor, in shock at his reversal of fortune. He raised his hands, dripping, and looked up at me, dark crimson welling from his mouth. The fact that he then smiled, showing bloody teeth, rather took the wind from my sails, but I carried on, trying not to let the uncertainty colour my voice. I knew enough about wounds to know the one I'd given him was fatal. "The necromancer who gives you your orders . . . she won't be pleased. I can't see your corpse getting a decent burial." I tried to smile back.

"That." Edris drew a rattling breath, some of it sucked in around my steel, bubbling blackly. "Was a mistake."

"Damned right! And the first mistake you made was going up against m—" A horrible thought interrupted me. I realized Edris had me trapped weaponless in the cell . . . "You're hoping when you die the necromancer is going to stand you up again to finish the job!"

"Are all royalty this stupid? Or did that bitch mother of yours breed with her brother to make you?" Edris straightened away from the door jamb, grinding his teeth against the pain, and took hold of the hilt of my sword where it jutted from his body. "There's no necromancer watching from the hills, you moron." He pulled the blade clear and the wound bled black. "I *am* the necromancer!" A laugh or a cough tore from him spattering blood between us. A few droplets hit my upraised hands and burned there like hot metal poured from the crucible.

My only chance lay in speed and agility. Edris might be gaining strength but he still moved with a certain stiffness, awkward around his injury. I backed a step, another, and prepared to spring when he cleared the doorway. Something caught in the back of my tunic. I tugged but found myself firmly snagged. Edris stepped into the cell, my short sword black and dripping in his fist.

"The closer to death we are the harder it is to kill us." He smiled again, his face in shadow with just the glimmer of his eyes to hint at the murder there.

"Now—wait, just let's stay—"

He didn't wait but came on unhurried, sword held without a tremor, point level with my face. In desperation I risked a glance back to see what I'd caught myself on. Tuttugu glared at me from the table, the familiar hunger of the dead burning in his eyes. The hand secured closest to me at the corner of the table had twisted inside the metal band about its wrist and locked fingers in the loose material of my tunic.

I pulled harder but I'd paid handsomely for the garment and the linen wouldn't rip. Looking back toward the door I found Edris directly in front of me now, sword arm drawn back ready to punch my own short sword through my head.

"No!" A hopeless wailing appeal for mercy as I fell to both knees, head bowed in supplication. Not perhaps the best way for a prince of Red March to die, but all my audience were dead or halfway there. "Please . . ."

The only answer I got was the wet thunk of steel cutting flesh, and blood spilling about my shoulders. The pain came intense and searing, a burning that engulfed my neck and back, blood ran everywhere, and immediately a sense of faintness engulfed me, a deep weariness reaching up from somewhere to drag me down. I stayed where I'd fallen, waiting for the light to fade or beckon or whatever it's supposed to do in your last moments.

"Bitch." Edris, but in a choking voice.

I puzzled over "bitch" but realized I had to let go of questions and slip away . . . The legs before me moved, perhaps to let me fall, but beyond them I saw another pair . . . more shapely . . . emerging beneath a dirty skirt. That made me look up. Edris had moved toward the doorway, his neck at an uncomfortable angle and spilling blood from a cut that looked to have made a decent attempt to reach his spine. Kara circled with him, sporting a magnificent black eye and holding her own stolen short sword, as black with gore as the necromancer's.

The blood that drenched me had belonged to Edris, burning me with its necromancy. I remained on my knees, blood dripping from my hair and hands, still anchored by Tuttugu's grip.

Despite his second mortal wound Edris took a quick step toward Kara, sword questing before him.

"Better run, Edris Dean, or I'll finish the job. Skilfar always told me how it would please her to drink from your skull and toast the Lady Blue." Kara swatted at his blade, the two swords clashing.

Edris made some reply but the words he gargled from his throat came too broken to interpret.

Kara laughed. A cold sound. "You think dead things scare me, Dean?" And as she spoke the lantern grew dim, every shadow thickening and reaching, the darkness writhing in each corner as if the blackest of monsters stirred from slumber there. Edris feinted to the right, threw the short sword at her, then staggered, ungainly, toward the doorway. Kara made to follow, her own blade ready to thrust into his back but she stopped short, fixated by something on the wall opposite. Another mirror, identical to the first. Quite how I'd missed it I didn't know. She seemed fascinated by her reflection. Glancing at Edris I saw him slowing, starting to turn. A third mirror hung above the doorway, I caught a glimpse of something blue, darkly reflected, a swirl of robes?

"Jalan." Kara spoke between gritted teeth, adding nothing to her declaration of my name.

"What?" Looking to the left I saw more mirrors I hadn't noticed, two of them hung at head height. Edris completed his turn. He would have been facing Kara if she hadn't been staring at the mirror that first caught her attention. Edris grinned, black blood welling over his jaw. He started to draw the knife at his belt, a wicked bit of Turkman iron, nine dark inches of it, thin and notched.

"Break. The. Mirror." Kara forced each word past her teeth as if it were a struggle she was barely equal to.

"Which mirror?" There must have been a dozen and it made no sense. I couldn't have missed them. "And with what?" I caught sight of blue robes again, fleeting reflections, here, then there, and eyes, eyes in the shadowed infinity behind the glass, just a gleam, but watching.

"Now!" All she could manage.

Edris had the blade out, arm awkward from the large hole I'd put through his pectoral muscle.

With a lunge, still held by my jerkin in Tuttugu's dead hand, I caught hold of the broken jug on the floor, and spun to throw it at the mirror I first saw. At least six mirrors hung there now, clustered together. Their reflections showed nothing of the cell but instead revealed some other dark space where candles burned, as if each mirror were some small window onto a chamber beyond. Those half-seen eyes found me, made me their focus, robbing the strength from my arm, fogging my mind with a blueness deeper than sea, brighter than sky. I threw anyway, blind, guessing my target. The sound of shattering glass came loud enough to knock me down if I'd not been on my knees already. I threw my arms up, expecting to be drowned beneath a deluge of shards. But nothing came.

I looked around and found Kara halfway across the cell still looking dazed.

Edris stumbled out through the doorway.

"Hennan's out there!" I shouted, intending it for Kara but realizing as I said it that I'd just reminded the necromancer too. Without pause, Kara went after him—decent of her since the last thing the boy did for her was slug her around the back of the head with a sock full of florins.

Her exit left me on my knees in a pool of my own distress, belly on display to the world with my tunic hitched up under my armpits, a handful of it still gripped by the dead thing secured on the table. I glanced around wildly, looking for the black shape of Loki's key, lost amid the filth on a floor cast into deep shadow. By luck, sharp eyes, or some trick of the key itself, I saw it, tantalizingly close but out of reach. I strained, stretching my arm until the joints threatened to pop, waggling my fingertips as if that would close the six-inch gap.

"Let go, damn you!"

It might have been coincidence but in the moment I made my demand something gave and I lunged forward, almost flattening my broken nose on the flagstones. I rose with the key in hand and hid it in my waistband as Kara returned, lantern held before her, guiding an unsteady Hennan at her side.

"Edris?" I asked.

"Got away," she said. "There's a pair of clockwork soldiers fighting two levels down. He didn't look fast enough to get past them." She shrugged.

"Shouldn't you be chasing him? Doesn't your grandmother want to drink her nightcap from his skull?"

A grim smile. "I made that up."

She sat Hennan against the wall. "Stay there." And crossed to the table. I managed to stand as she reached it. She stretched out an arm above Tuttugu's face and he strained to bite her.

"Don't—"

She turned her head toward me, a sharp motion. "Don't what?"

"I—" I wasn't sure. All I knew was that he'd been my friend and I'd not saved him. "You're dark-sworn!" The best accusation I could find.

"We're all sworn to something." She reached out with care and set a finger to Tuttugu's forehead. His corpse went limp, and when she drew back her finger it revealed one of her small iron rune tablets, remaining where she touched. "He is beyond their use now." She straightened, eyes bright. "Tuttugu was a good man. He deserved better."

"Will he go to Valhalla?" Hennan asked, still sitting hunched on the floor. He looked as though his head had yet to clear from its collision with the wall.

"He will," said Kara. "He died fighting his enemies and didn't give them what they wanted."

I looked down at the mess they had made of him. My eyes prickled unaccountably. He must have been beaten every day. The soles of his feet were raw, toes broken. "Why?" It made no sense. "Why didn't he just tell them where the key was?" The bank had no interest in killing the Norsemen. If Tuttugu had given up the key early on they might have been banished and sent off on the north road before Edris Dean even knew they'd been captured.

"Snorri," Kara said. "If he gave up the key he would have been giving up Snorri's children. Or at least he knew that's how Snorri would see it."

"For God's sake! He couldn't have been *that* scared of Snorri."

"Not scared." Kara shook her head. "Loyal. He couldn't do that to his friend."

I pressed the heels of my hands to my eyes and tried to clear my thoughts. As I took them away I became aware once more of the muffled bellowing from down the corridor. It hadn't stopped—I'd just blocked it out. "Snorri!"

The others followed me as I ran to cell ten and unlocked the door. They had Snorri chained to heavy iron rings set into the wall, his mouth bound by a leather gag. He showed no signs of torture but the wound he'd borne with him from the north, the cut from the assassin's blade, was now a strip of raw flesh an inch wide, a foot and a half in length, crusted with salt that grew in needle-like crystals, some as long as a fingernail.

Snorri strained at the restraints, wrists bleeding where the manacles bit them. Kara crossed the room, taking a small knife from her belt and reaching up for the northman's gag.

"Wait!" I ran forward to catch her arm. "I'll do it."

She met my gaze with furious eyes. "You think I'm going to cut his throat?"

"You wanted to leave him here!" I shouted, wrestling the blade from her hand.

"So did you!" she spat back.

"I didn't want to— I just— Anyway, you wanted to take the key to that witch up north!"

"So did you. Just to a different witch and not so far north."

I didn't have an answer for that so I sawed away at the strap binding Snorri's gag in place. Tough leather gave easily before the keen edge. That's how Tuttugu should have given. The idiot should have saved himself. I pulled the gag away and Snorri slumped forward, choking.

Kara came forward, reaching up to hold his head. I watched her and realized it made no sense. "If Skilfar wanted the key why didn't she just take it when Snorri was right there before her? It's . . . *you* who wants it?" Kara's own greed or Skilfar using her to steal it so as to avoid the curse? In the end it made no difference.

"Get the shackles off." She gestured with her head.

"I can't, they're held with rivets. It needs a blacksmith." I kept my eyes on her, looking for signs of treachery.

She turned from Snorri, concern hardening into something else. "You still haven't understood what you have in your hand. Use it! And use your head."

I bit back a curt response and decided not to remind her who the prince was here. I had to stand on tiptoes to reach the manacle on Snorri's wrist and expecting little I took the key, still shaped for the cell door, and pushed its end to the first of the two iron rivets that had sealed it shut. The thing resisted. I applied more pressure and with a screech of protest it slid out and fell to the floor. I repeated the operation and broke the manacle open. Snorri slumped forward.

"Where's Tutt?" He managed to raise his head but whatever strength had kept him battling the chains had gone.

I let Kara answer him while I removed the manacle on his other wrist.

"Valhalla." She turned away and went to stand by Hennan, setting a hand to his shoulder. The boy flinched but didn't shake her off.

Free of the second manacle, Snorri collapsed to his knees and fell forward to rest his head on his arms against the floor. I removed the manacles on his ankles and reached out to set a hand on his back but withdrew it before I made contact. Something about him made me think I might be safer putting my hand into a box of wildcats.

"Can you walk?" I asked. "We need to get out of here."

"No!" Snorri thrust himself off the ground with a roar. "We're not leaving until they're all dead! Every last one of them!"

Kara stepped up to him as he got to his feet. "And where does it end? Which is the last one? A jailer from the ground floor? The man who delivers food to the Tower? The banker who signed the arrest order? His assistant?"

Snorri pushed her away, snarling. "All of them." He pulled the short sword from my belt, too quick to stop.

I held the key out before him. "Tuttugu died so you could use this. He stood against hot irons because they thought him the weaker man, the man they could turn from his course." I pressed it into Snorri's palm, though careful to remove it again—it was, after all, all I had. "If you stay clockwork soldiers will come—you'll die here—Tuttugu's pain will have meant nothing."

"Pain never means anything." A growl, head down, face framed by dirty straggles of black hair, a glimpse of burning blue eyes behind. He made to leave.

"Tuttugu remembered your children," I told him. "Perhaps you should too."

His hand seized my throat, so fast I didn't see it coming. All I knew was that somehow I'd been pinned to the wall and breathing had stopped being an option.

"Never"—the point of his sword stood just inches from my face, aimed between my eyes—"speak of them." I thought he might kill me then, and in the surprise of it I hadn't time to be scared. But my words seemed to reach him—perhaps because I couldn't add any more—and a moment later he let go, his shoulders sagging. I found that my feet had left the ground, and dropped down, jolting my spine.

"Enough now?" Kara glanced between us, frowned and led on out of the cell. Hennan followed, then Snorri, with me to bring up the rear.

We got as far as Tuttugu's cell. Edris's long sword still lay on the floor close to the entrance. I picked it up, tentative, half expecting it to bite me. The thing had bitten me before.

"A pyre." Snorri pointed in at Tuttugu's corpse. "We build a pyre. Big enough so his smoke reaches Asgard."

"Where in the hell—"

"Doors." Snorri cut me off. "Open the cells. Use the key to undo the hinges. Bring them in here."

And so we did. Door after door opened and taken down. A tap of the key had the hinge pins flying out. Kara enjoined each occupant to find keys on any dead jailer and to release the prisoners on the upper floors. They all agreed, but then again they were all in for fraud so whether any of them did put their own escape second and fellow prisoners first I've no idea.

Within ten minutes Tuttugu lay on his table surrounded by a sea of doors. Snorri took rags and straw, doused them with lamp oil, and set the flame. Snorri said the words as the fire took hold and smoke began to coil thick above us, louring beneath the ceiling in a dark blanket.

"Undoreth, we. Battle-born. Raise hammer, raise axe, at our war-shout gods tremble." He drew breath and carried on in the old tongue of the north, Kara joining him on the litany's refrain. The light of the fire flickered across them both. Snorri touched his fingers to the tattooed runes picked out across the thick muscles of his arm, set there in black and blue, still visible beneath the dirt. It seemed as if he were spelling out his farewell to Tuttugu, and perhaps to the Undoreth too, now that he stood the last of their clan.

Eventually with the smoke thick across the ceiling, low enough to touch Snorri's head, and with the flame blistering our cheeks, he finished.

"Good-bye, Tuttugu." And Snorri turned away.

I stood a moment longer and watched Tuttugu through the wavering haze of the flame, his clothes starting to burn now, skin withering before the heat. "Good-bye, Tuttugu." The smoke choked me so I couldn't speak the words unbroken, and got into my eyes making them water. I turned away and hurried after the others.

We found Guardian waiting, victorious but too damaged to accompany us into the city without drawing undue attention. But I decided to keep him close until we were ready to leave.

On the ground floor the inmates had done a thorough job of looting, but one heavy door resisted them. I hurried across to unlock it. We needed whatever assets we could gather.

"Come on!" Snorri heading for the main exit.

Kara grabbed my shoulder then stopped to stare. "What in—"

The room beyond held shelves floor to ceiling, deep and partitioned, each laden with all manner of goods from paperwork to vases, silver plates to odd shoes. "Praise the Lord for Umbertide's bookkeepers!" I reached out for a gilt urn gleaming close by. Even as they tortured the fraudsters in the cells above, all their possessions lay ordered, catalogued, and untouched down below, waiting for the full process of the law to be completed.

Snorri strode past me, knocking my greedy hand aside. Kara behind him. The place, although cluttered, held very few weapons, both Norse made straight for them. Kara snatched a spear from its place on the far wall, Gungnir, her own work.

"You don't still think that will scare Kelem, do you? It didn't even keep the city guard from taking you!"

Kara cocked her head at me then looked over to Guardian in the doorway. She pushed by Snorri and slowly moved the spear until its point engaged with the solitary hole in the clockwork soldier's armour. A perfect fit. "They had two soldiers with them. The one that took Snorri came from behind us, through the wall, and wrapped its arms around him."

Snorri continued his inspection of Hel's blade. His father's axe had been hung among the other weapons. Satisfied he looked up with a grim smile, the first since I found him. "Now we're ready."

THIRTY-THREE

A crowd had started to gather by the time we left through the Tower doors. The whole top half of the Frauds' Tower belched smoke through its windows. Before we left I set Guardian to checking the building for Edris Dean and explained how many pieces he was to tear the corpse into. "Oh, and let everybody out," I added. The idea of leaving anyone to fry didn't sit well with me, but mainly I wanted as many fraudsters let loose on Umbertide as possible. That way the authorities might have too much on their plate to put great efforts in recapturing me.

No one challenged us, surrounded as we were by other inmates all pouring into the street and vanishing down alleys into the maze of Umbertide. If Edris Dean had escaped the building he must have had more important things to do than raise the alarm because there were no more than two city guardsmen in the road and both of those were trying to look inconspicuous in case anyone suggested they stem the tide of escaping prisoners. I sincerely hoped Edris had crawled away to die but at the very least it seemed likely that even a necromancer would require some time and resources to repair the kind of wounds he had sustained.

With the morning sun climbing above the rooftops we hurried along narrow streets following Hennan who had learned the ways in and out of the city that honest folk didn't use or know of. The easiest way to leave Umbertide proved to be by climbing over the walls rather than scrambling through the sewer pipes that got Hennan into the city. It would have been a tight and malodorous squeeze for Kara—Snorri and I would not have fitted. Besides, the walls of any city not at war are poorly watched, and with the column of smoke from the Frauds' Tower to draw the eye of any guard who might actually have been watching, it proved easy enough to find a stretch of wall we might escape over.

The only real problems were in buying a rope and grapple. It's damn hard to come up with a good reason for wanting a grapple in the first place and even harder to find a blacksmith who doesn't tell you to pay now and come back in three days to collect it.

"Throw it higher," Kara urged as the iron hook narrowly missed my head on its second descent.

I paused and favoured her with a narrow-eyed stare, remembering I'd not forgiven her for breaking my nose. "*Throw it higher?* That's the wisdom of the völvas speaking is it? All those years of arcane study . . ."

I threw it higher on the third attempt and snagged the wall. Climbing a thin and unknotted rope turned out to be a lot harder than I had imagined and I spent the best part of five minutes jumping, lunging, and straining, without getting more than a yard off the ground. Finally I got the hang of it, at least partially. Driven mostly by embarrassment I managed to shin up the rope to the top of the wall as two toothless elders and a growing crowd of local urchins watched on. Kara and the boy followed with no discernible effort, Kara with the spear, Gungnir, strapped to her back. Snorri brought up the rear, his wound making his climb an awkward one, though only once, when he slipped, did he snarl out in pain. I found getting down the other side proved both easier and faster. Also it hurt more at the bottom.

Once gathered outside at the base of the walls we hurried away across the dusty and hard-baked earth toward the margins of the nearest olive grove and lost ourselves among the trees.

"Well?" Kara spoke first. We'd followed the gradient down through the dappled shade to come in sight of the Umber, the river without which the city behind us would be nothing more than badlands flecked with mesquite bushes and picked over by scrawny goats.

"Well what?" I asked, swatting at the flies, already too hot and too sweaty.

"Do you know the way?"

"Hennan knows the backpaths. I came by the Roma Road." Before long much of the Umbertide guard would be fanning out around the northern stretch of the Roma Road. It wouldn't matter to Snorri. He was heading south, to the sour lands where Kelem made his home in a salty gash in the earth known as the Crptipa Mine.

"Do you know the way to the *mine*?"

"To Kelem's mine? Why the hell would I? I'm in Umbertide because my uncle sent me to attend to some banking affairs not to find some wizened magus and . . . and beg him to let me do something incredibly stupid." I actually did know the way, at least roughly, but given I'd no interest in going there I kept the fact to myself.

"Snorri?" Hennan looked up from his own misery at the Norseman in his. Seeing such a sombre look on so young a face reminded me that Tuttugu lay dead—a fact I'd been trying to push to the back of my mind into the place where things get forgotten.

"I know the way." Snorri looked up, eyes red, jaw set, scary as hell. "I'll have the key now—you can stay or go."

I studied the broad palm he held out toward me, and pursed my lips. "I didn't break Hennan out of one prison and storm another single-handed just to give you a key that we earned, all three of us, me, you, and Tuttugu. I came in to save your lives. And given that I could have just walked off with the key instead some might say I've got a pretty good claim to owning it now. So the least you can do is ask rather than demand, and perhaps show a little fucking gratitude." I regretted the profanity the moment it left my mouth. Partly because a prince of the realm doesn't want to be seen lowering himself to gutter talk with commoners but mainly because of the sunlight burning on the edge of the axe fixed across his back in a leather harness I'd recently paid for.

A dangerous silence stretched between us, slowly tightening every muscle I had in anticipation of being imminently hit. Snorri reached out and I flinched so violently that I nearly struck his hand away. He took hold of my shoulder, deep blue eyes finding mine, and sighed.

"I'm sorry, Jal. I don't know how you got to us but it took guts, and skill. I thank you for it. Tuttugu will be telling the tale over the tables at Valhalla. The north won't forget it. You are a true friend, and I was wrong to speak to you like that."

We stood there a minute, him with his head bowed, looming above me, hand heavy on my shoulder, me puffing up with pride. Some men can just lift you with a few words. Snorri was one of them, and although I knew how it worked, and had seen it before, it still worked.

I put the key into the open palm of his other hand and his fist closed about it. The sense of loss was immediate, even though I knew the thing to be ten kinds of poison.

"I have to do this," he said, sounding for all the world as if he actually did.

I tried to fathom that one. He had to take the key to the man who had sent assassins to kill him for it? He had to take the key to the man who wanted it badly enough to reach out more than a thousand miles for it? He had to enter the lair of a deadly mage and face ridiculous odds . . . and the "prize" was to open a door into death and start another suicidal quest that couldn't possibly give him what he wanted?

"You really don't."

"I do. And there's no man I'd rather have with me than you, Jalan, Prince of Red March. But this is my journey and I won't ask anyone to share the danger. I took you north against my enemies—I'm not going to lead you into Hel."

Dammit if I didn't find my mouth opening to contradict him. I managed to strangle off a defiant declaration that I'd stand by him against all the hordes of the underworld.

"Look. Kelem *wants* you there. He's been pulling you south with that wound in your side. He blocked you from the door in Eridruin's Cave and would have shut any others you went to. You know he's reeling you in. Christ, you're only out of that tower because of the dreams!"

"What dreams?" Kara stepped closer, eyebrows raised.

My shoulders slumped. "Kelem hired a dream-witch, Sageous, we met him in Ancrath, Snorri and I. He plagued me with nightmares about Hennan until I found him. Hennan led me to Snorri. There, I didn't come after anyone out of heroism. I came because I couldn't sleep. Weeks of not sleeping will have a man ready to try anything for peace."

"Weeks?" Kara smiled and turned away.

"Weeks!"

"But we were only captured five days ago," she said.

I stared at her retreating back, trying to re-evaluate myself. Perhaps I did have a conscience after all . . .

Snorri took his hand from me and stepped back. "We both know the key is a curse, Jal. There's no happiness in it, only trickery. You'll save yourself more sorrow than you can imagine if you give it up."

He held Loki's key out to me, compassion in his eyes. "But you're right—you earned it. I had no right to demand it from you." Kara turned and stared with such intensity that I thought at any moment she might leap forward and snatch the thing from him.

Part of me suspected Snorri had it right—I should refuse it. Even so, if I had a future in Vermillion it probably started with me placing Loki's key into my grandmother's care. And more than that I just plain didn't want to give it up.

I took the key from him. "I'm not going through the door if we find it, but I'll come with you and carry this burden until the last. And if you stand before that door and ask me to unlock it . . . I will." I made it a bold and manly speech, meeting him eye to eye. "It's what a friend would do." Also keeping his company while heading in an unexpected direction would probably be my best chance at not being caught by Umbertide's authorities and thrown back in jail. Kara shot me a suspicious glance as if she could read my mind, but if she could then after all those weeks lusting for her in that boat her opinion of me probably couldn't be lowered. I gave her a winning smile, slapped Hennan on the back and led off, the key deep in my pocket once more.

"Where are you going?" Kara asked as I passed her. "I thought you said you didn't know the way."

She had me there so I veered toward the river and knelt to wash my hands. "Cleanliness is next to godliness, dear lady, and since I'm keeping the company of heathens I should at least aspire to washing the dirt off."

We camped by the river that evening beside a slow meander where the Umber snaked across its floodplain. All of us took the opportunity to wash off the best part of a week's worth of prison filth. I had to remind myself several times that Kara was a treacherous dark-sworn heathen witch because she looked damn good dry and dirty and a whole lot better clean and wet. I'd been far too long without a woman. Being so focused on gambling does that to you. It's the only drawback. Well, that and the losing.

I say "camped" but "lying down in a vineyard" would be more accurate. Fortunately the sky was clear and the air kept warm with the memory of the day's heat. Kara sat with Snorri, cleaning his injuries and applying a paste made from some herb or other found along the riverbank. The cuts he'd taken from the manacles were deep and ugly and like to sour if not treated. Even with a chirurgeon wounds are apt to turn bad in the heat and once ill humours are in the blood they'll drag you to an early grave no matter who you are.

The main wound, the one Kelem's assassin put on Snorri, Kara couldn't treat. I could see it would give him no peace, and the way he kept looking to the south-east let me know where it drew him. How much of his thinking was his own now, I wondered. If Kara truly had sealed Baraqel away from Snorri so as to give her more chance of working her charms and stealing the key then she had done him a double wrong. While he was light-sworn his own magics had worked against the wound. With Snorri undefended the rock-sworn infection would only grow until either it killed him or claimed his will.

When Kara had finished with Snorri I tried to get her to see to my nose, after all she broke it, but she claimed it wasn't broken and if anything I should be tending her eye.

"Jal gave you that?" Snorri looked up from the grapes he'd been trying, wincing at their sourness this early in the season.

"Long story." I lay back quickly and stared up at the first stars, just piercing their way through the deep maroon of the sky. My shoulders burned where Edris Dean's blood had soaked them and had started to blister and peel as if I'd been out in the sun too long. It hurt but I consoled myself with the thought it probably hurt the necromancer more. If I'd had to let another gallon flood over me to know he was dead and done it would have been a price worth paying.

I wondered if the Silent Sister had seen this when she looked into a future so bright it blinded her. Or perhaps she'd not looked past the destruction of the unborn seeking the key beneath the Bitter Ice. Had she moved to stop the Dead King gaining Loki's key only to have her two agents of destruction, one her own flesh and blood, deliver the thing to Kelem? From what Grandmother told me Kelem was closely tied to the Lady Blue and hers was the hand that sought to steer the Dead King. We'd carried it a thousand miles and more from frozen wastes to the dry and burning hills of Florence, bringing it to the very door the Silent Sister never wanted to open . . . In the end it seemed that Loki's key had tricked even my great-aunt, reaching back through the years to fool her.

As the sun set I heard knocking. I looked around, but the others were settling down, Hennan already with his head buried in his arms. It came again, as if on all sides. I'd heard it before, in the debtors' jail, for a minute or two . . . The evening seemed full of whispers as the sky flushed crimson and the sun sank behind the mountains. The knocking came louder, then faded. I thought of Aslaug, of her dark appetites and the long-limbed beauty of her. It occurred to me, too late to act even if minded to, that I'd heard this knocking only since I held the key. Kara had somehow locked Aslaug away from me—did I now hold the means to open the way once more?

I noticed Kara watching me and decided to hang the key about my neck on a thong. Pockets are too easily picked and I didn't trust her not to try. I'd scarcely finished tying the knots when exhaustion leapt on me from the shadows. I hadn't slept in what seemed like days and felt as tired as I had ever been. I thought of Sageous, waiting to walk my dreams, and with a shudder I pulled the key from my shirt. I pressed it to my forehead. "Lock him out." A whisper, but heartfelt. It seemed worth a try. I shoved the key back, yawning those huge yawns that stretch your jaw and fill your ears with the sound of sleep.

I lay down and let dreams wash around me while the stars came out in force and the hills throbbed with the song of crickets serenading the night. My grandmother's war had swept us up, me, Snorri, Kara, the boy, Tuttugu, all of us—her sister had set us on the board and they played us. The Red Queen making her moves from the throne about which I orbited, slung north, slung south always seeking to return, and the Lady Blue watching from her mirrors, her own pieces upon the gaming table. Was Kelem hers too, I wondered, or another player?

All day, since near-choking on the blood that Kara's punch brought flooding from my nose, the dream I'd escaped had continued to run its course, whispering at the edge of hearing, painting itself on the back of my eyelids if I blinked. Now I closed my eyes and listened hard. In my time I'd been both a player and been played. I knew which I liked best, and I knew that learning the rules is a vital first step if you intend to leave the board. One more yawn and the dream devoured me.

The banqueting hall of the great palace at Vermillion lies below me, though grander, more full, and more merry than I have ever seen it. I'm standing in the musicians' gallery, a place I've crept to before to spy on feasts when I was too young to attend them—not that Grandmother is given to hosting such things, save for the great mid-winter banquet of Saturnalia, which she holds mainly to annoy the pope. Uncle Hertet on the other hand will honour any festival, pagan or otherwise, that gives an excuse to broach wine casks and summon his proxy court to the palace so they can all pretend the queen has died and play out their roles before age diminishes them further.

The hall below me however has more nobles shoulder to shoulder than Uncle Hertet ever attempted to dine, and on the walls garlands of holly and ivy festoon in profusion, berry red upon glossy emerald, chains of silver bells, and displays of swords and pole arms fanning out enough sharp iron to equip an army. I look left, then right. Alica stands to one side, a child of eleven or twelve, Garyus and his sister to the other, with me occupying the gap the twins have put between them and my grandmother. The girls stand, gripping the carved mahogany of the banister; Garyus sits, resting his ill-made legs.

The glittering crowd below hold my eye, the finery of a departed age, a fortune in silks and taffeta, each lord glittering with wealth displayed for every other. Hardly one among the hundreds would be alive when I woke, claimed by age, the children beside me old beyond my imagination. For the longest time I'd believed my grandmother had come into the world creased and seamed, carrying her wrinkles from the womb, the iron grey in her red tresses as ancient as the lichen on statues. To see her young unsettles me in ways I can't explain. It tells me that one day it really will be my turn to be old.

The feast is almost over, though food still mounds the platters and servants scuttle hither and thither to refill and replenish. Here and there are empty seats, a lord stands, unsteady, bows toward the host, and walks toward the great doors with the overly careful gait of a man in his cups. Elsewhere guests are flagging, pushing back plates. Even the dogs at the margins of the hall have lost their enthusiasm for dropped bones, barely prepared to snarl their ownership.

At the head of the great table, presiding over fifty yards of polished oak near hidden beneath silver platters, goblets, candelabras, tureens, and ewers for wine and water, sits a man I know only from paintings. His portraits are rare enough to make me wonder if the Red Queen burned them. Gholloth, second of his name, a blond giant of a man, sits there— red-faced from the drink now, his tunic elaborately embroidered and blazoned with the red banner of the March, but wine-stained and straining at the seams. On canvas they paint him forever young and glorious

as he looked on the beaches of Adora, or was imagined to look. They
show him at the start of the invasion that was to tie the dukedom to the
Red March throne. The War of Barges they called it because he took his
forces on river barges across the sixteen miles of sea to reach Taelen
Point. Now he looks to be fifty or more and wearing his years poorly, as
old when he sired my grandmother as his own father had been when he
sired him. Where the elder Gholloth might be I can't say, dead perhaps,
or a toothless ancient hunched upon his throne with a bowl of soup.

The twins aren't watching their father though: the Silent Sister is
staring at someone with unusual intensity, even for her, and Garyus
follows her gaze, frowning. Alica and I join them. We're watching a
woman about halfway along the table. She doesn't stand out to me, neither
old nor young, not pretty, more motherly, modestly covered, her gown a
lacklustre affair of black and cream, only her hair sparkles, raven-dark
beneath a web of sapphires held on silver wire.

"Who is she?" Alica asks.

"Lady Shival, minor nobility from one of the Port Kingdoms, Lisboa
I think." Garyus frowns, raking his memory. "Has King Othello's ear, an
unofficial adviser of sorts."

"Elias is watching her," Alica says, and Garyus blinks, looking across the
room to where a man stands by the wall in the shadows, away from the
diners, ostensibly filling his pipe. There's something familiar about the fellow.
It's in the swift and restless movement of his hands. He reaches up to light
a taper from the wall lantern and his upturned face catches the glow.

"Taproot! By Christ!" They don't hear me of course. I'm not here, just
a dreamer floating in the memories my blood carries. It can't be Taproot.
This man is in his forties, and the Dr. Taproot I know can't be past his
fifties. Besides, how would my great-grandfather's courtier be traipsing
across the Broken Empire at the head of a circus? This must be an ances-
tor of his. But just observing him, seeing the quick and bird-like motion
of his head as he scans the tables, always returning to our lady beneath
her net of sapphires, I know it's him. I know when he opens his mouth
I'll hear "watch me" and restless hands will conduct the conversation.

"Elias will—"

"This woman is beyond him. —— says she's here to kill . . . someone." Garyus cuts Alica off, waving her away with irritated jerks of his over-tight arm. Again their sister's name escapes me, just a silence where it should sound.

"I didn't hear her say anything," Alica says, peering at her sister who is still fixated upon the woman below, her gaze unwavering. "Who is this woman to kill?"

"Grandfather," says Garyus, half a whisper. "She seeks to change the destiny of our line."

"Why?" It's not the question I would ask, certainly not at eleven. I'd be asking where we should hide.

"—— won't say," Garyus replies.

The Silent Sister breaks her staring at the woman below to glance my way. For an instant I'm sure she sees me—I'm transfixed by those mismatched eyes, the blue and the green. She returns to her study.

"She doesn't know?" Alica asks.

"Be quiet, child," Garyus says, though he's just a boy himself. He looks serious now, old beyond his years, and sad, as if a great weight has been laid upon him. "I *could* have been king," he says. "I could have been a good king."

My grandmother frowns. She hasn't it in her to lie to him, even this young when the whole world is half make-believe. "Why are we talking about that again?"

Garyus sighs and sits down. "—— needs my strength. She needs to see, or this woman will kill us all before we can stop her."

Alica's frown deepens. "——'s done that before . . . hasn't she?"

Garyus's nod is slight enough to be missed. "Even before we were birthed."

"Don't do it." Alica is speaking to them both. "Tell Father. Set the guards on her. Have her thrown in—"

"—— needs to see." Garyus hung his head. "This woman is more than she seems. Much more. If we don't know her before we act, we will fail."

The Silent Sister leans over the balustrade now, staring at the woman with such intensity that it trembles in each line of her over-thin body, staring so hard that I almost expect to see the path between them light up with some recognition of the energies being spent. Garyus hunches in on himself, a slight gasp escaping his lips.

Unseen forces mount. My skin crawls with them, and I'm not even there. Down below the sapphires in the woman's hair seem to return more than the light of lanterns, sparkling with some inner fire, a vivid dance of blue across the blackness of her hair. She sets down her goblet, and looks up, half a smile on wine-dark lips as she meets the Silent Sister's gaze.

.   "Ah!" Garyus cries out in pain, limbs drawn tight to him. The Silent Sister opens her mouth as if to scream but, though the air seems to shake with it, there is no sound. I watch her face as she stands, her gaze still locked with the woman's. For a second I could swear there is steam rising from the Silent Sister's eyes . . . and still she won't break away. Her nails score the dark wood as some invisible pressure forces her back, and finally, like a branch snapping, she is flung back, reeling, arrested only by the wall behind her. She stands bent double, hands on thighs, pale hair about her face, drawing in shuddering breaths.

"What . . ." Garyus's voice is weak and croaky—more the voice I know. "What did you see?"

There is no answer. The silence stretches. I'm turning back to see what the woman is doing when suddenly the Silent Sister straightens up. Her hair parts and I see that one of her eyes is pearly blind, the other darkened beyond any memory of blue skies.

"*Everything.*" The Silent Sister speaks it as though it is the last word she will ever utter.

"We need to do something." Alica, seeming a child for once, states the obvious. "Get me close enough and I'll stick a knife in her." The illusion evaporates.

"It won't be easy." Garyus doesn't raise his head. "—— saw enough before to poison her drink."

"And?" Alica turns back to observe the feast.

"The man slumped on the table beside her? He's dead. She swapped goblets."

I don't ask myself how the Silent Sister had known hours before which goblet to coat with venom, or where she'd obtained such a thing, silent and young as she is. She knew the same way the woman below knew to exchange with her neighbour. Both of them carry the same taint.

"Jesu." Alica leans against the banister, eyes hard. The woman hasn't moved: she picks a last sweetmeat from her plate as she talks to the man beside her—the one who's not dead. She laughs at whatever he just said. "So if not poison, then what?"

Garyus sighs, an unutterably weary sound, and lifts his head as though it weighs a man's weight. "The men I have around me—they're mine. I replaced Father's with hires of my own, expensive, but they're mercenaries of the highest quality, and their loyalty runs as deep as my pockets. We'll wait for her in the Sword Gallery and . . . she won't leave."

Alica raises an eyebrow at this piece of information. A moment later she hastens to the door and raps against it. A man in palace livery enters, pushing a wheeled chair. He's a solid fellow, watchful, a thin white seam of scar below his right eye as if underscoring it. I'd like to say I would have spotted him as more than a flunky, but I don't know if that's true.

The Silent Sister helps Garyus into the chair and he waves to be wheeled out. He's weaker now, more twisted. It's more than exhaustion— his sister has spent his health to buy what she needed. A second hard-man waits in the chamber beyond amid the instruments too large to be taken away with the musicians, a harp, drums, long tubular bells. He helps carry the chair down the stairs. Any aristocracy who are staying at the king's pleasure will be housed in the guest wing, and to reach that from the royal banquet hall requires you walk the length of the Sword Gallery. If the woman is planning murder she must have been invited to stay the night, or else she is cutting things fine.

I wonder for a moment that neither of Garyus's men are armed—but of course he's unlikely to have permission to have his own hires wearing blades in the king's house, relative or not, especially not as a displaced heir. The mercenaries may be paid well enough to risk concealed knives, but they'd have to be damn small to pass unnoticed. It seems unlikely that my great-grandfather or his sire are so lax as to not have regular inspections—certainly Grandmother has become very keen on them in later life. Still, the pair of them could strangle this woman with a cord swift enough.

We walk through the palace, Garyus trundled ahead, rattling in his chair, taking familiar passages that have changed remarkably little in sixty years. Just before we reach the gallery Alica pauses, then the others, then me. The Silent Sister has stopped some way behind us, beside a black oak door. She's pointing.

"What does she say?" Alica asks her brother.

"I . . ." He seems lost. "I can't hear her any more."

The message is clear enough without words, silent or otherwise. We go through and find ourselves in a tall but narrow chamber lined with cabinets, each fronted with thin sheets of Builder-glass, and each sporting a score or more of butterflies, speared through with pins to keep them in place. In dusty legions they haunt the room, the brilliance of their wings muted through neglect, a dozen lost summers impaled behind glass. I've not been in here before, or if I have the insects have been removed.

"Did we miss her?" Alica ventures, pulling a small but wicked knife from the pleated folds of her cream skirts.

The Silent Sister shakes her head.

"Gwen! Is she safe?" Garyus tries to straighten in his chair, remembering their little sister. The one who Alica will put an arrow through from the walls of Ameroth Keep six years from now.

The Silent Sister nods, though there is a sadness in it, as if she now shares my knowledge.

Garyus turns his head with effort to look at the man beside him. "Grant, there's a woman that needs to be killed. She'll be coming down the Sword Gallery shortly. She's a threat to me and to my family. When the deed is done both of you will need to leave the palace and my service immediately. You'll be taking three hundred in crown gold with you."

Grant glances at the man behind Garyus. "Will she be alone?"

"There may be others with her, but no guards, nobody armed. The Lady Shival is the only one who should die. The one with sapphires in her hair."

"Blue lady. Got it." Grant puts a hand to his chin. His fingers are blunt and scarred. "Three hundred? And you're sure, my lord? Killing in the palace is no small thing. Not an end to be pursued without certainty. Unless your sisters can hide you you'll be found at the scene."

Garyus tolerates the questioning—it's well meaning after all, if insolent. "I'm certain, Grant. Johan, is it a fair price?"

"It is, my lord." The other man, darker, older, inclines his head. His voice, soft and high, surprises me. "The money will reach us where?"

"Port Ismuth. My factor there, Carls. Within two weeks."

We wait in silence then, amid the dead butterflies, dry wings unmoving within their cases. Five minutes pass, ten . . . an hour?

The Silent Sister raises her hand. Grant and Johan go to the door, we follow them out, Alica pushing Garyus along.

Double doors lead into the Sword Gallery and here I see a difference between the present day and the gallery of sixty years before. Grandmother has hung the length of the hall with oil portraits of swordmasters practising their art. Her father had his art in iron rather than oils, with a hundred and more swords lining the walls, each pointing to the ceiling, each different. Grant breaks a fine example free from its restraints, a long sword with a blade of black Turkman iron, and hands it to Johan. He takes another for himself, a shorter but heavier sword in Teuton steel, and advances toward the double doors at the far end.

The doors open a second before the two mercenaries reach them. And there she stands, Lady Shival, behind her a maid in royal colours escorting her to her rooms. The lady seems entirely unsurprised to see two men advancing on her with blades drawn. Her smile, on a face just a few years shy of being matronly, is almost a mother's, reproachful but indulgent.

"Look at yourselves!" she admonishes, and lifts her hand revealing a small silver mirror.

Johan's advance is arrested as if he'd walked into something solid. He lifts his off hand, grappling with something I can't see. The muscles in his neck stand out, corded with the strain. To the left Grant finds himself similarly caught, horror crowding his face as he struggles, his sword hand trapped, his off hand trying to close on something. Lady

Shival walks between the pair, leaving the maid standing stunned in her wake.

"Should you children be up so late?" She leans forward slightly to address the trio.

Alica doesn't waste any time on small talk or threats, just springs forward, knife concealed at her side.

"No." The lady is faster, a tilt of her hand and her mirror is aimed at the child, stopping her as effectively as it stopped both mercenaries. "And that leaves Gholloth's twins . . ." She faces them: Garyus hunched in his chair, the Silent Sister beside him. She ignores the boy and meets his twin's gaze. "We've met already, dear." Again the motherly smile, though I see something harder behind it now. "Quite the stare you have there, young lady. But if you go looking in places we're not supposed to look . . . well, let's just say the future is very bright."

The Silent Sister makes no reply, just stares, one eye pearly blind, the other dark and unreadable.

"This whole thing." Lady Shival waves her arm at the mercenaries, still struggling, grunting with effort, making quick readjustments of their feet. "It's very inconvenient. I have to move quickly now, so you'll forgive me if I don't stop to talk." She moves her mirror into the line that joins her eyes with the Silent Sister's. "It's a hole," she says. And it is. In place of the silver and reflections there's nothing but a dark and devouring hole, sucking in light and sound and air. I feel myself drawn forward, drawn in, the very essence of me bleeding from my skin and pulling away toward that awful void.

The Silent Sister holds her open hand toward the mirror, blocking it from her view, and closes her fingers with slow purpose. She's a yard short of touching it but the bright noise of breaking glass rings out and blood runs from the fist she's made. The hole shrinks, closes, and is gone.

"Remarkable," the lady says. She takes a step forward. Her eyes are blue. I hadn't seen it before. Deepest blue. A blue that bleeds into the whites and makes something inhuman of her. Another step forward and she holds out her hand toward the Silent Sister, clawed, palm forward. A blueness suffuses the light about her. "Impressive for one so young, but I don't have time to be impressed, child." Her lip trembles in a snarl. "Time to die." And something that was coiled tight inside her is released so suddenly that the shock of it runs through the air, pulsing out, almost visible as a ripple.

The Silent Sister reels back as if struck. Only her grip on Garyus's chair keeps her upright. She struggles back to her position as though walking into a high wind, her mouth set in a grim line of effort.

The Lady Blue raises her other hand and lets whatever venom is in her pour out onto the girl before her who falls to one knee with a noiseless gasp. The Lady Blue advances, my great-aunt bent and helpless before her.

"Get back!" My shout goes unheard and I stand, impotent, wanting to run but having no place to hide in these blood memories.

As the Lady Blue looms above her the Silent Sister reaches one hand up to clasp her brother's arm just above the elbow. Garyus lolls his head toward her. "Do it." Two words croaked out, thick with regret.

The Lady Blue stoops, clawed hands closing toward the Silent Sister's head from either side to deliver the coup de grace, but something stops her, as if the air has thickened. Garyus groans and twists in his chair, his body spasming as his twin draws power from him. They were born joined together these two, and though sharp steel cut them apart there is a bond there that remains unbroken. It seems what makes the Silent Sister stronger makes Garyus weaker, more broken, and given how this boy appears to me, decades later as an old man, it seems that whatever she takes cannot be returned.

"Die." The Lady Blue snarls it past gritted teeth but the Silent Sister, though bowed, continues to defy her as Garyus sacrifices his strength.

"It's only a reflection." Alica pants the words out behind Lady Shival. "It is *not* my equal."

Whatever the child is wrestling with it appears to be getting weaker. The mercenaries are having a very different experience, each backed against the wall now, the edges of their swords being pushed inexorably toward their necks, though nobody's there to wield the blades but them.

Somewhere in the distance there's screaming. I glance away from the contest of wills to see the maid has fled. It can only be moments before palace guards converge on the battle.

The Silent Sister raises her head, slower than slow, her hair sweat-soaked, her neck trembling with effort, and on her face, as she meets the Lady Blue's eyes, a grin that I know. Alica has her small knife raised now, her wrist white as if a hand were wrapping it, just as her free hand clasps empty air with a desperate intensity. With tiny steps, each the product of huge struggle, she is advancing on the Lady Blue's back.

Deeper shouts ring out, closer now, an alarm bell starts to clang further back in the palace.

Cursing in a tongue I've not heard before, the Lady Blue breaks away, sprints along the Sword Gallery and vanishes between the two mercenaries, veering left past the double doors. As she passes them both Grant and Johan lose their battle and slide down the walls clutching their throats, blood drenching their chests.

I stand, overwhelmed by a deep sense of relief, although I was never in danger. Alica's already running, but in the wrong direction: she's chasing the lady. The Silent Sister is on all fours, her head down, exhausted. Garyus flops in his chair, as broken as I ever knew him, his last vestiges of health sacrificed to his twin's power, drawn along whatever fissure still connects them. His eyes, almost hidden in the shadow of his monstrous brow, find me, or seem to. I meet his gaze a moment, and a sorrow I can't explain closes a cold hand in my guts. I know I'm not the man ever to make the kind of gesture this boy has made. My siblings, my father, Red March itself, all of them could go hang before I'd take the blow meant for someone else.

I run, though whether to get clear of Garyus's scrutiny or to follow Alica I don't know.

The Lady Blue's path through the palace is littered with guardsmen struggling against reflections that only they can see. It's late at night and apart from the guards the palace is deserted. In truth the palace is largely deserted at any time of the day. Palaces are an exercise in show—too many rooms and too few people to enjoy them. A king can't afford to let his relatives get too close and so the Inner Palace is nothing but luxurious chambers enjoyed by no one and unseen save by the cleaners who dust and the archivists who ensure that the dust is all they remove.

We pass more struggling guards. The dangerous men will be wherever the king is. Not in his throne room, not at this hour, but they won't be walking the corridors, guarding vases and rugs, they'll be close to the man who matters.

I catch up with Alica, though it takes some doing. I've run these corridors myself—well mostly corridors further away, the Red Queen isn't that fond of her grandchildren, but on occasions as a child I've scampered down these halls. But, stranger or not, the Lady Blue is ahead of us both. She'll need luck, however, and lots of it. This wasn't her plan, this is desperation, or anger, or both, and it's being made up on the spot.

As I run alongside Alica I try to remember what I've been told about my great-great-grandfather's death. I draw a blank. I never gave a damn about any of the dead ones, unless it was to file away some impressive fact about my lineage that might give me an edge in pissing contests against visiting nobility. Surely I'd have remembered if he'd been brutally murdered in the palace by some crazed witch though? One of them died hunting . . . pretty sure. And another of "a surfeit of ale." I always found that one amusing.

Although Alica looks grim, and there's murder afoot, I can't help feeling the worst is over. After all I never knew either of the elder Ghol-loths, One and Two as the historians call them, and I've had my whole life to come to terms with the fact that they were both dead. And frankly five minutes would have been more than enough for that. We'll find the Lady Blue has killed him, or we won't, but either way she's run off and I'm feeling far more relaxed than I was when confronted with her back in the Sword Gallery. Not that I was in any danger there either . . . All in all I'm relaxing into these memories quite happily and—I glance back over my shoulder. I'm sure I heard a dog bark. I shrug and catch up with Alica as she turns a corner and starts up a flight of stairs. *There it is again.* The baying of a hound. Surely none of the mutts from the banquet hall have been allowed to run loose in the palace. *Again, and closer.* Intolerable! Mongrels from the hall prowling the corridors of power! A sudden tremor puts me off my stride. Earthquake? The whole place seems to be shaking.

"Slap him!" A woman's voice.

"Get him up!" A boy's.

I open my eyes, confused but still outraged about the dog, and a large hand smacks me across the cheek.

"What the!" I clutched my face.

"Hounds, Jal!" Snorri let go of me and I sunk to my knees. The ground dusty, the night dark, the stars many, and strewn in such profusion they made a milky band across the heavens.

"Dogs?" I heard them now, baying in the distance, but not distant enough.

"They're tracking us down. After the key still." Snorri helped me up again. "Sure you want to keep it?"

"Of course." I pulled myself up to my full height and puffed out my chest. "I don't scare that easily, old friend." I slapped him on the shoulder with as much manly vigour as I could muster. "You're forgetting who stormed Fraud Tower unarmed!"

Snorri grinned. "Come on, we'll lead them higher up, see if we can't find a climb they won't manage." He turned and led off.

I followed before the darkness had a chance to swallow him entirely, Kara and Hennan flanking me. Damned if I was going to give up the key now! I'd need something to give them if they caught me. And besides, even if I gave the key to Snorri and ran off in another direction the bastards would still hunt me down. These were bankers we were talking about, and I owed taxes. They'd hunt me to the ends of the earth!

THIRTY-FOUR

Snorri led us immediately to the river. A fact I discovered by losing my boot in unexpected and sucking mud.

"What is it with Norsemen and boats?" Now Snorri stepped to the side I could see the water, revealed where ripples returned the starlight.

"No boat." Snorri strode down the long gentle bank.

I pulled my boot out of the mud. I appeared to have stepped into a small tributary stream. "I'm not swimming!"

"Could you lead the dogs away for us then?" Snorri called back over his shoulder. Ahead of him Kara and Hennan were already wading into the current. Damned if I knew where the boy learned to swim up in the Wheel of Osheim.

Cursing I followed, hopping as I tried to get my boot back on. The hounds sounded close one minute, distant the next. "Is it true that thing about water spoiling the scent?"

"Don't know." Snorri strode in, pausing a moment as the water reached his hips. "I'm just hoping they can't get across, or won't want to."

I've never seen a dog that didn't like to throw itself in a river. Perhaps Norse dogs are different. After all, for half the year doing that would just get them a bruised head.

"Damnation it's cold!" I've yet to meet a warm river, no matter how fierce the day.

We set off swimming, or in my case, thrashing at the water and attempting to move forward rather than down. Edris's long sword, now scabbarded at my hip, kept trying to drown me, pointing toward the riverbed and heaving in that direction as if it were made of lead rather than steel. Why I'd not bought a new blade in Umbertide I couldn't say, save that this weapon, already stained with my family's blood and my own, was my only link with the bastard who murdered them, and perhaps it might one day lead me to him again. In any event, swimming with a sword is to be even less recommended than regular swimming. Quite how Snorri stayed afloat with an axe across his back and a short sword at his hip I didn't know. Kara too must be struggling under the weight of Gungnir. I'd held that spear and it felt far heavier than any spear should.

The Umber was a wide and placid river at that point in its course but even so the current took over soon enough and carried me ten yards closer to the sea for each yard I managed to struggle toward the opposite bank. Somewhere in the dark the others were making quicker and quieter progress. I'd seen them for a while by the whiteness of the broken water in the starlight, but before long I fought my battle alone, unable to see either bank and imagining the river to have swollen into some estuary so wide-mouthed that I might be swept to sea before finding land again.

When my hand struck something solid I panicked and swallowed an uncomfortably large amount of river whilst trying to inhale the rest. Fortunately the water around me proved to be little more than two feet deep and I splashed my way out to lie exhausted on the mud.

"Quick, get up!" Kara, tugging at my shirt.

"What?" I struggled to all fours. "How did you find me so fast?"

"We've been walking along the bank following the noise." Hennan, somewhere in the dark.

"Probably covered half a mile." Snorri, close at hand, hefting me to my feet. "Kara didn't think you were going to make it."

We walked on through the night, making what sense we could of the rising contours highlighted by the stars, avoiding the ink-dark valleys where possible. The warm air and exercise dried me off quick enough and fear kept me from feeling the lost sleep, my ears straining against the night sounds, always dreading the distant voice of the hounds.

I can't say how many times I stumbled in the gloom—enough to twist my ankle into complaint. I fell several times, my hands raw with cuts and lost skin, coarse grit bedded in both palms.

I saw the others as dark shapes, no detail but enough to see Snorri hunched around the pain of his wound, hugging his side.

First light showed grey then pink above the Romero Hills in whose hollows the Crptipa Mine nestled. I heard the hounds again before the sun cleared the horizon. At first they seemed part of my imagination but Snorri stopped and looked back along our path. He straightened with a wince and put an arm around Hennan.

"We fought a Fenris wolf. A few Florentine dogs shouldn't prove much challenge." The shadow hid his face.

"Let's move." I strode on. Hunting dogs work together: half a dozen can bring down any opponent. And there would be men following. "It can't be much further now." I needed it not to be much further but what I need and what the world gives are often at odds.

"We should split up." The baying sounded closer by the moment and, as always when things come to the sharp end, my thoughts turned to how I could win free. Hennan was slowing us down, no doubt about that. The fear wasn't so deep in me that I was ready to leave the boy, but going our separate ways seemed a good alternative. He wouldn't be slowing me down any more, and yet I wouldn't be abandoning him—there was an equal or better chance the pursuit would follow me, and that, with the benefit of the doubt, could even be construed as saving him! "If we split up they can't follow us all . . ."

"What's that?" Kara ignored me and instead pointed ahead.

The land had risen beneath us, becoming barren and drier as we climbed into the hills. With little more than a general direction to head in, and a blurred memory of some maps I'd perused in the House Gold archives, it had seemed that our chances of finding the particular hole in the ground we sought depended upon meeting some local to guide us. Unfortunately the Romero Hills appeared to be entirely devoid of locals, probably because the place was rather less hospitable than the surface of the moon.

"A trail." Snorri lowered his hand from shielding his eyes, the grim line of his mouth twitching toward something less sombre, just for a moment.

"And there's only one place to go out here!" I started forward with renewed energy, wetting cracked and dry lips and wishing I'd managed to drink a little more of the Umber while struggling through it.

Something about the acoustics of the valley made it seem as if the hounds were on our heels at each moment, though by the time the trail had taken us to the far side there were still no signs of pursuit on the slopes down which we'd come.

"Not much of a trail." Snorri grunted and pushed Hennan up the incline. "Shouldn't we have met some traffic?"

"Umbertide imports most of its salt up the Umber River, you would have followed its banks to the city after you docked at Port Tresto."

Kara turned around at that. "I heard the Crptipa Mine is one of the largest—"

"It's huge—it just doesn't produce any salt worth a damn," I said. "It's got Kelem in residence. Apparently he doesn't like company, and since the place preserves him, he's not likely to be going any time soon."

We carried on another few paces before Snorri commented again. "But these tracks would be washed away in a few years if they weren't used."

"There's a small operation, working around the entrance chambers." I lifted my head and pointed. "There, look!" The rise revealed a scattering of shacks, storage sheds, stables and several carts, all clustered around a black and yawning hole in the base of a rock-face where the valley became suddenly steep.

We picked up the pace and jogged up the dusty road, burdened by exhaustion. Falling behind, I turned and saw, emerging from the dry gullies on the far side of the valley, the foremost of the hounds, tiny in the distance but fearsome even so.

I'd moved from last to first by the time we stumbled gasping into the clearing ringed by the buildings before the mine entrance. I stood there, hands on knees, hauling in a dry breath, my shirt sticking to my ribs. I heard rather than saw Snorri unlimber his axe behind me. A moment later the ringing of an alarm went up, someone spinning a stick against the inside of one of those iron bars bent into a triangle that they use to call men to sup.

"E-easy." I straightened up, reaching out to lay a hand on the thickness of Snorri's arm. He didn't look up to a battle in any case, dark lines beneath his eyes, sweat on his face, still bent around the agony of the salt-edged slash in his side. Miners from the night shift began to stumble out of one of the dormitory huts, rubbing the sleep from their eyes, yawns cracking their jaws. A couple more awake than the rest took hold of long-handled hammers from a stack beside the door.

Kara stepped forward. "We just need to visit Kelem. There's no need for trouble."

The miners stared at her as if she were some strange creature unearthed from the salt. The men might be paler than typical Florentines, labouring all day deep in the salt caves, but Kara's skin was like snow, preserved from the sun by one of the witch's unguents.

The foreman among them found his wits at last, just as I was about to chivvy him along. It could only be a matter of minutes before the hounds caught up and barks turned into bites. "Can't do that ma'am. Kelem's got his own ways. No one goes down less he sends his servant for them." He watched us with eyes narrowed against the brightness, a shrewd look on his gaunt face, tight-fleshed as though the salt had sucked all but the last drops of moisture from him.

"We could pay." Kara glanced my way, over-tired and leaning on her spear.

"Ain't enough in your pocket, ma'am, no matter how deep it is." He shook his grizzled head. "Kelem's rules aren't to be broken. Play by them and he's fair. Break them and you'll think the Inquisition kind."

"And you're going to stop us?" Snorri frowned. I knew it would be reluctance to hurt them that worried him, not their numbers.

The miners stiffened at the challenge in his tone, straightening up, awake now, some taking up crowbars, the last few emerging from the long hut to bring their strength up to fifteen. Their numbers worried me plenty, and Snorri looked done in.

"Wait! Wait . . ." I raised a hand above my head and threw what princely authority I could into my voice. "By the rules you say?" I reached into my jacket and riffled through the papers still packed into the inner pockets, the deeds and titles of various acquisitions so minor I hadn't had either time nor inclination to cash in when amassing the gold that Ta-Nam had taken from me. Of late they had served as nothing more than insulation from the night chill in the dungeons. I found the one I wanted and carefully unwadded it from the others. Thankfully it looked as though the ink hadn't run too badly after my dip in the Umber. "Here!" I drew it forth with a flourish. "Notarized by House Gold." I ran my finger along the scrolled title and wax seal. "I own thirteen twenty-fourth shares in Crptipa Mining Corporation. A grand name for this godforsaken collection of shacks and the trickle of salt you fellows manage to send to the city. So whilst . . ." I searched the document. "Antonio Garraro . . . is your paymaster and manages the running of this operation from his desk in the city, it's actually me, Prince Jalan Kendeth, heir decimal to the throne of Red March and her protectorates, who owns the controlling interest in this hole in the ground." I paused to let that sink in. "So, I'd like to take a tour of my holdings, and I can't think that such an action would break any rules set by Kelem. Rules which, after all, allow my employees to do exactly that, seven days a week."

The foreman came over, keeping a wary eye on the axe in Snorri's hand. He glanced at the faded and water-blotched ink work on the parchment and reached out to tap a nail against the wax seal. He let his gaze fall to the dirty rags adhering to my body. "You don't look like you own a mine, Prince . . ."

"Prince Jalan Kendeth, heir to the Red Queen, and don't try to pretend you've not heard of *her*." I raised my voice to the near-shout that works best when commanding menials. "And I look like exactly the sort of man who would own a played-out, worthless hole like Crptipa, which hasn't made a profit in six years."

The foreman paused, teeth against his wizened lower lip. I watched him weighing up various odds behind his eyes, the sums evident in the furrowing of his brow.

"Right you are, yer majesty. I'll take you down presently. The night shift will be up within the hour and then—"

"We'll go now, no guide required." I started walking toward the cavern mouth. The others joined me. The distant baying had started to grow rapidly louder.

"But . . . but you'll get lost!" the foreman called at my back.

"I doubt it! It's my mine after all, a man should know the way around his own mine!" A guide would only try to keep us in the company-controlled areas and wouldn't know how to navigate Kelem's caverns any more than we did.

"You're not even taking lanterns?"

"I . . ." Swallowing your pride is always difficult, especially if it's as indigestible as mine, but fear of the dark won over, and executing a sharp about turn I marched back to collect three glass-cowled lanterns from the hooks beneath the hut's eaves. I stalked across to the others, my dignity demanding I take my time. A dog's howl, the kind they give when sighting prey, chased away all traces of dignity and I sprinted toward the mine entrance, lanterns clattering together in my hands.

Rickety wooden ladders, lashed together with salt-crusted rope, vanished down the rocky gullet that opened in the cavern floor fifty yards back from the entrance. Directly above the shaft an ancient hole of similar diameter pierced the roof, a blue and dazzling circle. I shoved a lantern at Snorri, another at Kara. "No time to light them! Down!" And fear of the hounds had me leading the way, pulling Hennan along behind. Not even the ominous creaking of the ladder beneath my weight gave me pause. I climbed down in a fever and let the darkness rise to swallow me. Up above I caught the sound of snarls, of claws on stone, and Snorri's roar, as fearsome as any beast's. Something plummeted past me. A dog I hoped. I felt the wind of its passage. A touch closer and it would have plucked me from the rungs.

An age later, hands raw and unbearably parched from the salty rungs, I jolted down onto solid ground.

"Are you coming?" My words lost in the void overhead, its darkness pierced by a single patch of sky impossibly high above me.

"Yes." Hennan, high above me.

"Yes." Kara's voice. Closer to hand. "Do you have the orichalcum?"

I backed from the ladder to give her space and fished for the metal cone. I stepped into foul smelling mud, slippery under foot, and almost lost my balance. The orichalcum eluded me and I became convinced I'd lost it in the river, until my fingers brushed against the metal sparking such a response I half blinded myself. The pulsing illumination revealed several facts: firstly, the curves of Kara's behind as she descended the last few rungs, secondly, the splattered remains of a large dark-furred hound, and thirdly, that what I'd taken to be mud was actually the innards of the aforementioned dog, the beast having burst on impact. The fourth and least welcome fact proved to be that this wasn't the end of our climb, rather a narrow ledge from which a new set of ladders descended, the whole thing being less than six square yards and mostly coated in mushed dog. My heels rested perhaps an inch from the dark and endless fall behind me, and the shock of realizing it set me slipping once again. Both feet shot out from under me and skittered over the edge. The orichalcum flew from my grip. My chest hit the stone with a rib-crunching thud, arms reached out, driven by their own instinct, fingers scrabbled for grip and for a trouser-wetting moment I hung, with the corner of the ledge under my armpits, body tight to the cliff, feet seeking any hold on offer.

"Got you!" Kara threw herself forward, hand encircling the wrist of my right arm in the heartbeats before the orichalcum glow died.

We hung like that for what seemed an age, me too winded to undermine any claim to heroism with cries for help or pleading with whatever gods might be watching. Eventually, as air started to seep in past bruised ribs, I heard the sound of flint on steel and a lantern flicker into life. Snorri and Hennan stood by the ladder, Kara lay stretched out through the dog's wreckage, one foot hooked around the bottom rung, the only connection keeping us both from a fatal plunge.

It took a while for Snorri to haul me up—he seemed to lack his usual strength and groaned with the effort of raising me, his shirt stained dark on his injured side. Kara was still cleaning off the larger chunks of dog meat when I finally got up. I discovered I also had a few pieces of my own to pick off. Hennan recovered the orichalcum and I pocketed it. Kara and I had lost our lanterns over the edge and soon enough I might need my own source of light. Whatever the dog handlers were up to I could see no signs of them against the patch of brightness overhead. I wiped my mouth and found it bloody. I must have bitten my tongue when I slammed into the edge of the drop.

"Let's go." This time Snorri led off.

I followed after Kara, making my descent gingerly, boots still slippery and my chest one large ache from top to bottom.

The second leg of the climb proved longer than the first and the circle of sky seemed to grow as small and distant as the moon. A weight settled about me—an echo of the unimaginable tonnage of rock around us. I'd come from the frozen mountains of the north to bury myself beneath the baked hills of Florence, and whatever waited for us down there it seemed that our journey must be coming to its close. All those miles, all those months, and Loki's key accompanying us every step, the sole reason for our long migration. I wondered if the trickster god watched us from the wilds of Asgard, laughing at the joke which only he truly understood.

The visions came at the worst possible moment, when my arms ached from too many fathoms of climbing, my hands ran slippery with sweat, and the darkness folded around me on every side. A vast thickness of rock stretched above my head, and an unknown fall beneath me. The taste of my own blood brought the memories rushing in. It shouldn't have been a surprise. The remnants of Kara's spell still plagued me, burning with whatever magic I held in my veins, amplifying her simple casting into something that threatened to unravel the whole history of my line into my dreaming. The suspicion that the völva had planned this outcome still lingered. Certainly plunging me into weeks of dream-sleep had given her far more opportunity to work on Snorri and to steal the key if he wouldn't relinquish it.

The vision drew my thoughts from present suspicions to past ventures. We had been chasing the Lady Blue, Alica and myself, chasing her through the palace into the private quarters of the elder Gholloth, he whom legend had it was the true heir of the last emperor Adam the

Third, albeit a bastard nephew. We never spoke that story too loud, indeed it hadn't been told to me until my twenty-first birthday, little more than a year ago. There's nothing more likely to unite the enemies of any kingdom than a legitimate claim on the Empire throne.

Memory painted my grandmother's pursuit on the darkness as I descended, so vivid that it overwrote my sight and I sought the rungs utterly blind, all the while with corridors flashing through my mind, felled guards, broken doors, Alica Kendeth sprinting ahead of me, fearless and swift.

We wove past the carnage, speed our only goal, and still we came too late, past the wreckage of Gholloth the First's elite bodyguard stationed at the doors of the old man's bedchambers. The Lady Blue had felled three men in plate armour. God knows what magics she used and what it cost her. These would have been swift warriors, seasoned, loyal beyond question, deadly with sword and knife. They lay shattered as if each had been turned to glass and struck with a hammer, the sharp edges of their injuries softened by what leaked from them.

In the old man's bedchamber, its wall hung with paintings of the sea, we found the king, the emperor if not for lies, treachery, and war. He lay at peace among his linens, clutching the red flower of his lifeblood to his chest. If you had lived somewhere where the emperors' statues haunt every turn you would know at a glance that their blood ran from him. I saw it in the line of his jaw, the angle of his nose, the broadness of his shoulders, even slumped in death.

Alica's cry held more rage than grief, but both were present. Then she saw it, and I followed her gaze. In the corner of the room a tall mirror stood. Silvered glass within an ebony frame. Such a thing would cost you a hundred in crown gold should you seek it in Vermillion today. But instead of reflecting the room it stood like a narrow window into some other place. A place where a figure ran, marked by the sapphires twinkling across her hair as she crossed a dreamland where crystal shards longer than lances and thicker than men jutted from the bedrock like the spines of a hedgehog.

My grandmother reached the mirror, and I swear she would have run headlong into it, but it shattered before her, a thousand glittering pieces of it filling the air, sliding down one across the other against the ebony board behind.

Alica Kendeth fell to her knees then, careless of the glass, and set her head to the ebony planks. She swore an oath. I saw it on her lips, but the words eluded me as I stepped down, foot questing for the next rung, and jolted to a halt against the mine floor.

THIRTY-FIVE

The salt mine took me by surprise. I had expected some kind of grubby burrows where men scraped the stuff from the rock. Instead we found ourselves in a space huge as any cathedral, cut entirely into a seam of crystal-white salt, shot through with darker veins to give a marbled effect in places, like the grain of some vast tree, as if they'd cut into Yggdrasil that the Norse say grows in the empty heart of creation with worlds depending from its boughs.

Immediately before us lay a circular plate of silver-steel, thick as a man is tall, ten yards across, and pitted with corrosion though I'd never seen corruption lay a finger on such steel in the few places I'd encountered it.

"This must be ancient." Kara stepped around it.

"The Builders knew this place before Kelem ever did," Snorri said.

The floor beneath our feet was crushed salt, but here and there the poured stone of the Builders could be seen, slabs of it, cracked and broken.

"Let's have a better look." I took the orichalcum from my pocket and let the light pulse. Huge pillars stood where the salt remained untouched, supporting the roof, each carved all about with a deep spiral pattern so they looked like great ropes.

"A whole sea died here." Kara breathed the words into the void about us.

"An ocean." Snorri strode forward into the cavern. The air held a strange taste, not salt, but something from the alchemist's fumes. And dry, the place ate the moisture from your eyes. Dry as death.

"So how do we reach Kelem's part of the mine?" Kara looked about her, frowning at the lanterns burning in niches on the distant opposite wall.

"We're in it," I said, putting the orichalcum away. "The miners must pass on through to where they dig. They wouldn't leave this much salt so close to the entrance if this weren't barred to them . . . also they'd make a profit. And those lanterns . . . who wastes oil like that?"

"We're being watched." Hennan pointed to one of the dozen corridors leading off the main chamber. I squinted along the line of his finger. Something twinkled, there in the shadows.

Snorri started to advance in that direction, and as he did the thing that had watched us emerged into the light. A spider, but monstrous in size and made of shining silver. Its legs spanned a diameter of two yards or more, its gleaming body larger than a man's head, studded with rubies the size of pigeon eggs and clustered like an arachnid's eyes. It came on swiftly, its limbs a complex ballet of motion, reflecting our light back at us in shards.

"Odin." Snorri stepped back. The only time I had ever seen something give him pause.

"Why silver, I wonder?" Kara held her blade before her.

"Why a bloody spider? That seems just as good a question." I stepped behind Snorri. I don't mind spiders as long as they're small enough to fit under my heel.

"Iron corrodes." Kara kept her eyes on the thing. "Clockwork soldiers wouldn't last long down here. Not unless they were made of silver-steel like our friend here."

"Friend?" Snorri took another step back and I moved to avoid being trodden on.

The spider stopped short of us and started back toward the darkness it came from, moving with exaggerated slowness.

"It's a guide," Kara said.

"To what?" Snorri made no move to follow. "A web?"

"It's a bit late to worry about walking into a trap now isn't it?" Kara looked around at him, anger and exasperation mixing on her brow. "You walked us a thousand miles for this, ver Snagason, against all advice. It's been a trap the whole time. The web had you the moment you laid hands on that key. It should never have left the ice. Kelem sent assassins to take the key from you—now you've brought it to him yourself. His mark is on you and he has drawn you to him." She gestured to his stained shirt, now pierced by the crystalline growths about his wound.

Kara shook her head and set off after the spider, turning up the wick in the last of our lanterns.

For the longest time our journey reduced to the whir and click of the spider's clockwork, the *tick-tick-tick* of its metal feet on the stone, and the glimmer of long limbs in motion at the margins of the lantern light. It led us down salt-walled corridors, opening from time to time onto dark and cavernous galleries whose dimensions our light could not reveal. We descended by steps and by gradient, every turn leading down, never up. Twice we passed across broad chambers, the high ceilings lost in gloom and supported on columns of the native rock-salt left in situ. The remainder of the salt had been cut out in slabs long ago and transported to the surface uncomfortably far above us.

In one of these pillared chambers salt miners, now long dead, had carved a church and set it about with saints. Paul the Apostle stood before the arched entrance one white and glittering arm raised before him, fingers half-spread as if pointing out an important truth, the bible clasped to his chest, the expression on his face hard to see in white on white.

Once we travelled a corridor of Builder-stone, smooth and perfect for a hundred yards before crumbing away and returning us to the caverns. It seemed as if they had made some complex here, not valuing the mineral wealth around them, just digging into it to hide themselves away, only for later men to excavate around them.

The deeper the corridors took us the stronger the alchemy in the air, stinging my eyes, scouring my lungs. After what must have been a mile or more of corridors and galleries we started to see doorways, carved into the salt, the arches elaborately worked but lacking any door, instead just filled with a crystalline wall of the native salt, as if a new chamber were to be excavated but plans had changed.

The air grew thicker by degrees, and warmer, as if with Hel's promise, for surely the infernal fires could not lie much further below us. The salts changed too—from tasting like the salt of the sea to something sour that burned the tongue. The colours changed, the white adopting a taint of deepest blue that seemed to lend depth to every surface. The air lost its dryness, becoming humid as our path led deeper, so that where earlier on the sweat had been sucked from my skin before it had a chance to even show, now the air refused to take it and left it running down my limbs in trickles that did nothing to cool me.

At last the spider brought us by a long flight of steps and a short corridor into a natural cavern where rock occasionally showed through the salt-clad walls and everything had a rounded, lumpen look to it. Another turn revealed a bleached wooden bridge crossing a fast-running rill that carved down through the salt, hot and steaming as it ran. Beyond the bridge lay a chamber of wonder.

"Holy Hel!" Kara invoked the heathen goddess that rules the Norse in their afterlife should death not take them to Valhalla. A cold bitch by all accounts, split nose to crotch by a line dividing a left side of pure jet from a right side of alabaster.

"Fuck me." I feel Christendom provides the more apt responses in such situations. The cavern ran before us in a wide and writhing tunnel, as if some great wyrm had burrowed here, and on every side the salts lay in vast crystals, forests of them, some a yard long, hexagonal in cross-section and so thick I might not get my hands to meet around them. Others were ten yards long and thicker than I stood tall, each face flatter than anything man can make, the angles sharp and perfect.

I knew this place. I had seen it in the visions Kara's magic gave me. I had seen it in a mirror in my grandmother's memories. The Lady Blue fled to these caverns after she murdered the elder Gholloth, first of my line. That bound them, Kelem and the Blue Lady. But which had been the hand behind the move I didn't know—only that both had played the game and played it against my family. However I turned it this placed Kelem's hand on Edris Dean's shoulder on the day he came to Vermillion.

The spider moved between, beneath, and over the crystals without interrupting its pace, flowing around each obstacle in a whirring interplay of legs. We moved more slowly, struggling to extract any use from each lungful of scalding, over-moist air, and sweating water faster than a man could piss it away. A lethargy wrapped me, like a hot wet blanket, and I found myself paused halfway across a massive crystal shard that Snorri had just struggled over. The crystal plane beneath me returned the light of Kara's lantern, tinting it deepest indigo. The whole shard seemed to glow with some inner fire, burning at its core impossibly far beneath me. It felt for a moment that I sat upon the surface of a calm sea, fathoms deep, with only the thinnest sheet of some brittle substance to hold me up, to keep me from sinking down to where that fire burned . . . Exhaustion bowed me, a great weight, dragging my head down toward the crystal's surface. Loki's key slipped from my wet shirt, dangling on its thong, the blackest I had ever seen it, its tip just a finger's breadth above the surface that supported me . . .

"Jal!" Kara barked the word from behind me, her voice seeming to scratch like fingernails on a slate, filling me with irritation. "Jal!"

I turned my head to her, reluctant, and met her stare.

"Don't," she said. "The world is broken here." She frowned, sweat running down her brow, plastering her blond hair to her forehead. Her eyes seemed defocused . . . witchy I'll call it for lack of a better word. She tasted the air. "This is a place of doors."

"Well . . . so they say." I waved a hand around us. "I haven't seen one damn door since we left the surface."

She glanced at the crystal beneath me. "There's a portal here. An almost-door . . . to let that key touch it would be a mistake. I don't know where or when it might take you."

"When?"

But she didn't answer, just looped her hands so Hennan could scramble over the shard. The boy had wrapped rags about his hands. A good move. Mine were cut from sharp edges and already stinging with the salts.

The spider led us away from the crystal gallery, past a steaming pool of cobalt blue water, and into a hall equal to any we had yet seen but hewn from the bedrock. Along each side stood massive salt crystals, vast octagonal columns retrieved from some deep place by an artistry unknown to men, or at least to any since the Builders. Each would barely fit along the passage that brought us here and would take a hundred elephants to haul.

What salt had formed the columns I couldn't say but each held a limpid light that sprang from no source I could see and illuminated the clear depths of them where webs and veils of ghostly white fault lines suggested shapes, hints of horrors and of angels, held forever within the heart of the crystal.

"Listen." Kara held up her hand and even the spider paused, frozen in mid-step.

"I can't—"

"They're singing." Hennan gazed around him.

Singing was too grand a word for it. Each crystal emitted a pure tone, just on the edge of hearing. As I drew near to one then the next I could discern a subtle change in the pitch, as if each were like one of those tuning forks the musicians use to set their strings.

"*These* are doors." I set a hand to the surface of the one before me and the key on my chest rang with the same note, making my skin tingle with the vibration.

I counted thirteen of them, all translucent save for the one dead centre of the left row. That one stood black as lies.

Snorri came to stand beside me. He seemed diminished in this place where the scale made ants of us all. He held his axe before him, the manacle cuts on his wrists burning red and angry. His whole body curled around the assassin's wound and a crystal excrescence clad one side of him from hip to armpit, sharp with spiky outgrowths. "Which is mine? The black one?"

"They are none of them yours, northman." The voice rang behind us, a grating atonal thing that reminded me of the clockwork soldiers.

Turning, we saw first a throne of salt, carved in pillars and roundels, grand as any king's. The oak boards, upon which it sat, rested on the backs of several more of the silver-steel spiders, the meshing forest of their legs moving quick as bards' fingers across lute strings to propel both platform and throne smoothly on.

Hunched in the salt chair like a stain against the whiteness of it, a wizened figure, a corpse I took it for at first, grey and naked, sunken, emaciated, the skin pierced in many places by sharp white crystals of salt, growing in clusters like frost on frozen twigs.

"These are my halls." The head on that corpse-like body raised itself to view us, the glimmer of what might be an eye far back in the darkness of its sockets. Around a neck of bone and skin a device of silver-steel, bedded in the grey flesh and facing a perforated grille toward us. Similar contraptions sat in the necks of clockwork soldiers, generated their voices for them.

"Kelem—"

"You were not wise to come here, witch." The mechanical voice cut across Kara. "Of Skilfar's brood are you? Her judgment is usually better than this." As Kelem spoke more spiders came into view, smaller ones, flowing over the back of his throne, some with bodies the size of hands, others no larger than a coin. They moved about the mage in a complex tide, shifting his body, changing the position of his arms, so that like a marionette he became animated in some dreadful approximation of life.

When you invest in self-deception as heavily as I do there come points at which a swift audit of the truth is forced upon you and I can attest that the sudden realization of what a fool you have been is as cruel as any knife thrust. In my mind's eye we had sneaked into the mines and found the door Snorri sought while Kelem dreamed. Even with the spider leading us to Kelem I thought we might find what we needed before we reached him. Now it seemed that Snorri must trade away my last hope of salvation just to visit a place any knife could dispatch him to. And if Kelem chose not to bargain but simply to turn us into four columns of salt . . . then all our hope lay in Kara's spear.

"You sent assassins after me." Snorri spoke past teeth gritted against agony. I could almost see the slow march of the salt growing across his flesh.

"If you believe that then it was foolish to come here, Snorri ver Snagason."

"In Eridruin's Cave you tormented me with a demon in the shape of my daughter." Snorri lifted his axe.

"Not me, Norseman. Maybe some ghost of my past, feeling my will that you should come here to my home. But the past is a different country, I'm no longer responsible for what happens there. Age absolves a man's crimes."

Kara interjected, perhaps worried Snorri might attack and steal her chance with the spear. "But you sent no more assassins, no more shades. Did you think to bargain instead?"

"It is true—I do like to bargain." Some rusty sound that may have been a laugh escaped the voice grille. "And it would seem you need something from me, Snagason. I could help you with this problem you have . . ." A larger spider moved Kelem's hand along his side, a gesture mirroring the line of the wound eating Snorri up.

"I seek a door. Nothing beyond that." And Snorri straightened, his mouth set in a tight line of pain, the crystals cladding his side cracking, plates of salt falling clear.

Kelem scanned each of us, his sunken eyes lingering on me, then on Hennan, the legs of the spider that first raised his head now visible among the pale straggles of his hair. "I don't believe you have the key, Snagason. Though it is a mystery why a man would give up such a treasure if he did not have to." His gaze settled on Kara, lingering on the black and silver spear in her hand then moving to her face. "Give me Loki's gift, little völva."

Kara moved fast. Faster than when I punched her and she knocked me flat. Two short steps and she released Gungnir with a crack of her arm. The spear hammered into Kelem's chest, pinning him to his throne, a throw Snorri would have been proud of.

None of us moved. Nobody spoke. A spider tilted Kelem's head to look down at the spear. Another raised his arm to rest his forearm across the haft. "You took the wrong door, völva. They call me 'master of the ways.' Did you not wonder if I might not notice you passing through such portals as stand close to the Wheel of Osheim? I gave you this." A salt-crusted finger tapped Gungnir's dark wood. "I gave it to you to make you brave—"

"Sageous helped you." I clamped my mouth shut on the words, not meaning to draw attention to myself.

Kelem looked my way, head tilted in acknowledgment. "My skills detected you. I guided the dream-witch to sew this into your visions. He was well paid. A hireling, no more than that. You've no idea how hard it was to lead your slow and plodding minds to this plan, to guide you to the tools, to place them in your hands . . ." He returned his gaze to Kara. "And now that you have attacked me Loki will not mind if I simply kill you and take the key from your body. Even so, out of respect for your grandmother, I give you this last opportunity to hand it to me of your own free will."

"I don't have it." Kara let her arms hang at her side, as limp as her hair, defeated.

A noise like nails on slate rasped from Kelem's voice grille, perhaps as close to fury as he could come, this desiccated imitation of a man. His head turned sharply back to Snorri. "How . . . how is it that the one with the greatest power does not also bear the greatest weapon? You gave Odin's own spear to a witch when she didn't even own the key. Are you mad?"

"It isn't Odin's spear," Snorri said. "And when I face what lies beyond death's door I will be carrying my own axe, the axe my fathers bore, not somebody else's spear."

"Say your piece, Snagason. You've come far enough to say it." Kelem's mechanical voice held a twang of amusement.

Snorri looked my way, eyes dark, no sign of blue in the curious glow of the crystals. "You should speak with Prince Jalan Kendeth, heir to the throne of Red March. My friend. The key is his."

Kelem made a noise of disgust and jerked a dismissive arm at us. "The key you bear leaves a mark in the world. The longer it is still the deeper that mark. The more it is used the deeper that mark. Once you started your journey I had no good idea where to seek it. But now you stand before me . . . I see it is true. The princeling has the prize." His eyes, glittering deep in their dry sockets, settled on me. "I will buy the key from you. Shall we . . . haggle?"

Kelem had wanted the key-bearer to attack him. He'd dropped the spear into our laps to make us bold enough to do it. If his plan had worked he could have killed us and avoided Loki's curse just as Snorri had avoided it when the Unborn Captain had attacked him. Now his plan had failed the mage needed to have me give him the key willingly, or else steal or trick it from me. I doubted he was any good at picking pockets, but he did have deep ones of his own . . . I wondered quite how deep he would dig to own it.

"I'm sure we can reach a deal." I clutched the key tight, not intending to lose it to some thieving mechanical arachnid. As I squeezed it I saw a flash of another place, a room of many doors, just wooden ones, with Kelem standing before me, younger even than the shade we saw of him at Eridruin's Cave. "What's your offer?"

Kelem didn't speak as spider legs rotated his salt-crusted skull to stare directly at me. Even while he turned to face me though I glimpsed that small square room again and heard a younger Kelem speak, "Are you a god, Loki?" His eyes on me, hard as stones.

"Wh—" I started to speak but the vision came again, cutting me off.

"Your death lies behind one of these other doors, Kelem." It seems I'm speaking the words in that room, so many centuries ago that Kelem looks no older than Snorri.

That younger Kelem had sneered. "God of tricks they—"

"Don't worry." My voice, but it's not me. "You'll never manage to open that one."

The vision passed and I became aware that Kelem, ancient and wizened in his throne, was addressing me.

"The Red Queen's child?"

"Her grandson, sir. My father is cardinal—"

"Skilfar's spawn and Alica's, waiting on my judgment, deep in the salt earth with old Kelem. How strange the world does turn, and so swiftly. It seems only yesterday that Skilfar was young and fair, the flower of the north. And Alica Kendeth, surely she's a child still? Must everyone grow old each time I blink?"

The spear fell from him, several spiders had been working to free it. The weapon slid to the ground.

I raised the key, cold, hard, slick, and yet somehow seeming to writhe worm-like in my grip. "Do you have an offer?" A vision of crystals growing from the rock flashed before my eyes. A mirror, white crystals, the Lady Blue fleeing, the blood of my line on her hands. It would have to be a damn good offer.

"Long before they called me door-master I was master of coin. The golden key will open almost as many doors as the black one. Hearts too."

Those hollow eye-pits studied me a moment. "Every man has his price, boy. Yours is easy enough to guess. I'll pay for calling you 'boy,' but not much. I *am* rich, boy, did you know that? Rich enough to make a beggar of Croesus, to make Midas's wealth look modest. Money, boy, is the blood of empires." Spiders raised his dry hands, tugging on tendons, manipulating bones, a silver web of them across his sunken flesh. "Money flows through these hands. Name your price."

"I . . ." Indecision paralysed me and greed took my voice. What if I asked for too little? But asking some ridiculous sum might enrage him.

"Knowing your own price is quite a thing, Jalan Kendeth. Know thyself, that's what the philosopher said. A wisdom that has lived through the Thousand Suns. Easy to say, hard to do. Knowing your own price is most of knowing yourself, and who can expect such a thing from the young? Ten thousand in crown gold."

"T-Ten . . ." I tried to imagine it there, glittering before me, the weight of it spilling through my hands. More than I'd lost, more than was stolen from me, more than I owed. Enough to pay off the grasping hands of Umbertide, and clear my debt to Maeres Allus, with a thousand and more left over.

"Ten thousand would be an insult to a man of your breeding, Prince Jalan." The mechanical voice dragged me from my vision. "Sixty-four thousand. Not a clipped copper more or less. We have a deal."

Always take the money. Sixty-four thousand. A ridiculous sum, a preposterous sum. I could buy back Garyus's ships, set myself up for a life of debauched pleasure among Vermillion's elite, seduce the DeVeer sisters from their husbands . . . I could buy Grandmother a squad of sword-sons or a warship or something equally violent to take her mind from the loss of a key she never owned . . .

"The money will be waiting for you in credit at the House Gold. I will ensure all charges against you are dropped and when you've cleared your debts you may leave the city," Kelem said.

"It's not here?" That disappointed me. I wanted the mound of gold I had imagined.

"I'm not a dragon, Prince Jalan. I do not sleep upon my hoard."

"Sixty-four thousand—in crown gold—and you undo what you've done to Snorri." I hesitated then sighed. "And he gets to open death's door before you take the key." I glanced over at the Norseman, standing, hunched, with his hand on Hennan's shoulder, a father's touch. "Though I pray he finds the sense not to use it."

"No." Just that through the silver grille on Kelem's withered neck, then silence.

I drew in a deep sigh and wiped the sweat from my brow. "Sixty-three thousand, fix Snorri, and he gets to open the door." There's an exquisite pain involved in the loss of a thousand in gold. Not one I'll ever get used to.

"No."

"Oh, come on." I knuckled my brow. "You're killing me here. Sixty-two, the cure, and the door."

"No."

I wondered how far I could push him. Kelem clearly feared Loki's curse more than he feared losing sixty-four thousand in gold. But perhaps less than he feared opening the door into death.

I held up a hand and stepped to Kara's side, leaning in close to whisper in her ear. Damn but I wanted her, even there, even then, even sweat-slick and with the suspicion in her eyes. "Kara . . . how dangerous is this curse?"

She stepped back, her fingers on my chest. "Why didn't Skilfar take the key from Snorri?"

"Um . . ." I battled to remember. "The world is better shaped by freedom. Even if it means giving foolish men their head—that's what you said?" I looked from her to Snorri. "She let him keep it because . . . she's wise. Or something."

Kara raised her eyebrows. "Doesn't sound very likely, does it?"

"Skilfar was scared too?"

"It's Loki's key. God of trickery. Nothing as straight forward as strength is going to decide its ownership. Or it would have been Thor's key an age ago!"

"It has to be given," Snorri said. "Olaaf Rikeson took it by strength and Loki's curse froze his army, ten thousand strong."

"So . . . when you gave me the key back in the olive groves . . ."

"I trusted a friend, yes."

"Hell." Snorri had placed his future in my hands. That was far more trust than I could hold on to. It was like telling a dog to guard a steak. It was stupid. "You don't know me at all, Snorri." Somehow, even with sixty-four thousand in crown gold glittering in my immediate future I felt low. A fever perhaps, or poisoning from the sour salts of the lower mine.

Maybe it was the way Snorri didn't even argue his case but just stood there like the huge over-loyal idiot he was, having the gall to expect the same foolishness from me.

"Thirty-two thousand, the cure, and the idiot gets his door open."

"No."

"Oh for Christ's sake! How much to open that damned door?"

"That door shouldn't ever be opened. Even if you took no gold, only offered me the key to show you death's door, I would hesitate. There's a reason the ghosts of my youth are scattered across Hell. It wasn't just chance that one stepped out to oppose you when you approached Eridru-in's door. Opening that door is dangerous. Passing through still more so." Kelem's jaw moved as the voice issued from his neck. In his mouth something glittered, silver across the black thing that had been his tongue.

"Why? Why would a dead thing like you care?" I didn't even want that door open—why I was arguing rather than wondering how to carry my gold back to Red March I didn't know.

"I'm not dead." Kelem tilted his head. "Merely . . . well preserved."

I stood, the key tight in my hand, watched by the witch, the warrior, the boy, and the old bones in the chair. Something in the quality of the light from the crystals changed, as subtle as a slight shift in the wind, but I felt it.

"What would you do with this key, Master Kelem?" I asked him, starting to pace from one column to the next.

"I have a palace of doors. It's only natural that I should want one key that could unlock any of them." Kelem's throne rotated to allow him to track me. "Without a key the opening and closing of such doors is a complex and tedious business, dangerous even, and one that can exhaust an old man like me. These thirteen before me. These are difficult, but over the years I've managed all but three. The doors to darkness and light still defy me. Those on the far side hear me trying though, oh yes." A scratching sound that might be laughter. "They fear me, hate me, and hold the doors tight against my efforts. The dark knows that if I control the door, I own them. The light knows it too.

"Long ago I was told that one of these doors would never open for me, that my doom lay beyond it. Loki himself told me this, the father of lies. And I believed him because he is always honest. He takes pride in it—knowing that a partial truth cuts deeper than a lie." Kelem waved a desiccated hand in my direction. "The key will unlock the doors, and the last one—that will be the one I will leave closed. That one I will lock again, and lock so well that it will never open, not in the lives of men."

It's unnerving when the person you're bargaining with lets you know how valuable what you have is to them. In the market we pretend not to care, we insult the thing we desire, denigrate it. Kelem's honesty told me two things. That I could trust his offer, and that I would be a fool to refuse it because one way or another he would own the key.

"That black one." I pointed to it. "It's death's door? The gate to Hell?"

"No, that is one of the three that defy me still. The gate to Hell is opened easily enough, the Day of a Thousand Suns left it hanging off its hinges—it's the first of the thirteen that I learned."

I stared at the black crystal. "It's the night gate then." Even as I said them the words felt wrong.

"Do you think so, Prince Jalan? Has your connection to the dark grown so weak?"

"No." I shook my head. "It's not that one . . ." I passed another pillar, trailing my fingers across it.

"That door is Osheim, Prince Jalan. The door is the Wheel, the Wheel is a door. It's the door I need to own."

"The Lady Blue would open them all," I said. "She thinks the time for doors is passing and soon all worlds will bleed one into the other. She wants to open the ways and marshal the destruction to ensure her place in whatever hell results."

"I've been misinformed about educational standards in Red March," Kelem said, two spiders the size of silver eyeballs tugging at the dry corners of his mouth to make a smile. "You've been well taught, Prince Jalan. But the Lady Blue really only wants to turn the Wheel. She could do that by opening the black door, but the black door is opening by itself. It has been for centuries. Ever so slowly, but speeding up. Each door that is opened, each thing that passes through from one world to another . . . it weakens the walls between those places, and as the walls start to crack, the door of Osheim opens, the Wheel turns. With Loki's key the Lady Blue could end the world today by opening that door before us. Without it she must rely on the Dead King opening death's door wide enough to fracture the walls around it . . . and, by doing so, turn the Wheel and herald the end of all things."

"And where do you stand, Master Kelem?" The conversation had grown too big for me. I just wanted to escape with my money and enough years to spend it in.

"I'm a financier, a man of trade, Prince Jalan. Everything has its price. I buy, I sell. There's no harm in this surely? Buying what can be bought, selling it to those with the need and the means to pay. The rich must have what they crave—surely you agree with that?

"On this point my position should be clear enough. I'm refusing to open one door, just briefly, to save myself tens of thousands in gold. That hardly paints me as a man who would be overly keen to set them all open wide, now does it? I might want to own the darkness and the light and the creatures therein, but ending creation? What good would my wealth do me then? True, the Lady Blue and I have interests in common, but I am not her ally in this ambition."

You were her ally in another ambition, equally bloody, and long ago. The words twitched behind my lips. He had been part of the plot that killed the first Gholloth. Maybe the second had died by his command also. Had he directed the Lady Blue, or she him? Either way both of them had stained their hands with the blood of Kendeths. Snorri's family too counted among their crimes, his whole clan, the Undoreth, gone, just one man remaining now that Tuttugu had died beneath Edris Dean's blade. And Edris was the Lady Blue's creature, my mother's death her plan, my unborn sister just something broken in the process. I saw again the vision of the lady vanishing into the mirror, the Red Queen kneeling there among the shards, her grandfather slain, the linens of his bed crimson. Perhaps it was Alica Kendeth's legendary anger that infected my blood, perhaps my own, a pale flame to be sure, but feed any such spark enough fuel and it will blaze.

I heard the knocking again, that knocking I'd been hearing every once in a while since the debtors' prison. It sounded louder here, reverberating among the columns. None of the others looked up.

"Do you—" I broke off, the knocking came from my left. I turned and walked back toward Kelem and the others. Kelem, master of doors. Kelem, sender of assassins.

Knock. Knock. Knock. Steady, rhythmic, louder by the moment. I'd heard it every day of late. Was it sunset a mile above us . . . had I heard this sound every sunset since I took the key? Had Snorri heard it when he held the key, sounding each dawn since the wrong-mages' door had closed Aslaug and Baraqel off from us? *Knock. Knock.* Knocking had woken me from my dreaming that spring morning back in Trond. *Knock.* Some doors are better left unopened.

Kelem turned his head to watch my progress. I saw his dry hands drip with my mother's blood. I saw the Red Queen, a child, kneeling before the ruin of her grandfather. I felt the pain that cored me when I woke from the blood-dream that showed me Mother dying and returned her to my memories.

"You carry something I have bought and sold, Prince Jalan." Perhaps

Kelem could see the wheels turning in my head. Perhaps he knew he was losing me.

"I do?" I continued to hunt the sound, moving between the pillars.

"The sword at your hip. I recognize its taint. I procured it from a necromancer named Chella decades ago. It didn't come cheap, but the Blue Lady paid me ten times that price and more."

I paused, hand on the hilt of the weapon, glancing back at Kelem. "This? This was yours?"

"The Lady Blue had allies aplenty among the necromancers, long before there was a Dead King or any hint of him. She has been building their strength for years, seeding the unborn with such toys as that which you bear."

"If I have a price, Kelem, this is not lowering it." I cast about, straining for direction, willing the knocking to sound again. "Edris Dean tried to kill me with this blade."

"You were not his target, though," Kelem said. "Neither was your mother."

I stopped and faced him.

"Your sister." The spiders moved his jaws. "The planets aligned for that one. The stars held their breath to see her born. The Silent Sister thought the child would grow to replace her, to exceed her, to make this empire whole. And more . . ."

"To heal the world," I breathed. Grandmother thought I might be the one to undo the doom the Builders had laid upon us, but it wasn't me: our salvation had never been born.

"The sword you carry put your sister in Hell. Unborn. Sell the key to me and the author of her death will be thwarted in her ambition. With Loki's key I will own creation, and what I own I do not allow to come to harm."

My fingers flinched from the hilt as if it had grown too hot to touch. Edris's blade hadn't just cursed Snorri's son as it slew him in the womb, marking him to be unborn . . . it had done the same to my sister.

"What do you think the unborn were doing in Vermillion, Prince Jalan?" Kelem asked, silver legs stretching the leathery skin across his skull's grin. "The Dead King's captain, and the Unborn Prince, both of them in the same place, practically in the shadow of the palace walls? Both daring the Silent Sister's magics . . ."

"They were bringing an unborn into the world . . ." Even now the memory of the Unborn Prince made me shudder—just his eyes upon me through the slit of that mask.

"All that for a single unborn?" Kelem's head tilted with the question. "Haven't the Dead King's servants brought forth unborn in all manner of scattered spots, none of them half as dangerous as Vermillion?"

I recalled a grave horror rising in the cemetery where Taproot's circus had camped.

Kelem spoke again. "The older the unborn, the longer it has spent in Hell, the more powerful it is . . . the harder to return. And this one . . . this one needed a hole torn in the world, a hole so large a city might fall through. This one needed the strength of the two most powerful unborn this side of death's veil. This one . . . she needed the death of blood relatives to open her path. The death of a close relative best of all. A brother perhaps . . ."

"My . . . my sis—" The horror of it took me in its grasp, my feet rooted.

"Your sister was to be the Red Queen's champion. The Lady Blue took that piece and made it hers. As the Unborn Queen she might be the Dead King's bride, she might be his fist in the living world, the unknowing servant of Lady Blue, heralding the end of all things. That is who is waiting for death's door to open. That is why you should sell me the key and leave it closed. She needs your life, Prince Jalan. If she destroys you in the deadlands it will tear a hole through which she can be born at last into this world. If she comes through by some other path then killing you will cement her place here and stop her being cast back by the enchantments that might otherwise banish her." Kelem's chair moved closer, legs clicking beneath it. "You've no real choice here, Jalan. A sensible man like you. A pragmatist. Take the gold."

"I—" Kelem made sense. He made sense *and* offered a pile of gold so large a man could roll about in it. I could see it in my mind's eye, heaped and gleaming. But . . . the old bastard's hands were dripping with my mother's blood.

The knocking sounded again, close by. None of them could hear it but me. I came closer to the source of the noise. BANG. BANG. BANG.

Almost deafening. Kara said something but I couldn't hear her. A flicker of motion drew my eye, a black fist pounding against the surface of the crystal pillar closest to me, *from the inside*, the arm lost in a darkness that had polluted the column's clarity like ink drops in water.

"Every man has his price." Somehow Kelem's voice reached me through the din. I wondered what Snorri's price was, what my grandmother's price might be. Even Garyus, the third Gholloth, with his love of gold, his mastery of commerce . . . even he wouldn't sell a friend for as little as money. I didn't think it of Garyus—I both did and did not want to think it of me.

Sixty-four thousand . . . Kelem wouldn't show Snorri the door even if I sacrificed all those thousands. And even if he did Snorri would just march in to die—horrors would spill into the world, my unborn sister among them. Snorri would die and I'd own nothing but my rags, a tiny worthless corner of a salt mine, and a few other dribs and drabs that would be lucky to sell for fifty florins in total. There wasn't a choice to make here. Always take the—

Blood. It seemed the whole floor swam with it, ankle deep and rising. I saw it drip from Gholloth's bed. I saw Garyus twist in the crimson swirls as the Silent Sister took his strength. It ran red from Tuttugu's opened neck. I saw it drip scarlet from Edris's blade as Mother slid from the steel. And I saw the hands behind each act, the blue and the grey, each stained with what I held precious, sacred.

BANG. BANG. BANG.

This whole nightmare had started with Astrid pounding on my door, dragging me from a good dream. Every part of my return had been about the opening of one door or another. It had been a mistake to open that first door too. I should have stayed in bed.

And yet . . . somehow my hand found itself reaching out to the crystal column towering above us. Somehow I found myself drawing forth Loki's key.

"No!" Kelem's shout.

The clatter of metal limbs as his spiders raced toward me. The roar as Snorri threw himself into their path, heedless of his injury and pain, swinging his father's axe.

Against all reason I found myself pressing the jet-black key to that impossibly flat surface, driving it into the neat dark eye of the keyhole that appeared beneath it . . . turning it as the voices rose behind me amid the din of combat.

The door blasted open with a force that sent me skidding across the floor. Midnight boiled out of it, imps of ebony, all horns and hooves and curling tails, huger and more terrible shapes rising behind them, wings canopied, bat-like creatures, serpents, shades of men, and in the midst of it all, surging forward, Aslaug, wrought in night-stained bone, her lower carriage a frenzy of arachnid legs that made Kelem's toys seem delicate and wholesome.

"Take him through!" I screamed, pointing at Kelem, compelling the forces of night with whatever magic and potential lay in me, calling on the bond I had been sworn to. The horde, sighting their tormentor and would-be lord, surged through the narrow portal, borne on a wave of liquid night. Aslaug fell upon Kelem in an instant, a howling, tearing fury as if my own rage had infected her. The rest followed and in their frenzy the creatures of darkness flooded over the ancient mage, black imps sinking fangs into each wizened limb, inky tentacles reaching from the portal to whip around him. They hated him anyway, for presuming to rule them, for his endless attempts to open and own the night door, and for so nearly succeeding.

The dark-throng dragged Kelem away, a riptide of horror, his throne and platform scraping through the face of the column, a mess of stained and twisted silver-steel legs left twitching in his wake. In the silent moment that followed a faint laughter echoed, not in my ears, through my bones— a laugh both merry and wicked, the kind that infects the listener and makes them smile. It came from the key. A god laughing at his own joke.

Snorri and I lay where we threw ourselves in the moment, sprawled on opposite sides of the deluge.

"Die, you bastard!" I shouted it after the door-mage, scrambling to my feet. I hoped Kelem would suffer there in the endless dark and that as he did he thought of the Kendeths and of the debt he owed us.

Aslaug remained, the crushed body of a mechanical spider in her hand, silver legs giving the occasional jerk. She towered above Kara, her face furious. Snorri got to his knees and shoved Hennan behind the next pillar. "Stay there!" A handful of night-imps still prowled the perimeter of the darkness smoking around the portal and other, less wholesome, things writhed half-seen behind them.

"Send them back," I hollered. Kara might have dealt harshly with Aslaug before but the völva was dark-sworn and the forces of night were hers to command if she had the will. Their allegiance hadn't shattered just because she had crossed one of their number.

I didn't need to urge Kara—the effort of her working showed in every line as she raised her arms in rejection.

"Out, night-spawn. Out lie-born. Out daughter of Loki! Out child of Arrakni!" Kara repeated the incantation that had once driven Aslaug from her boat, her hands held before her, clawed in threat. All around her the darkness drew back, as if sucked through the doorway by a straw, down into the realms of night.

"I don't think so, little witch." Aslaug speared Kara with two black legs, pinning her to the next column, her robe tenting up around the impaling limbs.

Kara raised her head, bloody about the mouth and snarled, "Back!"

"Go back, Aslaug!" I shouted, and she turned that beautiful, terrifying face toward me.

"You can't just use me like that, Jalan. I'm not something to be cast aside once you've had what you wanted." I could almost believe the hurt on the stained ivory of her face was real.

I held my hands palm up in apology. "It's what I do . . ."

Snorri's short sword, thrown point over hilt over point, hammered between Aslaug's shoulder blades.

"Back!" Kara screamed.

"Back!" I shouted. I couldn't even feel bad about it.

And with darkness bubbling around the sword blade jutting from her chest, with her hands clutching at the sides of the column, with her black legs scrabbling for purchase against the retreating tide, Aslaug fell back, shrieking, into the night from which she came.

I rushed forward, tripping on a spider leg, and almost pitched head-first after the demon. In the last moment I managed to catch at the door, invisibly thin, and slam it shut before me, smacking my face into it a split second later. Clinging on to consciousness, I fumbled the key forward and locked the door again.

"Christ on a bike." I fell back into my own darkness and didn't even feel my head hit the ground.

THIRTY-SIX

I dreamed a pleasant enough dream, recalling the heady days when I'd traded on the floor of the Maritime House, those early days when it seemed I could do no wrong. The first lesson I'd learned there had been the most important. It concerned the value of information. No other currency held such worth in Umbertide. A rich man's wealth could be won and lost on a single pertinent fact.

I hadn't bought a controlling share in the failing Crptipa Mine on some nostalgic whim. I hadn't bought it against the possibility that one day I would want to get into it in a hurry. I'd bought the concern because I had a pertinent fact. A fact that represented long odds on a very significant change. I knew something. Something important. I knew that Snorri ver Snagason meant to go there.

I came round to find Hennan slapping me with considerably more enthusiasm than the task warranted, and the tatters of my dream were swept away.

"Kara?" I struggled into a sitting position.

Snorri knelt beside the völva. She lay, propped against the pillar where Aslaug had pinned her. Snorri had stripped her layers and lifted her undershirt to reveal ugly red weals across her ribs left and right. Some charm or spell must have denied her flesh to Aslaug's touch because the legs had thrust right at her. They must have seared Kara as they skidded over her skin, diverted from her vitals and left just pinning her by her clothes.

"A bitten tongue is the worst of it." Snorri looked across to me and abandoned Kara. He took my arm and hauled me to my feet.

"Jal." He brushed me down and stood back, looking solemn. "I knew you couldn't be bought."

"Hah." I rubbed my forehead, expecting my fingers to come back bloody. "You know I'm a man of honour!" I grinned at him.

Snorri gripped my forearm in the manner of warriors, and I held him back. We had a little moment there.

"What happened to your—" I pointed at his side, his jerkin holed in a score of places, ripped and discoloured, the crystal growths gone.

He patted his side and winced. "I don't know. When I threw that sword a chunk of the stuff cracked away. I pulled off the rest. It didn't seem . . . attached any more."

"Kelem's spell is broken." Kara hobbled over, supported by Hennan. "We could leave now?"

Snorri looked over at the völva and the boy, red-haired like his middle child. I wanted him to see the wife and son he could have, the life that could lie before him, not to replace what lay behind, but something . . . something good. Better than Hell in any case.

Snorri bowed his head. "I can't leave." He looked down at his hands, as if remembering how they had once held his children. "Show me the door. I've come too far to go back."

"I don't know which it is." Kara waved her arm at the columns marching away from us, the distance stacking them closer and closer until the eye lost their meaning. "That was Kelem's speciality. We came here to find Kelem, remember? Not the door. That lies everywhere. We just needed someone who could see it. And Jal has given him to the dark."

"He would never have told you, Snorri," I said. "He wouldn't have let us leave either, not with this." I held the key up. "Thank God sunset came when it did."

Kara gave me an odd look. "It's not sunset for a couple of hours and more."

I laughed at her. "Of course it is."

"I don't think so, Jal." Snorri shook his head. "Time gets turned around down here, true enough. But I'm with Kara. I can't believe I'm out by that much."

"It's you, Jal." Kara nodded. "You don't understand your potential. You bind yourself about with these rules, with lies you tell yourself to avoid responsibility. But you made Aslaug come. You found the door to her. You made it happen."

"I . . ." I closed my mouth. Perhaps Kara had it right. Now I considered it I would be surprised to find it dark if I climbed out of the mine right now. "Snorri has potential too. You said it yourself. He lights the orichalcum brighter than you do."

"It's true," Kara said without rancour.

I looked up at Snorri, not sure whether to say it or not. "If you want death's door badly enough, then in this place you'll find it." I shook my head. "Don't look for it, Snorri. But if you do, and you find it, I will open it for you." And then madness took my tongue, "And go with you." I think it's a disease. Being treated like a brave and honourable man becomes an addiction. Like the poppy, you want more of it, and more. I'd eaten up the cheers offered for the hero of the Aral Pass, but to be treated as an equal by the Norseman made those cheers dim, those thrown petals pale. There's a sense of family in that warriors' grip. A sense of belonging. I understood now how Tuttugu, soft as he was, got drawn along with the rest of them. And God damn it, it had got to me too.

"Come with me, brother!" Snorri started to stride down the hall like a man with purpose. "We'll open death's door and carry Hell to them. The sagas will tell of it. The dead rose up against the living and two men chased them back across the river of swords. Beside our legend Beowulf's saga will be a tale for children!"

I followed, keeping a brisk pace so the uncertainty nipping at my heels couldn't catch me. Kara and Hennan hurried along behind. My sister waited beyond the door, unborn, altered, hungry for my death. But Snorri had released his own child from that fate . . . surely a Kendeth could do the same? My head swam with visions of the parades they would hold for me in Vermillion on my return, the honours Grandmother would heap upon me. Jalan—conqueror of death!

• • •

It didn't take long for the foolishness to start to fade. I just had to remember the Black Fort to realize how little appetite I really had for this nonsense. For the longest time I hoped my over-enthusiastic boasts wouldn't be put to the test, that Snorri's search would be fruitless, but in time he stopped, one hand set against a pillar that to my eyes looked exactly the same as every other.

"This one."

"You're sure?" I peered into the depths of it, trying to see something amid the pale fault lines stacked one on another, reducing its clarity to a misty core.

"I'm sure. I've stood a moment from death so many times. I know the feel of its threshold."

"Don't do it." Kara pressed between us. "I beg you." She looked up at Snorri, craning her neck. "The unborn could be waiting for you on the other side. Would you really unleash such things into the world? You've no weapons to stop them save steel. And once they hold it open . . . how long before the Dead King comes?" She turned to me. "And you, Jal. You heard what Kelem said. Your sister will hunt you down and eat your heart. Go through that door and how long do you think it will take her to find you?"

Snorri set both hands to the crystal. "I can feel it."

"They'll be waiting for you!" Kara grabbed his arm, as if she could hold him back.

Snorri shook his head. "If we were in the deadlands and I asked you where the door to life lay . . . what would you say?"

"I—" She pursed her lips, seeing the trap before I did. "It makes no more sense for it to be in one place there than it does for it to be in only one place here. It would be everywhere."

"And the unborn will be waiting . . . everywhere?" Snorri offered her a grim smile. "There will be nothing waiting for us. Jal will give you the key. Lock the door behind us."

I saw the calculation cross her face. Quick then gone. Skilfar had sent her for no reason other than this moment—the key offered freely, no trace of Loki's curse on it.

"Don't go." But the conviction had left her voice. That made me sad, but I suppose we're all victims of our ambition.

"Stay." Hennan, his first word on the subject, his bottom lip pushed up as if to steady the upper, eyes bright but refusing to say more, too used to disappointment. His years seemed too short to have beaten the selfish out of him, but there it was.

Snorri bowed his head. "Jalan. If you would do the honours?" He gestured to the crystal plane before us.

I always thought that phrase about blood running cold was a flight of fancy but the stuff seemed to freeze in my veins. There's a thing about being stuck between fear and pride, even though you know fear will win in the end it seems impossible to let go of the pride. So I stood there frozen, my face a rictus grin, the key trembling in my fist as if eager.

"Kara, Hennan." Snorri had them both in his arms in two quick steps, swept from their feet, lifted tight against his chest. "I would stay if I thought I could be the friend you needed." He held them close, squeezing any question or protest from them. A moment later he let them go. "But this thing." He pointed at the key, at the door. He waved at the world about us. "It would eat me away until nothing was left but a bitter old Viking without a clan, hating himself, hating whoever had kept him from his task. Fool's errand or not, it *is* my errand. It is my end. Some men have to sail to the horizon and keep going until the ocean swallows their story—this is the sea I must sail."

"All men are fools." Kara spat the words at the floor, wiping at her eyes. I agreed with her in this instance. She sniffed angrily and passed Snorri her last rune. "Take it!"

Hennan watched Snorri, a single tear cutting a channel through the dirt across his cheek. "Undoreth, we. Battle-born. Raise hammer, raise axe, at our war-shout gods tremble." He said it high but firm, without a waver, and I swear, that whole time it was the only moment I thought Snorri might crack.

But he pointed at the key, waving me forward, not trusting himself to speak. I advanced on the door, my mind screaming at me to run, thoughts colliding in their attempt to find a way out. Perhaps Kara and Hennan needed an escort, perhaps they wouldn't be safe. The men who hunted us from Umbertide must be in the tunnels, searching.

I set my fingers to the crystal, trying to sense something there, trying to hear the note and understand what had drawn Snorri to this pillar. Nothing. Or so I thought, until the moment I moved to draw my fingers away, and in that second I felt it, saw it, a dryness, a thirst, an emptiness. No sense of anything waiting, just a hunger that I'd seen before in dead eyes.

"God save us." I set the key to the crystal and there was the keyhole, as if it had always been there, waiting since time started. The others watched me. "Shouldn't you take the boy, Kara, get away from here?"

"I need to lock the door," she said.

I set the key in the keyhole. Turned it. And felt a year of my life take flight. I used the key to draw the door back, just a fraction, just enough for a line of flat orange light to show. The hall's air hissed into that crack as if Hell drew in a breath, and I struggled to keep the door open, taking hold of the edge. Where my fingers reached around I felt the dryness, as if the skin were peeling back, my flesh already withering on the bone.

I took the key out and, with a reluctance so thick it seemed I reached out through molasses, I set the key in Kara's outstretched hand. I almost snatched it back. It seemed too final. Perhaps she saw that in me for she tucked it into her pocket quick enough. The moment passed—the moment which Kara had waited a thousand miles for. Had Skilfar truly sent us to the ends of the earth just to give Kara time to work that magic, to have the warrior fall for her charms, or failing that to come to terms with the wisdom of her counsel, and give over Loki's key of his own free will? Might not Skilfar have shown Snorri the door then and there in her cavern on Beerentoppen if she'd wanted to? Surely that cold bitch knew her own paths to it?

"Gods watch us," said Snorri. "We ask no aid, only that you witness."

"Damn that, God help me! The heathen can make his own way if he wants!"

Snorri shot me a grin, took the door and heaved it open. The light seemed to shine through his flesh, offering only his bones, the broader grin of his skull. And in a moment he was through.

The door slipped from my grasp and slammed shut behind him. I'd blame it on sweaty fingers if they weren't more parched than they had ever been. I should have reached to open it again but my arms kept by my sides.

"Oh God, I can't do it." My voice broke.

"There's no shame in that." Kara reached out to touch my shoulder and in that moment I fell into her, wrapping both arms around her, wracked by a sob, half of it shame and half the mourning of another friend, perhaps my only friend, now as good as dead.

I'm not proud of what my hands did at that point. Well. Just a little proud, because it was clever work, no doubting that. I knew that Loki being a fellow of tricks and thievery, if he existed—which he doesn't because there's only the one God and he's quiet enough that I'm not always sure of him even—anyway, I knew that his curse prohibited the strong taking the key by force but surely Kara had already shown me that a bit of stealing would be in the spirit of the thing. I stepped back sniffing, one hand rubbing at my eyes and the other concealing Loki's key now grown conveniently small as if it approved of the deception. I'm not sure how long I expected it to take for Kara to notice it was missing—unless she forgot about locking the door she was pretty much bound to discover its absence within moments. Frankly, I wasn't thinking very clearly. All I knew was that there was no way in Hell I was walking into Hell and that now I had the ticket to Grandmother's good books in my hand, quite possibly the ticket to the throne when she vacated it. Moreover, I was now the owner of a salt mine that had suddenly gained access to the largest and most lucrative deposit of salt north of the great Saha in Afrique, thus making me a very rich man indeed. It wasn't a salt mine any more, it was a gold mine! Adding those two to the other thousand or so reasons not to go with Snorri left me convinced that any personal shame was well worth the price. After all . . . always take the money! I had my price, and it turned out to be "everything." And my shame had only two witnesses, both of them heathens. If they didn't like it I'd just take to my legs and not stop running until I reached home.

Home—there's a magic word. I hadn't properly appreciated it on my first return but this time I would be going home the rich and conquering hero and I'd damn well enjoy it. After all, did I not say: *I'm a liar and a cheat and a coward, but I will never, ever, let a friend down. Unless of course not letting them down requires honesty, fair play, or bravery.*

Consistency! That's the finest virtue a man can possess. Somebody famous said that. Famous and wise. And if they didn't then they damned well should have.

Somehow all these thoughts managed to cram themselves through my head in the moments of silence that stretched between me, Kara, and Hennan. Warmed by the memory of home, I even started to think everything would all be all right. Kara would probably soften to me on the way back . . . show me her northern delights . . .

When the door banged open and a thick arm grabbed the neck of my shirt, hauling me backward through it, I didn't even have time to scream.